The Kindness of
Strangers

Also by Julie Smith

THE KINDNESS OF

STRANGERS,

A SKIP LANGDON NOVEL

JULIE SMITH

FAWCETT COLUMBINE • NEW YORK

A Fawcett Columbine Book
Published by Ballantine Books

ISBN 0-449-90937-9

To Elisa Wares and Leona Nevler,
as brilliant and sensitive a team as a writer could hope to work with

ACKNOWLEDGMENTS

As always, so many people assisted so generously I've probably forgotten some—I apologize if I have. My deepest thanks to Tracy Johnston and Jon Carroll for a great idea over dinner; to New Orleans Police Captain Linda Buczek, John Gagliano of the coroner's office, Sergeant Andrew Clark of the Louisiana State Police, Mike Andrews of Reed Brothers Security, Betsy Petersen, Kathy and Ken White, Kit and Billy Wohl, Chris Wiltz, Steve Holtz, Jim Alexander, two librarians—Robert Burke and Mairi McFall—and Bob Breck, who talks about weather in a way even I can understand. Thanks also to those who helped in Southwest Louisiana—Alison Owings and Stanley Dry, the kind people at the *Teche News*—especially Henri Clay Bienvenu and Gladys de Villiers—and Lee Pryor, with whom I would travel to the end of the earth.

The Kindness of
Strangers

1

• •

Some find it amusing that the coroner of New Orleans is a gyne-cologist. Few know that the city's first black mayor is buried next to Marie Laveau, the voodoo queen—by request, the tour guides say.

Even those who have lived there for years and those who were born there and those with the sensitivity of a barnyard beast and those who have spent the last twenty years drunk in the gutter can feel the strangeness of the city, its seductive perversity.

It hangs in the air like the cooking smells that pervade the streets and the old houses. Sometimes when you enter a Creole cottage, you could swear there's a pot of red beans simmering some-where, but the scent comes from the brick itself perhaps, or from the ghosts that everyone talks about as freely as they gossip about their neighbors.

The smells are unmistakable and complex; mysterious; elusive. Yet oddly pleasant and reassuring—delicious, even.

The strangeness is like that. After you give in to it, it is a warm embrace, and more than that. It is like the endless variations of a lover's fingers on your body; familiar and yet different; titillating, yet safe and warm.

1

Each new discovery, each seeming contradiction is surprising, yet perfectly expected. Because they're pieces of the crazy quilt, even the repugnant aspects, like the city's (indeed the whole state's) cynical style of political corruption, and the stupid ones, like drive-in daiquiri stands, are somehow tolerable. If you are not willing to give in to it, you generally leave town in a hurry.

Skip Langdon had done that, almost the minute she was old enough. Eventually she had come back, and bit by bit she had begun to give in, to let the thing wash over her, an inevitable tide of events.

For months now she had felt as if she would drown.

Becoming a cop was in some ways the most constructive thing she'd ever done; it had given meaning and focus to her life.

Lately it had turned on her.

Some days were better than others, but this wasn't one of them. It was Sheila Ritter's fifteenth birthday, and Sheila was the closest thing she had to a daughter. If ever there were a reminder that life goes on, this should have been it, and was.

That wasn't the point. The life cycle wasn't in question. The problem was that it simply didn't cheer her up to remember that.

She couldn't explain it any more than she could predict when she was going to burst into embarrassing tears. All she knew was that a feeling of hopelessness had come over her and would not leave.

Sheila was the niece of Skip's landlord and best friend, Jimmy Dee Scoggin, who had become Sheila's guardian and that of her younger brother, Kenny, when his sister died. Though he had now had nearly a year and a half to adapt to fatherhood, Jimmy Dee hadn't. Sheila was having her first boy-girl birthday party, and he was a wreck. Railing about the impossibility of making it through a teenage party alone, he had invited no fewer than four adults to help him weather it.

Skip's presence and that of Layne Bilderback, the man Jimmy Dee loved but barely saw anymore, due to Layne's fierce allergy to the children's dog, were *de rigueur*. But he also required assistance from Darryl Boucree and Cindy Lou Wootten, or said he did. *It was just an excuse to have them over*, Skip thought, and indeed they were all

2

fulfilling their responsibilities by eating pizza and drinking wine around the kitchen table. Music of a sort issued from the room where Kenny and Sheila usually watched TV.

The adults were talking about the upcoming mayoral election, a subject that made Skip's stomach clench for reasons she couldn't get anyone to understand. She knew something about one of the candidates that terrified her—knew it, didn't imagine it—but when she brought it up, everyone dismissed her. She found this puzzling and alienating, so she kept her mouth shut tonight, and tuned out the conversation. That left her with her own thoughts, which weren't pretty.

"I'll go check on the kids," she said, and slipped away, aware that she was making people uncomfortable, the way she'd forget to laugh when anyone said something witty or got to a punch line.

The lights were on in the elegant parlor Jimmy Dee called the family room. A few kids were dancing, but most were just talking. Sheila was standing very close to a tall, short-haired, slightly over-weight boy whose chubby cheeks flamed. Skip could see panic in his eyes and despite her mood, it made her smile.

Sheila was tall and a little too heavy—like Skip herself—but even at thirteen she'd had a sexual presence. At fifteen she was developing confidence.

She had dark, shiny long hair, luminous skin, and cheeks nearly as bright as her shy swain's. Skip had often noted that adolescence will cause some feature or other to gain temporary prominence— noses or Adam's apples on the unlucky. Sheila had been lucky— ripe, pouty lips dwarfed her other features.

Another boy came up behind her, touched her lightly on the waist, and she turned to him, a belle accepting her due. The other boy, the panicked one, looked hugely disappointed.

You never know what you want, Skip thought, *till it's taken away.*

She checked the room for Kenny, who had been bribed to stay in his room and not embarrass Sheila with his puerile, if exemplary, presence. Apparently, the promise of a fishing trip had worked.

Music blared, conversation buzzed. All seemed in order except for the girl on the sofa who looked like Skip felt. She was beautiful,

3

this girl, as slight and wispy as Sheila was opulent. Her hair was dark and hung to her shoulders, a little messy, as if she never thought about it. Her skin was light—much lighter than Sheila's—and her oversized feature was her eyebrows, which were bushy and strong, and which most kids would have plucked. She wore jeans and a white T-shirt, and looked as if she'd just lost her best friend.

Which is possible, Skip thought, remembering her own youth. *I wonder how bad I'll embarrass her if I talk to her.*

But there was something so sad about the girl that Skip was drawn to her. *If misery loves company, she'll adore me.*

She sat down, not next to the girl, but close enough to talk. "Hello. I'm Skip."

"Oh. Auntie."

That was what Skip liked the children to call her, but they seldom did. "You know about me."

"Oh, yes. Sheila talks about you all the time. I'm Torian, by the way. Torian Gernhard."

"Oh, of course." Torian was a neighbor, one of the few kids in the French Quarter. She and Sheila had met that summer when Torian saw her walking Angel, the black and white dog that Layne was allergic to; they were best friends, Jimmy Dee said, but this was the first time Skip had seen her.

She was looking neither at Skip, nor apparently at anything else. Gently, Skip touched her arm. "Torian. Is something wrong?"

"Wrong?" She seemed genuinely puzzled. "With me?"

"You're sitting here all alone."

"Oh. I'm just tired."

Skip smiled. "Okay. I didn't mean to be pushy."

"Oh, you weren't." Torian smiled back, warming to Skip, perhaps. "It's okay. Sheila says you're a cop."

"Does she talk about all of us?"

"Sure. But I know Jimmy Dee and Layne. Is Darryl here tonight?"

"Uh-huh. Do you want to meet him?" Of course Sheila would have talked about him—he was her grown-up crush, and Skip had a thing for him herself.

4

Torian nodded serenely, suddenly interested, not nearly so sad.

Skip took her into the kitchen. "This is Cindy Lou Wootten. Do you know about her?"

Torian nodded. "The psychologist. Also known as Lou-Lou."

Skip said, "Sheila talks about us."

"Woo. I hate to think," said Lou-Lou, and everyone laughed except Torian.

"And this is the famous Darryl."

Darryl gave Torian a grin that would probably cause her to run a fever. "Famous for what?"

"Sheila said you found her that time."

Sheila had once run away, and Darryl had tracked her down. Skip was in the rescue party as well, but apparently Sheila hadn't noticed.

Darryl was a tall, lanky black dude, with glasses and fabulous teeth. He was a bartender, high school English teacher, and musician, the last of which would have made him cool even if he hadn't had the mercurial charm of a con man who'd missed his calling. Skip figured his female students would never forget him— she knew Sheila wouldn't.

"Sit down," said Skip. "Want some pizza?"

Torian nodded, not taking her eyes off Darryl.

"Hey, Darryl. Wanna dance?" It was Sheila, galumphing into the room as if she were Kenny.

"No way. I'm too old for that stuff."

Sheila came up behind him, dropped a hand on each shoulder, and squeezed. "Oh, come on."

"Uh-uh. That's for young people."

"You're young." She slid one of her hands to his neck and moved her fingers ever so slightly.

Skip gave Jimmy Dee a discreet look, and saw something like terror on his face. *Probably afraid he's going to have to stop it,* she thought, *but not to worry.*

Darryl said, "Is there a bug crawling on my neck?" and slapped at Sheila's hand. "Ooooh, what's this?" He grabbed it and stared for a moment, holding it suspended. Then he brought up the other hand and touched the palm. "Hey, you're a Virgo. Right?"

"Oh, right, Darryl, it's September fourth, of course I'm a Virgo."

"It's right here in your palm. See that? Know what else? It's gonna rain. See? It's right there."

"Oh, great. We've had hurricane warnings for days. Big deal, it's going to rain."

"We're not getting Hurricane Faye. Uh-uh, it'll be another. See that little line?"

"Hey. My palm's supposed to be about *me.*"

"There's your life line—look. It's *real* long. You might make it to sixteen."

Giving up, Sheila jerked away. "Okay, don't dance. Come on, Torian."

Obediently, Torian followed, big sad eyes raking the adults as she left.

As soon as they were out of hearing range, everyone except Jimmy Dee burst out laughing.

He covered his eyes. "One day I'm going to kill her."

Skip said, "What's the matter with the other one?"

He shrugged. "She's a real serious kid, that's all."

● ●

Skip slept most of the next day, which was the way she spent most of her free time these days.

On Monday her sergeant, Sylvia Cappello, gathered up her brood like some mother animal taking them out to forage: "Hey guys, back to the scene of the crime."

They'd been to the St. Thomas Project the day before, and three days before that. Homicides were getting to be so common there it made you wonder who was left alive.

Skip piled in the car with the rest of her platoon—there were so few police vehicles, they traveled in a pack.

The victim would be a kid, she thought. The motive would be drugs.

It was an article of faith among Homicide detectives that kids in some of the projects didn't care whether they lived or died, and more or less expected the latter. Skip thought that was probably right, and it depressed her to see the same thing day after day—kids killing kids, misery in their mamas' eyes, hardness in the survivors'.

But then, *everything depresses me.*

Her stomach flopped. *Everything except my job. What's happening to me?*

She sat up straighter, hoping that would help.

It was raining, the tail end of a weary storm that had once been a hurricane, but had cooled down. Nonetheless, the car window was open. Skip turned toward it for air.

Someone poked her in the ribs. "Ain't that right, Langdon?"

" 'Isn't,' Dickie, 'isn't.' "

"Well, idn't that right?"

"Isn't what right?"

"Perretti gets elected, we're out of a job—he'll burn the damn place down."

The car shook with police humor. Perretti was the right-wing candidate for mayor—or so he wanted to be perceived. He wasn't going to burn the projects, and he wasn't going to stop crime by hiring a neo-Nazi police chief who could "get the job done," but he was probably going to wear out his vocal cords promising he was.

Skip hated him and was probably going to vote for him, which made her hate herself.

There was a knot of people in the courtyard of the project, some of them witnesses Skip knew from other homicides. It made her slightly sick to realize she'd interviewed a couple of them three or four times.

The body was crumpled up in a doorway, Lloyd Rogers, a young man in jeans and a T-shirt that didn't cover his belly, a fat young man with short hair and a pair of running shoes that had probably cost a hundred dollars or more.

A child of seventeen or eighteen.

He had been shot in the chest with an automatic weapon.

It wasn't Skip's case, it belonged to the one named Dickie, a young, cocky dude just transferred from Robbery. He asked Skip to talk to the guy's wife.

"Wife! He's barely old enough to date."

He pointed. "She's the one over there. In the pink shorts."

Her name was Kiva, and she looked about Sheila's age.

She said "Let's go to my auntie house. She stay over there." They walked across the courtyard.

"How long were you married?" asked Skip.

"Oh, we ain' married exactly; we just always be together."

Skip thought: *What's "always" to someone her age?*

Her aunt looked fifty and was probably thirty-five. She had the stringy-necked, flat-assed body of a longtime crack addict. A baby clung to her, a light-skinned girl of about two or two and a half, chubby legs sticking out from blue rompers trimmed with red plaid ruffles, her hair decorated with barrettes in crayon colors. She had on a Barney T-shirt stained with chocolate milk.

"Mama? Mama!" She ran to Kiva and grabbed one of her bare legs. She looked up at Skip and said gravely, "My daddy dead."

Skip felt feathers start to fly in her stomach, the beating of wings in there.

The child nodded. "Daddy dead. Daddy day-edd." She seemed taken with the rhythm of it.

"Somebody told her?" Skip said inanely.

Kiva looked at her as if she were speaking Russian.

"I have to sit down for a minute." Skip's knees were buckling, her neck was wet with sweat. Her heart pounded.

● ●

Later, in her office, Cappello paced, the twin lines between her eyes drawing closer together.

Skip sat, a hand over her eyes, speaking raggedly. "It was like a flashback. I swear; I saw Shavonne. Crawling. I saw her like it was real."

Cappello held up a hand, palm out: *Don't tell it.*

"Look, it's never happened before. You know it hasn't. It's not going to happen again."

"Skip, I'm worried about *you*, don't you see that? This case has about as much chance of getting solved as Jimmy Hoffa's murder. But Dickie just arrived—he doesn't know about Delavon, and he doesn't know you. What he knows is, you couldn't do a simple interview today. What if he talks about it? You want it to get back to

8

O'Rourke?" O'Rourke was her nemesis, a sergeant who hated her for no reason.

Skip shrugged helplessly. "Sylvia, it happened. I can't take it back."

"Skip, you've got a problem. If you don't do something about it, I'll have to send you to Cindy Lou." Cindy Lou worked for the department on a contract basis.

"She's my best friend—how can she be my psychologist?"

Cappello made her voice low, so Skip would have to pay close attention. "I'm your friend, too, and I'm trying to tell you something. If I send you to Cindy Lou, this becomes a departmental matter. Do you follow?"

Skip realized she hadn't really understood. If Cappello sent her to Cindy Lou, it wouldn't be for a friendly pep talk—it would be to have her fitness for duty evaluated.

She stared at the sergeant, thinking, I didn't know I was that bad.

"Skip?"

"I need to think, Sylvia. Can we talk again after lunch?"

Cappello smiled, and Skip understood that she really was her friend. "Sure."

She needed to think and she needed to talk—with her good friend who happened to be the department psychologist. Cindy Lou's familiar voice floated over the phone: "Hey, girlfriend. Lunch?"

"My treat. I need advice. Bad."

"Girl, you're right about that."

"Somewhere private."

"No such place."

They ended up whispering, at Semolina. "I blew it on a case today. I had a flashback of some kind."

"Uh-huh." Cindy Lou didn't even look up from her pasta, seemed to shrink into herself—just a friendly pair of ears, non-threatening, nonjudging.

Skip told her what had happened at the project, but there was no need to fill in the background. Lou-Lou had been around when it happened, had spent hours talking to Skip about it, had been there through the long months of depression.

"I think," Skip finished, "Cappello wants me to take a voluntary leave of absence."

"Tell me something. Are you enjoying your work right now?"

"No. But I'm not enjoying anything. You know that."

"Do you want to take a leave?"

"No! God, no."

"Why not?"

Skip thought a minute, thought of the long days with nothing in them, days in which her mind could wander and hark back, showing her Shavonne again, crawling across the floor; days when the image wouldn't leave her. "I'm afraid to," she said.

"Afraid of what?"

But Skip couldn't say it, not even to her best friend. "I don't know," she said. "What would I do all day?"

Cindy Lou crossed her legs and pinned her with a hard stare. "Go into therapy."

"What?"

"You heard me. Why haven't you done it already?"

"I don't know, I thought . . . I guess every night I thought I'd wake up fine the next morning." She was quiet a moment. "I guess it just didn't occur to me."

Lou-Lou snorted. "It's not like no one suggested it."

"What?"

"Skip. I've mentioned it a million times. So has Jimmy Dee."

"You have?"

"Those very words: 'Maybe you should go into therapy.' And you usually say, 'Maybe I will if things don't get better.' "

"Oh. Well, I . . ." She was so surprised she couldn't go on.

"What?"

"I don't know why I haven't. I don't know; I really don't."

"Listen, I haven't wanted to say this before, because I know how important your job is to you. But I think you should know how precarious things are. Here's a little statistic—eighteen months is the average amount of time policemen stay on the job after killing someone."

Skip felt her mind go blank. "Why? What does that mean?"

Cindy Lou shrugged. "You should know better than I. Think about it."

"I don't have to. My job means everything to me—I'll do anything to keep it."

Cindy Lou rifled her purse and came up with a card. "I've got a friend who just moved to your neighborhood—she's a fantastic therapist, and I think you'd like her."

Skip took the card. "Joanne Leydecker."

"She's called Boo."

"Her clients call her Boo?"

"Probably. She's smart and incredibly down to earth—absolutely no bullshit about her. She just might be right for you."

At the moment, doing anything at all, going anywhere, seemed such an effort that the fact that Boo lived five minutes away was the most appealing thing about her.

Suddenly, the idea of not having to go to work, to go through the motions of her life, to pretend she was really living it, seemed like a soft, warm bed.

2

• •

Boo approached her phone, as always, with a towel for the dust. It was sawdust and plaster dust and brick dust and the dust of old paint, sanded away for the new. Dust was her life these days; dust and contractors and Joy, her baby. Her husband and practice were secondary.

She dialed and was almost relieved when her husband wasn't in his office. She had one tiny thing to tell him, and he hated it when she wouldn't chat. He'd been brought up the New Orleans way; you took things slow and easy. He made friends with waiters when Boo just wanted them to take her order. He knew every shop owner in the French Quarter, and they'd only moved here a few months ago. Boo didn't even know the clerks at Matassa's, though she popped in for something nearly every day. To her husband, any conversation that lasted less than ten minutes was plain rude.

It was convenient, but slightly odd that no one answered, she thought. It was mid-afternoon. He was always there. Was anything wrong?

She smiled at herself. When she couldn't get someone, or

didn't hear from them—even when they didn't return her call—
she was always sure something was wrong.

Real well-adjusted, Boo. Some shrink you are.

She'd left herself five minutes for chitchat. Now she could have
a yoga break before the new client. She was feeling refreshed by
the time the doorbell rang.

"Skip? Hi, I'm Boo. It's this way—we're sort of under
construction."

"Beautiful house. And it's going to be gorgeous. Omigod, is
that what I think it is?"

Boo had led her client nearly halfway to the back entrance.
She saw that the workmen had left open the door in the living
room wall.

"Uh-huh—the lady who owned it before turned the porte
cochere into a garage. Can you believe it?"

"Do you know how rare that is—a garage in the Quarter?"

"We didn't when we bought the house, but everyone remarks
on it." She kept walking, out the back, across the courtyard, and
into the outbuilding.

Her client looked it over appraisingly. "So you made the slave
quarters into an office."

Boo nodded. "It's the only thing finished so far. That and the
baby's room."

The office was pale pink, furnished with antiques that were
good but not pretentious. The chairs were covered with chintz—
cheerfulness was the least she felt a therapist ought to offer.

"What a pretty room," Skip said, and Boo motioned her to a
chair containing a longhaired gray and white cat.

Skip picked the cat up, producing a soft protest.

"Melpomene! What are you doing here?" Boo shooed the cat
and looked sheepishly at Skip. "Hope you're not allergic."

"No, I love cats."

"Cindy Lou tells me you're a police officer."

"Uh-huh. Also your neighbor. You can't have lived here long."

"We moved from Uptown about four months ago—why, with
a year-old baby, I'm not sure. Well, yes, I am. We fell in love with
the house."

"Ah. You're a real estate junkie."

"We used to just look—but this place got us."

"I love Creole townhouses—I'd like to do what you're doing, restore one."

"You do need a therapist."

They both laughed a little nervously, as each party contemplated the segue from pleasantries to the business of the hour. Finally, Boo said, "How can I help you?"

"Well, I've been depressed. Do you know any jokes?"

Boo smiled, acknowledging the stab at humor.

"I had a couple of real bad things happen at once. I lost my partner . . ."

Boo gasped. Most of her clients had relationship problems.

"And I went after the asshole who killed him."

She paused so long Boo prompted. "He got away?"

"It would have been better if he had."

Is she saying what I think she is? Boo waited.

"I found him. And he tried to kill me. And I shot him."

Boo nodded, trying not to show emotion. "You did what you had to."

"He had a seven-year-old daughter."

"My God." *What would it do to Joy if something happened to her father? And me? How would she possibly cope with it?*

The young cop told the story in detail, her green eyes troubled, and as she talked, Boo developed an affection for her, a respect that she often felt when hearing a client's story, seeing her suffering laid out as if on a gurney. It was amazing what the human mind could cope with, how it could wrap itself around a problem and find a way out.

But the woman before her had killed a man in front of his wife and child, and she had no previous experience to help her through it, no psychic armor to protect her.

I wish I could build her some. I wish I could mend the hole in her.

She was a big woman, at least six feet tall, and a little overweight—twenty pounds, maybe. But the weight looked good on her; gave her substance. Her brown hair was wild and curly—Boo thought she must wear it up on the job.

14

She was young—probably slightly over thirty—but she gave the impression of strength and intelligence. Boo was willing to bet certain men were threatened by her, probably some of her colleagues included.

Her eyes were what impressed Boo the most—those green, compassionate, troubled orbs that looked as if they had seen too much.

I want to make her smile. I want her to be happy.

It was her weakness and she knew it—as a human being that is, because she gave too much; but in her job, it was her strength. She could not rest until she saw the glint of laughter return to her clients' eyes.

"I don't know what to do," Skip was saying. "Being a cop is my identity; it's my life. It's the only thing . . ." She stopped.

"Go ahead, tell me."

"I was going to say the only thing I've ever loved."

Boo waited.

"But that isn't true. I love my friends and the children, my best friend's children . . . and . . ."

"And?"

"My boyfriend, I guess."

"You're not sure?"

"Oh, of course I'm sure. Sure I love him. I'm just insecure."

"Is there a reason to be?"

"I don't know." She sounded impatient. "Could we get back on the subject?"

"Whatever you like."

"Well, I don't know that I did love anyone before I had this job."

"Not your parents?"

"I guess, but that's another story. What I mean is, this job sort of solidified things for me. It made me . . . I don't know—it made me want to live, I guess."

"Ah."

"Well, I hate to sound clichéd, but I guess I mean I get my self-esteem from it."

"Do you think that's still true?"

"Maybe not. Maybe it isn't, but it's still my life."

"Of course."

15

"What would I do if I didn't have it? I can't even think about that."

"I don't think you have to. You still have it."

"Not for now I don't. I'm on leave for six months." She brought a hand down on her thigh. "*What* am I going to do all day?"

"What do you want to do?"

She sat back, and Boo thought the pain in her eyes was searing. "I don't know."

"Do you ever find that sometimes you know things you don't know you know?"

Irritation flashed across Skip's face: *Don't give me that shrink-talk.* And then her expression smoothed into thought. Finally, she said, "Maybe. What are you getting at?"

"You could look at this as an opportunity."

This time she didn't bother to conceal her annoyance. "Well, I don't."

I guess I'd feel the same, Boo thought. She said: "What would you think of doing a little exercise with me?"

"Sure, why not?"

"Okay, get comfortable. Now close your eyes and leave the morning behind you." She spoke slowly, to induce a light trance. "Let go of the past and the future, and take a breath . . ."

She led Skip, in imagination, to "a beautiful place where all things are possible."

"See if there's anyone there," she said.

"Yes. There's a woman wearing a diaphanous gown. A muse or something."

"Good. Ask her to give you what you need."

Skip was silent for a while. "I'm not getting anything."

"Okay. Let's go deeper. To your left, find a path that leads downward. Follow the path and tell me who you meet . . ."

Almost instantly, Skip gave a little gasp and a jerk. She kept her eyes closed for almost a minute, and then let them fly open. "I did get something."

"Good." Boo was a little taken aback. She'd planned to lead her client gradually back up the path to consciousness, ever so nurturing and gentle, but Skip had taken matters into her own hands.

"It's not what I expected. It's the last thing I expected." She was shaking her head. "It was Errol Jacomine."

"The mayoral candidate?"

Skip nodded, licking her lips, excited. "This worked, you know that? There really is something I care about—I just forgot about it, that's all. I mean I didn't think I could do anything, but I have all this free time."

"Tell me about it."

"What do you know about Jacomine?"

"Just that he's the minister of a multicultural church. He seems to have done a lot for drug addicts and people down on their luck—I mean, really a lot. My impression is, he's a real grassroots, serious kind of guy who puts his money where his mouth is."

"My God." Skip was shaking her head, a hand over her mouth in horror. "I think that's what most people think."

"And what do you think?"

"He's a psychopath. He's dangerous as hell."

She was so adamant Boo started to wonder if this was a projection. Was there more to Skip Langdon's emotional state than she'd thought?

"I met him last year on a case. He was sitting down with eight or ten members of his flock. When he stood, they stood, and I've never been so sure in my life that something was badly wrong. I mean *badly*."

"I'm not sure I understand."

"They were obviously under orders to watch his every little move and carry out some prearranged scenario."

"Every organization has rituals. Especially churches."

"Maybe you had to be there—trust me, this thing was sinister as hell. And sure enough, I found a disgruntled member who left because he abused her. She spilled something, and he made her wear burlap underwear or some damn thing—which he called sackcloth. And there were sexual things."

"Rape?"

"More like *droit du seigneur*. The church ladies were just sort of on call."

Boo raised an eyebrow.

"So I told the department's intelligence guy—you know, the one who's supposed to know about cults? And he said Errol Jacomine's a good guy, and I should leave him alone."

"Jacomine's got a following," Boo said, trying to keep it neutral. In fact as far as she could tell, he was beloved by those who knew him.

Skip was looking more lively than she had at any time during the session.

Boo asked, "How does all this affect your life?"

"Well, I think it's preying on me—it's contributing to my general black, dark mood. And I realize the thing I want most in the world right now is for him not to get elected. I could work on Perretti's campaign, or Jackson's . . ." She stopped. "Uh-oh. No, I can't. I'm still a police officer. I can't work on a campaign." She looked utterly dejected. "For a minute there, I thought I could actually do something useful for once."

"I'm sure you've done many useful things in your life."

Skip gave her another cut-the-shrink-talk look. They were all like this at first, till they got used to the vocabulary.

And the nurturing.

Boo felt strongly that there wasn't enough nurturing in the culture, and that most people had a hard time accepting it—but then, perhaps those were just the ones who ended up in therapy.

Still, there was her husband . . .

Stop that, she thought. *You're too smothering, nobody could take it.*

Skip was saying something. "Do you think I'll ever get over this?"

She was so pathetic, this huge, competent woman, obviously so unlike herself right now, that Boo wanted to hug her and tell her that yes, everything would be fine; but she wasn't sure of that.

Probably Skip would never get over it completely. But she would stop being depressed.

"Of course you will," she said. "People do."

It just takes time, and it's incredibly painful.

"It's taking so long."

Oh, God, why can't I put a bandage on them or something?

"Want to come back Wednesday? We could do twice a week for a while."

Skip nodded, looking pathetically grateful, this large woman, so defeated in her triumph. If a woman's gotta do what a woman's gotta do, she had—and now she was flat as a busted balloon.

Boo thought: *We never know what life will bring us.*

When Skip had gone, she realized how much the other woman had affected her. She had ways of closing herself off from her clients' pain—all therapists do—but there was something about this one, something like seeing a wounded lion.

She went to find her daughter. She had ten minutes before the next one.

3

• •

They went to the Burger King on Canal Street because Noel thought nobody else would be there. Torian had heard her mother say that if you didn't want to be overheard by the people you were talking about, you had to go to Hooters. Burger King was good if you didn't want to be seen.

Anyway, she preferred it to PJ's or the Croissant D'Or because she wanted a Coke instead of coffee.

Noel said, "I brought you the poem. May I read it to you?"

Asking her permission.

He was so diffident, so shy with her. She didn't really know how to respond—nothing had prepared her for this—but she thought it best to accept the role he assigned to her, that of lady receiving her troubadour.

It felt odd. It felt downright absurd.

She was just Torian Gernhard, who had the worst clothes in the class and got tongue-tied when a cool boy spoke to her, and here she was with Noel Treadaway. That in itself didn't make any sense, but the way he treated her was madness—like a queen, yes, but not the way a king treats a queen, the way a servant does.

Of course it made her uncomfortable, because it was too weird and too unlikely and made her feel like she was in a dream. But in a strange way, it also seemed her due. Usually, she felt rattled, but there were moments when she felt she brought it off pretty well.

She was about to say that of course he could read the poem when he said, "You have no idea how cute you are with those glasses on."

She felt her cheeks flush and her right hand tear them from her face. She'd forgotten she was wearing them.

"No, leave them on."

"I'll put them on later. If you ask me *real* nice."

She leaned forward a little, seductively, she hoped, though she hadn't had much practice at this sort of thing.

He laughed. "What a *grande dame*."

How many of her friends even knew that phrase? Her heart swelled with gratitude that this was happening, that he'd noticed her.

She made her neck and spine long and looked haughtily down her nose. "You may read the poem now."

His hair was gold in the sun, his blue eyes kind right now, but sometimes she thought they would burn a hole through her.

We are the opposites that attract, she thought. *Light and dark, tall and short, thick and thin.*

Sunny and sad.

But she wasn't nearly so sad when he was with her. Sometimes she thought he'd been sent from heaven to save her, to give meaning to her life.

They'd known each other four months now, but this magic, this love between them, was new, now going into its fourth week—its twenty-second day, to be exact.

She had wanted him from the first, but that was nothing. She got hardly anything she wanted, unless you counted the occasional Coke.

She had written poems about him. He *liked* poetry. She'd never in her life met a soul who did, not even Sheila.

Poetry and classical music. It was too much to ask.

21

"Are you sure you're ready?"

She nodded slowly, grandly.

Tears stood in her eyes when he had finished. The images were so crystalline, so pure and clean she felt her body tingle, as if she had dived into a mountain stream. They made her wish she lived in a place where there was snow, wish she could have her own house with her own bowl, in which there would always be carnations.

Wish she could get away from Lise and live with Noel.

She had fallen in love with him long, long before he noticed her, and for months had not gone to sleep without his face in her mind. She'd been beside herself when they started seeing each other.

But the way she felt right now, at this moment, was so much more intense that she thought it threatened to explode her body.

"What is it?" he said. "What's wrong?"

"The poem . . ." How could she tell him it wasn't the poem, it was him?

"It reminds me of you."

She didn't answer.

"So pure. So lovely in your purity."

She smiled. "So simple."

He took her hand, which had been obsessively folding a napkin. "Don't."

"Oh, the napkin. Nervous habit." But even as she spoke, she saw that he was shaking his head.

"Not the napkin. I meant don't be ironic—don't cheapen the meaning. You heard what I said. I want you to take it in, not push it away."

No one had ever talked to her that way.

The tears had fallen now and were running down her face, so that she could see clearly again. He was still holding her hand. She stared up at him, unable to form words, and he stared back, their eyes locked like necklaces that had tangled.

Lise would die. My father would die. It would kill him.

She couldn't look away.

"Let's take a walk," he said, and she thought, *He needs air, too,* barely surprised to realize once more how much they were in tune with each other.

But she was wrong this time, and if they had needed air they wouldn't have found it in the steamy embrace of early September, which pressed on Torian's chest as she stepped onto the sidewalk. She was still trying to adjust when she felt herself pushed against a wall, Noel's mouth on her, his huge hands in her hair.

Before Noel, she had never tasted anyone's tongue, never felt hands on her body, except her mother's when she was tiny and her dad's when she hugged him. Just one of Noel's hands could reach from her waist to her breasts, could cover her entire shoulder. To feel them on her was to feel safe from the world, from Lise, from the penetrating sadness that informed her life.

His tongue was silk and velvet at the same time, and all the perfumes of the East, and the sparklers that had so enthralled her as a child, and yet it was also something soft and wet for which she could think of no simile at all. She had tried to write about it, and there simply was no analogy in her experience. It was soft and wet and delicious, and yet certainly not like the soaked cake of a trifle or the plump thrill of an oyster, both of which sounded revolting when you put them down on paper. Nothing at all like the satin, electric ecstasy his tongue could produce, nuanced and gentle and delicate and maddening in its purposeful slowness.

She thought: *Caramel, maybe. Butterscotch.* But that conveyed only the sweetness of it—not the aliveness. The joy.

He was hard and huge and overwhelming, and yet if she focused only on the caresses, minute feather touches in her invaded mouth, it was like falling into a golden cloud, encompassing and infinite and softer than the air itself.

"I needed to kiss you," he said, and pulled away, walking now, holding her hand. They were on Canal Street and could have been seen, yet he did it anyway, and she did not stop him.

They walked toward Woldenberg Park, and when they reached the levee, there was a breeze from the river, which lifted her hair off the dampness of her face.

He touched her cheek. "You're so beautiful."

She might have said, "You are a god. You are Apollo. You are the golden light of my soul, and the sun itself," if she could have spoken, but a hunk of steel wool had grown in her throat and lodged there like a cancer.

She stared up at him again, into the pale blue of his eyes, cold, pale blue she had thought at first, but hot now, lit with the heat of something she didn't understand, and wanted.

"It's going to rain."

"It's going to storm."

"The storm is here, Torian. Inside." He touched his heart.

She understood so completely it embarrassed her, made her feel naked in public. She said, "Sometimes you don't talk like an American."

"Don't I?" He looked surprised. "Only with you. I don't know why."

"Don't you?"

"Yes. I do." He said no more and, knowing, she didn't ask. She liked the rhythm of the exchange. With him, every word was a poem, every moment a haiku, a minute a sonnet, an hour an epic.

They walked until they came to a place where there was no one close, and he pulled her down to the grass. She slid under him, holding him tight, feeling the hard muscles of his legs, the rock of his chest harsh on hers, like the Earth itself, above her and below her, enfolding her.

He had rolled onto her reluctantly, she had had to pull him, but now he plowed his fingers once again into the silk of her hair, and raised himself on his elbows, his breath hot in her face.

"I love you. Oh, God, I love you so much."

She closed her eyes, taking it in, knowing it was true and yet not believing it.

He pinned her wrists, but gently, so that she would not be frightened, yet in such a way that she could not mistake his mastery, and she thought that if she died in that second she had lived fully.

"Make love to me," she said, and he rolled off her, staring up at the sky, hands on his chest.

For a moment, she stared at the sky herself, and saw that it was darkening. Lightning flashed, so perfectly matching her mood, and disappeared. She waited till the thunder before she touched the gold hairs on his arm.

He didn't respond.

"What is it?"

He seemed to go deeper inside himself, and she could have kicked herself for causing it.

He's afraid he'll hurt me, she thought, and whispered to him. "I want you, Noel, I want you; don't treat me like a child. I know what I'm doing."

Her breath was ragged, her throat raw; she was dizzy from the effort of it. She felt soft, open, like a white petal, yet somehow there was power in this. It was deeply confusing, but heady, and she could not stop.

She threw an arm over his chest and buried her lips in his neck. "Noel. Don't turn away from me."

He threw back the arm and pinned her again, this time not gentle at all, angry. "Stop!"

Tears came again. She couldn't follow her emotions, or his, could understand nothing at this point.

The rain started then, a few soft, fat drops at first, then a stinging flood.

He jerked her to her feet and pulled her to him, jeans against jeans, her soggy hair straggling. His face, slick with rain, tense with the pain of his struggle, was unearthly beautiful, yet oddly familiar. She realized, finally, where she had seen it. In final acts: onstage, in movies, even on television.

He's a Montague, she thought, and her head whirled with the import of it. *My age is even right.*

Yet she knew, deep down, that there was something skewed about the analogy. She just didn't want to think about it.

• •

Once more, lightning split the sky, and Noel thought what a strange, pathetic sight they must be, clutching each other like runaways, too dumb to get out of the rain. But here on the levee, both soaked, no one would see them or recognize them. They could clutch and cling as if it were the most natural thing in the world.

And maybe it was. All kinds of people fell in love with each other. Mobile people and paraplegics. Retarded people and those of normal intelligence. People who spoke different languages. Dolphins, even, fell in love with human beings.

Why not Torian and me? Why not? Why not?

He could think of no good reason except the conventional: only pedophiles fall in love with children.

But he wasn't a pedophile and hadn't the least interest in children—only in Torian, who happened to be fifteen, but who looked like an adult and had the serene wisdom of a lithe young Buddha. He hated the New Age phrase "old soul," but he felt that he knew one. There was nothing of the child about her except her age.

He remembered the first time he saw her, how surprised he had been at her beauty—those huge eyes and thick, dark eyebrows, her serious jaw, her thinness. She had taken Joy from Boo and held her and fed her as if she had already raised seven children of her own, and he had known instantly that his child was in good hands with her.

They'd gone to a fund-raiser that night, he and Boo, and gotten home early, at Boo's insistence. Boo had been worried about the new babysitter. Even then—it seemed ironic now—he'd told her not to worry, said Torian looked like a kid who could handle it if the house burned down, and Boo had started to worry that she'd left her curling iron on.

They'd developed a system: Boo would go in and shoo Torian out while Noel waited in the car to drive her home, two blocks away. He could have walked her, but that had seemed awkward, and it had been pouring rain that first time.

Her face was wet and shining when she got in the car. "My God, it's the most beautiful thing I ever saw!"

"What?" he had said. "It's just a Honda."

"The night. The French Quarter! Look how beautiful." And she had almost literally pressed her nose against the window, luminous in her appreciation.

He had fallen in love with her at that moment, he could see that, looking back.

"Should we drive around a minute?"

26

"Yes. Oh, yes. Let's go down Dauphine. There's a building there I love."

It was the one at the corner of Toulouse, sand and rose with age, cracked and watermarked, elegant in its decrepitude. It was a favorite of his as well.

After that, he collected jokes for her, even making up riddles. She did it too and was good at it.

When he saw her with a volume of poetry—an anthology for school, he thought—he felt a funny leap in his chest, and couldn't rest till he brought out all his old books.

And he thought: *What became of me? How did I get from there to here?* He had once thought he would have an academic career.

One night she couldn't babysit, and a friend of hers had come instead—Sheila, he thought her name was, though he hadn't the least recollection of her. A strange moroseness had come over him when he came downstairs, expecting to see her, a new joke on his lips, and she wasn't there.

He had been strangely out of sorts that night, and he and Boo had fought.

Not until one bizarre moment a month ago had he put any of this together, had he had the least understanding of it. Boo had gone early to an afternoon party, having arranged for Noel to meet her there after a business lunch. He'd come home to change into shorts and get the car, and Torian was there, of course. For some reason, he was surprised. He'd never seen her there in the daytime, hadn't somehow, expected her. Yet there she was, reading in the living room, (which hadn't yet been torn apart), bare feet on the coffee table.

She was all in white—T-shirt, shorts, and sweatband catching her dark hair. She looked up and smiled. "Oh. Hi, Noel. Joy's asleep."

She turned the book over: *Sanctuary.*

Noel said, "Not his best."

"I love it. I've read it three times."

"Temple Drake," he said, understanding in some uncanny way. *"C'est moi."*

"Are you Brett Ashley as well?"

She nodded. "And Nicole in *Tender Is the Night*."

"Emma Bovary?"

She made a face. "Never. Not in a million years. Emma's a dingbat."

She has to be more than fifteen, he thought, and went to change.

He remembered perfectly well what he had sung in the shower: "Sergeant Pepper's Lonely Hearts Club Band." He wasn't thinking of her at all, or of anything in particular.

He had picked up his keys, his hair wet, walked into the living room, sat down on the sofa beside her, put his keys on the coffee table, and said, "Anna Karenina?"

As she turned toward him, before she could speak, he had kissed her. It was fast, he didn't push it, but he thought she responded, just a little. When he let her go, she looked as if she'd been struck.

He pulled away, not acknowledging that it had happened, and said, "What about Scarlett O'Hara?"

"Who's that?" she had said, and given him an ironic smile.

"See ya." He got out as fast as he could, sweat beaded on his forehead, not able to believe what had happened. It seemed so strange, it had happened so fast, had been so utterly unexpected, that he almost thought it hadn't. He had no idea what to make of it, hadn't planned it, hadn't even considered it. It was as if some part of him he couldn't control had taken over.

Why? Why did I do that?

He knew the answer. He just couldn't believe it.

And what of Torian? Would she tell her parents? Boo?

Would she call the police?

If, somehow, word got back to certain people, he wouldn't get the job he wanted.

Fuck the damn job! I'll finish my Ph.D. and be happy. I'll marry her if she'll have me.

Marry her? Hold on, old buddy. She's fifteen.

"What is it?" said Boo, when he got to the party. "You look like you've seen a ghost."

"I don't feel too great."

She had brought him a drink and been solicitous all afternoon, but he pleaded illness and left early.

He came in from the garage and there was Torian, standing with her back to him, holding Joy up in front of the big mirror over the fireplace. "There's your nose, and here's your eye . . ."

He saw his own reflection behind theirs, and Torian's face took on a look of such beatific happiness it was as if the babysitter and his daughter had become the Madonna and child.

"Hello, Noel," she said, and put down the child. "Joy, honey, go get your Pooh. Show Daddy your Pooh."

He watched his child toddle out of the room. At the same moment, he and Torian stepped towards each other, their arms going round each other as if they had done it a thousand times.

"I love you," he said.

"I know."

He hadn't realized how much he loved her, or what love would feel like. She made him ashamed of every relationship he'd ever had. He was a taker and a user. He knew how to get women, and he did. In this arena, at thirty-three, he was as much a virgin as Torian.

The job had come through—just today—and that only confused things. He wanted desperately to leave Boo, to get out from under the lie he was living, but he couldn't do that now, not for months.

His life was split by lightning as jagged as the flash that bisected the sky. It was killing him.

Boo was waiting for him in white shorts and T-shirt, the way Torian had dressed that day, and the sight made his throat constrict. It was like a parody.

She was tall, nearly as tall as he was, and slender, though not so thin as Torian. But where she was dark and mysterious, Boo was blond and ordinary. Where Torian was languid, Boo was brisk. Where Torian was sensitive, Boo was mindlessly cheerful.

"You got caught." She smiled at his bedraggled appearance.

He shrugged. "I was walking. I couldn't see stopping."

"Want a beer?"

"I'll get it."

He went quickly into the kitchen, hoping she hadn't seen his face. Living with her, keeping his real life from her, was getting harder and harder. Every day he felt less like her husband, more oppressed by their life together. He was increasingly aware how few decisions he made, how much of their life was about what Boo wanted.

For instance, she had wanted to buy this house. "Do you realize we'll be under construction for two years?" he had said, and her eyes shone.

"Oh, please, Noel. Think how much fun it'll be to bring it back to life."

So far she had brought only one room back (besides her office)—the baby's, which she had painted peach, a color he loathed. They both liked antiques, they could agree on that. But her taste was fussier, and when they disagreed she always won. As a result, the rooms already seemed too full, too formal, too overdone. He couldn't get comfortable in them.

He got his beer, changed into dry clothes, and rejoined Boo, flopping in a chair that was too small for him. This room, the living room, now had only a few items in it, just a table and chairs, to perch on really, while sanding and painting went on.

"I got the job."

"The one you wanted?"

"*And* the other one."

"Whee!" She jumped up and hugged him. "You got both of them! I knew you could do it."

"This is something I really believe in, Boo. Frankly, I never thought I'd get it. It means more to me than anything I've ever done."

"Oh, come on. I'm going to die of suspense." He hadn't told her because so many things had fallen through lately—he no longer talked of details, just of interviews and meetings, to let her know he was trying.

"Are you ready for this? Errol Jacomine's press secretary."

"No!"

"Yes. Isn't it wonderful?" But she was wearing a look he didn't understand—he could have sworn it was distress.

"What's wrong?"

"Nothing. That's great." But she looked oddly tense. He wondered if, deep down, in a place she didn't even know about, she wanted him to fail. "It's just that . . . I thought he had a press secretary. I never dreamed it was even a possibility."

He shrugged. "She's left the campaign."

"Why?"

" 'Personality conflict,' Jacomine says. Probably incompetence and he just doesn't want to say so. He's a very ethical, very fair man—he wouldn't go out of his way to ruin someone's reputation."

She nodded.

"Do you realize we actually have a chance to have a decent mayor? Somebody who's not a crook, not a racist, not tied up with any machines, and doesn't owe anybody. You know what that could mean to this town?"

"I thought you liked Perretti."

He took a swig of beer. "Never. Not for a minute. I just thought he was the best of the ones who could win. But I'm starting to look at things differently. People are so damn fed up. Errol could win, Boo. He could really win."

"Nonsense. He will win. With you at the helm." He thought the way she said it sounded slightly insincere. She smiled. Forcing it? There was something very odd about her demeanor.

"What was the other job?"

"You're not going to believe this—Perretti's press secretary."

She raised her glass to him. "When you bounce back, you really bounce."

4

• •

Skip had come back from the therapist's feeling oddly cheated—as if she'd finally discovered an escape hatch, only to find it locked. She lay down on her bed, supine, assuming the position in which she'd spent so many hours since her depression began.

Maybe I should quit. Just quit and go to work for Perretti anyway. Maybe it'd be worth it.

What am I saying? I don't want to work for any of those assholes.

There were seven candidates in the race, but four were considered out-and-out losers. That left Seymour Jackson, a mob-front black man; Perretti; and Jacomine.

A crook, a possibly racist wild card, and a psychopath. Great.

What do I care who gets elected?

She lay there and let the question seep through her.

Maybe Jackson was the best choice, representing as he did machine politics as usual.

But he's not going to win.

The big money was split between him and Perretti, which diluted their influence and gave Jacomine a huge advantage. *Jacomine could do it. He's got people mesmerized.*

I've got a real bad feeling about it. I think the guy's capable of murder and worse. He's crazy, and you don't know what crazy people will do.

Even that didn't satisfy her, couldn't justify the violent reaction she had to him, the urgency she felt about knocking him out of public life.

Why do I feel this way?

He's evil.

He's got to be stopped.

Oh, come on, you don't even know what evil means.

I don't have to, I can smell it. I can feel it.

She thought her heart beat faster.

She sat up, feeling oddly excited. *Okay, you're alive—on leave, but not dead. Good.*

And then: *So what? Where does that get you?*

Wait a minute. Hold on.

Just because I'm not a cop doesn't mean I'm not a detective.

I could treat this just like a case.

She thought back to the time she'd first met Jacomine, how suspicious she'd been, and how she'd been sure she'd find a disaffected church member who'd confirm what she thought. She had lucked out, in spades, with a woman named Nikki Pigeon.

Suddenly, thinking of Pigeon, her place in politics was so clear she couldn't imagine why she hadn't thought of it earlier. All she had to do was locate Nikki and a few more like her, turn their names over to the *Times-Picayune*, and she could stop the juggernaut. It was elegantly simple; preposterously easy.

For the first time in weeks she felt like getting out of bed.

● ●

Skip had cleaned up Nikki Pigeon's story for her therapist. Seeing Boo's incipient skepticism, she wasn't about to present it in all its gore and ugliness. Nikki had talked to her with a swollen mouth, the result of a blow from Jacomine, she said.

Skip could remember her words: "I honestly think he's evil. I don't know if I ever met anybody else I felt that way about."

Skip knew what she meant. Jacomine made her scalp prickle as no human being ever had and only one thing could: tarantulas.

Nikki had said he got people "under his control and made
them do things."

"Like what?" Skip had asked.

"Sex."

"What else?"

"Causes and shit. Like work the phones for some politician he
wants to get elected. You know? That kind of shit. Then, the politician gets elected, I bet he makes him do what he wants."

And now Jacomine was running for mayor himself, probably
having called in quite a few markers. If he won, he wouldn't stop
there: he'd go for the governorship.

"They plannin' somep'n," Nikki had said. "What, I don't
know. But somep'n. Gotta be. Why else put together an army of
zombies?"

Maybe she was just being paranoid. But maybe this had been
the plan all along: political power.

All that was speculation, but Nikki had also told tales of com-
pulsory sex, sadistic punishments, public humiliation, and violence.
But she'd been unwilling to file a battery complaint on grounds Jacomine would kill her.

It would make great reading in the Times-Picayune. The hard part
would be talking Nikki into it.

Skip had originally found her by calling all the Pigeons in
the phonebook. She went down the list again until she found
Tanya, on Baronne Street. Best to go over there, she thought,
though probably no one would be home in the daytime.

Still, what else have I got to do?

She remembered the once-proud house gone to ruin, the depressing apartment within. To her surprise, a woman's voice answered her knock.

"Nikki?" she said. "It's Skip Langdon."

A woman she'd never seen opened the door. "I remember you."

"Tanya? I don't think we've met." Tanya was too thin, addict-
thin, and Skip's heart sank; she knew Nikki's sister had children.

"I remember your name. You the only one Nikki talk to. She
hate them bastards. Precious Lamb or whatever." She meant Ja-

comine's church: Blood of the Lamb Divine Evangelical Following. He'd recently shortened the name to the last three words.

"How's Nikki doing?"

"Don' know."

"You don't know?"

"Nikki ain' been home for a while."

"You mean she's still living with you?" Skip had pictured her with a place of her own by now.

"Ever since she lef' the nutballs. Oh, she had boyfriends; gone for a while now and then. You know. But this time she been gone a good while. She mighta got married or somethin'."

Skip's neck started to prickle. "How long's a good while?"

"You mean how long she been gone?"

"Uh-huh."

"Oh, le's see. Befo' the fo'th, I know that."

"The fourth of September? That was two days ago."

"The fo'th of July. We was s'posed to go see our people that day, out in the country. Nikki gon' drive, but she ain' home."

"The third? That was the day she didn't come home?"

"Sometime befo' that, I b'lieve."

"Has she called or anything?"

"No. She ain' called."

Skip wanted to shake her. She said, "Aren't you worried at all?"

She was instantly sorry. Tanya said, "I got my chirren to worry about. I got myse'f, my house, how I'm gon' pay the rent."

And where you're going to get your rock. "Did you report her missing?"

"No. I ain' report her missin'." She might be an addict, but she hadn't completely numbed her feelings. Her eyes were so full of tragedy Skip's heart went out to her. She rummaged in her purse. "Could you use some money for your children?"

"Yes'm, I could."

Skip handed over thirty dollars, hoping it would get spent on groceries, and wishing Tanya hadn't felt a sudden servile need to call her "ma'am." "By the way, how did Nikki happen to leave?"

"I don't remember. Guess she went out, just didn't come back."

"Went out with a man?"

"I s'pose."

"Any idea who? Was she dating anyone in particular?"

"I don' know." That was probably right. Skip was having less and less hope that any of her money was going to get to the kids.

"To tell you the truth, what I really want to do is talk to people like Nikki, who left that awful church. Did she have any friends like that?"

An odd new look came into Tanya's eyes, something almost like hope. She nodded several times. "Yes'm, sho' did. She had a friend like that.

"He was from our neighborhood. Young boy, barely out his teens. Nikki brought him into the church I b'lieve. And then he come to her when he got out, 'cause he need a friend. See, he wadn't no boyfriend, jus' a frien' boy. People's all messed up when they come outta there." She contorted her face. "*All* messed up. Some bad things happen to Jamal. Ummm. Ummm. Real bad things."

Nikki had told Skip that Jacomine forced not only the women, but the men as well to have sex with him. She supposed that was what Tanya meant.

"Jamal who?"

"You know, my chirren ain' had nothin' but cereal all week."

Skip realized what the look like hope had been about. She opened her wallet for Tanya to see. "I have one twenty left. But I really need to find Jamal. Can you tell me how to find him?"

Tanya looked downright triumphant. "Yes'm, I can. He Jamal Broussard."

Skip handed over the money.

"And he drive a tow truck."

"Uh-huh. And where does he live?"

"I ain' know that."

"Okay, who does he drive for."

"I ain' know that. But he drive a tow truck. Sho' do."

Oh, well. She needs the money more than I do. She thanked Tanya for her time and went home for another session with the phone book.

• •

A Jamal Broussard lived on North Prieur, but there was no answer, no machine, and no assurance in the world it was Nikki's Jamal. That meant four pages of "Towing" listings.

She had said, "May I speak to Jamal?" fourteen times when someone finally said, "It's his day off."

"Oh. Well, this is Lorraine at Federal Express. Does he still live on North Prieur?"

"Yes, ma'am, I b'lieve he does." The voice was that of a young female dispatcher, slightly husky, strong New Orleans accent: probably a completely guileless person. *How refreshing*, Skip thought, *and thank God it's only me pulling this shit.*

Jamal's house was a rundown shotgun in a black neighborhood where there was quite a bit of foot traffic. Skip got out of the car and knocked. No answer, but lots of stares from the neighbors.

She could have waited for him, but she couldn't see the point. She knew where he worked, and she could catch him there. For the moment, she contented herself with a note in his mailbox: "Jamal—Nikki Pigeon may have mentioned me. She told me what happened to her in the Following, and I hear you had a bad time, too. Maybe we can help each other." She signed it, thought twice about leaving her phone number, but in the end couldn't see any harm in it—it wasn't her address, after all, and right now she wasn't a cop.

She went to the coroner's office and found her favorite deputy, Wayne Kerlerec. He was a short man with hair in a brush cut, stocky but soft, a man who obviously believed in lots of fried seafood and no exercise. He was married with two children, and remained relentlessly cheerful despite the gory nature of his work.

When she arrived, he was mopping up blood after an autopsy. "Hey, Miss Skip. You missed the excitement. Six homicides in twenty-four hours."

"Drugs?"

"Oh, yeah. Drive-bys, a couple of 'em. Gangs, prob'ly. Young

37

kids. Mmmmm. Mmmm." His lips set only briefly, before he smiled again. "What can I do you for? I thought you were on leave?"

"I am, but you know—there's always something."

"A little moonlighting?"

"Something personal."

"Well, I'm sorry to hear that."

"Young, black Jane Doe—late last June sometime, or early July. Before the fourth."

He finished his mopping up. "Let me get to my list. How old did you say she was?"

"Not sure, exactly. Between twenty-five and thirty-five."

"Here's one. I got one for you. June twenty-eighth exactly—that be about right?"

Skip nodded.

"Somebody found her lying on the sidewalk with a cracked skull—like she tripped and fell. Okay, it was off Jackson Avenue, near the St. Thomas Project. No purse on her, but you know what that place is like. Wouldn't put it past half the bozos live there to take it off a corpse. The other half would mug her for it."

Skip got a sudden tight feeling in her stomach—if Jacomine had done her, he'd done her right. Without witnesses, there'd be no point in reopening the investigation. "Can I see the video?"

"Sure."

When the office first instituted the videos, it struck Skip as a little odd, since a picture of a corpse is a still by definition, but she had to admit it made all the difference—photos wouldn't do it, and this saved the family the actual sight of their smashed-up loved one.

The tape showed what the office called a face and bust shot—more or less head and shoulders.

"That's her."

"Who?"

"Her name's Nikki Pigeon. She had one sister, Tanya, on Baronne Street, but lots of luck with Tanya. She's probably too strung out to make it over here."

The investigation was undoubtedly closed, and she could think of absolutely no argument to take to Cappello. It was just another piece of the dark, tortured picture she was forming of Errol Jacomine. Without much hope, she phoned Tanya herself.

No one answered.

That was probably the way it was going to be—Tanya was probably going to make herself pretty scarce to official personnel.

I'll have to go see her, Skip thought, and found the idea depressed her.

• •

"Potter. Potter, got a minute?"

Potter loved that about Daddy. His politeness, the way he always asked, as if he weren't paying Potter for his time, as if he didn't know Potter Menard would lay down his life for Errol Jacomine.

He couldn't call him Daddy in public anymore, though. They had decided to forego that during the campaign—actually, during Daddy's entire public life, which was projected to be long and distinguished. It sounded too "fundamentalist cornball," Daddy himself had said, and chuckled. Another thing Potter liked about him: He could laugh at himself.

He'd never thought he'd feel about a white man the way he felt about Daddy—almost as if Jacomine were his real father. God knows he could have used one once.

"We all need our daddy," Jacomine said. "And we need our mama too. We don't ever outgrow it."

Potter had been a Christian for a long time, ever since he was a teenager, since long before he found Daddy, and he had wanted God to be enough. But he wasn't, he was too distant, too pie-in-the-sky. Daddy said you needed a *symbol,* some kind of symbol of God-on-Earth to bring it all together for you. For his flock, Daddy was that symbol, and Potter had never known such certainty, such a sense of purpose as he did now, working for Daddy.

Potter stepped into his office. "Yes, Mr. Jacomine."

"Potter, for the Lord's sake, call me Errol."

Potter grinned. He just couldn't, but he wasn't going to say that to Daddy. He spoke to the other man in the office, the new press secretary. "Hey, Noel."

"Sit down, Potter," said Daddy. "Look, I just got a call that worries me. Somebody out there doesn't like us."

Potter sat and crossed his legs, his pulse speeding up a bit. He was about to get a problem to solve, and he thrived on problem-solving. Liked it best of anything in the world because you could take care of something small. You couldn't save the world or maybe, in some cases, even your own family members, but some things you could do, as long as you did them one at a time. That was what Potter liked and what he did well: He had a teacher once who called him Potter the Plodder, and he took it as a compliment.

"Don't know if I ever told you about this funny thing that happened last year. A female detective came to see us, big, fat girl, but skittish . . . didn't want to tell us what she was working on, couldn't wait to get out."

This was for Noel's benefit; Potter knew as much about it as he knew about Daddy's daily schedule. He'd been promoted now, but he was still Daddy's sometime bodyguard and chief of security—at least that was how he thought of himself—and he made it his business to know what Daddy was doing every minute of every day, just in case.

Daddy was looking at Noel, bewildered, as he always was when he told this story. "We'd had someone make cookies for her, and we had tea all ready. But she just rudely spurned our hospitality—we never even found out why."

Noel asked, "What did she want?"

"She was looking for a former member of our flock. Unfortunately we were unable to help her, though we did try. We tried to be as nice to her as we knew how to be. But for some reason, she seems to have taken a dislike to us. You know your Bible, Noel? Bible says it'll be this way. It is written, it is predicted, and it should come as no surprise to us: 'My enemy is like a lion eager for prey, like a young lion crouching in ambush.' "

Potter knew there was going to be more. Daddy never stopped at one Bible verse. " 'The Israelites cried out to the Lord their god. Their courage failed, because all their enemies had surrounded them and there was no way of escape.'

" 'All nations surround me, but in the Lord's name I will drive them away. They surround me on this side and that and in the Lord's name I will drive them away.'

"This is my life, gentlemen—our lives, if you will. This is what we must bear if we walk the path we have chosen. I regret to say that this young woman is out to discredit us. This is the call I have just received. Potter—any questions?"

Potter thought. "No sir. I'll take care of it."

"Of course you will. Noel, I just wanted you to be alert to the situation. Mr. Menard knows what to do, you need not concern yourself."

Noel looked confused. "But what is she doing, Errol?"

"The information we have at present is that she is trying to discredit us. Exactly why is not clear, though I expect the answer is quite simple—she is undoubtedly a Perretti supporter."

"Wait a minute, wait a minute. If she's a cop, this could be serious. Are you saying she's got something on you?"

"It will be Mr. Menard's job to find that out."

"Okay, but I'm still confused. How do we know about this in the first place?"

"Oh, we have quite an organization, as you'll find out. Quite large and quite impressive, if I do say so."

Potter was itching to get to work. "Mr. . . . uh, Errol, do you mind if . . ."

He didn't even get to finish. Daddy read his mind and waved him out of there.

He got on the phone to a volunteer: "We have a situation here. A very disturbed person is harassing Daddy. We need information and we need letters. I want you to call ten people and have each of those people call ten people, and so forth. . . . Get each of them to report back to you with the names of the ten they called, and get each of them to get reports from their callers and get them to you. Then you get them to me."

"Potter," asked the volunteer, "what exactly are we trying to do here?"

"Why, nip this thing in the bud, Culotta. Any way we can. Do you understand what I'm saying? This person is a white police officer named Skip Langdon. She lives on St. Philip Street in the French

Quarter. Her best friends are a homosexual named Jimmy Dee Scoggin and a black woman who works as a psychologist for the police department. Get each of your people to contact anyone they know in the police department or the French Quarter or the homosexual community or anyone who's a psychologist or even in therapy. They're to find out anything they can about her and write letters. Call me if you find out anything damaging or helpful in any way. Do you understand?"

That was the small stuff. After he got that going, he settled down to the serious business of damage control. He dialed a number in the police department. "Hey, Rosie. Potter. Been thinkin' about you, baby. She's fine. Yeah, the kids are fine, too. Alexa's taking riding lessons. Yeah, can you believe that? I'm scared of horses, too. She's only ten and a half. Listen, baby, I need a couple of favors. Who do you know in the chief's office?"

He wrote as she talked. "Uh-huh. Uh-huh. How about personnel? I need somebody's file.

"You can? Terrific. Now about this Tony in the chief's office— how well do you know him? Think I could call him directly?"

Next he called the man in the chief's office. "Tony, this is Potter Menard over at Errol Jacomine's. You know, we think the chief's doing a really great job. Errol asked me to call and just let you know how much we admired your handling of that little PR problem you had last week—yeah, with the officer who put out the contract on that woman. Whooo-ee, talk about a tough one.

"We loved what you said—just *loved* it. Errol said, 'Now there's a man who's doing a great job. How many city officials can you say that about?' He had me there, Tony, what do you say? How many could you say that about? So we just wanted him to know, that's all."

"I'll be sure and tell him," said Tony, and Potter knew he would. The police chief was appointed by the mayor: a new mayor could mean a job in jeopardy.

"Say, Tony, while I've got you, I came across something kind of odd a couple of weeks ago—forgot all about it till right this minute, but I just happened to think, 'Maybe Tony can shed some light.' Do you know a detective named Skip Langdon?"

Tony laughed. "Everybody knows that one. That's kind of a high-profile cop you're talking about. On the news every other day, it seems like."

"A real hot dog, huh?"

"Damn good cop, though. Had some bad luck recently. Her partner got killed, and she ended up shooting the guy who killed him—kind of a double whammy for her."

"Hey, I'd have thought she'd be thrilled she got the guy."

"I'm sure it was better than not getting him, know what I mean? But he had a little girl, and Skip felt real bad about it. Matter of fact, I think she's on leave right now."

"Oh, well, if she's mentally unstable, that would explain everything."

"I didn't say that. She's on leave, that's all."

"Well, all the things coming down, I kind of wondered."

"Hey, what's happenin', Potter? Talk to me." Tony sounded suddenly alarmed.

"Well, it's very confusing. Frankly, we don't know what to make of it. But she seems to be trying to discredit Errol."

"Why would she do that?"

"We have absolutely no idea. Maybe some personal reason of her own—we just can't figure it; but now that I know she killed someone, I'm going to be doubly vigilant."

"Listen, Potter. Maybe I can help you. Let me ask around and see what I can come up with."

Potter hung up smiling: a satisfied man. He loved stuff like this.

He was perfect for this job, technically called "campaign aide," but really what it was about was two things—protecting Daddy's butt and destroying Marvin Perretti's credibility—and Seymour Jackson's, if he had any left. Detective Langdon, rogue cop, might prove very useful indeed to the Jacomine campaign. The thing was like karate—you used the other's strength against him.

Satisfied with a good day's work, Potter called his wife:

"Honey? Yolanda, honey, I'm coming home early today. Why don't you send the kids over to Oliva's? Why? Because I want some time alone with my wife, that's why. I'm bringing home a nice bottle of white wine—now what do you say?"

The kids were still home when he got there, but they weren't as scruffy as usual, had obviously been combed and groomed to go over to their aunt's. Potter had brought not only wine, but also flowers and a cake. The cake was for Alexa and Mark to take to their aunt's.

Eight-year-old Mark ran toward him and grabbed him around the waist. "Daddy, Daddy, Daddy, guess what I did today?"

Potter couldn't help smiling. "What did you do today?" When the boy's hands went around his waist, Potter's mind went back in time, to those same hands around his calves, then his knees, and then his thighs. They were growing up so fast, Mark and Alexa. It made him sad, made him wish he could turn the clock back, or somehow make more time to be with them.

He fondled the top of Mark's head. "What did you do today?"

"I scored three goals. Joey scored one and I scored three, and we won four to two."

"Who'd you beat?"

"The Pandas! Yaaaaay. I hate the Pandas."

"Well, I'm proud of you, son. That's really fine."

Alexa put her hands on her hips. "Well, guess what I did?"

She was jealous.

When Potter had been duly brought up to date and the kids complimented and petted, he drove them over to their aunt Oliva's and returned to find his wife stepping out of the shower. "Hold it right there," he said and opened her robe.

"I was going to put on something sexy."

He pushed the robe off her shoulders, let it fall to the floor. "Now that's sexy."

"What?"

"This." He cupped a breast. "And this." He kissed her.

Yolanda leaned away from him, making him bend her backward, so that her body curved back gracefully, a reverse C, smooth and brown. Her hands kneaded his shoulder blades, and then found his zipper. She started to unfasten his trousers, but he grabbed her hand. "No."

"Why not?"

He didn't answer. Instead, he slipped a hand under her knees, picked her up, and carried her to bed. Then he undressed slowly, knowing she liked to watch. He sat on the bed for a moment, stroking her breasts, and then he changed position. She reached for him, to pull him up by the shoulders, but he pulled away, parted her legs, and buried his face between them. Instantly, she began to moan. She liked this almost better than fucking—or better maybe; she loved it. And he could do it for her for hours. He felt like that tonight, like licking her until it was time to pick up the kids, forgetting entirely the nice bottle of wine, simply getting lost in her wet, slippery, pink-and-brownness.

"That's enough! God, Potter, that's enough!" She was half laughing. "Come here." And now she did pull him up by the shoulders, so that he was on top of her, his long, lanky body stretched against her soft one.

She gave a little scream as he entered her, as she used to do, as she had always done until they had both become conscious of noise, of keeping quiet because of the children. He didn't know how long it had been since he had heard it, and a shiver passed through him. "I love you," he said. "God, Yolanda, I love you."

She screamed again, this time because she was coming. She often came like that, at first, almost the second he entered her, or she used to. It hadn't happened in a long time, and the thought of that filled him not with regret, but with greater, deeper love for her, as the weight of their years together settled comfortably on him.

It was as if they had always been together—she was as familiar to him as his fingers and toes—and he knew they always would be, that nothing could separate them.

Some people, he thought, never get to love anybody like this, and he nearly exploded with gratitude.

● ●

Afterward, they warmed up the étouffée Yolanda had made and drank the wine. When they had progressed to coffee, Yolanda said, "What is it, Potter? It's not our anniversary."

He put a hand over hers. "I was just feeling grateful to the Lord, that's all."

"For what?"

"Oh, I've got a beautiful wife and a great job—and of course, the campaign's going good."

"That's all?"

"I swear, honey. I just wanted some quality time."

"Did I ever mention I love you?"

Potter thought: *You never thought you could do it, did you? You are one lucky sonofabitch.*

She said, "The campaign's *really* going good?"

"Great. Except ..." He furrowed his brow, thinking. "I don't know about the new press secretary. Noel Treadaway—remember him?"

"From where?"

"Think."

"Oh, yeah. Pretty boy on TV."

"That's him. Quit to write a book, and now he's decided to go into politics."

"He's famous in this town, and he's pretty. All he has to do is issue statements, right?"

Potter laughed. "He's really got to control the flow of information."

"You don't think he can do it?"

"He's competent. He's just a little green. I don't know how tough he is."

"I'm sure he'll be okay."

"I'd feel better if he were a Christian."

"Oh, what difference does it make?"

"It's about commitment, honey. It's all about commitment."

"I don't see what you mean."

He patted her again. "I mean doing what you have to do. That's all. I don't mean anything more than that."

5

• •

Sheila's house was so beautiful, Torian was almost embarrassed to have her over. The apartment in which she lived with her mother was only part of a building the size of Sheila's—about a quarter of it, probably. It didn't even have charm. It was one of the French Quarter buildings with low ceilings, part of an apartment complex owned by one of her mother's ex-boyfriends who was probably letting them live there for free. Torian didn't know the details, but if she knew Lise, she'd probably bullied him into a free apartment.

It didn't get much light, which depressed Torian, and it was furnished with any old thing they could scrounge, most of it beyond tacky. At least Torian's room was better than the rest of the house. She had gone to the flea market and found a few things—some antique lace curtains and some old pictures—but she had very little money and no way to get more. While Sheila had everything money could buy.

"Except my mother," Sheila would wail. "At least you have your mother."

"But I don't have my dad."

"Yes, you do, on weekends."

It was true, but Torian still felt orphaned. Lise was never home—all she cared about was her damned boyfriend—and her dad lived in Old Metairie. At first she'd been furious that they'd moved to the French Quarter—the mingy little apartment, the crummy school, no other kids around, her dad on the other side of the planet—but things had worked out.

There was Sheila now, and most of all, Noel. How she felt about Noel was indescribable. It was love, but it was beyond love; it was passion, but it was . . . so much finer, so much sweeter, so much rarer. It was the tenderest, most fragile, and yet it was also a strong, sinewy bond that nothing could break.

Nothing!

Torian had never been so sure of anything.

The buzzer sounded, harsh, like most things in her life. Good—Sheila. She was coming over to work on a science project, but Lise was gone, so they could talk. That was the good thing about having her come over—total privacy; an adult-free zone.

Sheila was in a snit. "God, Uncle Jimmy's a dork."

"What's he done now?" Torian led her into her bedroom, where she had lit candles and incense. It wasn't dark yet, but the shadows were lengthening, and the effect was almost Anne Rice–ish. If only the ceilings were high and the walls were peeling; it was hard to live a romantic life in a modern box.

"Cool," said Sheila, noting the decorative touches. "You know Layne—Uncle Jimmy's boyfriend?"

"I don't think they say boyfriend. I think they say 'lover.' "

"Ewwwww. Gross."

"I don't think it's so bad."

"It just . . . I don't know . . . it just makes you think about . . . what they do. I mean, what they actually do."

"You don't have to think about it. Anyway, it's kind of fun to imagine."

"Torian!"

"Well, he's not my uncle. I guess that makes a difference. What about Layne, anyway? I think he's cute."

"Not Layne. He's cool. Uncle Jimmy's the dork. See, Layne's

allergic to Angel, and Uncle Jimmy says he should get a healing from these witches Skip knows."

"Weird."

"It's not me, right? I mean, are these people weird, or what?"

"At least he doesn't stay out all night with his boyfriend." She couldn't keep the wistfulness out of her voice.

"Well, I think he'd like to have Layne stay over sometimes. Which would be fine. Layne's really cool—he knows lots of games nobody else ever heard of. But he can't, because of Angel. But witches! I mean, really."

Torian shrugged. "I don't know. If it's not expensive . . ."

"He actually believes that stuff!"

"Oh, he probably just thinks it's worth a try."

"Torian, you have no idea how weird my uncle is."

Torian shook her head. "You want a cigarette?" She walked over to her bureau and brought out a pack of Virginia Slims.

Sheila shook her head. "Not today." She had coughed for ten minutes last time she'd tried.

Torian lit one and inhaled. "How's Danny?"

"Oh, *Danny!* What a child. Danny has all the sophistication of those asshole tourists who pee on the buildings at Mardi Gras."

Torian giggled. She was nervous because of what she'd decided to do. "Last week he was your main man."

"He's just such a . . . *baby.*" She walked over to the window and looked out, moody, and then turned back to Torian. "What about you? Do you like anybody yet? You've got to forget about Billy and get out there."

Torian had known Sheila would ask her. She'd been nagging about this for weeks now, and Torian couldn't stand it anymore. She had to tell her, even though Noel had asked her not to tell anyone. You had to tell your best friend—that didn't count as anyone.

She smiled. "I do like someone."

"Really! Who? Tom from English class? He likes you, I'm pretty sure."

"No. No, it's no one like that." Now she turned toward the window, gathering courage. On the slate roof next door, just on the peak, were two doves. She took it as a sign. "I'm really in love, Sheila. This is it. This isn't a teenage crush."

"Torian." Sheila's voice was awestruck. Torian turned back and saw that her face was serious; she wondered if it reflected her own.

Sheila said, "Your face! It's different. Torian, have you done it? We said we'd tell each other . . ."

"No, no, no. Nothing like that. Do I really look different?" She walked over to the mirror, one she'd salvaged and painted the frame. She looked at her features, slightly indistinct in the dusk, but even she thought there was something romantic about herself.

She turned to Sheila. This was the part that might hurt her feelings, and she wanted to see her friend's face while she talked. "I'm sorry I couldn't tell you . . . he made me promise."

"Oh, no. Not one of my exes."

"Of course not! What kind of friend do you think I am?"

"Well, who is it? I'm going to explode if you don't tell me."

"It's Noel."

"Noel? Who's Noel?"

"Noel Treadaway."

"Mr. *Treadaway?*"

"I swear to God."

"The guy you *babysit* for?"

"Do you think I'm horrible?"

"Could I have a cigarette?"

"I mean it. Do you think I'm horrible?"

Sheila lit her Virginia Slim slowly, apparently considering. She shook her head finally. "I just think it's a little weird."

Torian shrieked, "Sheeeela!" She was aware of the panic in her voice.

"I'm trying to think this through, that's all. I think you've got to fill me in." She puffed nervously, not inhaling, Torian could tell. "Okay, let me see if I can get it. You're in love with Mr. Treadaway, and he knows it, right?"

"Noel. Yes, he knows it. He started it. He's in love with *me*."

"But he's married."

"He's got a kid, too. I think that's the hardest part for him."

Sheila was leaning her head on a hand. "Wait a minute. Why would a married man with a kid . . . ?"

She obviously couldn't bring herself to say it. "What? Fall for the babysitter? He didn't plan it, Sheila. It just happened."

"You mean, he . . . like, saw you and got to know you, and then one day just declared himself?"

"Something like that."

Sheila threw herself backwards on the bed, landing with a plop. "God, that's romantic."

"Isn't it? Isn't it? I think it's the most romantic thing in the world."

"What do you do with him?"

"Oh, we have dates after school. He reads to me. Poetry." She hoped she didn't look unattractively smug.

"Oh, my God."

"And we kiss. And talk about things. We just talk and talk and talk. I never thought anybody could understand me like . . ." She saw Sheila's hurt look and stopped. "I mean a man. And without having to be told. He just knows things about me. Like he'll say, 'I'll bet you're the kind of person who likes poetry.' Or 'You're going to love this movie. Know what? This movie is meant for you.' And he'll be right. He knows me, Sheila. It's like he sees down to my soul. And he feels that way too. It's like he's always saying that. That he really sees me; like no one else does. We're . . . you know . . . God, we're lucky."

Sheila was quiet, apparently still trying to take it all in.

"You could go all your life without meeting your soul mate, and here I am fifteen and I've met mine."

"You sure he's your soul mate? I mean, he's pretty old."

"Age doesn't matter when you're really in love."

"Oh, come on, you don't know everything."

"But I know so much more than I used to. I feel like I've learned half the stuff I know in the last month."

"Like what?"

"Oh, like all the good poets of the twentieth century. And . . . other stuff."

"But what other stuff? I mean, if you're not even doin' it, then what?"

"What it means . . ." Torian faltered, tears coming, her voice thick. "What it means to be loved." She almost screamed it. Sheila was sitting up now. She shrank back against the headboard, cheeks seeming almost to sink, as if withdrawing into an imaginary shell.

"Sheila, you just don't *know!* You just don't understand. My mother doesn't give a shit about me, do you understand that?"

Her cheeks were flaming. She dumped her ashes, and when she raised her eyes, they were afire as well. "My father deserted us. Did you forget that?"

Sheila was almost pale.

"Oh, I'm sorry. God, I'm sorry. It's just that you can't know what it's like living with Lise. She's such a bitch. All she cares about is her goddamn boyfriend, who probably couldn't give a shit about her and certainly doesn't about me.

"My dad . . . well, I know my dad loves me, but he's got all these responsibilities—huge responsibilities—that he wouldn't have if Lise hadn't left him. I mean, he has to support us, and his new wife and kid—I don't blame him for getting married again, do you? I mean, who wouldn't? She dumped him—just threw him out like I didn't matter and he didn't matter and . . . I don't know . . . *nothing* mattered. You just don't even *know* what a bitch she is.

"And Noel cares about me. It's so sweet." She felt herself calming down, the tears subsiding as she thought of him. "I'm dying to make love to him. *Dying* to! Wouldn't you be? But *he's* the one who won't do it. He's trying to protect me, do you see that? He doesn't want me to do anything before I'm really sure. He won't drink with me either, or even buy booze for me, and when he found out I smoke, he threw away my cigarettes."

"Gosh, with him you don't need a mom."

"You don't have to be so sarcastic."

"Torian, it's illegal for him to make love to you. He could get in big trouble for that."

"Well, he wouldn't want to anyhow. That's the kind of person he is."

Sheila grabbed another cigarette, but she was smiling. She'd gotten a grip on herself, though Torian had no idea what her true opinions were. All she saw, all that mattered, was that Sheila was still her friend.

"So," said Sheila, "are you going to marry him?"

"Uh-huh." Torian nodded, sure her love was making her radiant. Her pale skin probably looked gold in the candlelight. "Sure. Of course we're getting married."

"Torian! He's got a wife and kid."

"Well, he won't always." She must look like a cat licking cream from its whiskers. But she didn't even care if Sheila thought her smug. This certain knowledge, this perfect trust made her feel happier, more secure and satisfied than anything ever had.

Sheila looked skeptical. Torian could feel her slipping away. "Hey, will they let you sleep over?"

"Uncle Jimmy, you mean? I guess so. Sure."

"Well, let's call him. We can drink my mom's booze. Madame Lise has a date—she probably won't even come home tonight."

• •

Lise was giving the goddamn service test, the most demeaning of the host of humiliating tasks her job entailed.

"Did you find I got to you quickly and promptly? What?" She felt herself flushing. "Well, I know it's redundant. I'm sorry. Did you feel the service was prompt? Oh? Why not? But you see, we couldn't process the claim until . . . I'm sorry, I know I asked. Let's start over. After the claim was processed, did you find . . . why is that irrelevant? Okay, why don't we go on to the next question. Did you find me polite? No? But . . . oh. Slight edge to my voice. Okay. What about efficiency? Did you think . . . ? Oh. You'd give me about a five and a half. Well, I want to thank you for your . . . uh . . . well, I . . ." She couldn't bring herself to say she enjoyed working with the asshole. "Umm, thank you, I hope, uh . . ."

The asshole hung up. Shit. Why in the hell had she majored in history when she could have gone into computers or something useful? Sixteen years of marriage was her entire work experience. She wasn't trained for a damned thing except loading dishwashers and making sandwiches.

She picked up the phone again. "Homelife Insurance." She tried to give her voice a lilt. Feigning cheerfulness was harder and harder these days. "Oh. Wilson. It's you."

"Don't sound so thrilled," said her ex.

She said nothing, hoping her silence was eloquent.

"Look, you're the one who called me. If you're going to talk, talk."

"You know what I called about. The same thing I call about every month."

He didn't answer.

"I need my support check, Wilson."

"Look, I've had a lot of unexpected expenses. I just don't know if I'm going to be able to . . ."

"You don't know if you're going to be able to! On your goddamn corporate lawyer's salary. Do you know Torian had to go back to school with three T-shirts and one new pair of jeans? That was it, Wilson! That's all she had."

"So? What else does she need?"

"How can you be like that? Just tell me—how can one man be so goddamn selfish?"

"Torian could have gotten a summer job. You spoil the kid rotten, and she's getting worse every day."

"She looked for a summer job. Nobody would hire her."

"You're telling me she couldn't have gotten a job at McDonald's? Her grades, and McDonald's wouldn't hire her?"

"Wilson, I am not going to discuss this matter with you. I'm telling you now we're eating beans."

"Best diet there is. Beans and rice. What are you complaining about?"

She couldn't keep the tears out of her voice. "I'm begging you. I'm begging you."

He couldn't keep the hostility out of his. "I'll do the best I can, Lise." He hung up.

Lise closed her eyes. She thought, *Thank God I'm seeing Charles tonight.*

Charles was a contractor, a little rough around the edges, a bit of the good ol' boy about him, but he had a sweetness that Lise had seen right away and realized she craved after sixteen years with a well-educated asshole.

Charles had gone two years to LSU and flunked out. That was the extent of his formal education, but he did okay; he had a little shotgun in the Bywater, which was more than she could say for herself. True, it was a bit run-down and needed paint, and the backyard was full of old lumber and rusting tools, but Charles had never been married. He wasn't domesticated, but he was such a sweetie-pie he'd probably catch on quick, Lise thought.

She thought that sometimes. Other times she thought, *What kind of life can Charles give Torian and me? I ought to dump him and find someone with some money.*

And then she would think: *But they're all such assholes.*

Charles was about fifty pounds overweight and had sandy hair that showed streaks of head underneath when he combed it back. His neck and belly were too large, and he had more sagging flesh under his chin than Lise really cared for. But he was tall, and Lise loved to wrap her legs around his thick body. She even loved the soreness the next morning in her inner thighs, which she would feel all day and sometimes part of the next, a reminder of their passion. Passion with Wilson had died before Torian entered kindergarten.

She called Torian. "You doing okay?"

"That depends."

"Don't be surly, Torian. What have I done to piss you off? I haven't said a word yet."

Silence.

"Did you remember I'm going out with Charles tonight?"

"Yes." The word was more or less spat at her.

"Well, darling, sweetheart, honeydew, what is there to eat at home?"

"What do you care? You're going out."

"I'm your mother, remember?"

"Oh, yeah. I remember."

"What's that supposed to mean?"

"Mom, would you cut to the chase?"

"I'm checking on your welfare. I'm calling to make sure you're fine and you have enough to eat."

"Thanks a lot."

Lise made her tone severe. "If you don't like anything in the house, you can order from the Verti Marte."

"I hate the Verti Marte."

"Royal Street Grocery, then. I don't care where you order from. You're a big girl, why don't you act like it?"

"Will that be all, Mommy dearest?"

"Torian, that'll be enough. I'll be home late."

By the time she left to meet Charles, she needed a drink in the worst kind of way. They had a couple of beers at a bar Charles knew, a neighborhood joint that frankly gave Lise the creeps, then they decided to go out to the West End and get some boiled seafood.

Over dinner, she told him about Wilson.

"I'll tell you what," he said. "I'm gonna go out to Old Metairie and break both his legs."

"Oh, Charles, don't be silly."

"He can't talk to you that way."

She didn't answer, wondering what the alternative was.

He upended his beer and stood. "Let's go. I'll drop you off, then I'm gon' go do it."

"Charles, you're such a gentle man. You're not going to do that."

"Bullshit. I'm sick of this crap. I'm gon' go break his legs."

She hated it when he started posing. He would no more break Wilson's legs than those of his twelve-year-old dog, Buzzy, but let him get a few beers in him and he more or less went crazy.

"Charles, sit down for heaven's sake."

"Lise, you keep whinin' and whinin' about that sonofabitch, and I'm goddamn sick of hearin' it. Le's *go!*"

"Charles, you're making a scene."

"I'll pick you up later," he said, and started toward the door.

"What about the bill?" She hated herself. She'd have loved to let him go, pay it herself, and take a taxi home. But she didn't have the money.

"Oh, yeah." He turned around, threw down some bills, and started once again for the door.

She got up and followed, fuming.

When they were in the car, he gathered her in a bear hug and stuck his face in hers, nuzzling, breathing beer fumes.

"Let me go." She beat on his shoulder blades. "Goddammit, let me go." She could have killed him.

He unwrapped her, and she saw that he was laughing. "Had you goin', didn't I?"

She was too astonished to answer.

He took her chin in his hand. "Baby, I just wanted to get you alone, that's all. I wouldn't hurt a fly, you know that."

"Why couldn't you have just said, 'Lise, baby, I want to be alone with you.' Wouldn't that have been more romantic?"

"Nah. You liked it this way."

"I did not, Charles. I assure you I did not."

"Oh, listen to Miss Priss." He spoke in an old-maidish falsetto: "I did not, Charles. I assure you I did not."

She turned and stared out the window. "Take me home."

He grabbed her elbow and turned her toward him, pulling her against his body. He stuck his tongue in her mouth and she opened her lips against his, forgetting everything except the taste of him, the gentle velvet of his mouth.

When he finally started the car, she kept a hand on his thigh, cursing bucket seats, wishing she could lean her body against his.

She thought they were driving to his house, but he stopped at the same bar she hadn't liked in the first place. "What are we doing?"

"Let's have a nightcap."

"I have to get home, Charles. I have a kid, remember?"

"Come on, just one."

He ordered a Rusty Nail, and so, more or less in self-defense, did she. Then he ordered another.

"Charles, come on. I've got to go home."

He said, "God, you're beautiful," and leaned toward her. They kissed in the bar, unmindful of who saw, and then they had another Rusty Nail.

Finally, he took her home, it being far too late to go to his house by then, and she thought she heard noise from Torian's room.

"Torian? What are you doing?"

"Just talking. Sheila's sleeping over."

Lise opened the door. Sheila was on the floor in a sleeping bag, candles were burning on Torian's dresser, and the room reeked of cigarette smoke.

"You've been smoking again."

She crossed to the window and opened it.

"Mom! The AC."

"We'll talk in the morning, young lady."

As she left, she heard her daughter say, "Did you smell her? She's drunk as a coot."

6

Skip rang the doorbell promptly at four. She had arrived early, but out of politeness waited till the hour.

It was a long time before she heard footsteps. Finally Boo opened the door, hands grubby, in a dirty T-shirt and shorts. She'd obviously been gardening.

"Omigod, Skip! I didn't call you."

Skip said nothing, too confused to speak.

"Omigod, come in. I spaced it. I can't believe I spaced it."

Skip followed her in, but stood barely in the doorway, knowing she'd be leaving soon. Evidently, Boo couldn't see her now.

"Listen, I'm so sorry, but something very unfortunate's come up. I'm afraid I've got a conflict." She spread her arms, palms up, contracting her shoulders. "I promise I didn't know this at the time we talked, I really didn't, but my husband has taken a job with Errol Jacomine's campaign. I don't know what you're planning to do"—she put up a hand—"Don't tell me. Please. You see what I mean? We just can't talk freely right now. So I'm afraid I really can't see you anymore, but I'll be glad to recommend someone I think you'll like. I'm really sorry about this."

Oh, no. Not my shrink too.

She took the name of the person Boo recommended, knowing she wouldn't call her.

Okay, I'm paranoid, but I'm not telling my deepest secrets to someone recommended by the wife of one of Jacomine's henchmen. For all I know Boo's involved with them too.

Here's what I don't get—how does he do this? It's like he can get to anybody. Or am I being paranoid, as advertised?

And she wondered, *Who can I trust?*

Jimmy Dee, always.

Cindy Lou.

Or not?

She's Boo's friend and she's a shrink. Also, she's black and Jacomine's got that phony brotherhood thing going. Worst of all, she knows my lately unstable history. If Boo tells her I've gone off the deep end, she might believe her.

Steve Steinman. No question there.

Okay, good. All I need is one person, and that's two. I can get through this.

●　　●

An emphatic sneeze, audible from the far side of the courtyard, issued from Jimmy Dee's kitchen as Skip stepped across from the garçonnière.

Layne's eyes were watering. He held a tissue to his mouth and nose.

Skip said, "Uh-oh. Did we forget to take our meds again?"

"They're wearing off."

Angel, the dog, was now apparently shut up somewhere in the back of the house, in deference to her pal's infirmity. This was the second prescription that had worked for a while and then stopped.

Jimmy Dee looked panicked. His relationship with Layne was already the longest running of his life, he'd recently told Skip, and to his amazement, it was going beautifully.

"Magnificently," he'd said, beaming, not even being slightly ironic, which was nearly unheard-of where Dee-Dee was concerned.

But then he'd said, "Except, of course, for the Celestial Furball."

Dee-Dee, perennially depressed Dee-Dee, was happy for the

first time since Skip had known him. When they first met, he was in a funk she thought was permanent. Many of his friends had died, but he never talked about it. He covered up his grief with campy chatter and weed, but she knew.

The kids and Layne, who'd arrived nearly simultaneously, had made all the difference. He'd had to give up pot because of the bad-example factor, and he still chattered campily, but he smiled a lot more. He was softer, somehow. He'd fallen in love with three people at once: or, to be more accurate, three people and a dog.

And then Layne's allergy had come up.

"Something smells great," Skip said.

"Crabmeat Extravaganza. You're going to love it."

"Extravaganza?"

"You wait."

Layne looked miserable. "Wish I could taste it."

Dee-Dee said, "Set the table, will you, Kenny?"

Thirteen-year-old Kenny, sitting quietly at the kitchen table all this time, got up and began gathering silverware. "This one, or the one in the dining room?"

"Sheila's not here, so we can be intime, I guess."

"What's that mean?" Kenny looked so earnest Skip wanted to kiss him. He was desperate, as usual, to do nothing wrong, to make sure everything was perfect.

"It means the kitchen."

He nodded, a man with a mission.

Skip said, "Layne, remember those witches I met a couple of years ago?"

"Oh, for heaven's sake," said Layne. "Don't start on the witches again."

Kenny said, "I like witches."

"You do?" Layne said. "Well, if you like 'em, old buddy, you get your mojo workin'. I'm afraid of them myself."

"Oh, Layne, you've got it wrong. They're gentle as kittens. What can it hurt? I'll call them and ask if they can do a healing."

"Just so I don't have to meet them."

"Well, I don't know whether you have to or not."

"They probably have to lay on hands or something."

Kenny said, "I want to go if you go to a coven meeting."

Skip was surprised. "Why? Are you expecting vampire makeup and black fingernails? Believe me, it's not like that."

"Oh, Auntie, I know what a witch is." He sounded disgusted. "We had one come in and talk to our class. They're into goddesses and myths."

"And you *like* that?" She would have thought a thirteen-year-old boy would prefer some fantasy form of Satanism.

He shrugged. "Yeah. I think it's cool."

Jimmy Dee ruffled his hair. "I think *you're* cool."

Kenny was the gentlest of children, unlike Sheila, who could be rambunctious. As a result, he got more rewards from adults, which bothered Skip sometimes—she hated seeing him work so hard to be perfect. "Why do you think it's cool?" she said.

"All those stories. Mythology and stuff. Oh, yeah, and magic. Everybody likes magic."

"Okay. I'll see if I can get you in." *He really is too cute for words.*

Dee-Dee sighed. "You're going to call them?"

Layne sneezed again. "Yes. She is."

The Crabmeat Extravaganza was something with cheese and eggplant and artichokes (besides crabmeat, of course): "My own concoction," Dee-Dee said proudly, but Kenny left half of it on his plate.

When he had begged to go, been chided for failure to eat, and finally been excused, Layne said, "Oh, well. Sheila probably wouldn't even have pretended."

"Where is she, anyway?" said Skip, who had been invited at the last minute, on grounds that they had too much because Sheila was out.

"At Torian's." Dee-Dee and Layne exchanged a look. Skip noticed they'd been doing that more and more lately, like married people.

"What is it?" she said.

"What did you think of Torian?" Dee-Dee asked.

"Nice. Shy but nice." She shrugged, trying to figure out what he was getting at. "Inoffensive. Why?"

"I don't know. I just notice Sheila's getting weirder and weirder lately—maybe since she started hanging with Torian."

"More obstreperous, you mean. That's called adolesence, Dee-Dee darling. They just get that way."

"I don't know. I think she's *less* obstreperous. She's even a little withdrawn; she spends a lot of time in her room."

"Teenagers are like cats—they have important business that doesn't involve mere humans."

Layne said, "Tell her what's really bothering you."

"Oh, all right." Dee-Dee turned to Skip. "That business with Darryl the other day. What's with that child?"

"Oh, that. Well, you're right. She went too far."

"You know how I feel about Darryl—"

Layne said, "I don't want to hear about it."

Dee-Dee gave him a flirtatious look. Skip said, "Quit being cute, you two."

"Darryl's the man I'd marry if it weren't for Layne—"

"He handled it really well."

Dee-Dee nodded. "A gentleman to the core. But she can't make a habit of that shit."

"So why are you telling me and not her?"

"My, don't we cut to the chase."

"Uh-oh. I don't like the way you said that."

"The poor child has no mother. Who's going to give her motherly little talks?"

"You are, Dad."

"How about some chocolate cake? I've been baking all day."

"You have not. And don't think you can bribe me."

"Hush or I'll give yours to Kenny." He plopped a huge slice in front of her. "Of course I'd never *dream* of bribing you. But I know you're as concerned about the girl's welfare as her mother and I are—isn't that right, Laynie?—so naturally you'll do the right thing. I offer cake merely to fortify you."

Skip sighed. "I don't have to talk to her tonight, do I?"

"She's not even coming home tonight. She's sleeping over at Torian's." He made a fist and slammed it gently against his forehead. "God knows what those two are plotting."

"Okay, I'll do it. I don't know when or how—and I've got no earthly idea what I'll say, but if you want a completely unqualified cop on the case, you've got it."

"You're not unqualified, you're a woman."

Layne said, "Just tell her we're going to beat her butt if she doesn't stop it."

Skip laughed. Sheila at fifteen was nearly as big as Skip—over five-eight and a hundred and forty-five pounds. Layne was an inch shorter and probably weighed less.

"I've got to go, guys. Got a phone call to make."

Dee-Dee said, "You go hug that bear," knowing she was about to call Steve Steinman, her long-distance beau.

● ●

It was two hours earlier in Los Angeles, about seven o'clock. "Hang on a minute," said Steve. "I was just making some pasta." When he got back, he said, "You okay? How are you feeling?"

She was taken aback, having almost forgotten he'd been worried about her. "Better." She thought about it. "I'm actually feeling better."

"Fantastic! What's happened?"

"Oh my God. I don't know where to start. First of all, I'm on leave from the department."

She heard him breathing in. "Is that really a good idea?"

"I lost it when I saw a kid whose father got killed. People saw."

"Yikes. Not good."

"Cappello said she'd make me go to Cindy Lou if I didn't do something drastic, so I went to Cindy Lou myself—not officially, I mean, just as a friend. And she said take a leave and go to a shrink."

"It must be working. You sound a hundred percent better."

"Well, in a way it is, I guess. But the therapist dumped me. What happened was, the first session was great. She got me thinking about what I ought to be doing, and that worked out so well I almost feel . . ." she stopped to assess ". . . well, not my old self, but better than I was. But then, because of all that, she dumped me." She realized she was more or less gibbering. The whole Jacomine thing scrambled her brains.

"You're not making sense."

"I know. I just caught on."

"But you do sound more upbeat."

"I really think I am." She took a breath. "Okay, let me start from the beginning. Remember that preacher-man I met last year? Errol Jacomine?"

"Sure. He's running for mayor."

"Right. I'm trying to kick his ass."

"*That's* what you got out of therapy?"

"Well, yeah. She hypnotized me, and I realized that's what I wanted most in the world."

"I thought you wanted to be with me."

She laughed. She had been withdrawn for weeks, and he had put up with it and gotten past it in his own mind, understanding it had nothing to do with him.

"Then I went back for my second appointment—having done quite a bit of work already, I might mention—and she said she couldn't see me anymore—her husband's his press secretary."

"She should have thought of that before."

"He only got the job the day I saw her."

"Sounds fishy, doesn't it?"

"Everything about Jacomine's fishy. That's why I gibber when I try to talk about it. It's like some giant kids' game run amok."

"I don't see what you mean."

"See? I'm not making sense again. It's like the way kids play fantasy games. They agree to play certain parts to keep the game going. Jacomine's getting people to play parts—like that time when I met him and all those people stood up together. Each one was a recovering something-or-other his precious church had saved from the gutter."

"Isn't that 'testifyin' '? I thought it was an old Protestant tradition."

"I can't explain it. My brains are scrambled."

"Exactly how do you plan to kick Jacomine's ass?"

"Using my police skills, of course." She was suddenly sick of the whole subject. "Listen, how's the project going?"

"So glad you asked. I'm coming into town next week."

"You are? When?" She heard excitement in her voice, and she wondered at it. Not even Steve Steinman had been able to make her voice rise for a long time.

"You sound like you might be glad to see me."

"I'm always glad to see you. What day are you getting here?"

"How about a week from today?"

"Fantastic! Still have your key?"

"Uh-huh."

"Okay. Tell me about the project."

"I think I want to do two things—all part of the same piece. Kids who've been shot by other kids."

"And the kids who shot them."

"You got it. What do you think?"

"Powerful. Depressing."

"Sometimes I don't know if you can have one without the other."

"Yes." Her voice was almost a whisper. There were times when it took only a nuance of thought to swing her back into sadness. Her life before her depression had been powerful; she was paying for it now.

● ●

The next morning she awakened with a sense of something unpleasant to do. Rolling over, she thought of it—go tell Nikki Pigeon's sister that Nikki was dead; try to persuade her to make a positive ID.

It can wait, she thought, and turned her mind once more to Steve Steinman, her favorite early-morning diversion. She liked to think of him in the zone between sleep and full awareness—she reveled in his voice; his laugh; his happy, kind face.

His body, heavy against hers.

She wasn't ready to come out of her trance when the phone rang.

"Skip? Cappello here."

"Sylvia. What is it?"

"You tell me."

"What?"

"Nobody can get through the switchboard, we've had so many calls about you."

"Calls about me? From whom?"

"From people trying to get you fired. They say you're a racist, and a cop has absolutely no business in politics, and how dare you try to tear down a good man like Errol Jacomine."

"What?"

"What are you doing, and why? You're home because you're supposed to be resting. What the hell is going on here?"

"Sylvia, who's getting these calls?"

"Me. Joe Tarantino." Her lieutenant. "Every other lieutenant in the building. Every captain. Every officer who anyone's brother-in-law knows. The superintendent. And the mayor. And guess who they all called? Joe."

"You've got to be kidding."

"You're jeopardizing your job, Skip. Tell me you're not working on Perretti's campaign."

"Of course not. But—how to say this?—I've been trying to get something on Jacomine. Not for any candidate. Just because the guy scares me to death." She realized how lame that must sound to a working police sergeant—people didn't do things for free, certainly not scratch for dirt on a candidate. The concept of "concerned citizen" hardly applied in a state as corrupt as Louisiana. "Look. This is the one thing in the world I want to do right now. I met him last year and it shocked the hell out of me. We talked about it—remember?"

Cappello ignored the question. "Did I mention you're supposed to be taking a rest? You need to go to the beach and cool out."

Skip was silent, trying to think what to make of all this. "How many calls have there been?"

"I don't know. Dozens. Call after call since seven A.M. No letup."

"Doesn't this strike you as an organized campaign?"

"What does that have to do with it?"

"Tell me the truth. Have you ever seen or heard of anything like this?"

"No. But the guy's running for office—what do you expect? And you're vulnerable right now."

"Sylvia, this is scary as hell. Political candidates aren't this organized. These people are a bunch of robots."

"I really don't think it's up to me to comment on that. I'm telling you as a friend that people here are hot under the collar. Think about it. Our lines are tied up, and people's time is being wasted. And you're doing what you're not supposed to do—"

"I've got a right to . . ."

The sergeant raised her voice. "Skip, I'm telling you as a friend. I really think you should listen."

How to make them stop? she thought. *I haven't even started yet. How do they even know about me?*

There could be a leak somewhere—maybe in the coroner's office.

Surely not. But what else? How else could they know?

Jamal Broussard. The note in the mailbox.

But to know about that, they'd have had to follow me.

She got dressed and went to the towing company where he worked.

• •

Jamal Broussard was slightly shorter than she was, and a body builder. He had a neck like a five-gallon can and a chest like a fence. His hair was short, but he had a mustache, which gave him a bit of Aaron Neville sensuality.

"Skip Langdon," she said, and realized she couldn't produce her badge. For a moment she was tongue-tied. Finally, she said, "Did you get my note?"

"What are you talking about?"

"You didn't?"

"Lady, I got a job to do. You want to tell me what you want?"

"I wonder if I could talk to you about Nikki Pigeon."

"I don't know no Nikki Pigeon."

"Her sister says you do."

"I don't know her, and I don't know her sister, and I don't know you. What you mean comin' down to my place of bi'ness, tryin' to get me fired?"

"She's dead, Mr. Broussard."

"Who dead?"

"Nikki."

He gave her a long look. She thought she saw something flash a second in his eyes, just for a second, something more like fear than sorrow. "I don't know no Nikki, and I don't appreciate you comin' down here. You gon' go now?"

"I know you were friends, Jamal. Don't you even care how she died?"

"You get out of here." His voice became a roar. "You get out of here *now*." He'd gotten so angry so fast there had to be something there.

He could still be in the church, she thought.

• •

Tanya Pigeon came to the door in dirty khaki trousers that hung on a frame that looked ten pounds lighter than a day or two ago. Her T-shirt had been pulled on with no bra, and her hair hadn't been combed. Skip didn't think she was going to live long.

"You gon' give me some money?" she said, and she sounded half-loaded.

"Why should I give you some money?"

" 'Cause I'm hungry. I ain't had nothin' to eat all day."

"Come on. I'll buy you lunch."

"I don' feel good right now."

"Okay, I'll give you some money. But I have some bad news for you."

For a fraction of a second, Skip thought she saw something besides dullness in her eyes.

"It's about Nikki, ain't it?"

"She's dead, Tanya."

"How you know? You see her?"

"I saw a video of her. The coroner would like you to come down and look at it."

"I have to do that?"

"No, you don't have to. I just thought you'd like to know what happened to your sister."

"She gone now. Nothin' else matters." Her voice was softer, as if the news were actually sinking in. "She never did no drugs or nothin', and now she gone. I thought she did good when she went off to the quarters to dance. Then she come back, she got a job at a restaurant. She was doin' real good." She sniffed. "And now she gone."

"She's been gone for a couple of months." *And you never even noticed.*

"*He* done it. That holy father of hers. He the one did Nikki. Oh, yes. He the one."

"Who's that?"

"You know. The one she runnin' from last year when you come aroun'. You know the one."

"Errol Jacomine."

"Yeah, he the one. Nikki afraid of him. She never get over bein' afraid."

"I didn't even say how she died."

"Well? What happen?"

"She was found with her skull cracked. Could have fallen, might have been mugged."

Tanya snorted, "You don't think he done it, you blind in one eye, cain't see out the other."

"How do you know it wasn't a drug dealer?"

"You listen or not? Nikki didn't *do* no drugs. I already tol' you that."

"Maybe it was someone who thought she was you. Or someone trying to get at you."

"Oh, no. No way. Look, I be a mess; no two ways about it, I be a mess. But I jus' buy, I don't do no sellin'. I don't owe nobody nothin' 'cause I'm so fucked up ain' nobody gon' give me credit. Nobody in hell be bothered killin' me or any of my kin jus' 'cause they related to me. You put that idea outcha head, Miss White Po-lice."

"Tanya, it just doesn't compute. Nobody who was clean could live with somebody as bad off as you."

Tears came to Tanya's eyes and she wiped them away with a fist. "Well, my kids had to. See, I be like this when Nikki come back from that church thing. She stay to take care of the kids. She mighty nice to me and the kids both."

"Where are the kids now?"

"They gone."

"What do you mean they're gone?"

"They just gone."

"You mean they died?"

"No. They just gone. I b'lieve Ms. MacAlou got 'em right now."

"Who's Ms. MacAlou?"

She just shook her head, more tears flowing, and stepped back inside the house.

● ●

Without giving it a second thought, Skip headed for Headquarters, having failed to heed the morning's warning. Cappello and Tarantino had to be filled in—this was too serious to keep to herself.

She wasn't prepared for a reception that would have frozen a team of huskies.

Cappello first looked puzzled. Then, manipulating her body subtly, like a yogi about to move into a pose, she withdrew from Skip, wrapping herself in an invisible cloak of separation. "What are you doing here?"

Skip noticed she didn't use her name.

"I need to talk to you and Joe."

"Langdon, you need to go home."

"Can we go into your office?"

Cappello turned and walked toward it without answering. Skip had never seen her so angry.

When they had entered the sergeant's private space, Skip said, "Yesterday I ID'd a body—remember Nikki Pigeon, that witness in the Hebert case?"

Cappello shook her head. Her voice was glacial. "You're not supposed to be working."

"Actually, I did this before we talked. I would have thought you'd be glad to have a Jane Doe ID'd. She was killed around the end of June."

The sergeant said nothing, if anything pulling her muscles tighter against her skeleton, further from Skip.

"She had a cracked skull. Her sister says Jacomine did it."

"Does she have any proof?"

"Of course not." Skip was beginning to get royally pissed. "Last I heard, it's our job to get proof."

"Not your job. Nothing is your job right now. That case has been investigated. Go home."

"Don't you want to even—"

"I want you to stop persecuting a perfectly decent man who may be the only honest politician in the state of Louisiana. If Jackson's elected, we've got the same old machine as we ever had; the same old asleep-at-the-wheel chief; the same old institutionalized corruption. If Perretti is, God knows what could happen—he'll probably start a race war. With Jacomine we might have a chance."

"Sylvia, he's a psychopath."

"Get some help, Skip. You're a damn good officer and I don't want to lose you. For Christ's sake, get some help."

"As a matter of fact, I was trying, but Jacomine seems to have co-opted my therapist, along with everyone else in this goddamn town."

For the first time, Skip saw compassion in Cappello's brown eyes. Pain almost.

7

• •

The day got no better. Scarcely believing she'd said what she had to Cappello, practically accusing her, she'd literally gone back to bed, hunkering in embarrassment. She slept the sleep of the depressed.

Now and then she woke and thought she should get up and eat something, but instead she closed her eyes again.

She might eventually have turned on the television and fallen into its socially acceptable but druglike haze if she hadn't had dinner plans approaching a command performance.

Her dad, who had barely spoken to her since she went on the job, was finally coming around. Three of these invitations had come lately—to dinner at the family home on State Street—and she'd successfully fielded them all. But this time she felt sorry for her mother when she called, and she realized it was childish anyway, putting off the inevitable, acting as cranky as her dad.

But it was going to be a strain, and she didn't feel up to it now. Yet she was stuck with it. Her mother had even called to remind her.

She got up with half an hour to spare and then dithered over what to wear, finally settling on black linen slacks, a green silk T-shirt, and a cream blazer. She wasn't sure the blazer worked, but it was all she had.

Sheila and Kenny were in the courtyard with Angel, a white blur with one black eye and one black ear, racing about like a type A on a deadline.

Kenny said, "You look nice, Aunt Skippy."

Angel, who'd grown nearly as large as Napoleon, Steve Steinman's shepherd, leaped up on her, leaving a black smear on the blazer.

"Damn!" she shouted, and the terrified dog, possibly thinking she'd said "down," yelped and retreated.

"Oh, Auntie, I'm sorry."

Skip sighed. "It doesn't look that bad, does it?"

"It looks shitty," said Sheila.

"Sheila, could you *please* refrain from four-letter words?"

She heard the testiness in her voice and saw that Sheila looked nearly as hurt as Angel.

"I'm sorry, honey. It's not my day."

"Well, you don't have to yell."

That made Skip mad again. "And you don't have to be snotty."

She left without saying good-bye, the smear still on the jacket, her whole being out of sorts.

● ●

Her mother met her at the door, dressed in beige linen—dressed up, in fact, and Skip wondered if she'd misunderstood, if it were someone's birthday.

She pecked at her mother's cheek. "You look nice. Is someone else coming?"

"Oh, yes, didn't I tell you? Camille and Conrad are already here. And the Gilkersons are on the way."

Skip strove to keep her face under control. The Gilkersons were her parents' age and her brother Conrad might as well be, for all the youthful exuberance he exhibited. Just being around them made her feel like a criminal, so constricted were their likes and dislikes, so strongly did they disapprove of almost everything.

On the other hand, she liked Camille, her brother's wife.

Camille might share the beliefs of the others—Skip had no idea—but she was too polite to let it ruin the conversation.

Her father came in and pecked her. "Skip. How's it going?" As if there weren't years of partial estrangement between them.

Camille gave her a hug, Conrad barely nodded. "How're things at the cop shop?"

"Actually, I'm taking a leave of absence."

She watched as her father's face fell, thinking how ironic it was that he'd stopped speaking to her because she had joined the police department and had seemingly only started again because she'd done so well it reflected on him.

Her mother handed her a glass of white wine and went to answer the door.

"Why is that?" her father asked, trying to keep the disapproval out of his voice.

This is about the way it looks, she thought. *It's always about that.*

As a child, she had been used as a lever to pry the Langdons into desirable social circles. She had to go to certain schools, attend certain birthday parties, join particular clubs, and reflect well on the family. It was this last that—not knowing what was expected of her—she had trouble with.

Her mother came in with the Gilkersons. Nan had a perfect small-waisted body, brown hair that had been lovingly labored over, and a face that hadn't yet been lifted, but was probably being regularly peeled. Ted had white hair, a slightly too-pink face, and a middle as convex as Nan's was concave.

"Ah. The prodigal daughter." Ted kissed her and she realized he'd been drinking.

Her father looked disconcerted, and she could see that he didn't want to continue the conversation, didn't want even Ted, his best friend, to know the bad news, whatever it might be.

"How are things on America's worst police force? When are they making you chief?"

Conrad said: "I'd be ashamed to say what I do if I were you."

"We're mighty proud of Skip," her father said, his face red.

Skip thought: *Hoist on his own petard*, and felt sorry for him.

Her mother, who spent most of her time fighting with her

father, seemingly for sport, rushed to his defense as she always did when a third person attacked. "It's not her fault the cops are killing each other. Is it, Skip?"

Skip smiled. "I'm innocent."

She wondered if her parents, too, had been drinking. It was nice to have them on her side for once. She hoped it would continue awhile.

"What's the inside story on that?" Nan asked. She accepted a drink and settled on a sofa.

"You know as much as I do. This young cop's accused of robbing a restaurant and shooting her former partner, who was on a paid detail there."

Conrad said, "And that was the same week a Tulane student claimed she got raped by a cop."

"Hey, nobody's perfect." They laughed, but Skip was stung, not so much by their jibes as by the fact that she had to defend a department that really was as corrupt and inept as they thought. She was suddenly touched by her father's pride in her accomplishments—he probably had to put up with this kind of garbage a lot.

She tried to keep it light, obediently telling war stories until her mother called them to dinner.

Ted Gilkerson, who'd now had a couple of martinis in addition to whatever he'd swizzled earlier, wouldn't leave her alone. "It's the mayor who appoints the superintendent, right? If we had a decent mayor, we might get a decent chief."

"I like the mayor," said Camille, but he bulled on ahead.

"Only reason we got the kind of police we do is, the powers that be want it that way. Right, Skip?"

"I don't know, Ted. I think the problems are ingrained over generations."

"Good mayor could stop 'em. We gotta get that asshole outta there."

"Well, since he's not running for reelection, I don't think it'll be a problem."

"There's always a machine guy. Jackson's it this time." Jackson had been accused of taking kickbacks when he served on the city council. In fact, he'd resigned over it.

"Know who I like?" said Camille. "I just love Errol Jacomine. Now *he* talks sense."

Skip felt her stomach turn over.

Her mother said, "At least he's not a racist. Perretti might be."

"My man!" said Conrad, raising a clenched fist. Skip couldn't conceive how the two of them could be made of the same genetic material.

"I agree with you, honey." Their father addressed himself to Camille. "I really think he's got something to offer."

Skip said, "I know him. There's something wrong with him. He's a very, very bad man. And I don't think Perretti's really a racist." She shrugged. "Just another Louisiana opportunist."

"I think he believes what he says, and I think he's going to kick ass," said Conrad. "I'm voting for him."

"Sweetheart, you can be so heartless sometimes," said Camille. "Jacomine's done stuff the others only talk about. He's gotten people off drugs, he's cleaned up neighborhoods, he's worked for good candidates . . ."

Skip noticed everyone was nodding except Conrad. "I'm voting for him," said her father.

She was losing her appetite fast.

●   ●

Lise had gotten stuffed peppers somewhere, and some broccoli. She had supplemented these with frozen corn and called it dinner.

I could have cooked, Torian thought. I could have shopped. I could have made something real. She won't do it herself and won't let me do it either. She doesn't have any idea what I can do or who I am.

"How was school today, dear?"

Torian shrugged and pushed some of the pepper around on her plate.

"Torian, for heaven's sake. The least you can do is answer when I speak to you."

With a huge effort, Torian heaved her shoulders up. "School was school," she said. "Just like always."

"What are you taking this year?" School had started a week ago.

"Mother, please! I've told you six times."

"Then you'd better tell me a seventh, young lady, because it suddenly slipped my mind."

It's because you drink so much, Torian thought.

She said, "English, P.E., algebra two, piano, ancient history, and French."

"I don't think I like your tone of voice."

"You *asked* me what I was taking."

"Fine. And you answered me."

They ate in silence for a while, awkwardness spread before them like a picnic cloth.

Lise couldn't stand it—Torian knew she'd blink first. "I wish you'd have a little appreciation for what I try to do for you."

Torian said nothing. What was there to say?

Lise said, "Well?"

"I do, Mother. I really appreciate what you're trying to do for me." She had to say this at least once a week. Lise never let her forget what she was fucking trying to do for her, as if Torian had asked for it, as if her greatest desire in the world was for prefab stuffed peppers and frozen corn, and a mother who'd go out later and fuck her brains out, leaving Torian to watch television or drink Lise's booze or rob convenience stores if she felt like it.

I wish I was fucking my brains out.

It bothered her a great deal that Noel didn't consider her adult enough to have sex.

"There are laws, darlin' girl," he'd finally said. "They'd toss my ass in jail and throw away the key."

As if she would tell. As if she, Torian Gernhard, who loved him, couldn't be trusted. That distressed her as much as anything else—that he didn't trust her. It frustrated her so much she wanted to bite something.

Lise is over forty—why does she get to fuck and not me? She's too old to enjoy it.

But then, why does she do it?

Why does she consider that more important than behaving like a mother?

Because she's pathetic, that's why. She probably confuses sex with love. She thinks if she sleeps with old Charles he'll keep coming around.

Which I cordially wish he wouldn't. Who would want him, anyway?

Lise's eyes filled. "I wish you really meant that."

Really meant what? Torian could barely remember what she'd said. Oh, yes, that she appreciated Lise's efforts.

God, I wish I lived with my father!

She said, "I wish you'd stop asking me to say it."

Lise said nothing for a while, just ate mechanically. Torian thought it was possible she'd get off light, but out of the blue, her mother started sobbing. "You heartless little bitch! You don't understand anything and you don't know anything, and you don't care about anyone. You haven't got a decent bone in that skinny little body you're so goddamn proud of. You haven't got a second for anyone but your own selfish, pathetic little soul. Well, let me tell you something, young lady—you're not nearly as smart as you think you are!"

Torian gasped, terrified. What had set her off? What was wrong with her?

It's so unfair, she thought. *She must be crazy.*

I've never said a word to her about my body. I'm not proud of it—where on Earth did she get that idea? I'm ashamed of it—I don't have any boobs, and my legs don't even go together at the top and my butt's too big. How could she think something like that? And where does she get off saying I don't care about anybody? I love Noel. Love him. I'd do anything for him. And Daddy, too; and Sheila. How could she say something like that?

And I don't think I'm smart at all. Certainly not compared to Noel. I mean, I'm smarter than Lise, but that's nothing. It doesn't mean I think I'm smart. Why does she think all this stuff?

Lise got hold of herself long enough to stare at Torian for a long time, nearly a minute, Torian thought later, tears rolling out of eyes so hurt you would have thought Torian was dead, not sitting here being berated by a crazy woman.

Torian stared back, afraid to look away, afraid Lise might hit her or jump out a window, or pick up a frying pan and throw it— she had no idea what was going to happen next, she just knew her mother had flipped her wig and might be dangerous.

Should she run?

Instead, Lise ran. Got up, overturning her chair, and fled the room, her butt wobbling in the cotton pants she was wearing.

Torian sat stunned for a minute, not at all sure what was happening.

I'm eating dinner, she told herself. *Dinner is what's happening.*

She forked a bit of the pepper and chewed for a long time.

Eating was definitely not what was happening.

Feeling dazed, she got up and scraped the plates into plastic bags, which she tied and dumped in the garbage. She put the lid on tight, the whole procedure being designed to guard against the roaches she hated so much and which pervaded the Quarter. There wasn't a single roach in her father's house in Old Metairie.

Mechanically, she washed the dishes, and put away the plates, listening for any noise at all from her mother's room. She heard nothing.

Finally, feeling curiously empty and lonely, her throat tight, she went to her own room, wishing she could call Noel. She did her homework, which took about forty-five minutes, and then she did hear her mother stirring about the apartment. Her body tensed. She wondered if Lise would knock on her door. When she didn't, Torian's muscles let go, and she fell back on her pillow.

She wrote a poem, which was what she always did when she felt sad, but it failed to satisfy her. It was a poem about confusion, which was all she knew right now, all she could write about, and that wasn't helpful.

She thought about Noel, about what it would be like to live with him, but the thought was so frightening she had to stop. She had to wait at least three years. Wasn't that it? They could have legal sex when she was eighteen, he had said, and there was absolutely no chance they were breaking that particular law—he had been clear on that.

She felt the ache between her legs that she always felt now when she thought of him.

I can't wait three years.

I have to wait three years to graduate, too—to get away from Lise.

Why is everything always in the future? Why can't I have anything now?

She lay there awhile, her cheek against the pillow, wondering how long she would have to be unhappy until one good thing came to her.

I can't stand it. I just can't stand it. There ought to be something I can do.
It occurred to her that there was.

There was a way she could stand side by side with Noel, a way she could function in the adult world, a way she might even get to see him every day, or at least sometimes, in a perfectly normal way. No one would suspect a thing, and she'd be doing something useful with her life, maybe even something fulfilling.

Noel had told her how much he thought of Errol Jacomine, what his becoming mayor could mean to the city. And Torian could help. In some small way, she could help. She would go down tomorrow and volunteer as a campaign worker.

• •

Boo had put on a pot of red beans that afternoon. All that remained was to cook the rice and put together a salad. She was bustling about doing that, having put Joy in her Johnny Jump-up, and thinking about Noel.

Something was wrong with him, but she didn't know what. She had the vague feeling it was her fault.

Oh, come on, Boo, you're a shrink.

That doesn't mean you aren't supposed to be a good wife.

I have this weird feeling I haven't been lately.

She heard the garage door open and the car drive in. Her hand went to her hair, straightening.

Noel came in. "Aren't you a pretty picture."

"A little wilted from the heat." Automatically, she kissed him. "Are you hungry?"

He shrugged. "Not really."

"Good, let's have a drink before dinner. I'll just finish up the salad."

Noel took Joy out of her seat and did Daddy things—throwing her in the air, making her laugh. Boo felt almost happy with the three of them in the kitchen, for a few minutes able to forget her disquiet.

Noel went to change, and she cut up a tomato. She was thrilled with this new job of his, thinking it was just what he needed at the moment. He'd been a very good, extremely respected television reporter who quit to write a book—not journalism, but fiction, something he'd always wanted to do. She wasn't sure what the story was, or even if Noel knew. She just knew it was important to him.

But he hadn't seemed to be making that much progress, and then they bought this house, and that distracted him further. It was deemed that Boo's office needed to happen first, and so it would be awhile before Noel's was finished.

Consequently, he'd taken a small office in a building owned by friends of theirs. It was a little damp, a little depressing, at least to Boo's mind; she much preferred fresh paint to noble rot.

She had no idea if he was getting anything done there—he didn't talk about it, and had even snapped at her when she tried. But what she thought was that he was used to the daily ego massage of being on television, and, even if he was writing *Moby Dick* in there, he needed a quick fix to keep him going.

Consequently, this press secretary thing was just what the doctor ordered.

Especially since she was so distant lately. It wasn't easy overseeing the contractors and taking care of the baby and also keeping her practice up. Still, that shouldn't take away from her marriage.

Why am I putting it last? she wondered. *I swear to God I'll do better.*

She had changed into an ankle-length, flowing dress, and pinned her hair up, for openers. And she had gotten ice cream for dessert, despite the fact that she hated to have sweets in the house, due to her penchant for eating things she shouldn't.

What a selfish person I am, she had thought as she bought it, realizing how seldom she did something extra.

She poured Noel a glass of wine, a Chardonnay of which he was particularly fond, and which she'd also taken the trouble to get today.

Returning in shorts and polo shirt, he kissed the back of her neck.

She said, "How was the first day at work?"

"A little weird. I have a feeling it's going to be a thrill a minute. And maybe not in a good way."

"Woo. Let's go in the living room."

She waited until he was comfortable in one of the chairs, and then sat on the floor, looking up at him. They had sat like this a lot, early in their courtship; for some reason, it appealed to her.

"Tell me everything," she said.

"Did anyone ever tell you politics is a dirty business?"

"That's somewhere else, right? Certainly not in Louisiana."

"Apparently some cop is trying to discredit our boy."

"How?"

"I don't know exactly. She's got a wild hair about him, for some reason. I'm not sure exactly what went on, but I think she met him on a case and took a dislike to him. Probably just your basic redneck racist."

Boo's heart had speeded up when she heard the pronoun. "What's her name?" she asked.

"Langdon, I think. And some nickname. Skip, maybe."

"Ah." Confidentiality required that Boo keep her mouth shut.

"Have you ever heard of her?"

Boo shrugged. "I think so. She gets her name in the paper now and then."

Noel nodded. "So I gather. But since I never covered police—" He shrugged. As a reporter, he had considered crime beneath him.

"Anyway, there's a lot of stuff I don't know about the way campaigns are run. Jacomine's got this scary-looking aide named Potter Menard—sunglasses, power grooming, like the Ton Ton Macoute."

"Or the Farrakhan guys."

"Yeah." A shadow passed over Noel's face. "Anyway, Jacomine said to him, 'You know what to do,' and Menard gave this kind of curt nod like, 'Sure, Godfather.' "

"What? You think she's in danger?"

"Of course not. I'm sure they'll tell me what's happening, as soon as I start catching on to things. But it did have this sort of eerie feel. Kind of like a contract killing."

Boo was fighting panic. "You're kidding, right? Tell me you're kidding?"

He leaned over and touched her cheek. "Hey. What's wrong, baby? This is me, Noel. Am I a bad guy?"

She shook her head, trying to smile.

"And this is just a crummy mayor's election, not the governorship or anything. It's not important enough to bother doing anything criminal—you know what I mean?"

"I'm not so sure, Noel."

She sipped her wine. How could he be so naive?

In a town like this, which is more like a banana republic, it's probably all about who gets appointed to what and how much they pay to get access to a particular till.

"Oh, come on. I'm a hardened newsman, remember? Believe me, there is nothing bad going on with Errol Jacomine. He's a prince among men, and I'm going to get him elected. Everything's all right. Do you believe me?"

She smiled. "Go get 'em, Tiger."

But she had purposely avoided her husband's query. She wasn't at all sure everything was all right. The hairs on the back of her neck were standing up.

8

• •

There was a phalanx of volunteers in the office when Noel got there. They were making phone calls and writing letters, Potter overseeing them.

When he could catch Potter's eye, he said, "What's going on?"

"Come in here." Potter led him to his private office. "This is our organization in action. You want to know how we're going to stop that cop? We're going to work at it."

"Doing—uh—what?" Noel felt a little flustered.

"I'm going to give you a lesson right now." He gave Noel an appraising look. "I think you're going to be good at this."

He dialed a number and spoke to Noel again. "Listen up."

"Sergeant Sylvia Cappello," he said, and waited.

Then: "Sergeant Cappello? This is Potter Menard with the Jacomine campaign. I understand you have an officer named Skip Langdon in your platoon. You know, she's working with Marvin Perretti's campaign, and I've—"

"She's not? Well, I don't mean to contradict, but I believe she is." He listened a moment. "We know perfectly well she is, Sergeant.

85

"How do we know? Why, people call us and give us information—people from all over town. Sergeant, I don't know if you realize it, but that woman is creating quite a disturbance in this town. Look, I wouldn't bother you with that, it's our problem, really. It's just that I'm disturbed by some of the rumors I've been hearing. She can look all she wants and she won't find any dirt on Errol Jacomine—that's just not going to happen—but you understand, a candidate has to be—frankly, Sergeant, according to our information, this particular officer has an unhealthy obsession with sex."

Of all the things Noel expected to hear, that was the last. He could imagine the sergeant's puzzlement. *What does that have to do with anything?* she must be wondering. *What is this guy getting at?*

She'd probably tell him that.

In a moment, Potter hung up, looking satisfied. "What'd you think of that?" he asked.

"To be honest, I didn't see the point of it. If I'd been the sergeant I'd have told you to fuck off."

"Oh, she did. She did." He chuckled, obviously extremely pleased with himself. "Yeah, she must be a straight arrow. Not many of 'em out there—most people would have wanted to know what I meant by 'obsessed with.' They'd want to know how the rumor got started—you know, just what their officer had been doing and what she was likely to do.

"You see what I'm gettin' at here? It makes her sound unstable. That's because she's a woman. Now if it were a man, I'd have said I'd heard he was violent. But sex is best for a woman."

Noel was wondering if campaign work was really the right career path for him. *Maybe I'm just naive,* he thought. *I don't know anything about how campaigns really work. Maybe this stuff is just routine for these guys.*

Trying to keep an open mind—at least to keep the ice out of his voice, he said, "Look, I don't see the point. She hung up on you, right?"

"Yeah, but she's going to think, 'Where there's smoke, there's fire.' She's going to know her officer's been up to no good, but she ain't going to know what kind of no good. It's brilliant, you see that? 'Obsessed with sex' could mean anything. Maybe it means she says unprofessional things; maybe nothin' like that; maybe she sees sexual misbehavior everywhere she looks—maybe the sergeant better be above reproach herself with that woman around."

Noel was trying to sort out this information in his own mind. He said, "What about all those other people who're placing calls—are they spreading the same rumor?"

"Oh, hell no, my man. Hell, no. We got a lot more than one trick up our sleeve. Some of 'em are callin' all over, trying to get some real dirt on her; some are just complaining that she's doing such a thing to a fine man like Errol Jacomine; some are saying they heard she's really unreliable." He chuckled again. "Yeah. 'Unreliable's good. Even 'unstable'—I got a few people on that one. Alcohol and drugs, we got some folks on those. Actually, not drugs so much because she probably isn't on 'em. But alcohol and sex are good, because everybody fucks and most people drink a little. If they don't it's because they're in AA, which means they used to, and that's even better—sounds like they fell off the wagon."

Stunned, feeling his way, Noel said, "You must have worked in a lot of campaigns."

"This is my first, my man. What do you think? Am I a strategist?"

"Where'd you learn this stuff?"

"Oh, I've had some teachers." He laughed, a more expansive laugh than the smug chuckles he'd been emitting.

"What are you saying? Are you spying on Perretti's people spying on us? Is that what it is?"

Potter nodded. "We got some of that going on. Don't think we don't."

"So they're doing the same thing."

"All that and more, my man. You can take that to the bank. I'm gonna teach you, too. I'm gon' teach you everything I know."

"Well, there are some things I think I'd rather not know."

"What, you don't want to be in on this? This is the fun stuff."

"I think I'd better stick to writing press releases." He got up and went into his own office, feeling disoriented and a bit unbelieving, not sure if things were coming apart at the seams or if he, hardened reporter that he was, was getting exposed, for the first time, to the real world.

He sat there for a while, covering his face with his hands, not sure what to make of anything. He had looked for some stability in this job. It was a time in his life when he couldn't write, he wasn't sure why. The book had been going slowly, painstakingly, more a matter of grinding pain than creative fulfillment.

Then he had met Torian, and all work had stopped. He simply couldn't think of anything or anyone else—that is, anyone except Boo and Joy and his guilt toward them, his sadness that his marriage would end, his fear that he would lose his child.

He sat there in his office, his computer on, trying to focus on his novel, and he found sometimes that an hour or more had passed and he had not typed a word. Sometimes, when that happened, he gave in to it; he thought it best, as long as he was going to think of Torian, to do it in a creative way. He wrote poems to her, poems that he hadn't yet had the courage to read to her. He was working on a short story as well, but that was like the novel. It was happening slowly, at its own pace. He knew it would come together eventually, but for the moment life was confusing. Things that had seemed permanent were suddenly transient, fragile as crystal.

His job, on which he'd leaned for so many years, was gone, at least for the moment. Boo and Joy were floating figures, bobbing on the horizon. And Torian, so much in the forefront, so Colossus-like in his brain, could disappear at any moment; he was aware of that. If someone found out, anyone at all, she could be forbidden ever to see him again, watched like a prisoner, though they'd done nothing sexual.

His whole life was hanging by a hair.

A job was supposed to give him a sense of security, of permanence, of once again belonging—maybe even a sense of self. And this was like stepping into a strange, upside-down world where he didn't know the rules and people might be cheating.

He felt not only at a disadvantage, he felt a strange sense of foreboding.

Someone knocked at his door.

"Come in."

The candidate himself came in. "Got a minute?"

"Sure." Surely there could be nothing wrong—that was impossible. Here was a man so humble he came to Noel's office instead of summoning him, and then he asked if Noel had a minute, as if being there for Jacomine wasn't his job.

Suddenly he saw what was happening. He saw it as clearly as if the sky had lit up and revealed it: Jacomine didn't have a clue what was happening. Potter Menard was running the show and it was out of hand.

Jacomine said: "We need to talk about the white honky media."

Noel nodded, a little surprised by the epithet but relieved to discuss a subject about which he felt confident.

"Here's a list of reporters we need some dirt on."

Jacomine handed over a piece of paper with seven names on it, all but one people Noel knew. All of them he respected.

Three were good friends, another two were casual friends, one was a friendly associate. He had had dinner in the homes of most of them.

"I don't understand," he said.

Jacomine's eyes looked suddenly small and beady. He shrugged. "Well, you're the press secretary."

"Errol, I don't think you quite understand how things work. The media isn't dirty."

Jacomine laughed, prompting a rueful smile from Noel.

"I mean, relatively speaking. Nothing like politics is."

The other man sat back in his chair. "Oh. Well, I've been misinformed."

I'll just bet you have, and I think I know who your informant was.

"If we tried to blackmail them, they'd just put that in the paper. You see what I mean?"

"Oh. Well. We don't want that, do we?" He seemed embarrassed. Noel was trying to think of something to say to get them over the social hump, something casual and reassuring, when Jacomine stood and turned toward the door. He looked over his shoulder and smiled. "Guess we'll have to kill 'em then."

• •

Skip's phone rang again, for the third time in five minutes. "Hi, it's Tricia."

"Tricia Lattimore. God, I'm glad to hear from you. You're the only person who knows me that's called this morning."

"Lots of wrong numbers?"

"No, it's something else. How's every little thing?"

"Well, I don't know how to say this, but I'm a little worried about some things I've been hearing about you."

Skip sighed. "What have you been hearing?"

"Just that you haven't really recovered from . . . uh . . . what happened last year, and you're on leave."

"Go on." Skip felt her heart pounding, angry and a little panicked.

"Well, I hear you're going around spreading rumors about Errol Jacomine. Listen, he's . . ."

"What am I supposed to have said?"

"I just heard you're saying really crazy things . . ."

"Like what?"

"I don't know, I just . . ."

"You didn't ask?"

"Well, no. But the person who told me is totally reliable. It's someone who knows we're friends and was worried about you—and thought I ought to know. Thought someone ought to be taking care of you."

"Who?"

"I can't tell you that."

"Why not?"

"They asked me not to."

"Why?"

"Listen, it's complicated. I just can't do it."

"Is it someone I know?"

"I'm sorry, Skip, I just can't break the confidence."

"They didn't tell you what I was actually doing . . ."

"They did! They said you're saying crazy things and acting paranoid."

"How am I acting paranoid, and what did I say?"

"Look, Skip, this is a person of goodwill. They were concerned about you."

"Okay, a person of goodwill comes to you about a very close

90

friend, says things that could damage the friend's reputation, and won't let it be known who he or she is. Does that strike you as normal behavior?"

"Skip, you're really overreacting. I just wanted to know if there's anything I can do, and you come at me with this."

"I'm sorry, Tricia. I'm in the middle of something very confusing and uncomfortable."

"Let me help you. Why don't I come over and we can talk about it?"

"I think I have to work this through by myself."

"Come on. I'm your oldest friend."

"Tricia, I really can't."

"Look, it bothers me that you're trying to make something out of this—"

"Make something? I'm not trying to make anything."

"Would you let me talk, please? I called up for the reason I said, and you made a big deal out of who the person was and what did they say . . ."

"So?"

"So I'm sorry to say it, but it really does seem paranoid."

"Look we'll talk about it when this is all over."

"Now you're the one talking in generalities. When what's all over?"

"I'm a police officer. You know I can't talk about my work."

"Skip, you're on leave. Right now you're not a police officer."

"My doorbell's ringing. I've really got to go."

She hung up, breathing hard, her heart beating. This was crazy-making. How on Earth had they gotten to Tricia, who really was her oldest friend?

Or had they?

Maybe I am paranoid, she thought. *Could it be I really am going nuts? Is she right? It makes as much sense as some perfect stranger telling my oldest friend some cockamamie story, and her believing it. Why did she believe it? That's the part I don't get.*

The answer came to her with a nasty jolt: *Darryl!*

Her friend Darryl—the one Sheila liked so well—tended bar in the same place Tricia waitressed. Could Jacomine have gotten to him through one of his followers? Many of them were black, as was Darryl. Was there someone he trusted implicitly who had fallen under Jacomine's spell? A relative, even?

Tricia's informant could have been anyone, of course, but Darryl was her best friend—she'd believe him without a second thought. That might explain why she was so insistent.

This thing is so insidious. If I wasn't paranoid before, I am now. I feel like all my best friends are in a conspiracy against me.

● ●

Her phone rang again. "Detective Langdon? This is Emily Warford. I'm a friend of Sergeant Milius, who works with you."

"I don't really know Sergeant Milius, I've only heard of him."

"Well, listen, I think it's important to the police department for Errol Jacomine to get elected, and so does Sergeant Milius. The Reverend Mr. Jacomine's such a fine, fine man, Detective. I wonder if you know how much he's done for this city? With his day care programs, and his drug treatment programs, and—this is real important to me, because I have a teenage daughter who's a mother—he has a special program that helps girls like her stay in school. I'm sure I don't need to outline each and every one of his contributions—"

"No, indeed. I'm well aware of them, I think."

"But I just wanted to tell you how good Sergeant Milius thinks he's going to be for the police department."

"I really appreciate your calling, but I'm afraid I've got a call on my other line."

As she cradled the receiver, the phone rang again. This time she let the machine pick it up. She hoped the deluge wasn't going to last too long—it would be so irritating to have to get a new phone number.

How did they get my number anyway?

It was Cappello's voice on the machine. Skip picked up.

"Hi. I'm screening today. Jacomine's flock is calling in, one at a time, and so is everyone any of them have ever heard of."

"I know what you mean. We're still getting it down here. Even me."

"Why not? You're my sergeant."

"Look, I've already asked you to stop whatever you're doing. Now I've been officially designated to ask you again. I won't say who asked me—"

"Oh, no, not that again."

"Not what again?"

"That's how he works. Everything's always a big secret."

"Hey. Nothing's secret. I was just being discreet. This request comes straight from Captain Giannini. Is that open enough?"

"Sorry. I guess I was being paranoid."

"Listen, Skip, the brass is very fed up with this. For your own good, please think about that. Will you?"

"I will, Sylvia. I promise."

"Good. Then I'll tell you about the call I just had—the guy sounded like a nut case. I think you might be on to something."

Skip let out her breath so hard it was almost a whistle. "Sylvia. You don't know how much that means to me."

She unplugged her phone, and no sooner had she done it than her doorbell rang. It was Henry, the mailman.

"Got a few letters for you, Skip." He had an armload. "What you been doin'—answering chain letters?"

"Don't knock it, Henry. There's a five-dollar bill in each one of those."

As she talked to him, she looked up and down the street, hoping she was being reasonably discreet—if they were writing to her, they had her address, which meant they probably had her under surveillance.

As usual, every available parking place was taken, but she thought she saw the top of someone's head in a dark red Saturn. Even that was no big deal. Here in the Quarter, people seemed to sit around in cars for hours sometimes—talking, resting, maybe selling drugs.

She went back in and opened a few letters. They nearly all started out the same way: "Dear Detective Langdon, I want to tell you how much the Rev. Errol Jacomine has done for the community."

She counted them. There were sixty-three.

When she left the house, she glanced once again at the red Saturn. There was definitely someone in it.

She picked up some things at Matassa's and returned. The car was gone.

• •

If there were such a thing as protesting too much, Jacomine was certainly doing it. He had to be guilty of something—else why bother trying to stop an investigation?

Skip knew what he would say: "Our people have just had so much trouble, they're so disenfranchised that, frankly, we're used to being abused. That's all we expect anymore, and we've learned to cope with it."

But everybody had trouble, everybody was disenfranchised, and nobody behaved like this. There was a big scandal somewhere, and it wasn't only in the future, she was sure of that. It could be happening in the present—political skulduggery was probably going down even now at a rate she couldn't even imagine. But she didn't know what form it would take or (since they knew her and were probably watching her) how to investigate it. Her gut feeling was to go for whatever he was trying so hard to cover up.

She phoned a friend in Records. "Jeanie? I need a big favor."

"I heard you were on leave."

"Yeah, but no one's gonna know."

Jeanie sighed. "You'd do the same for me, right? Whatever it is."

"I need a sheet on somebody."

"Easy enough."

"And an NCIC search." The National Crime Information Center was a federal wanted system—a little hit-or-miss, but the only service available.

"Okay. Give me a name."

"Errol Jacomine."

"You got to be kidding."

"Hey. Would I do it for you?"

Next, there was nothing like her good old hometown sources. When she was looking for a missing person who'd once been a

member of some off-brand sect, she'd called the religion editor at
the *Times-Picayune* to ask about three churches she'd narrowed it
down to. He hadn't known a thing about them, but one had
turned out to be Jacomine's.

She felt a twinge of conscience now at never having called him
back. Realizing there was something badly wrong with Jacomine,
she'd reported him to the department's intelligence officer, who'd
brushed her off. But she hadn't even thought of nice Stanley at
the T-P.

Never too late, she thought, and dialed him. "Stanley? Skip
Langdon from NOPD."

"Ah, yes. We talked about a year ago."

"I'm calling because one of those churches I asked you about
was Errol Jacomine's."

"Oh, was it now? My, my. Now *there's* a development. What
did you think of him?" She heard keen interest in his voice, but
by now she'd had enough Jacomine experience not to go blurting
indiscretions.

"Well, I had opinions. I'm wondering if you've done any work
on him lately—in view of his emergence in politics."

He sighed. "If you don't know the answer, you must be on the
right side."

"Oho. Calls and letters? Pressure on your boss and your boss's
boss? Maybe even your wife? Is that what we're talking about
here?"

"And how would you know about that?"

"I think we better talk."

9

• •

Stanley came out to meet her and took her into an interview room. So far they'd only talked on the phone, and she had to admit surprise at seeing him. He was no one's idea of a religion editor.

He was a black man—short, rotund, wearing the kind of baggy print trousers for sale in health clubs, though if he'd ever been in one it wasn't doing much good. He had on a Dr. Dre T-shirt, and his bald head was so shiny it looked waxed.

"You're looking at me like you think I'm weird. You think I'm weird?"

"Not exactly. But I'll bet the archbishop does."

"Yeah, I bet he does." He laughed. "I'm so weird the paper didn't even want to give me any kind of job, despite my fabulous credentials and affirmative action potential. So they offered this little gig to get rid of me, never knowing I had family here, and sickness in it. It was either take their dirty job or get me one as a bartender or something.

"But guess what? I love it. And I'm great at it. Love to go to voodoo ceremonies; crazy for priests who can't keep their hands off the kiddies." At Skip's look, he said, "Journalistically speaking, of course. Why should the police guys get all the exposés? You should pardon me, but that's one hell of a department you've got over there. My successes aside, cracking this Jacomine thing's another ball game. Tell you the truth, I've only been nibbling around the edges of it.

"When the big man decided to run for mayor, a young reporter came to talk to me about him, a young political wanna-be—don't ask, to me it's the world's most boring beat. Anyway, she came in here, all full of piss and vinegar and said she'd talked the powers that be into letting her do little features about everybody who'd filed for mayor. A pretty tiresome chore, so I guess the regular political guys were happy to let one of the youngsters do it.

"So she wanted some background on Jacomine. I told her what I must have told you—that I didn't know him at all. She said she'd looked in the clips and there wasn't a damn thing on him, but then she got a call from somebody talking about his work in the community." He stopped himself. "You got to let her tell it. She needs to talk about it; in fact, if you want to know the truth, she could probably use a good therapist right about now."

"So could I—mine quit because her husband works for Jacomine."

Stanley's demeanor changed so suddenly Skip was startled. Thunderclouds settled over his sunny features. "Who is this guy?" he shouted. "How the hell can he be everywhere at once."

Seeing her shrink back in her chair, he said, "Oops. Sorry. He's got us all a little on edge."

"I think I know what you mean."

He left and came back with a woman in her late twenties, with long brown hair and blue eyes. The hair had a funny sheen to it, and Skip could see roots—obviously she was prematurely gray, but unwilling to live with it.

Skip liked her looks—high cheekbones, but a round face, very friendly; a good smile. "I'm Jane Storey," she said. "I've heard of you."

"From Jacomine's people?"

"Oh, no, they don't communicate with me directly. Though there was a time when Errol called me nearly every day. I've read about some of your cases. And of course Eileen Moreland did that great piece about you."

The story she meant was done almost over Skip's dead body. It was shortly after the shooting that had changed her life, that had her so depressed; it made a hero of her at a time when she would just as soon have put her head under the covers and stayed there.

Today I don't feel that way, she thought with surprise. *Too bad Boo's gone. She was a great therapist.*

"Stanley here says you've had a little trouble with the Blood of the Lamb people."

"Trouble! I'm a mental case. There's something so crazy-making about these people . . ."

"Jane, I have to interrupt for a minute. I need to tell you I'm not here in any official capacity. I'm on a leave of absence from the police department."

Both Jane and Stanley looked puzzled. "What's this about, then?"

"Last year I met Jacomine on another case and I thought he was bad news. Not just bad, but real bad. Like psychopathic. A megalomaniac. I'm not crazy for Perretti or Jackson, but Jacomine's more dangerous than David Duke—only in a different kind of way. So when I went on leave I started investigating him—just because nobody else was doing it." *And to save my sanity.*

Jane said: "Just as a concerned citizen." Skip couldn't tell if she was being sarcastic.

Jane's eyes narrowed. "Is this inside information?"

"I'm not part of anybody's campaign, if that's what you mean. I'm investigating because I think it's important. Period."

Jane gave her an oddly knowing look. "Okay. I think I know how you feel. I'd be happy to pool information."

"Stanley?"

He stood. "I'm turning it over to you lovely ladies. 'Scuse me, but I've got to go scare up a lady rabbi who's into Hebrew goddesses."

Jane said, "What would you think about grabbing some lunch? I've found it helps a lot if I have a drink when I talk about this stuff."

When she had one before her, and they were sitting at an isolated table at an unpopular restaurant, she still spoke softly, both she and Skip remembering that even in normal New Orleans circumstances it wasn't safe to talk about private things in public.

Jane drained off about a third of her wine at one gulp. "I gibber when I try to do this," she said. "I absolutely can't be coherent about it."

Skip looked at her, inviting the tale.

"Nothing bad happened to me. I mean, like bad bad. Like terrible. I don't know why I'm such a basket case."

Skip waited, letting her get her thoughts together.

"There's something about it I can't wrap my mind around. Maybe I just can't believe anybody could go through something as elaborate as the show they put on for me. It's crazy, it's not what adults do." She gulped some more wine. "I've been toying with the notion of evil. I'm not sure what that is, but this might be it."

"How would you define it?"

"I don't know. Being so self-involved, so controlling, so power-hungry that you could mobilize a virtual army just to stop one newspaper story that would have probably been more flattering than otherwise—certainly would have been objective and no more damaging than any of the stories on the other candidates."

She took a deep breath. "Okay. Let's see if I can do it. All I did was call for the interview, and I started getting calls—'Let me tell you all about the Reverend Mr. Jacomine, a giant among men.' And my boss got the calls and so did his boss. And furthermore, some of the calls came from people I knew—even from friends—and these people seemed to be—I can't explain it—on his side." She pushed her hair behind her ear, in the process tilting her chin far up, as if to disconnect her mind from her heart, to stop the flow between the two organs.

"I mean, there shouldn't have been sides at all. I wasn't even aware that there were. But somehow—I can't tell you how—it was as if we were squared off against each other, Jacomine and me, and he'd gone and recruited all my friends to fight against me. Does that make any sense at all?"

"It wouldn't—I'd probably think you were on the edge—except that a similar thing is happening to me. Similar, but not exactly the same—because he and I are enemies. I really am out to get him."

"How did he get to my friends? I still don't get that."

"Tell me about it."

"You, too?"

Skip nodded. "It really hurts my feelings."

Jane laughed. "I know what you mean.

"Anyway," she continued, "it was obvious something was up. And here's what the paper said—that I couldn't write about any of my personal experiences. Okay, I can kind of see it, because he's running for office and we wouldn't want to single out any one candidate, but it wasn't even put that way. They said nobody cares about how you get the story, they just care about the story. Now I ask you—is that responsible journalism? Surely when someone tries to influence a story in a way that no one's ever even seen before, that's a story. What do you think?"

"I don't know anything about journalistic ethics, but yes. Sure. I'd say that's a story."

"Well, I wasn't allowed to breathe a word of it. So if that wasn't the story, there was still a story to get beyond just 'here's who the candidate is'—which, by the way wasn't available, because they were blocking it. I started calling up everybody in town who I thought might have been involved with Jacomine in any political kind of way to see if anyone knew anything. And I got the same thing every time—or anyway, one of two stories. One was, 'Oh, we better not talk about that'—no explanation, just a polite refusal. The other was what a great guy Jacomine was. Nothing else. Nothing!

"But I had an ace in the hole. There's this one city councilwoman who'll talk straight with the press. I'm not saying she isn't self-promoting, but she's very down to Earth and she doesn't bullshit. So I called her. She said, 'Listen, Janie, it's very simple. Here's a man who can mobilize votes. If he says I'll have fifty people over there tomorrow to put up signs, he does. A hundred people to stuff envelopes—no problem. He delivers what he says he will, and it's usually something big. And then he does it again. Are you getting the picture?'

"Well, what could be simpler? Of course that had to be it—everybody wanted him on their side because of what he could do for them. And now that he was running for mayor, people owed him a lot of favors—I was just beginning to see how many—and if he won, he was going to be in a position to dole out favors to them. So I had what I needed—something to make sense out of the whole thing.

"Of course, this particular councilwoman had spoken off the record, as usual. No problem there. She said I could call her a 'high-up figure in city government' or something. But ten minutes later, I got a phone call from her. She said, 'Janie, I was just thinking. I think maybe I spoke too fast. I think maybe it would be better if you didn't use the quote at all.' Now who the hell could have gotten to her? No one could have known about the phone call—absolutely no one—except her assistant. Are we to believe this civil servant of thirty years is a member of the Blood of the Fucking Lamb? Is everybody's assistant in the whole city?"

Skip said without hesitation, "Your phone's tapped."

She looked as if she'd been bitten. "What? This is the *Times-Picayune* we're talking about—how the hell could the phone be tapped?"

"It's either that or what you said—everybody's assistant is a follower of Jacomine. I don't know why I never saw it before—that's why he seems so ubiquitous. Or one of the reasons. Another reason is that he is."

"Can you imagine what my boss will say if I suggest the phone's tapped?"

"You're paranoid and crazy, and would you consider early retirement."

They both laughed. Jane was starting to look more relaxed. "You know, it makes sense. And it fits with—omigod, my home phone's tapped too."

"Why do you say that?"

"Jacomine used to call me at home a lot. But never—and I do mean never—unless I was working in the garden and had dirt up to my elbows. I used to wonder how he did it."

"He could have had you watched."

She nodded. "You know, one of my neighbors did tell me she saw a prowler going through my garbage."

"That was no prowler, that was a parishioner." This was doing Skip a world of good. When the same things happened to someone else that had happened to her, she could think them through, put a label on them. Jane was right—when you were the target, the overkill seemed so unlikely you didn't even consider it. Hence, the experience was crazy-making.

Jane was almost bubbly. "I feel better. I feel a lot better. And it isn't even the wine."

"Me, too. In fact, I'm ordering a glass to celebrate."

Jane said, "Good idea, because we're going to be here awhile. I'm barely started. The thing is, there was some merit to running any story at all because it might encourage disaffected followers to call, so I kept at it. I'd heard he was a healer, and that's news—I mean, it would be if he got elected. A mayor of a major American city who can heal the sick? This is worth investigating.

"So I asked if I could go to a church service, and they said yes, which surprised me. But meanwhile the pressure continued. I did another story on another public official, a man called Ferguson— just a day-in-the-life kind of profile—and first thing that morning, Ferguson called to thank me for the nice story. Next, Jacomine was on the phone, in the most incredible snit. He said he heard I was the *Picayune*'s hatchet woman and after seeing that story, he knew it was true. Ferguson and 'all his people' had been on the phone to Jacomine all morning, lamenting about my betrayal and warning him about me."

Skip said, "Well, that's easy. He was lying."

Jane nodded. "That's easy to say, isn't it? But do you see how it creates an atmosphere of paranoia and unease? I told Jacomine that Ferguson had called to thank me, and he said yes, Ferguson had told him that. He'd called me because he felt at my mercy and he was afraid if he didn't treat me with kid gloves, I'd go after him again. So, was Ferguson lying to me?

"I could have called him up and asked him, but I was damned if I'd get into that kind of fifth-grade, carrying-tales thing Jacomine was doing."

Skip nodded vigorously. "It seems so incredibly childish."

"Exactly. It's so inept you even feel a little sorry for him. Imagine my surprise when I saw how well it worked."

She paused. "I've thought about it a lot. I think the thing about crazy people is, they don't feel silly about doing whatever enters their heads. So they do things to get what they want that a normal person would be far too inhibited to do.

"My mistake was, I didn't realize it would work.

"Anyway, he gets me all in a tizzy about that, and then a couple of days later, he calls up and he says, 'Janie, I'm really trying to trust you, and I know there's nothing I can do to stop you from doing the story, but I'm having serious second thoughts about letting you come to a church service.'

"Naturally, I said, 'What's wrong now,' and he said, 'I was talking to a minister this morning and he warned me about you.' Now, Skip, I don't even know any ministers. So I said, 'Who was that?' and he said, 'I can't tell you; only that it was a black minister.' I said, 'What did he tell you?' And Jacomine said, 'He said you're obsessed with sex.' "

"What on Earth is that supposed to mean?" Skip asked.

"Exactly. So I start going back in my mind—have I ever interviewed a black minister? Done some church story? Did I wear a miniskirt? Was it something like that? Or was this just some conservative dude who saw some of the stories I did that did involve sex in some form or other? What on Earth was he talking about?"

"Did you ask him?"

"Of course. He said he didn't know, it was just what the minister said. Well, naturally, I was tempted to say, 'Well, then, why can't I come to church? Do you have orgies to the tune of "Onward, Christian Soldiers"? ' And maybe he was trying to provoke me into saying that. I did say, 'What does this have to do with my coming to church?' And he said it was a matter of trust. If I was the sort of person he couldn't trust, I'd twist things. Anyway, in the end he did agree to let me come, and I did go, and sure enough, he did a few healings, which I dutifully reported in my story."

Skip nodded, feeling a little overwhelmed, but Jane said, "And that's when the real stuff started. First of all, this weird thing happened at church. He was showing me around with a bunch of church members, and we ended up in this small room that he said was a meditation room, all white and decorated with hanging plants.

"It was really a tiny place, and all of a sudden I realized we were alone and the door was shut. All the people with us had melted away, and he started talking about how his wife had a bad back and couldn't have sex—can you imagine? I didn't know if he was going to try to grab me or what. My heart started pounding really fast, but I thought, 'No problem, all I have to do is yell, this building is full of people,' and then I looked at my watch and said a photographer was going to meet me, I wonder where he is, and Jacomine led me out as if nothing were out of the ordinary.

"But put that together with that whole 'obsessed with sex' routine and what does it spell?"

Frankly buffaloed, Skip shook her head. "It makes no sense at all."

Jane leaned back in her chair. "I'm so glad to have confirmation. It doesn't to me either. I've turned it over and over in my mind, and I can't make a coherent story out of it. It makes no sense. And yet it must have some kind of logic to it—have I used the word 'crazy-making' yet? By the way, you're the first person I've told that to. It made me feel defiled somehow. I know I was being manipulated, I just don't know what the object was. If I told it to a man, I guess he'd say Jacomine was trying to get into my pants, but that makes even less sense than any other theory—of which I have none, by the way."

"Well, if he were really, really crazy—"

"Which he is."

"Then he might think no woman can resist him—and if you didn't, then he'd have you in his power."

Jane's face twisted into a frown. "I've thought of that, but—is anybody that crazy? I mean, one minute he's telling me how dangerous I am and how he's sacred to death of me, and the next, he's making me his sex slave. How do you cram both of those things into one mind?"

Skip shrugged.

"Anyhow, I went back and wrote a first draft, which I finished right before I went home one night and showed to my editor. He said he thought it wasn't quite balanced enough in view of the delicate subject this obviously was, which I thought was completely wrong. Why should we bend over backwards when these assholes were so obviously trying to control what we ran? But I said sure, I'd be glad to put in some more community quotes saying what a great guy people thought Jacomine was.

"Then that night Jacomine calls me at home. He says he's heard the story's going to run the next day and it's a hatchet job. Now how could he know it was even written? So naturally I asked him, and he said that was just what he heard. The question is, who told him?

"My city editor? Stanley? He saw a copy.

"Whoever it was, it was probably someone I trusted and was close to."

"Wait a minute. Was it in the computer?" Skip asked.

"Yes."

"Maybe they got into it."

Jane shrugged. "It's possible. But, my God, it wasn't like there was a million dollars at stake, or even *anything at all*. It was a completely innocuous story that was about to get slanted in his direction.

"Anyway, the upshot was, I rewrote it six times. And every time I rewrote it, it had to go up the ladder to the top, and every time, it came back with orders to water it down a little bit more. Meanwhile, Jacomine was calling every day with versions of what he'd 'heard.' And that's just calling *me*. God knows who else's ear he was bending, but I've got a few ideas. Frankly, I don't even rule out blackmail on this one.

"Anyway, the story finally ran, six weeks later. All of the other stories in that series took an average of four hours' work—a one-hour interview, maybe an hour's research, and a couple of hours to write them. They all sailed through with hardly a word from any editor.

"When I went home the night before this one ran, I was pretty disappointed in the whole process. I had all six versions before me, and I could see it getting more and more sanitized in every version. The one I'd just turned in was unbelievably bland, didn't begin to scratch the surface of what we knew about him, and was really pretty one-sided in his favor. But I comforted myself with the fact that at least it had the healing paragraph in it. I had actually seen healings at his church, and I wrote about them—as I mentioned, that's pretty unusual in a mayoral candidate.

"But guess what? I got up the next morning, read the paper, and that paragraph wasn't there. It disappeared. Simply was not there. And I saw the final version right before I went home. I'll tell you I went into that paper livid. Absolutely loaded for bear. I asked every single editor what happened and you know what they did? Shrugged their shoulders. One of them said, 'weird.'

"That was it. That was all.

"After Jacomine had put us all through six weeks of hell, no one gave the tiniest damn. No one even cared. Now I ask you, what went on there?"

"Someone got paid."

"Or blackmailed. Or converted. God, I don't know. But whatever it was, I don't think it was simple."

"Was anything missing besides the healing paragraph?"

"Yes, but it was nothing that mattered. It was just a phrase in a sentence about what he'd been doing before he came here. I think it said he was in New Iberia—or maybe St. Martinville. I mean, why bother?"

Skip was sitting up straight, feeling a little like a bloodhound that's happened on a particularly redolent sock. "That," she said, "might bear investigating."

10

• •

Torian loved Friday nights—loved the first sight of her dad after a week, loved having dinner with him and Carol (who actually cooked, unlike her mother), then the ritual of getting her little sister ready for bed, and finally, talking to her dad while Carol disappeared discreetly for a while.

Marly was only her half sister, but Torian had never had a whole sister and Marly was good enough. In fact, she was one of the wonders of the world, as far as Torian was concerned. She was fair, like her dad and Carol and Noel, not dark like Torian and Lise. She had tiny, neat fingernails the size of cake crumbs, but they were getting bigger now—she was ten months old and about to walk, Carol thought.

She was a year younger than Joy, Noel's daughter, and infinitely more fascinating—to Torian, anyway. Every week, she seemed a different child. And Torian gloried in each of her tiny achievements—smiling, sitting up, drinking from a cup—as if Marly were her own child.

I wish she were, she thought sometimes. *I'd love to have a baby.*

But there were so many other things to do, too—live in Paris, write poetry, marry Noel and travel everywhere with him.

And finish high school, of course.

But maybe she didn't have to do that. Maybe she could somehow get her GED. Maybe she could just run away and worry about it all later.

Anything to get away from Lise.

But that would mean leaving Noel; therefore it was out of the question—unless she could somehow run away with him. How to do that? she wondered.

He wants to, too. I know it.

Her dad honked and she ran out, grabbing her backpack with its change of clothes. She was only allowed to stay two nights and one day. Sundays, she had to come back to the dreary old apartment in the Quarter. Theoretically, she and Lise were supposed to have quality time then, but her mother usually had a hangover and wanted to spend time with Charles anyhow. Torian was left to run the streets with Sheila, which wasn't her idea of a terrible time, but she'd rather have spent Sundays in Old Metairie, with her dad.

The carpets there were beige and soft under her toes. She had her own room, which was much nicer than the one Lise had given her. It had all new, white-painted furniture, and flower-print Roman shades. Torian and Carol had picked out the fabric, which was more expensive than everything in her room in the French Quarter.

There was a lot more light here, too, and the paint was fresh—it was gray with grime at Lise's—and she'd never seen a roach here. Not even when she raided the refrigerator in the middle of the night, which she couldn't do at Lise's, because there was never anything in it.

But here there were lots of things—all kinds of fruit, and Sara Lee cakes, and chocolates (which Carol kept refrigerated), and strange cheeses that Torian would never have heard of if it hadn't been for her dad and Carol, with a whole selection of crackers to eat with them. Sometimes there was leftover shrimp or chicken or ham, and if she wanted a sandwich, there was a choice of breads, whereas Lise bought only one loaf at a time, and there was never leftover anything at her house, because what's left over from a frozen dinner?

And sometimes there were special treats from weddings and cocktail parties Carol had catered.

Carol cooked for a living. What could be more feminine, more nurturing? So different from hard-edged Lise, with her set mouth and the nervous way a vein in her neck jumped.

Carol was a little plump, especially her hands, which were soft and lovely and often manicured, despite her job. Torian could never understand how she kept them that way, given her job, but she supposed Carol didn't take on as much work as she used to before Marly was born.

Her hair was two colors of blond, with lots of highlights, and it was curly as well. She wore plenty of gel in it, which made it seem both lionlike and sophisticated at the same time, never fluffy. She wore beige and taupe most of the time, sometimes a kind of gold color, and white in the summer, so that the effect was a pleasing monochrome.

She was nice to Torian, which was more than Torian could say for Lise.

Her dad had met Carol at a party she had catered, which made it no surprise to Torian that he had fallen in love with her—it was probably for her cooking. That and the fact that she was nice to him, after Lise had been such a shrew.

Everything in their house was new and nice, which wasn't Torian's favorite style—she would have much preferred beautiful antiques—but it was infinitely preferable to Lise's early Goodwill look. Not that she blamed her mother for not being able to afford better, but then . . . she did. She did and she always would.

Lise could have kept Wilson—Torian's father. She had chosen not to. Wilson wasn't the type to run out on his family—he'd have stayed and put up with Lise as long as she was willing. She had dumped him. How was Torian supposed to forgive a thing like that?

She slammed the car door. "Hi, Dad." He looked tired; his tie had been loosened.

He reached over and touched her cheek. Lise never did that. "Hi, baby. How's my girl."

She shrugged. "Okay, I guess."

"Listen, something's come up at the last minute. What would you think about babysitting tonight?"

"You're going out?"

"Well, we could. Carol has this opportunity . . . it's a potential client." He glanced at her, looking distracted. "But of course it's up to you, baby. It means a lot to her, but you know how important our time together is to me." He smiled. "It's just that these days you don't have much time for your old dad."

He meant last Saturday, when she had gone back to Lise a day early for Sheila's birthday party.

"Oh, Daddy, you know I . . ."

"I was just teasing you, sweetheart. I want you to do whatever you like. I just thought you might have something more important to do than hang with an old man, that's all."

"Well, I do. I'm going to hang with a young woman—a very young woman who can't even walk yet." She gave him a big smile, knowing she was being more of a baby than Marly to feel so disappointed. What he said was perfectly true—she bagged the adults when she felt like it. Therefore she couldn't expect them to hang around as if she were royalty or something.

Her mother's voice echoed in her brain: *Oh, is the princess distressed tonight? Perhaps we could just stop the world and start it again at the speed the princess prefers. Would that meet with her highness's approval?*

Her dad squeezed her knee. "That's my girl." He sounded so smug, so sure of himself that Torian almost wished she'd refused. *Don't be like that,* she told herself. *What's your problem? Can't you act your age?*

●   ●

Loud music was playing when they arrived. Carol was in her underwear, hair wet, flying between the hall bathroom—usually Torian's alone—and her bedroom.

"Hi guys," she called. "I'm late." The hair dryer went on.

Torian's dad looked at his watch. "Me, too," he said. "You can amuse yourself, can't you? Marly's in there." He pointed to the dining room, where Marly was cooing in a playpen, and he was gone.

Torian felt melancholy. Somehow disappointed without knowing why.

Some other feeling nagged at her, something she couldn't identify, but it had to do with a sense of things not being right. It reminded her of Noel, and that confused her.

Things were right with Noel. Things were right with her father. What was her problem?

Needing human companionship, she went in and picked up Marly, who smiled at first, but almost instantly began crying. She was wet and probably had been for a while.

Sighing, Torian went to the bathroom for a diaper, but Carol was still drying her hair. "What is it?" she snapped.

"I—uh—need to change Marly."

Without speaking, Carol reached into a cabinet behind her, pulled out a diaper and held it out, all the while staring in the mirror, scrunching her hair to keep the curl in.

She looked very beautiful in her lacy bra and panties, champagne-colored to match her hair and skin. Lise wore underwear that looked as if a nurse had chosen it—white and plain, often cotton.

Feeling small and in the way, Torian took the diaper and went back to Marly, who was fussy and not good company either. She hated the noise of the hair dryer, Torian thought, or maybe she sensed her parents were going out and she was cross about it.

Torian took her out of the playpen along with some of her toys, and sat on the floor, ready to cheer her up. Marly was restless. She flung a rubber pig at Torian, which glanced off her nose.

"No, Marly. No." She spoke louder than she meant to. Almost at the same instant, the hair dryer went off, and the baby wailed. Carol came running out. "Now what?"

Torian had leaned forward, and was starting to pick the baby up, but Carol tore her out of the girl's arms. "What is it, baby? Mmmmm? What is it, darling girl?"

Torian thought: *Lise never talked to me like that in her life.*

"What's wrong with her, Torian?" Her voice had a dangerous edge to it.

Torian shrugged. "Nothing. I just . . ."

"Oh, for Christ's sake. I haven't got time for this now."

She shoved Marly back at Torian, and the baby began to wail again. Carol disappeared on bare feet, leaving Torian the task of calming her.

Having had lots of experience with Joy, and some with Marly herself—and furthermore having quite a bit of patience—Torian went back to the rubber pigs and fuzzy kittens, until she had a calm baby again, happily drooling and exploring with her hands.

For some reason, Marly turned from Torian and her toys, back to the playpen. She pulled herself up and looked over her shoulder. Torian, sitting a step away from her, scooted back and held out her hands. "Come, baby," she said. "Come on, Marly."

With that inquisitive look that comes over kittens and sometimes babies, Marly stared at her and held out a hand.

"Come to Torian, baby."

Marly put a foot forward, so that she was standing sideways, one hand still clutching the playpen. Torian scooted back a little more and leaned forward, her hands moving towards Marly, barely out of reach.

The baby let go of the rail and stood there a moment, swaying. Torian half expected her to sit down hard, but somehow she found her center of balance. Her front foot moved forward and then her back one. She had taken a step.

Torian leaned back. "Come on. Just a little farther. Come on, Marly." The baby's front foot moved forward again and she fell into Torian's arms.

"Good girl! What a good girl, Marly. What a girl! Let's go see your mom and dad."

She picked the baby up and raced to her father and Carol's bedroom, smiling and excited. "Dad, guess what?" she said as she reached the door, and she saw motion as her father's head turned to look at her. But she never saw his expression. What she remembered most about that moment was the side view of his naked butt.

His shorts were around his ankles, his penis in the mouth of

Carol, who sat on the bed, still in her bra and panties. His hair was wet; he must have just come from the shower.

"What the fuck are you doing here?" he yelled, and then she did look at his face. It was red; furious. A vein in his neck worked.

Mortified, Torian gasped and ran, not knowing where to go. Finally, after a false step or two, she took the baby into her room and slammed the door, terrifying Marly, whom she dumped unceremoniously on the bed, and who began to howl inconsolably.

Torian, too, burst into tears, unable to contain her embarrassment and horror. Mostly what she felt, besides stinging humiliation, was anger.

What the hell are they doing, she thought, *when they're supposed to be in such a goddamn big hurry? Why couldn't they be bothered closing their goddamn door? How can he be mad at me? What did I do?*

She really couldn't get to the bottom of this. To her, it seemed that if anyone were at fault, it was they, certainly not her. Why had her father yelled at her? She couldn't fathom it, but she didn't think she was ever going to get over the pain of this.

Also the shock.

She had heard of what they were doing, even had some vague notion what it was called, but it hadn't really occurred to her it was something married people did before going out for the evening on a Friday night. And certainly not with the door open.

Her father came in, tucking a half-buttoned shirt into a pair of trousers, not bothering to knock. "Torian, I'm sorry you had to see that."

"Couldn't you have closed your goddamn door?"

"Look, don't give me any lip. You had no business being there. You were supposed to be taking care of the baby, not walking unannounced into people's bedrooms."

For the first time he looked at Marly, who was lying on her back, legs up in the air, knees at right angles to her body, yelling like she was being tortured. He picked her up.

"You're doing a lousy job of that, Torian."

Torian turned her face away from him. "I was coming to tell you she took her first step."

"What?" His voice was suddenly gentler.

Hearing the click of high heels in the hall, Torian turned to see Carol, dressed in a beige silk suit, the skirt short enough to reveal chubby knees and thighs that looked like nylon sausages. It was the first time Torian had found fault with her.

She was standing in the doorway, one hand on the jamb. Her eyes caught her husband's, and she echoed his question: "What did you say?"

"Torian says Marly walked."

Torian nodded and smiled, her embarrassment, in spite of herself, giving way to pride. "She did. She took two steps."

Her dad shook his head. "Honey, I'm sure you must be mistaken."

Carol looked panicked. "She wouldn't do that. Not for Torian."

"She did! I don't care if you believe me or not. Marly walked!"

"It's not that we don't believe you, Torian. I'm sure you're just mistaken." Carol entered the room and sat on the bed. Torian's dad held the baby out to her, but she refused, gesturing toward her outfit, which she obviously didn't want mussed. "Look, I know you need a lot of attention right now, and I don't blame you if you need to make up stories."

"Bullshit, Carol! Marly walked. Your baby took her first step while you were writing an addendum to the *Kama Sutra*."

"Writing *what*?" Her dad laughed as the penny dropped. "Hey, honey, that's pretty funny."

Carol's eyes were a storm-tossed sea. "Wilson. Didn't I tell you? She thinks she's in competition with me."

"Excuse me. She's in the room with you. She'd like to be addressed as 'you' if Mrs. Gernhard the Second wouldn't mind."

Carol stood up. "Mrs. Gernhard the Second! All right, Torian, that's it. You may not come into my home if you can't keep a civil tongue in your head."

"I beg your pardon. This is my dad's home. And he's known me a lot longer than he's known you."

"All right, ladies, all right. Chill out, okay? We'll talk about this later. Carol, we're late."

When they were gone, and she had put Marly to bed, Torian went into the kitchen and opened the refrigerator. There were only condiments in it, and some packaged ham. Carol must have cleaned it out.

Finally, Torian found a frozen pizza, and while she waited for it to heat, she thought about the time she had asked her dad why she couldn't live with him instead of Lise. "I wish you could, sweetheart, but your mama won't let you. It's as simple as that."

"Have you asked?"

He nodded vigorously. "Oh, yes. You betcha I've asked. It's Lise's decision."

Torian had never understood that. Lise hated her, so why would she want to live with her? Now it seemed that Carol hated her as much as Lise did. She wondered if that was the real reason she couldn't go live with her dad.

● ●

Skip had decided there was little point in heading to southwest Louisiana on the weekend. She could go first thing Monday morning. She felt fairly driven, but supposed there was something to Cappello's advice about resting.

Anyway, she had some things to do in New Orleans. She called a witch she knew and asked about Layne's problem. The witch said she'd consult the coven, and if they tackled it, Kenny could watch.

Skip went to find Jimmy Dee and the kids. He and Kenny were in the kitchen, Kenny stirring something that smelled like liquid gold.

"We're making pralines," said Jimmy Dee.

Kenny consulted a candy thermometer. "This thing won't get to the soft ball stage."

"Yes, it will. You just have to be patient."

Skip said, "I've got good news. The witches might magic Layne—they have to take a vote or something—and if they do, I think you're in, Kenny boy."

Kenny turned around, delight on his young features. "I can go? Cool."

"He can?" said Dee-Dee. "Did I say he can?"

"Maybe not, but you will."

"Yaaay. Soft ball, soft ball! What now, Uncle Jimmy?"

Skip went off in search of Sheila. She found her lying in bed with her shoes on, a book in her hands. Angel, curled up on the floor, got up and started jumping and licking.

"Hi. What are you reading?"

"*Pride and Prejudice*. I hate it."

"Angel, get down. Great first sentence, you have to admit."

Sheila flipped back to look at it. She turned up her nose. "Antifeminist."

"It's supposed to be funny."

"It is?"

"The whole book is—you didn't notice?"

"Uh-uh." She looked genuinely puzzled.

"Well, no wonder you don't like it. Rethink it with irony."

Sheila had put down the book and now began to eye Skip with suspicion. "You don't usually come back here."

"You mean I'm not welcome?"

Sheila pointed to a sign on the wall: ADULT-FREE ZONE.

"Oh, sure," said Skip. "When you see 'Drug-Free Zone' on a school, you know they've got a little substance problem. Mind if I sit down?"

Sheila moved a finger ever so slightly to signify reluctant assent, but Angel beat her tail on the floor to take up the slack. Skip sat.

"Honey, I want to talk to you about something."

Deliberately, Sheila turned her head away. "I figured."

"You sound like you know what it is."

Sheila said nothing.

Skip patted her shin. "It wasn't cool the way you talked to Darryl at your birthday party."

"What?" Sheila sat up, obviously outraged, cheeks flaming. "You're upset about that? Uncle Jimmy must be, too. He sent you in here, right?"

She's mortified, Skip thought, but now that she'd started it, she had to finish.

"Not upset, exactly. I just thought I'd mention you put Darryl in kind of a bad position."

"He said something to you?"

Oh. That's what she really cares about.

116

"Of course not. Darryl's your pal. He'd never complain about you. I just thought I'd mention that teenage girls aren't supposed to flirt with grown men."

"I wasn't flirting."

"Honey, I don't know what else you'd call it." She did, though—her own mother would have used the term "throw yourself at"; a bit strong, in Skip's opinion.

"Why not? Darryl's my friend. He knows I didn't mean anything." Her voice was sulky.

"Darryl happens to be a very hip, very together man who's had lots of experience with kids your age. They're not all that way, honey-pie."

"Well, what are they going to do? Leave their wives and children for me? I really don't think I'm that powerful, Auntie."

"Wives and children? Where's that coming from?"

Sheila was getting red again. "You wouldn't understand."

And I don't want to, Skip thought. *God, I hope this is bravado.*

She stood up. "Auntie the Great has spoken. Henceforth flirting with over-twenty-ones shall be considered rude."

"Well, that's just *special,*" Sheila said, picking up the book. Before Skip could answer, she hid behind it.

11

• •

On Sunday afternoon Skip headed for Iberia Parish armed with a picture of Jacomine cadged from the *Times-Picayune's* files. It was about a three-hour drive, and her plan was to stay overnight, get an early start Monday morning, then drive home that night.

Jeanie in Records had called her back the day before. Her search had turned up negative, which didn't discourage Skip at all, instead persuaded her all the more that Jacomine was using an assumed name.

After finding a Holiday Inn, she checked the phone book for churches. Curiously, though she was in the heart of Cajun country, there were pages of churches, only a few of them Catholic. This was evidently fertile ground for religion.

Her problem was, she didn't know how long ago Jacomine had been here, exactly what town he'd been in, what he called his church, or even what he called himself at the time.

There was a newspaper in St. Martinville. She decided to go there first thing in the morning and see if he'd made any kind of local splash.

● ●

The *Teche News* (so named for Bayou Teche) had its own building, a small but efficient and prosperous-looking operation with a staff of three currently in evidence. The publisher was out, but the lifestyle editor, Marie LeBlanc, was as friendly as small-town folk are supposed to be.

"I'm sorry I don't remember him," she said, as if it were her job to call to mind every stranger who rode into town. "Let me look him up for you."

She went to her computer and typed. After awhile she said, "Here we are. The Reverend Errol Jacomine, big as you please. I see he's from the Christian Community."

"That's a Protestant denomination, isn't it?"

Marie nodded. She had sharp features, dark hair, and fabulous ivory skin. "Uh-huh. We've got two of their churches here."

"So he's a real minister. I'll be damned."

"At least he was a few years ago." She scrolled down quickly through the first clip. "It just says he's been assigned here to take over one of the churches. Oh, here's something good—a picture caption. Looks like he had his picture taken with some NAACP honcho on Martin Luther King's birthday."

"That makes sense. He's got a big black following in New Orleans. Is the Community predominantly black?"

Marie shook her head. "I don't think so. I had an aunt who was a member and, knowing her, it had to have been mostly white."

Skip said, "What was the name of the man from the NAACP?"

"Ralph Washington." LeBlanc scrolled on. "I guess that's all. There's not even anything saying Jacomine's leaving town. So I guess we can't tell when he did leave. He came here in ninety-one, and this picture was in early ninety-two, so he was here at least a few months."

Without much hope, Skip decided to try Jacomine's successor at the Christian Community. He probably wouldn't say anything, but not talking to him was like failing to check the phone book if you wanted a number—it just wasn't good policy to overlook the obvious.

The Community had a phone number, and the person who answered said he was the minister and if Skip would come on over, he'd be glad to see her. He was a white man, at least in his eighties, Skip thought; a very old man who still had a preacher's voice.

"Adam Tardiff," he boomed, lifting one white and overgrown eyebrow. He still had quite a bit of flesh on his bones, most of it sagging, but he was healthy-looking. His eyes were blue and sharp. "Nice weather, ain't it? Think we're gon' get a hurricane this year?"

"Hope not."

He shook his head. "I think we are. Haven't had one since I came home. I just have a feelin'."

He ushered her into a neat but very tiny brick house. "Small, ain't it?" he said. "We've been having services here lately. Not that many of us in the Community anymore. My wife died last January, and a few others died as well. Only five or six left."

All the shades were down in the house, possibly against the heat, though Skip felt air-conditioning. The furniture was cheap and fussy, undoubtedly chosen by his late wife. It looked as if it could use a good vacuuming.

"I'm from Lafayette originally, so when that other fella left, I said I'd come back. Had more members then, though." He laughed. "Don't think I was what they expected."

"How's that?"

"Well, I'm just an ol' boy from around here, and that one could heal the sick. Sent down from Atlanta, I think—you know, our world headquarters? Guess he learned some real slick tricks there. Heard he could raise the dead, too, but maybe that was just a rumor." He laughed so hard you would have thought he was in a room with Steve Martin and Eddie Murphy.

"Is that part of the Community's usual program? Faith healing?"

"Noooooo." He drew the word out so there'd be no mistaking it. "We just preach the Word. Do a little Bible study, that's about it. That fella was full service." He laughed again. "Yes, sir, we lost members when I came here. I just haven't got the knack of raisin' the dead."

Skip wondered why he thought it was all such a joke. She said: "That must have been upsetting."

"Well, I didn't mean they got sick and died 'cause I couldn't heal 'em. I just meant they liked to think ol' Errol could. Anyway, it wad'nt specially upsettin'. The Community's kind of old-fashioned. I b'lieve that fella made 'em nervous."

"How did he happen to leave?"

"Well, now, that I wouldn't know. Just heard there was an openin' and I was welcome to come if I wanted to. I knew there weren't many people, but I'm eighty-four, startin' to slow down a little bit. And I had relatives here—perfect setup for me."

Skip wanted to get back to Jacomine. "Was Errol Jacomine asked to leave?"

"I wouldn't know about that. Didn't ask, didn't think it was my business. What you want to know for?"

She'd already told him she was a detective. "You know he's running for mayor of New Orleans?"

"Why, no, I didn't know that."

"I've got this feeling about him. I don't think he's on the up-and-up."

Tardiff pursed his lips. "What you think about faith healin'?"

Skip laughed. Considering she'd just asked a gang of witches to heal an allergy, she didn't think she could afford to be judgmental. She said, "Maybe it could work. The Bible talks about miracles. What do you think?"

"I think a man says he can do it's a charlatan."

"I see." She thought she was getting his drift, but she wasn't sure. "So maybe I should go talk to whoever told you about Jacomine's special talents."

"You catch on real fast, young lady. I don't want to do anything undignified. Fact, when tongues get too loose in front of me, I make 'em quit waggin'—there's ways I don't want to talk about another preacher."

"Ah. But I have no such scruples."

"Well, idn't that fortunate?" His blue eyes crinkled. He might be old, but he was enjoying the hell out of life. "What I think you might ought to do is is talk to some other preachers. Some of 'em don't have professional standards like yours truly. Or let me put it another way—they got different ones. I get the feelin' some folks around here thought he was givin' the job a bad name—I feel like it ain't none of my business myself."

Now we're getting somewhere. Skip felt her heart pick up speed. *I knew there had to be something. I wish I had Jane with me.*

He gave her the name of a Baptist minister he said might shed some light. She found Dr. Theon Cowan at a much more prosperous church than Tardiff's, one that had its own building, though it was old and wooden, with no air-conditioning.

Dr. Cowan was in his mid-fifties, and thick, thick through the neck and shoulders and belly, as if his mama had once told him to eat everything on his plate and he'd been obeying ever since. He was black, his hair was close-cropped, his glasses looked a little too small for his face, and he was sweating.

Skip thought there was the odor of snake oil about him, something that reminded her of Jacomine. *Maybe it takes one to know one,* she thought.

She identified herself, said Tardiff sent her, and stated her business. Cowan wiped his face with a white handkerchief, nodding vigorously.

"Yes. Yes. I knew Errol Jacomine. Mr. Tardiff is correct on that point. Exactly how can I help you?"

"I think he's a dangerous man; I gather Mr. Tardiff thinks you think that, too."

"I don't know that I'd say that. It depends what you mean by dangerous."

Skip waited, wondering why Tardiff had sent her. Finally, she shrugged. "Mr. Tardiff apparently thought you could help. Can you?"

"I really couldn't say."

Skip started to stand. "Well, I—"

Cowan surprised her by patting the air with his palm. "Sit down. Sit down. I have decided to tell you what I know."

Pompous ass, Skip thought.

"Mr. Jacomine came to my attention when a number of people from my congregation began to attend his church. Naturally I was upset by this." For the first time, he smiled. "Professional jealousy, perhaps. At any rate, I put out my antennae and I began to hear reports of miraculous healings."

He said the word "miraculous" as if he were delivering a sermon—singsonging it, with heavy emphasis on the second syllable, irony implied.

"I was skeptical, of course, and I began to ax questions." It was funny the way he so clearly prided himself on his enunciation, yet he still said "ax."

"I found that several members of my flock had been cured of dangerous illnesses, in fact that the Reverend Mr. Jacomine had pulled the tumors from their very bodies." He was singsonging again, as if at the pulpit, seeking to convince with the ironic tone of his voice.

"The problem was that in spite of her miraculous healing, Mrs. Hattie Morgan had the temerity to die! I visited her son Aaron the morning after she passed, and he was in deep mourning, as indeed the whole family was. Mr. Duplain Morgan, his father, was in his house, holding something in a jar, rocking back and forth, back and forth, in the agony of his widowhood. When I inquired what that something was, he held up the jar. It contained what appeared for all the world to be a chicken liver, preserved in alcohol. 'It is her tumor,' he told me, in as bewildered a voice as I have ever heard. 'It is the malignant tumor that Daddy removed from her blighted body. She has been healed and yet God has struck her down. It must truly have been her time.' "

Skip was now quite enjoying the way Cowan declaimed, understanding the honor of a performance for her benefit alone. Every once in awhile he even closed his eyes, squeezing them open only with great effort.

"Naturally, I was deeply concerned. I said to Mr. Morgan, 'What do you plan to do with that tumor? I wonder if I might have it?' I had in mind to submit it for laboratory analysis, of course, but Mr. Morgan said, 'It is all that I have left of my Hattie, and I shall never part with it.'

"Still, I was not satisfied. I asked him the name of Mrs. Morgan's doctor, and I went so far as to call the man and voice my concerns. I thought perhaps that she had suspended medical treatment in the belief that God had healed her through the hands of Mr. Jacomine." He steepled his fingers on the desk in front of him. "Now, Miss Langdon, I am a man of God and I believe in God. But he works in mysterious ways, not the least of which is western medicine. The preacher who claims to have healed when he has not healed is a dangerous man!" His voice got louder as the speech continued and at the end of it, he banged his fist on the desk.

Amen, Skip thought, but she held her tongue.

"Her doctor, alas, was bound by his own professional scruples. Naturally he could not reveal the details of the case, but he went so far as to volunteer that in his opinion he could not have helped Mrs. Morgan any further than he already had. I took comfort in that, Miss Langdon. I hoped that it was so, yet I could not help but worry that it might not be so in every case. This has weighed on my conscience, yet what was I to do?"

Skip said, "I wonder if you talked to other people who got involved with Jacomine?"

He nodded and dabbed at his left temple. "I can assure you that I did. Yet I was never able to elicit other than the highest praise for the man. And so I was forced to content myself with what I had done and to trust in God it was enough."

Despite his pomposity, he said it with such obvious sincerity that Skip felt herself developing a soft spot for him. She asked if he would mind if she went to visit Hattie Morgan's son.

Cowan nodded approvingly: "Mr. Aaron Morgan is a very intelligent young man. I would be happy to call him for you."

Young Mr. Aaron Morgan proved to be somewhere in his early forties, and at least as handsome as he was intelligent. He was working a construction job, his wife had told the minister, and given him the address.

Skip arrived to find Morgan shirtless and shining with sweat. She had now and then seen as good a torso of muscles, but not often. "Mr. Morgan. I'm Skip Langdon from New Orleans. Dr. Cowan sent me."

124

"Call me Aaron," he said, and gave her the smile, the welcoming handshake that made country people famous for friendliness. "Who'd you say sent you?"

"Dr. Theon Cowan over at the Baptist Church."

"That's my daddy's church. My daddy all right?"

"Oh, yes. It's nothing like that. I wanted to ask you about another minister—Errol Jacomine, the one who tried to heal your mama."

"You po-lice or somethin'? 'Cause he a fraud. He a fraud as sure as I'm standin' here."

"Dr. Cowan told me about the thing in the jar and all that."

"Hmmmph. Big ol' turkey gizzard. He say she 'pass' the tumor. She didn't pass nothin' 'cept away. Maybe his fault, maybe not, but one thing I'm tellin' you, he didn't help her none."

"I'm wondering what happened to that big old turkey gizzard."

He shook his head, disgusted. "Daddy had it buried with the body. Ain't that too much?"

Trying not to show her disappointment, she shook her head as well. "Mmm. Mmm. Mmm." It was the Southern expression most useful for keeping your feelings hidden.

As if as an afterthought, she asked if Aaron knew anyone else who'd had a healing from Jacomine.

"I don't b'lieve I do," he said. "But I bet I know somebody who would talk."

"Who's that?"

"Man named Ralph Washington. Baby doctor here in town."

The name was familiar. "I've heard of him. He's a honcho in the NAACP, isn't he?" He was the man with whom Jacomine had had his picture taken.

"Well, I wouldn't know about that. What I know is, after my mama died, he come around askin' questions just like you doin'. 'Bout whether she thought she was healed and where that ol' tumor went. Wouldn't say why, but I had a feelin' he had the same opinion I do of Mr. Jacomine."

Skip looked at her watch. It was eleven-thirty, the perfect time to show up unannounced at a doctor's office. He'd almost certainly be going out to lunch soon.

• •

Naturally, he didn't like being accosted on his way to a nice plate of catfish. Yet when Skip said the word "Jacomine," he slowed and looked at her for the first time.

He was a light-skinned man, beefy for a doctor, young for a community activist. He had a gentle demeanor, yet a determined glint in his eye. "Wait a minute," he said. "You're here about Errol Jacomine?"

"I am waiting. I was hoping you would."

He stopped. "Well, I will. I've got a thing or two to say about the Reverend Mr. Jacomine."

"I came here to listen. Aaron Morgan sent me. I gather his mother was unsuccessfully 'healed.' "

Washington's face was hard now. "Oh, yeah. Yeah, I tried to get that son of a bitch."

Skip waited.

"I'm a pediatrician, you know that?"

"That's what Mr. Morgan told me."

"I'm a children's doctor. I see some pretty ugly stuff. But this sickened me. About thirteen years ago, I started seeing a beautiful baby girl. Her parents didn't have much money, and I always treated her more or less for free. Her and her brothers and sisters. I got more than one case like that.

"But this little girl was one of the first babies I delivered after I went into practice. When that little girl was eight, she developed a brain tumor. It was malignant, but it was operable; the prognosis was good. If she'd had the operation, she'd be alive today.

"The only thing was, her parents got talked into going to this faith healer. At first they didn't put too much stock in what he was doing, but then they saw me in a picture with him in the paper and somehow, they got the idea from that he must be respectable. So they let him 'heal' their little girl and she died." He shrugged. "That's what they say now, anyway. I think they were just panicked; grasping at straws. And afraid of the expense. They never came back to me until it was too late.

"But you know what about them? Try as I might, try and try and try, I never could get them to report it, they never would do a damn thing. Now there's water under the bridge. Maybe they'd talk now. If they would, I would—but it would take both of us, I think." He took a deep breath and squared his shoulders. "Yes, I think it would."

"Dr. Washington, this man's running for mayor of New Orleans—or did you know that already?"

"Oh, yes." He nodded. "I knew it. I just didn't know what I could do about it."

"You could tell your story publicly. To a reporter from the Times-Picayune. Would you be willing to do that?"

"I don't see how I could. I don't have any proof."

"I don't think you have to accuse anyone of anything. Simply back up the parents, I would think—say that you saw the girl and she was ill, and that there was a very good chance of recovery if she had surgery."

"Let me think about that. Let me just think."

He crossed his arms and stared at the horizon for a few seconds. Finally, he nodded vigorously. "Yes. I'd be willing to do that. He caused that child's death as sure as if he murdered her. The buck's got to stop somewhere."

"Good. What would you think about my going to see the parents?"

"I can't give you their names, I'm sure you understand that."

"Of course. Confidentiality."

"Still, I could talk to them. Can you call me tonight?"

"Of course." He gave her a card and scribbled down a home number.

Skip went out and got her own plate of catfish, and then she went back to every single person she'd already seen to try to pull some more names out of them. Nobody had any.

She asked Adam Tardiff if she could have a list of his church members, and he said sure she could, he'd be glad to give it to her. There was Josephine Toups, then Dan and Evelyn Robichaux, and Robert Feran. That was everybody.

She spent the rest of the afternoon tracking them down and drawing blanks.

At seven o'clock, as soon as she thought it could properly be called "night," she called Ralph Washington. "Good news," he said. "I've been waiting for you. They're ready to talk. First time they've been this way."

"Fantastic. Can I call them?"

"Yes. They said I could give you their phone number."

"And you? Would you still be willing to talk to a reporter?"

"Yes, ma'am. Yes, ma'am, I certainly would."

The family name was Boudreaux. Judith and Bud were the parents, and the child had been named La Tarsha. Skip saw them only briefly, standing at the door of their light green asbestos-shingled house. They didn't tell their story, only confirmed what Washington had told her, and said they'd be glad to talk to Jane Storey. Two sadder-looking people she couldn't remember seeing.

"We think we did wrong," the father said. "We so sorry now. We just so sorry. We want our little girl back so bad, and ain' nothin' gon' bring her back.

"We prayed and prayed about this thing, and at first we thought, Reverend Jacomine, he be doin' the best he can, no reason to blame him, get him in no trouble he don't deserve.

"But now we mad. We think he shoulda known, at least coulda known he couldn't really save our little girl. We change our minds after we hear a preacher talk about somethin' we never heard about before. You know what hubris is, Miz Langdon?"

"Yes, I do."

"Well, we didn't used to, but once we hear the word, we jus' looked at each other and we said to ourself, tha's what it was with Reverend Jacomine. It was hubris kill our little girl." He nodded. "Yes, ma'am. We ready to talk about it."

12

• •

The girl stood uncomfortably in Potter's office, shifting her weight, trying not to look at the floor. She had been a drug addict and a prostitute the first time he met her. She was seventeen at the time.

She was a white kid, a skinny little thing. One of the boys in the church had found her in the French Quarter, sitting in a doorway crying. "Gimme some money, honey," she had said to him. "You gimme some money and I'll give you anything you want."

She was so dirty, the boy dismissed it as a sexual overture.

He said, "What you need the money for?" and she pulled up her dress to show him she had no pants on.

"I got somethin' you want," she said.

Later, telling the story, his eyes got big and he shook his head. "I'm a red-blooded boy, Reverend Jacomine, but this wadn't right. Just wadn't right."

"Are you on drugs?" he had asked her, and she shook her head. "Right now I'm shore not. Not even a little bit. Someone stole my money and I feel bad. I feel real, real bad. You understand what I mean?"

He was an innocent boy, the son of longtime church members, but he had known she meant she needed drugs. He said, "Listen, I've got a friend who can help you," meaning Paulette.

The girl said, "Your friend got any rock?"

He had ended up giving her some money and his phone number, which she had called eventually, and then he had taken Paulette to meet her.

Her name was Abby. She'd been clean and sober for a year and a half, and she had her GED. During one of those long talks Paulette always had with the kids (she was like their mother and shrink rolled into one), Abby had said shyly that she wanted to be a detective, but she knew it wasn't what real people did.

Paulette was always saying the kids could do anything they wanted if they just put their minds to it, but there were a lot of ambitions Abby could have had that wouldn't have been as easily satisfied.

Because Potter existed, it was only a matter of a phone call, and he was glad to have a white female to work with. Especially a young, skinny, relatively plain one—a girl you hardly noticed. She could go a lot of places Potter couldn't.

He had put her on Langdon because she was the only white female he had, and she was pretty good, usually. Not very experienced, but she could think fast and she desperately wanted to please. He absolutely couldn't do it himself—there was too much else to do right now, and most of his operatives were pretty ham-fisted.

There were a couple of good ones, but Langdon was a cop— she'd notice young black men in a car. So he had sent Abby.

He sat down and kept her standing. "How *exactly* did it happen?" he asked, his voice like a lit fuse.

The girl's lip trembled. "I don't know." Her whole body started to shake. "I don't know. There was too much traffic on the Interstate. She has this ordinary little car . . ."

"You don't even know what kind of car she has?"

"It's a . . . you know, a beige, uh . . . a light-colored—"

"You don't even know. Abby, Abby, what am I going to do with you?"

She squared her shoulders. "It's a little American car, sir. A Dodge or something." She shrugged. "So's every other car in Louisiana. I remember, you taught me that—people here like American cars."

"What else did I teach you, Abby?"

"Potter, I'm just as sorry as I can be. I just . . . lost her."

"Now how'd you do a thing like that?"

"Well, there were two or three of those cars all at once and, I don't know, someone changed lanes and I thought it was her."

"I taught you, Abby. You're a better operative than that."

"Well, sir, I . . ."

He leaned across the table and raised his voice. "What really happened?"

She jerked back, stung. Her voice hissed like a leaking tire. "I ran out of gas."

"You ran out of gas?"

"Well, I didn't know she was going to leave the city. I *got* as far as Breaux Bridge."

If Langdon had gone to Breaux Bridge, he knew where she was headed. But he wasn't done with Miss Abby. He could have killed himself for this. It was a reflection on his judgment, one of his troops messing up like this.

They just didn't do it. It wasn't done.

He said, "You on rock again, Abby?"

"No, sir."

"You act like you are."

She sat down involuntarily, as if falling into her chair, and her body began to shake with sobs. "I know I fucked up. I'm real sorry I fucked up."

"I will not have my operatives using foul language. Pull yourself together, Abby." He waited a moment while the sobs subsided. Finally, he spoke more softly, letting her off the hook. "Give me the rest of your report."

She pulled out a tissue and blew her nose. She straightened her spine and became businesslike, animated.

She has the stuff, he thought. *She'll never pull that one again.*

"Wednesday afternoon about four P.M., she went to an address in the nine-hundred block of Orleans Street, stayed a few minutes, and left."

"What address?"

Abby gave it to him.

"I'll be a son of a bitch."

It was Noel Treadaway's address.

"At approximately ten A.M. Thursday, she went to the offices of Caplano's Towing . . ."

"That'll be all, Abby."

"Hey. I've got some real good stuff. Don't tell me you're so mad you don't even want to hear it."

"Submit in writing, please."

He stormed over to Daddy's office. "We got a problem. Langdon's tight with our new boy, the press secretary."

Daddy raised an eyebrow, unbelieving. "Treadaway? Who says?"

"Intelligence."

"You sure about this? My press secretary's a goddamn spy?"

"Why don't we call him in here and ask him."

Daddy nodded very slowly, very slightly, flicking his eyes toward the door.

Potter marshaled his whole wiry body of energy, knowing full-out aggression was called for. He strode furiously to Treadaway's office, the entire thing an act. Actually he was cool as a cucumber.

"Treadaway!"

"Yes?" The press secretary couldn't have looked more shocked. Obviously, this wasn't a man who was used to being called on the carpet, especially by a mere "campaign aide."

"Get into Daddy's—Errol's—office. On the double."

He cocked an eyebrow but otherwise didn't move. "Something wrong?"

He was arrogant. Way too arrogant. Probably a racist. "On the double." Potter turned and stalked off. He was already seated, legs crossed by the time the other man arrived, nervous but not wanting to seem intimidated. He had moved the other chair out of the way, so Treadaway couldn't sit down.

Daddy didn't give him time to get his bearings, even time to cock another damned WASP eyebrow. "Noel, we had you in here to talk about our little police problem. You listened to us and you didn't even say anything."

"I beg your pardon? Police problem?"

"You know what I'm talking about." Daddy barked it.

"I'm afraid I don't."

"What kind of press secretary are you, Noel? You can't even remember a fucking talk we had earlier this week?"

"You mean the cop on leave? I wouldn't call that a police problem, exactly."

"Well, what kind of problem would you call it, Noel? You know more about it than I do."

Treadaway shook his head. Potter had to admit he showed a certain amount of guts. "Errol, I'm afraid we've got off on the wrong foot on this one. It seems as if we're speaking at cross-purposes."

Daddy rose up out of his chair, his face threatening. "We're not speaking at any cross-purposes, you son of a bitch. You're lying 'cause you're scared shitless."

Treadaway spread his hands, palms up. "Don't you think you should tell me what this is all about?"

To his credit, he wasn't scared and he wasn't mad; he was detached. A thoroughgoing professional. Potter was impressed; knew he'd underestimated him.

"It's about you being a goddamn spy in my camp. How could you have the motherfucking nerve?"

"Spy." Treadaway nodded slowly and folded his arms, a man trying to get the hang of things. A damn good actor.

Daddy turned to Potter and nodded at him. Potter consulted a small blank piece of paper he had in his hand, a prop. "Where were you at precisely sixteen hundred hours, Wednesday, September eighth?"

He never hesitated for a second. "None of your damn business."

"I beg your pardon," said Daddy. "You were on my payroll at that time. I b'lieve it's very much my business."

"I said it's none of Menard's damn business."

"Are you a racist, son? You're a racist, aren't you? That's what's wrong with you. You don't want Errol Jacomine to get elected because that would be a victory for the black man. You're working to defeat me. Right in the heart of my inner circle, and you're a viper—a poisonous viper who will sting me unto death." His voice didn't rise; it got lower if anything, and more and more dramatic, yet resigned, as if this was what Jacomine expected.

"Look, Errol, I'm working for you. If you don't get elected, it's just as much a defeat for me as it is for you. I don't see what you're getting at." Cool as a breeze off the river.

Daddy turned once again to Potter, who once again read from the fake cheat sheet. "At precisely sixteen hundred hours Wednesday, September eighth, Margaret (Skip) Langdon was seen entering your house in the nine-hundred block of Orleans Street, where she remained approximately twenty minutes, exiting at roughly sixteen-twenty hours."

"Langdon? The cop?"

Neither he nor Daddy said anything.

"Omigod. I think I get it. Do you guys have a tape recorder? I want to call my wife, and I want you to hear the conversation."

"Let's use the speaker phone."

"We can't. She's a therapist. She won't talk if a client can hear."

Daddy nodded at Potter, who got the recorder and attached it. Noel dialed, let it ring a couple of times, hung up, and dialed again. "Secret ring," he said. "She'll answer even if she's busy."

When they played the tape back, it went like this:

"Noel? Is anything wrong?"

"It's not that kind of emergency. It's about a client of yours. Skip Langdon."

She drew in her breath. "How do you know about that?"

"I don't know, she was seen going into our house. I'm asking you."

"I saw her once a week ago. Then you got the job and I realized I had a conflict. When she came Wednesday, I told her I couldn't be her therapist. But of course I couldn't tell you because of confidentiality."

There was a little more, in which they said conciliatory things to each other—he was sorry he'd interrupted, she that she couldn't tell him—but that was the gist of it.

When Treadaway had played it, Daddy said, "Potter, what do you think?"

Potter prided himself on being able to admit he'd made a mistake. A true leader could do that and move on. He said, "I think it's genuine. Mr. Treadaway, we owe you an apology."

Daddy said, "If you ever, *ever* cross me, Noel Treadaway, you're going to find out the meaning of sorry."

• •

Torian had almost gotten over her discomfort at having Sheila come over to her shabby apartment. Since she had told her about Noel, they'd achieved a new bond, almost of sisterhood. Nothing now could make her ashamed in front of Sheila, who was in possession of her deepest secret and therefore closer than anyone except Noel himself.

A pattern had formed. Torian had joined the campaign. After school, she'd go down to Headquarters in the Central Business District and work awhile, then come home and Sheila would come over. That was on days when she couldn't see Noel.

It was boring, dirty work in a scroungy little office, an office where Noel didn't work. That had disappointed her, and so had the work itself—mostly phoning or stamping and stuffing envelopes— but she found it fulfilling. It made her feel as if she was doing something worthwhile, and people were getting to know her. They appreciated her efforts, and so did Noel. He had been so moved he had to sit down when she told him what she was doing. That alone was worth it.

Another benefit was that she could always tell Lise she was at Headquarters when she was really with Noel. Not that Lise gave a damn what she did with her afternoons, but on the rare occasions she was home, they had to play that game where she pretended to be interested; it was good to have something to tell her.

Lise was home more and more seldom, it seemed to Torian. She and Sheila had the run of the house. They could smoke as many cigarettes as they liked, and drink Lise's booze if they were careful (though they didn't have to be that careful; she drank so much it was easy to convince her she'd done it herself).

Torian loved having Sheila around—such a relief from Loathsome Lise. And from her own tiresome, melancholy self. Fresh from a golden afternoon with Noel, alone in the shabby apartment, Torian could sink into such a depression she could only lie on her bed and stare at the ceiling with the lights off, so that the street light, through her lace curtains, made a lovely design on the wall, which only depressed her more. It was so beautiful, so delicate, in the face of so much misery. It seemed to heighten the minginess of the apartment and of her life, rather than to enhance them, to show them stark and drab by contrast.

And so the more she lay there, the more depressed she got. Too depressed, certainly, to get up. Too depressed to cry. Way too depressed to do her homework.

With Sheila here, she was happy. It was almost better than being with Noel. "Call Uncle Jimmy and say you're staying to dinner. We'll order from the new place."

Sheila could never resist. Her uncle made her eat pasta primavera and crawfish maque-choux and vegetable burritos—he was trying to turn her into a walking vitamin. At the new place, the place on Dumaine, they could get burgers and potato salad or po' boys or even fried chicken; but that wasn't the main attraction.

The delivery boy was to die for. Torian had discovered him, but Sheila'd developed a major crush.

Sheila hung up the phone. "Uncle Jimmy said, 'Are you sure it's okay with Lise, your hanging around there all the time?' I had to explain that kids are much easier with two of us, so he said come over there, and I said we couldn't because Lise was fixing something special."

Torian snorted. "I think she did that once. She burned it."

"I'm starving. Let's order."

"You just want to see Joe Eddie."

"I do not." Sheila's cheeks flamed. "I want some mashed potatoes and green beans. And carrot salad."

"Wait a minute. I thought you hated vegetables."

"I like good vegetables."

They ordered Sheila's vegetables, and some potato salad for To-rian. She hadn't felt much like eating lately, but she could usually get down white things—potatoes or pasta.

Joe Eddie was sweating when he came to the door. "Hi, gorgeous. Hello, beautiful. Boy, are you girls lucky you don't have to work. The humidity must be about four hundred and eight."

Sheila said, "There's going to be a hurricane."

He looked at her. "That's what my mama says. Says we're not gettin' off this year."

Torian didn't miss a beat. "Come in and cool off."

"I got two more deliveries to make."

"Big deal. No one expects anything on time."

"I'm not going to cool off around you two girls." Torian was sure he gave Sheila a wink. Her heart soared. She wanted everyone to be as happy in their love as she and Noel.

Joe Eddie had slicked-back blond hair and biceps that he must have had to work at. He always wore tank tops or some kind of shirt with the sleeves cut off. He had a smooth brown body, white teeth with one broken at the side, and a muscular, neat butt. A cobra was tattooed on one of his gorgeous biceps. That and the broken tooth gave him a raffish look. He was from Corinth, Mississippi.

He unpacked their food. "What'd you girls order? I'm hungry. Potato salad. All right! Mashed potatoes. Any meat? You girls religious or something?"

Sheila said, "We never eat anything with eyes."

He hooted. "Yeah, I know what you mean. All those little animals, like in *Fantasia*, with their foot-long eyelashes. Be a shame to barbecue 'em." He dug into the potato salad with a plastic spoon.

"Bacon's okay, though, 'cause pigs are so *ugly*." Sheila was leaning so close Joe Eddie had to lean away from her to keep his cool.

"I'm Torian. This is Sheila."

Sheila blushed, perhaps realizing they hadn't been properly introduced.

"I'm Joe Eddie."

"We know. You told us last time."

"I did? Well, I remember you two, too."

Torian said, "I'll be right back," and went in search of cigarettes. She found them in about two seconds, and smoked one, giving the lovebirds time alone. Then she looked in the mirror, messed up her hair, and put on her glasses, making the statement that she wasn't interested, Joe Eddie was Sheila's.

Joe Eddie was just leaving. "You be sure and call me now," he said, and she smiled to herself.

Sheila danced into the kitchen, leaping as she crossed the threshold, touching the doorsill with her fingertips. "Yes!"

"He asked you out?"

She leaped again. "Yes!"

"I told you he liked you." She turned her attention to the food. "Oh, shit, he ate all the potato salad."

"Have my mashed potatoes. I have to lose five pounds."

"When are you seeing him?"

"As soon as he finds out his schedule. How old do you think he is?"

"Eighteen or nineteen."

"Not older?" Sheila seemed hesitant.

"Maybe. Who cares?"

"Well, you wouldn't." They collapsed, giggling, and ate the rest of the mashed potatoes, then polished off the green beans, Sheila treating them as finger food, pretending to smoke them. She didn't touch the carrot salad.

Torian foraged in the freezer for ice cream, and dredged up some chocolate syrup. Lise arrived to find her topping the sundaes with cherries. Her arms were full of groceries.

"For Christ's sake, Torian, can't I trust you for five minutes? You know you can't have dessert till you've had dinner. What on Earth do you think you're doing?"

Torian raised her voice to match her mother's. "We've had dinner. We ordered from the deli."

"Well, that's fine. That's just fine. You couldn't even wait till I got home and fixed dinner?"

"Mother, I don't even remember the last time you made dinner."

Perhaps sensing an escalating scene, perhaps embarrassed already, Sheila mumbled something and left.

When she heard the door shut, Torian said, "Do you have to embarrass me in front of my friends?"

"I embarrassed *you*? You're the one with the mouth like a garbage can. You can't be trusted for anything, can you? You order junk food and invite your friends over whether you have permission or not." She fanned the air. "It smells like you've been smoking in here."

"What would you care what I eat? I wish I lived with my dad—at least there's usually food in the house. Here I have to order because you can't be bothered to shop, and you can't be bothered to cook, and you certainly can't be bothered to remember I'm here, because you're out every night drinking and fucking your fucking overweight boyfriend who nobody would fuck unless they were fucking *desperate!*"

Torian stopped and felt herself suspended in midair for a fraction of a second, later knowing it was exactly the sensation that falling people must have, people who know they are about to hit the ground with a splat that will rupture their organs and splinter their bones, who know they have made an irrevocable, fatal mistake.

Her mother whacked her so hard she fell backwards, hit the countertop, and bruised her lower back. For the moment, the pain of that nearly obscured the excruciating sensation of what could only be a broken nose. She felt her face, and came up with a handful of glasses so badly twisted she couldn't even wear them. There was a ridge on her nose, where the nosepiece had slammed into flesh and cartilage, but it hadn't swelled yet.

"My nose is broken," she cried, terrified, not merely in pain.

"I certainly hope so," said Lise. "And I'll tell you something. If it is, you're going to live with it. My insurance would cover having it fixed, but we're not going to do that. You're going to go through life with a big, ugly bump on your nose, to remind you of what a perfect little bitch you are. I hope you're satisfied."

She walked out of the room, almost with dignity, as if she were the one who was satisfied, leaving Torian to find some ice for her injuries.

When she had made herself two ice packs from threadbare dish towels, Torian limped to bed, moving with difficulty only partly because of her back pain. Part of her inability to stand up straight, to regain spring in her step, had to do with her mental state, the now literal feeling of being beaten.

She lay in bed with her ice, not even bothering to turn the light off, not able to bear the lace pattern on the wall, not caring anyway if she went to sleep with every light in the house on and loud music blaring.

She had thought she would fall asleep instantly, had looked forward to it, to escape her misery. Instead, she found her mind wandering to possible ways out. She hadn't thought of this before except as kind of a daydream—it had never occurred to her simply to bolt.

I could run away. But where would I go? I already live in the French Quarter. This is where people run to.

I could turn her in!

She sat upright. She knew that what Lise had done was beyond the pale; maybe she could go to jail for it.

What do I do? Just walk into the Eighth District?

Hey, wait a minute. Why not tell Dad? He'll come get me. He wouldn't want me living with this. Or Noel! He's five minutes away. He'll come now. I'm going to call him.

She reached for the phone, but some inner brake clicked on and stopped her. In her heart of hearts, she knew she couldn't do it. *Shouldn't* do it. Noel had a wife and family, she had no right. Besides, he might kill her mother.

She took some deep breaths and calmed down a little. Her mother wouldn't come back in tonight. Surely she'd go out and find Charles. It was okay to have a cigarette, no one would mess with her.

And if she does, I'll get another bruise that I can show the cops. If she hits me again, that's it. I'm reporting her.

She lit the cigarette, wondering if she possibly could. Lise wasn't responsible, she drank too much, she probably didn't deserve jail.

On the other hand, I could live with Dad.

In some ways, it seemed as if deliverance had been handed to her by Lise herself. But she knew she wasn't going to take the rope Lise had thrown, that she couldn't betray her mother.

She jumped when the phone rang, thinking it was too late for calls. But when she looked at her watch, she saw it was just eight-thirty.

• •

Boo had gone to her yoga class, and Noel was glad to be alone—that is, alone with Joy. What had happened that day had unnerved him, and his daughter was his anchor—a real, laughing, flesh-and-blood creature. So alive. So innocent.

He changed her diaper, something he thought he'd never do, but he found that he enjoyed it in a way. He was revolted on the surface, yet the sensation of being useful to his daughter, doing something she needed, something intimate, something vital, outweighed that.

Next he fed her, giving her food that Boo had left for her, playing little games to get her to eat. He'd pretend the spoon was a giant humming insect about to land in her mouth, and she'd laugh and finally open up.

This was something he loved, something he cherished, these all too few moments with Joy. Without Boo.

Moments when if he did something wrong no one would know, no one was there to correct him, to tell him that wasn't the right way to hold the spoon, or the bite was too big or too little. It was amazing she'd leave him alone with the baby, knowing he was as hopeless as she obviously thought.

Boo wasn't someone he could talk to. She was all too ready to solve his problems, to offer suggestions, to help him pull up his socks and get on with it. That had been appealing at first, until he realized it wasn't what he wanted. There was at least a chance he could work out his problems, and he'd rather try it before asking advice. Besides, by the time he told something to Boo, he usually had thought of everything that would occur to a person of normal intelligence. It was insulting, the way she treated him as if he had a two-figure IQ.

And she always jumped the gun on him. Tonight he didn't want to come to any decisions, didn't want to make any changes, just wanted to think about what had happened. Maybe get some tiny glimmer of understanding.

He heard Jacomine's voice echoing in his mind: . . . *a poisonous viper who will sting me unto death.*

Preachers talked that way. A candidate under extreme stress—meaning any candidate for any office—might talk that way.

On the other hand, it was worth noting that it was pretty weird. And the whole outburst might conceivably be called paranoid if you didn't blame it on stress.

Then there was Potter Menard, more robot than man. He was like some latter-day Green Beret, some commando run amok. His sangfroid, his chilly efficiency, gave Noel the creeps. But Menard had caught on that Noel wasn't a spy for the other side.

Jacomine hadn't seemed to. What disturbed Noel most was the way the man couldn't seem to take in information, couldn't let go of the notion of Noel as enemy. His parting threat was hostile and absolutely pointless.

You have to wonder if a person like that would really be a good mayor.

Maybe he's a little nuts.

Or maybe it's just the stress.

But being mayor's a stressful job. He's always going to be under stress.

Wait it out, Noel. Wait it out. You don't have enough information. Unless he's absolutely psycho, he's better than a machine cog or a racist.

Joy banged the table. Evidently, his mind had wandered for a moment.

"Okay, doll-baby, let's read a book. Want to?" He lifted Joy out of her high chair. "How about one of your pop-ups?" These were her favorites—they were so much fun to tear apart.

He settled her comfortably in his lap and read her one of the books, which took about a minute and a half. She was sleeping soundly when he came to the end of it.

"Guess you weren't up for a book tonight," he said, on the way down the hall.

He settled her in bed and was sure, in proper clichéd fashion, as all parents are, that an angel had landed on Earth.

142

How innocent she is. I'd kill anyone who tried to hurt her.

She was wearing a pink T-shirt and diaper. Her legs were open, as babies' are most of the time and women's are when they make love.

Because of that, perhaps, he took the thought further: *I'd kill anyone who tried to get into her pants.*

And then: *What a crazy thing I'm doing. Torian's someone's daughter. What if Joy were fifteen and a man my age tried to get near her?*

I'd kill him.

A married man with a child.

I'd torture him first.

But Torian's an angel, too—how can I? Of course, it's not like I'm having sex with her, but her dad probably wouldn't stop to ask the particulars.

I've got to stop.

I can't stop, I'm in love with her. I feel like her dad—I'd kill anyone who came near her.

He was seized suddenly with an overwhelming desire to talk to her, a frantic desire that was like a muscle contraction. He went back to the living room and waited for the cramp to subside.

But the pain, the desire only became stronger.

Why not? he thought. *She can't call here, but I could call there. If Lise answers, I'll just hang up.*

Torian answered, and her voice sounded oddly thin.

"Babe? You okay?"

"Noel. You did call."

"What do you mean? Torian, what do you mean?" There was some note in her voice he didn't recognize, something like hysteria.

"I'm okay. It's all right."

If he didn't know better, he'd have thought she was on drugs.

"What is it, honey? You sound so strange. Like you're afraid of something."

"I'm . . . sleepy. I'm . . . okay." She was saying words that had nothing to do with her tone of voice. She sounded terrified, yet oddly withdrawn.

"Are you alone, Torian? Are you frightened of something?"

"Mom's here."

"Anyone else?"

"Just us."

He was frantic. Something was badly wrong, he could feel it. "Torian, I'm coming over."

"No!"

"I want to be with you."

"You can't. You're with Boo." He thought there was a note of desperation in her voice.

"I love you, Torian."

She hung up, saying nothing, yet he heard a noise, perhaps a sob, maybe a sigh.

Surely he couldn't have caused this unhappiness. He was miserable, being in love with an adolescent while married to a therapist. But Torian had her whole life. He was a blip on her screen.

What if I just went over and got her?

Turn up on the doorstep with Joy?

I don't think so.

But what if she's in some kind of trouble?

How could she be? Her mother's there.

He poured himself a drink of single malt scotch, something he rarely drank—it was too hot in New Orleans. He saved it for times of deep melancholy.

13

It was nearly midnight when Lise left Charles's. She had cried for about three hours solid, occasionally throwing things and once or twice beating on poor, dear Charles, who was about the only person she could stand right now.

Even after investing three hours, she couldn't make him understand. He thought if he went out and "beat the shit out of Wilson," that would solve everything. It hadn't been that easy to keep him from doing it.

Wilson didn't need to be beaten, but he did need to be talked to. Things couldn't go on. Lise was a mess, and Torian was out of control.

She would never have hit Torian, never never never, if she weren't so stressed out. It was Wilson's fault that she was, and probably her fault that Torian was. A domino effect.

A car nearly sideswiped her.

"Motherfucker!" she shouted, putting her whole heart and soul into it, but the windows were shut tight for the AC.

Wilson's house was dark when she arrived. She leaned on the

horn as she turned into the driveway, ran to the door, and leaned just as heavily on the doorbell.

Wilson answered, belting his robe, followed by his bimbo trophy wife doing the same. She looked bewildered, he furious.

"Is Torian with you?"

"Torian? Forget Torian. This is between us."

He sighed. "What is, Lise? It's the middle of the night."

"I need to come in. We can't talk out here."

He looked at the trophy as if he had to ask her damn permission. She nodded and he stepped aside for Lise.

Anger raced up her spine like a flame. He had never asked her permission for anything—they hadn't communicated at all. And there was another thing. She could see that both Wilson and the trophy were naked under their robes. The last year or so of their marriage—Wilson and Lise's—he had pointedly worn pajamas.

She walked into their beige-on-beige living room with its Hurwitz-Mintz furniture and felt herself consumed by the flame inside her. It metastasized in the space of a millisecond from her spine to every cell in her body. Her tongue was a lightning bolt.

"Goddamn you, Wilson Gernhard. *Goddamn* you! Look at this place! Do you know what kind of squalor your only daughter is living in?"

The trophy—Carol, wasn't it?—looked as if she were about to wet her pants, and as if on cue, a baby wailed somewhere in the bowels in the house. Carol left, but not before shooting Lise a look—a very different look from the hateful one she expected. Carol looked terrified.

Wimp, she thought. *If she stays married to Wilson long enough, she'll end up this way, too.*

"Torian isn't my only daughter, Lise." He spoke in a perfectly modulated voice, the voice of someone trying to calm a mental patient. It made Lise want to rip his liver out.

"No wonder you don't care about her anymore. No wonder . . ."

"You're not making sense."

Lise heard noises in the kitchen, as if Carol were cooking.

"I'm sick and goddamn tired of your stinginess, your utter abdication of responsibility, the way you can never quite come up with our little bitty checks, paltry as they obviously are compared to any others you might be writing. Now that I see the way you live, I understand why you never have any money for us.

"Do you have any idea what I have to do for the few bucks a month I get from the goddamn insurance company? I have to sell my soul to some power-hungry supervisor the minute I get to work, and then five minutes later I have to turn around and sell it again to some numb-nuts who's mad at the world because he didn't have any better sense than to get drunk out of his skull and total his car. Half the time I have to work ten hours a day without overtime. And I still don't make enough to keep decent clothes on your daughter's back."

"Lise . . ."

But she wouldn't let him talk. "Wilson, I can't take this anymore. My life is the pits, do you understand that? I'm going nuts. This is driving me stark raving crazy."

"Something obviously is."

"Go ahead. Be fucking sarcastic; go ahead. I have no money, Wilson. Do you know what it's like to have no money? Not to know if you can afford to park your goddamn car? Or go to the movies? Hell, rent a video! My life is so awful I really think I'm going crazy. I swear to God I do." She put her face in her hands, trying to hold back what she had almost said. She must not tell him what she had done. She must not, no matter what.

"You're the one who wanted the divorce, Lise. You're the one who wanted to be on your own. You were the dumper; I was the dumpee." The sneer in his voice was so nasty she recoiled.

Perhaps it was the trigger, or perhaps the night of drinking had reached a plateau—suddenly, she began to sob into her hands. To her horror, she felt a soft arm go around her shoulders. Carol's. *Goddamn phony bitch!*

She jerked away, uncovering her face, and spilling the coffee the trophy had brought her.

While she and Carol stared at each other in mutual revulsion, Wilson marshaled his strength. Carol offered the cup, and for some reason, Lise took it.

When Wilson spoke next, it was in a new tone entirely, a

147

clipped, angry one. "Lise, why the hell are you here? What do you want?"

"I can't stand your damn hypocrisy." She screamed it. "That poor daughter of yours—your number two daughter, it would seem—honestly thinks you want her to come live with you, worships you and your phony wimp of a wife, when you don't even want to buy her a pair of jeans to wear to school."

He spread his hands, palms up. "Fine, fine. I'll take Torian. If you recall, you insisted on custody, but you can just forget it now. I'll fight you all the way on this. I'll tell the judge how you came over here drunk and abusive, and I'll get custody. Make no mistake, I'll get it." His lips were set in a nasty, grim line, one that Lise had seen before, maybe one of the principal reasons she'd divorced him.

The trophy was grim, too. She looked as if she'd lost her last friend.

"The hell you will," said Lise. "You'll give us enough money to live on."

He was smiling. He kept talking as if she hadn't said a word. "It'll really be better for Torian. We can send her to Country Day . . ."

"Country Day! The only reason she's not going to Country Day right now is because you won't pay for it."

"No, Lise, I don't think you remember correctly. We decided not to send her to Country Day because you didn't want to drive her in the morning." She hated his goddamn, supercilious, self-righteous, hyper-rational tone.

"You bastard!"

"She'll thrive here. She needs something to love. You should see her with Marly—like she's absolutely starved for affection. And Carol's a wonderful cook, and of course, her room's a teenager's dream. Let me show it to you."

Lise's jaw had dropped when he began, but the shock had worn off. The flame consumed her now, the anger that had been simmering in her cells for the last twenty minutes.

"You son of a bitch." She yelled so loud she saw the trophy flinch, and as she yelled, she flung the coffee at him, first the liquid, then the cup. It splattered his beige robe and a little of his chest. The cup thumped against his torso.

Balling up her fists, she went for him. She managed to land one blow, on his chest, but unfortunately in the robed area, before he caught her arms. He said to Carol, "I think we'd better call the police."

"No." Lise whispered the word. "Don't do that to me. Let me go." She sank to her knees, Wilson still holding her wrists.

Carol came up behind her, once again slipping a condescending arm around her. "Come on, Lise. You'll be fine." They started to lift her to her feet, Carol and Wilson working together.

● ●

Skip was awakened from a sound sleep by a phone ringing. "Hello."

"It's Jane Storey."

She sat up. "Jane! What's going on?" Her bedside clock said seven-thirty.

"I'm so goddamn mad I couldn't sleep. I spent the night in St. Martinville, or anyway I tried. I got up in the middle of the night and came home. I got here half an hour ago, had a cup of coffee and half a dozen cigarettes and finally couldn't wait any longer."

"What is it?"

"The sources dried up."

"What?" She didn't get it, wasn't fully awake yet. "Who backed out?"

"Ralph did. The wonderful Ralph Washington who just thought the story ought to be told. And the little girl's parents. All of them. Count 'em, three."

"Well, what excuse did they give?"

"They'd been giving it some thought and realized they'd been hasty. They'd slept on it and decided nothing would be served by 'digging up old bones.' That's what the parents said. Grisly, huh?"

"And Ralph?"

"Pretty much the same thing without the bones."

"Jacomine got to them."

"Of course Jacomine got to them. Jacomine always gets to them. I'm going to go nuts, you know that? This whole thing's going to drive me nuts. There's no way out. You just get caught in some sticky web that won't let go, and next thing you know, you're trying to chew your way out of a straitjacket."

"How the hell could he have known?"

Jane snorted. "That's as close as I get to a chuckle. He had you followed. Why should you be different from anybody else?"

Because I used to be a cop. Last time I looked I could spot a tail.

"Jane, I'm sorry about this. It's not the end of it, though. I'll get you something. I promise."

"Get me my sanity." She hung up, and Skip reached for the phone book.

An hour and a half later, she was on a plane for Atlanta. It was too early to check anything out by phone, so she hadn't. Just hopped on the first plane she could get, impatient as Jane Storey. Atlanta had been in her mind ever since Adam Tardiff said he thought Jacomine must have learned some "real slick tricks there."

Just to get warmed up, she started with "Jacomine" in the phone book, but that was no good. She'd known it wouldn't be. She didn't think that was a name he'd had for long.

Okay, then, Christian Community World Headquarters.

It had an address in Cobb County. The best plan, she thought, was to go there and produce her badge.

After driving for what seemed half the morning, she ended up at a tacky brick building barely off the expressway, and learned the Christian Community occupied half the third floor. Either the Community had fallen on hard times or it hadn't been much to start with. She suspected the latter.

The receptionist took up about half the front office. She was a white woman, maybe fifty or sixty, maybe forty or seventy—her skin had the smoothness obesity affords, and her face was as pretty as heavy women's are reputed to be. Her makeup was thick and shiny with the heat. Her hair was hennaed a delicate peach, and her dress was fuchsia. Her hands were carefully manicured, dainty fingers and perfect nails, feminine and lovely, adorned only with a wedding ring. Skip had noticed that a lot of fat women had perfect hands and wondered if that should be added to the pretty-face stereotype.

"Jesus loves you," she said. "I'm Mary Lou."

Skip was momentarily speechless. Finally, she stuttered out her name, and said she needed to ask some questions about a Community member.

"Why, sure," said Mary Lou. "I'd be glad to help you." She turned expectant sapphire eyes on Skip, eyes sooty with perfect mascara and liner. Except for her odd penchant for pinks and oranges, she was one of the best-groomed women Skip had ever seen.

"I wonder if I could talk to . . ." *Who? The director? The bishop?* She finally said, "Someone who'd know."

"Honey, I been here nineteen years. Know where every body's buried. Believe me, we got quite a history."

Skip wanted to ask why she wasn't worried about a stranger asking questions, but she certainly wasn't going to. Her quizzical look must have given her away.

"Honey, we got a policy. We were born naked before God, and tha's the way we're gon' leave this world. We don't mind talkin' about ourselves. Only thing is, we don't keep real good records, and the way things have been goin', we lose a lot of staff. So mostly, if you want to know anything, you have to ask Mary Lou."

Is she for real? Skip thought. But it didn't matter, because Mary Lou was very effectively placing herself between Skip and any other sources. In short, it was Mary Lou or nothing.

She drew in a breath. "The person I want to ask about may or may not still be connected with the church. His name's Errol Jacomine."

"I beg your pardon?"

"Errol Jacomine. He used to be assigned to St. Martinville."

Mary Lou looked stumped. "Why no, we never had a . . ." She stopped in mid-sentence and chewed her lip. "You don't mean Earl Jackson, do you? Come to think of it, I think Adam Tardiff called him something funny." She nodded a couple of times, then pushed back her chair, turned around, and went to a file cabinet. Skip saw that her dress fit immodestly over jiggling bottom cheeks, each the size of a small moon.

She brought back a thin file, from which she pulled a photograph. "Is this who you mean?"

It was a much younger Jacomine. Skip nodded. "He was called Earl Jackson?"

"First I've heard of that other name. 'Cept maybe once, and I thought Adam was just a little forgetful."

"May I ask his middle name?"

Mary Lou frowned. "Well, it's—" She seemed to be struggling with something.

"What?"

She frowned some more and said something that sounded like "fee." There was evidently more.

"May I look?"

Mary Lou turned the file around.

"Ah. Theophilus." Skip noted his date of birth as well.

"I wonder why he changed his name."

"Any idea?"

Mary Lou gave Skip a quick, sharp look. Her wonderment had obviously been rhetorical. She shrugged, looking through the file. "I guess we've lost track of him." She pulled out a letter. "He wrote us, sayin' he'd have to leave St. Martinville, which is our only outreach post in Louisiana—see, Earl started the church there. That's how we work—if a preacher wants to start a church, he just does. Anyway, we got this letter and that was it."

"What do you mean that was it?"

"Well, as far as I recall, we just never could reach him after that. So we sent Adam on out there—Earl started something, somebody had to finish it."

Skip was beginning to wonder if there really was any "we"; maybe Mary Lou was the entire administration of the Christian Community.

"He has a church in New Orleans now."

Mary Lou tightened her carefully painted mouth. "Not under our auspices."

"Tell me something. Is healing a normal part of your community?"

"Some of our ministers are gifted. God gives the power to some and not to others."

"What about Earl?"

She shrugged. "I don't know. I never attended one of his services."

"Why did he go to St. Martinville in the first place? I know Adam has relatives there. But why Earl Jackson?"

She stared at the file and pursed her lips. "It was his time to do outreach."

Skip waited awhile, hoping for illumination. None came, and she asked, "Why was that?"

"From time to time we call on a member to start a new church. Have you ever heard of the Buddha with the begging bowl? We think of it as somethin' like that."

"An act of humility."

Mary Lou nodded. Some kind of curtain had come between her and Skip; but when it had happened, Skip wasn't sure. She said, "Any particular reason?"

Mary Lou shrugged. "It was just his time, bless his heart."

It was a different story from the original—"if a preacher wants to start a church, he just does."

Skip asked: "Was it some kind of punishment?" *And did it work so well he decided to change his name, divest himself of his former life, and start over as a charlatan?*

Mary Lou looked uncomfortable.

"I'm sorry. Am I stepping on toes? I believed you about being naked in the world. Am I asking too many questions?"

Mary Lou closed the file and looked Skip full in the face. Her face was damper now, though it was no warmer in the office. She pulled a tissue seemingly from nowhere, and dabbed at her forehead. "This is a personnel file."

And I'll bet there's something pretty sensitive in it. "I wonder who could tell me more about Earl Jackson?"

"I'm afraid our executive director hasn't been here long enough to remember him."

But maybe he'd let me look at the file. "Just the same I wonder if I might talk to him."

"I'm very sorry. Mr. Moore is out of the country just now."

"I see. When will he be back?"

153

"I really don't know. I'm just a secretary." She seemed to have demoted herself. A few minutes ago, Skip could have sworn she more or less ran the place.

"Well, Mary Lou, you've been a big help. I want you to know how much I appreciate it."

"I don't get that many visitors anymore—'cept for the UPS man. I've certainly enjoyed talking to you. Jesus loves you and God blesses you."

"I'm sure she blesses you, too."

● ●

Skip left, found a telephone, and called Jane Storey. "I finally have a name for him. And I think something happened with the Christian Community. Do you have any contacts here in Atlanta?"

"I'll talk to Stanley. Call back in ten."

When Skip called back, Jane gave her the name of a reporter at the Atlanta Constitution. "Stanley didn't know a religion editor, but this is someone he went to school with. Education reporter or something—Charlina Digby. She'll do a clip search for you."

Skip called first. Charlina had already done the search. She sounded harried and uninterested. "You want printouts?"

"Sure."

"Well, come get 'em. Ask at the reception desk."

Half an hour later, wiping away September sweat, Skip presented herself at the Constitution's reception desk and was in turn presented with a paper-clipped pile of papers.

Unable to wait, she sat down and started reading, the most recent first, a little squib, that might have appeared on the religion page: *Rev. Jackson Transferred*, as if anyone cared.

Going back in time, she saw why some readers would—and when Mary Lou had dropped that curtain on her. She must have done it when she realized who Skip was really asking about. Earl Jackson had had a church in Atlanta for some years, and quite a big church, it seemed. In fact, Skip gathered he'd been rather a prominent minister.

Then a lady in the congregation had dropped a dime on him—in the form of a letter to Community headquarters saying he'd had an affair with her, gotten her pregnant, and dumped her. The matter might have ended there if her husband hadn't tried to kill Jackson, which got the police involved.

Once that happened, other ladies came forward. It seemed he had treated them to some fairly unorthodox pastoral counseling.

It wasn't a huge scandal, but it was a start. And she had Jacomine's real name.

14

• •

Noel was sitting sideways at his desk, talking to Boo on the phone. He had taken to sitting that way when talking to her, as if looking straight ahead were too painful.

He had flicked his eyes toward the dirt-encrusted window and flicked them back, so that he was now idly contemplating a pile of campaign brochures. He caught motion out of the corner of his eye, but later he thought that he had felt something, too—felt her presence as strong as a scent.

He turned toward the blur. It was Torian, in baggy white shorts and T-shirt, backpack slung over her shoulder, hair slipping from her ponytail. Her body was moving fast and so, he thought, was her face, or maybe just her eyes, which took in the scene quickly, then seemed to rake the room for escape.

He said, "Boo, I have to go. We've got a crisis here."

He hung up without waiting for an answer and nearly leaped over the table to get to Torian. Her arms went around him as if she were shipwrecked and had found flotsam to cling to. With one hand, he pulled her to him, with the other pushed the door closed. But as he pushed, he noticed Errol Jacomine, standing in the reception area, turn around and note the closing door. What else he had seen, Noel didn't know.

"What is it, darling? What's wrong?" He whispered it, hoping the softness of his breath would calm her. Her neck was uncharacteristically hot.

"Ohhhhhh, Noel!" Her voice was ragged with sobbing.

He squeezed her closer, held her tighter, until the sobs began to subside.

She pulled away from him and touched her nose, high on the bridge, where a nasty bruise discolored her delicate skin. "I can't stay with my mother anymore."

"She did that?"

Torian nodded and flung herself against him again, clinging like a toddler. "She hit me! Noel, she hit me! And then she left me all alone in the middle of the night." She began to sob again.

"It's all right, sweetheart, it's fine. Everything's going to be fine." He was horrified for her, distraught on her behalf, yet a part of him exulted because she was with him, this thing had driven her to him.

When he had stopped her sobs, he sat her down and got her a drink of water. "Noel, what am I going to do?"

"Let's think about it. Let's talk it out."

There was a light tap on the door, and Jacomine entered without being bidden.

"Am I interrupting something?"

Torian leaned back in her chair, withdrawing as if she were suddenly shy, but her face split in a smile. "Mr. Jacomine? Reverend Jacomine?" Her voice was eager.

She extended her hand. "I'm Torian Gernhard. You don't know how hard I've been working for you. It would mean really, really a lot to New Orleans if you got elected. I'm just so glad you decided to run." The words came out in a breathless rush, making her sound more like an awkward schoolgirl than she ever had in Noel's acquaintanceship. She flushed, apparently afraid she was babbling.

Jacomine smiled as if she had just conferred a knighthood on him. "I'm so very pleased to meet you, Miss Gernhard. I wonder if . . ." He paused, seemingly shy. ". . . if there's any way I might

157

be of service." He glanced suspiciously at Noel. "I mean I . . ." another gentlemanly pause ". . . I really couldn't help noticing your distress, and I wondered if you and Mr. Treadaway could use my assistance in any way."

He sounded so courtly that Noel almost forgot the things he had heard about "taking care of" Langdon, the cop. However, he was far from ready to put Torian's fate in Jacomine's hands.

But Torian was all innocence. Her face gave way again, and when she had enough control to speak, she said, "I don't know what to do; I'm frightened, and I just don't know what to do."

"What is it, child?"

"My mother hit me!" Again she rubbed the bruise on her face. "I'm afraid to go home, and I can't tell my father, he'll . . ."

Jacomine put a hand on her knee. Torian apparently took the gesture as paternal; Noel wanted to kill him. "He'll what, dear child?"

"I don't know what he might do to her!" The sentence was more like an explosion. Her cheeks reddened.

Noel started. She'd painted her dad as the next thing to a saint. Jacomine said, "Your father is violent?"

"No! I mean, he never has been, but—" The tears and sobs started again. Noel longed to hold her.

Jacomine looked at him curiously. "Mr. Treadaway, you're a relative?"

"Neighbor. Torian babysits for my wife and me."

"Perhaps she could stay with you for a day or two."

But Torian blurted, "No! I mean—I do need a day or two, but I need . . . I need . . ."

Jacomine patted her again. "I understand, dear child. You need to be away from people you know."

She gave him such a grateful look Noel was jealous.

"There's a very nice place called Covenant House."

"The one on Rampart?"

"Yes. They offer sanctuary for seventy-two hours, I believe. Before they inform anyone of your whereabouts."

She started to shake her head, and Noel knew that she was afraid. "I don't know . . ." she said. He knew she was thinking of the runaways who hung out on Decatur Street, the kids with multiple piercings and dreadlocks and three months' worth of caked dirt. "I don't think I could . . ." she shuddered, apparently unable to stop herself.

Finally, she said, "I think I need more time. I need a week, I think. Just one. To think. To consider my options."

Jacomine smiled what Noel thought was an exceptionally smarmy smile. "I think there was a reason you came to Mr. Treadaway."

Torian flinched; her face was like a baby animal's.

"You must believe he can take care of you." He turned to Noel. "Children have excellent instincts, don't you find?" Back to Torian. "And he can, my dear. Make no mistake, he can solve your problem."

Noel felt his stomach start to spin in his belly. Torian looked at him adoringly. Jacomine took advantage of the situation to wink at him: *Little white lie coming up; bear with me.*

Noel had no choice but to bear with him. He couldn't have found his voice if fire had broken out.

Jacomine said, "I'm thinking of that woman you told me about. The one who takes care of runaways. Did you tell Miss Gernhard about her as well?"

"I . . . uh . . . must have." He thought: *What the hell is he talking about?*

"Why don't you just take her over there? You know the church can't shelter a runaway. That's illegal."

"But it's illegal for me, too."

Jacomine ignored him and turned to Torian. "Miss Gernhard, would you like to stay with a nice woman for a few days who'll take care of you? While you think?"

"I have to go get my clothes." She sounded uncertain.

"Well, of course."

She said, "Noel, should I? Tell me what to do."

"I don't . . ." He stopped to clear his throat, barely able to speak. "I don't think this is a good idea at all."

Torian looked as if he'd slapped her. She started to cry again, and Noel would have given up anything he owned to be able to go to her.

Jacomine stood. "I think I'd better leave you two to talk about it."

When he had gone and Noel had made sure the door was safely shut, he took both of Torian's hands. "Darling. You have to go back home. Or to your father's."

She looked utterly panicked, a cornered animal, no place to turn. "I don't see why you won't help me." Her voice was high with the knowledge of betrayal.

He stared at her, helpless, unable to think of a thing to say. Finally, he settled for, "Excuse me a moment," and dashed into Jacomine's office.

"Who is this woman? What in God's name are you talking about?"

He was cool as vichysoisse, and just as smooth. "Noel, I don't know how much thought you're given to children's rights, but that happens to be a particular concern of mine. And of the Following. We feel very strongly about seeing a child mistreated, and even more strongly that there aren't enough options for them."

"Options," he said again. He stopped and seemed to be sipping the word. Holding it in a chalice. "Miss Gernhard used the word herself. A child like her has no options. Did you ever think that in some cases, it's not what the law is that matters? It's what's right? Did you ever think of that?"

He pointed to Noel's office, electricity practically sparking from his fingers. "Now that young lady in there is desperate. Somebody's been abusing her badly, and I can tell she means a lot to you. We happen to know a woman—that is, the church does—who is absolutely marvelous with these children. We've worked with her for years, and I assure you she's both reliable and discreet. That child will come out of there feeling as if she's been given a new mother and a new life. I've seen it over and over."

He stared at Noel for too long a time. "It's up to you, Mr. Treadaway; it's completely up to you."

He turned away and made a note on a small piece of paper, leaving Noel feeling as if he'd been slammed in the solar plexus. He handed the paper to Noel.

On it was written a name, "Paulette Thibodeaux," along with a phone number and address. Noel read it and said, "Laurel Street. Near the park."

Suddenly Jacomine's face began to turn purple. He spoke with venom that seemed to come from nowhere and nothing. *"What does it matter where it is? You're trying to find out if she's black or white, aren't you? That really matters to you, doesn't it?"* He shook his head, a man utterly disillusioned. "I'll tell you one thing, Noel. I'll just tell you one thing. I've been worried about you. Maybe this just isn't the job for you. I've been worried about that. I've talked it over with Potter, and we both agree you might not be working out."

Noel felt as if he were being given an order: *Send the girl to this woman.*

He said, "You know I can't take her over there. Anymore than you can."

Jacomine shrugged. "Send her in a taxi then." He picked up the phone and dialed. "Paulette? I'm sending you a baby."

Noel left, amazed, feeling dazed and manipulated, yet not knowing how to get out of the net he'd fallen into. He said to Torian, "You sure about this?"

She smiled, already looking as if she'd been given a new life. He had had some idea of trying to talk her out of it, but there was no hope now.

He gave her the slip of paper and some money. "Call me when you get there. Promise?"

She gave him a half-disgusted look, almost as if she were dealing with a parent.

● ●

Skip tried Jeanie in Records, but she was off.

Just as well. She didn't want to do it the first time. Who else can I call?

Jim.

The thought came before she could stop it. And a wave of pain, the first in a long time, made her gasp.

Jim Hodges was the officer who'd died backing her up—the person in Homicide to whom she'd probably been closest besides Cappello and Joe Tarantino—the person she'd have called instead of Jeanie if he'd been around. Due to her delicate status with the department, she couldn't ask either of the others for a favor.

She'd been standing, staring out at the courtyard. But she found the sudden tightening of her throat so painful, so evocative, that she stepped backward involuntarily, staggering a little. She turned around, groping her way to the sofa through a curtain of tears. For a few minutes she sat motionless, not really remembering Jim, just feeling sad, as if she had done it so long she couldn't remember what else to do.

This had happened to her before, and coming out of it felt like waking up—she never knew how long she'd been gone, and was always surprised that she seemed to have had no thoughts at all during the period she'd been away, and no sense memories of it.

Shortly after the two killings—Jim's and his murderer's—she'd spent her weekends in that state, coming out of it only to go to work.

This time she shook her head, as if shaking off the sadness, and got up to get some water.

Abasolo! she thought.

Adam Abasolo had come to Homicide only recently, but they'd been through a lot together and she knew he'd do her a favor.

She phoned him for access once again to NCIC. "I need everything you can get on an Earl Jackson," she said.

"AKA anything I should know?"

"Certainly not," she said. Abasolo was her buddy, but he was also a sergeant; she certainly wasn't mentioning Jacomine to him.

"It's kind of an ordinary-sounding name."

"It's Earl *Theophilus* Jackson. DOB June 14, 1945."

"Okay, ma'am. I'll get back to you."

In a couple of hours he called back. "One little assault, one tiny battery; that's it. Or almost it."

"Tiny battery? How do you manage that?"

"Well, he wasn't convicted. Some guy in Savannah said Jackson hit him with 'no provocation' during an argument—do you love that phrase? There weren't any witnesses, but the guy had a broken nose."

Skip was curious. That was more information than NCIC provided. "How do you know all that?"

"How do you think?"

"You called the Savannah cops."

"I got curious."

"I'm so touched I may send flowers."

"Do. It'll enhance my reputation."

"What about the assault?"

"He took a swing at somebody in Tampa. That time there were witnesses, but the other guy had the sense to step out of the way."

"Volatile dude."

"I don't know. Jackson was waiting for a parking place and the other guy sneaked in behind him. They must have some pretty hard-nosed juries in Tampa. You probably wouldn't convict on that yourself."

Skip had to admit she wouldn't. "What did you mean by that was 'almost it'?"

"Well, the Savannah policeman said there was also a fraud investigation, but it didn't pan out. He didn't really know any more about it."

"I think there's a juvenile record somewhere."

"Oh, great. You didn't mention you wanted me to get sealed juvenile records which cannot be gotten. What else can I do for Your Majesty?"

"Sorry, Adam. Just thinking aloud."

"Could I go back to fighting crime now? I hear some noise outside—I think it's the city falling apart."

"Listen, thanks a lot."

"Whatever I can do for you, kid. You know that."

"I know." He'd been with her the night she shot Jim's killer.

She called Jane Storey and ran down what she had. "Not bad," said Jane. "Not good, but not really bad."

"That fraud thing might be interesting."

"Libelous, however. What the hell, I'll call the cops in Savannah. Maybe it'll come to something or other."

"I wonder what he was doing there?"

163

Next, she called Mary Lou at the Christian Community and asked where Jackson came from in the first place. "Atlanta, I guess."

"You sure?"

Mary Lou sighed dramatically. "Let me go look at the file." Skip could almost see her waddling to get it.

"Savannah," she said in a minute.

"Bingo."

"What?"

"Thank you."

Twenty minutes later she was in the library, Xeroxing the 'Jackson' section of the Savannah phone book. There were six Earls and one Theophilus.

Back home, she called the Theophilus.

A woman answered—Mrs. Theophilus Jackson, also known as Perdita. "There've been Earls," she said. "Quite a few Earls in the family."

"This one became a preacher."

"Oh, yes. I know the one you mean. He's a few cousins removed, I b'lieve. Or something like that. His folks were—let me see—Blanche! Blanche and Harry. Or maybe it was Henry. Something like that, anyway."

As she talked, Skip scanned the Jacksons. "Henry on DeRenne Avenue?"

"Now that's his brother, I think. There were three of those boys. Henry and Earl and—let's see now . . ." There was a long silence. "Thomas! That's it. Henry and Earl and Thomas. Earl became a preacher, and Henry married Marcelline Sims from over at Port Wentworth. He's a pretty good car mechanic. We've always used him. Thomas, now. They say the good die young, and everyone said that about Thomas. Something sudden, I think. Heart attack. He was a bus driver, can you imagine? What if he'd been drivin' the bus at the time?"

"What about his wife?"

"Let me see now . . . Eva! Think she lives out at Wilmington Island."

Skip tried Eva first, but got no answer. Next she tried Henry.

Since it was daytime, the best she could hope for was Marcelline.
But a man answered, quite a young one from his voice.

"Is Mrs. Jackson there? Marcelline Jackson?"

"She isn't here right now. This is her son Theo—can I help
you?"

Why not? Skip thought. He sounded very young indeed. She
made her voice a little more Southern, a lot less confident, and
about an octave higher. "I'm calling for a newspaper in Louisiana—about your Uncle Earl?"

"Oh, Uncle Earl. Did he die or something?"

"Well, no. He's been elected president of the Chamber of
Commerce."

"Uncle Earl? You sure you got the right Earl Jackson?"

"Well, I must, because he said something along those lines. He
said, 'My family sure would be proud of me. Nobody would have
ever thought when I was growin' up . . .'

"Of course, him being a preacher and all, I didn't really believe
it, I thought it was just a kind of modest thing he said, but then I
thought, 'Wait a minute. There might be a pretty good story in
this.' We're just a tiny town, you know; even something like the
Chamber of Commerce is news. And I'm kind of—you know—
new here. So I thought . . . I mean, nothing much happens here, so
I thought . . ."

"Did you say Uncle Earl's a preacher?"

"Well, yes. With the Christian Community?"

"You *got* to have the wrong Earl Jackson."

"Earl Theophilus Jackson?"

"That's him, but—"

"You sound so nice. I know a boy from Savannah—Charlie
Kendall? You know Charlie?"

"No, I don't think . . ."

"He goes to Georgia Tech. Unless he's flunked out by now. I
went to Agnes Scott."

"Really? You know Patsy Scarborough?"

"Patsy! She used to live right down the hall from me. Nice girl.
Real nice girl."

"My roommate used to go out with her. We go to Georgia."

"Oh, yeah, I think I met him. Mike, uh . . . no, that's not right . . ."

"Jim. Jim Halsey."

"Oh, yeah. I think we all went tubing together once. You sound so nice. I can't believe your uncle isn't nice, too."

"I never knew him, to tell you the truth, but I've heard stories about him all my life. He was kind of the bad boy of the family. Oh, Lord! Know what he's supposed to have done? I hope this doesn't gross you out."

"Omigod. What?" She tried to get her voice to convey wide-eyed innocence.

"He buried baby chicks up to their necks and then mowed their heads off with a lawn mower."

"You're kidding! He couldn't have done that."

"My dad and my great Aunt Alice swear he did. And that's not all. He fried goldfish alive—"

"In cornmeal batter or what?" She managed a little giggle.

"I think he just sautéed them with a little butter and garlic."

"I bet they flipped their little tails around like baby whales."

Both of them got a fit of the giggles. "Oh, you're so baaad."

"You're pretty bad yourself."

"Know what else he did? He put a cat and a litter of kittens through an entire dryer cycle."

"Gross! Little bitty kittens—how could he?"

"I see you're a cat lover."

"I just don't see how anybody could be so mean, that's all."

"What about the fish?"

"Well, it's not like they have fur or anything! Somebody who'd hurt kittens would probably . . ."

"What?"

"Well, I'm wondering. Did he ever get in trouble with other kids or anything?"

"What kind of trouble?"

"You know. Fights maybe. I don't know. Maybe he built a tiny little guillotine."

"Oh, come on. He was just mischievous, that's all."

"You know, I think this could really be a fun story."

"Oh, yeah! Think how embarrassed he'd be."

"It'd be kind of like a roast. I wonder if I could talk to your dad about him?"

"Well, mom and dad are in North Carolina right now. I kind of have the house to myself. Listen, I was wondering, do you ever get over this far? We've got a great beach here."

"Gosh, I don't think I could right now. I've only had this job two weeks."

"Damn!"

"Is there anybody else who knew your uncle? Maybe I could talk to them."

"Well, there's Aunt Alice, but she's so deaf you have to write to communicate with her."

"What's her last name?"

"Sherman, but . . ."

"Oh, damn. A five-alarm fire. Listen, nice talking with you. Can I call you back?"

15

● ●

Throwing some clothes in a backpack, Torian thought she had never met a man like Reverend Jacomine. Someone who almost read her thoughts, who treated her like an adult—more so than Noel did.

She could have gone to her father; certainly she could have. But she didn't think that was the best strategy at this point. She wanted to up the ante on them both—her mother and her father. She could go to her dad now, with her slightly bruised nose—face it, despite her first fears, it wasn't broken or anything—and he might or might not take it seriously.

Maybe he'd use it as an excuse to try to get Torian back from Lise, and maybe he'd succeed and maybe he wouldn't; or maybe he'd just say Lise was high-strung and give her another chance. She wanted to do something he couldn't ignore. She wanted him to hear her cry for help loud and clear.

And if she ended up staying with Lise, she wanted to make sure it was on better terms.

I'm at the end of my rope, goddammit—nobody believes it because I'm only fifteen. But I can't do this; I can't live like this, even if I do have Noel.

168

There were adults in the world who would have nitpicked about logic and reason, but Reverend Jacomine had cut right through the bullshit, exactly as if he had known what she knew—that she had to make a statement. A big statement.

And he had been willing to help. How many adults would have done that? Not even Noel. Noel wasn't going to send her to Paulette until the Rev had suggested it.

He might be a great man. I don't think I ever met one before.

I'm so proud to have worked for him, to be associated with him.

When I go home, I'll join his church. I'll work for him that way.

She went outside to find a cab, too impatient to call one and wait for it.

● ●

A young woman was sitting on the porch when she arrived. Her house had once been painted gray, but it was peeling now. Still, it looked cozy and welcoming, perhaps because of copious petunias growing in large pots.

The woman on the porch stood up and waved. Torian couldn't imagine who she might be—she was too old to be another runaway, yet not nearly old enough to be the proprietor.

She wore jeans and a tank top that showed off heavily muscled arms. She was dark, with short hair, slightly sharp features, a benign demeanor.

Cajun, Torian thought. She had met only a few Cajuns, but she was always drawn to them—they seemed so gentle and soft-spoken; so friendly. She was drawn to Jews, too—and Italians. To almost anyone different from Lise.

"Torian? Paulette Thibodeaux. Do ya need me to cover the taxi?" Paulette started down the walk.

"No. I'm fine." She paid the driver and turned to face the woman. She was shocked that Paulette was so tall—as tall as Noel, and probably about as solid. She had a certain amount of weight on her, but she had muscles, too. Either she did manual labor every day or she worked out.

She looks like a goddess, Torian thought, feeling young and small beside her.

She blurted: "I didn't know you'd be so young."

Paulette laughed, and her laugh was rich, resonant, almost bass. "Everybody expects a mother. I'm more like an older sister. Is 'at good enough?"

Torian looked at her, instantly loving her. She nodded, smiling, realizing she hadn't meant to smile, just couldn't help it. "Yeah. Sure." She felt suddenly shy.

Paulette turned and led her up the walk. "Ya hungry? I got some ice cream bars. We don't eat supper till later." She looked at her watch. "We havin' gumbo tonight. Ya like gumbo?"

"Who doesn't like gumbo?"

"Tha's right. Nobody dodn't like gumbo." She laughed her rich laugh again.

Inside, the house was utilitarian, apparently furnished much like Lise's apartment—with whatever could be gleaned from Goodwill or Volunteers of America.

"Ya room's upstairs. Ya gon' stay with Faylice. She's makin' the gumbo right now." Paulette led her up into a greenish room with marks on the walls, many looking as if they'd been put there by hands. There was a rain forest poster on one wall, and a framed print of *The Last Supper* on another. Two single beds were covered with Indian print bedspreads, and a beat-up chest of drawers completed the furnishings.

"It's not fancy, but I think it's kinda cheery, don't ya?" said Paulette. "Ya wanna wash up or anything? Then come to the kitchen. I'm fixin' Faylice some iced tea."

Torian turned to thank her, but Paulette was gone. She was glad to have a few moments alone, to assimilate what she'd gotten into. This place was worse than Lise's.

But probably not worse than Covenant House.

She shuddered. She'd thought about Covenant House a lot. It was where runaways went, but surely they were runaways from Kansas or Missouri. Nobody ran away from the French Quarter; it was where you ran to.

Well, I did. I pulled it off, and I'm even in a place where they don't have to call my parents after three days. Maybe I could stay here awhile.

She was surprised at the thought.

Maybe I'm getting used to it.

Oh, hell, it doesn't matter. It's really no worse than Lise's—the main thing is, Lise isn't here.

She checked out the barely adequate bathroom (nothing interesting in the medicine cabinet), then the other two bedrooms. One, she thought, must be Paulette's, because it had a double bed and some cosmetics lying around, as if someone lived there full time. The other was much like Torian's. There was a suitcase on the floor, and underwear had been tossed on the bed. So there was probably at least one other kid there.

She wondered if Paulette had a lover.

Maybe the Rev.

She felt her cheeks go hot the minute she thought it. Well, she couldn't help it if she thought older men were more mature, and that the Rev was practically God.

Though of course, she thought, *I'm not attracted to him. Anyway, would you do it with God? The Rev's not eligible.*

She went downstairs, to find Paulette and a fat black girl sitting at the table. Both were drinking iced tea and the girl was also chopping vegetables and sausage, neat piles of which lay on the table in bowls.

A third glass of tea, its ice cubes starting to melt, had been set out on a napkin.

Paulette pointed to it. "For ya. Torian, this is Faylice."

Torian turned to the black girl, about to extend her hand, but she realized the girl's hands were gummy from cooking, and that anyway, this might not be behavior she'd learned in her neighborhood.

Faylice was very dark, one of the darkest people Torian had ever seen. Her hair was pulled back some way or other, out of her face, but it had no style and apparently hadn't been intended to. She had large boobs and she was big around, but not obese. Since she wore shorts, Torian could see that she had tree-trunk thighs and knees so well padded they hardly showed.

Her strong healthy teeth were lovely against her dark skin; indeed there was something about her smile that Torian found touching. Something sweet, something vulnerable, something needy—Torian couldn't put her finger on it. Perhaps it was the thing that Anne Frank wrote about—the faith that things would be okay, that people weren't so bad, despite all evidence to the contrary.

She was only thirteen or fourteen, Torian thought.

"How you?" said Faylice.

"I'm okay. You need some help?"

"No, I'm 'bout to make my roux soon as I finish my tea. It's a one-person job, but boring as shit."

"You stir awhile and then I will."

"No, I don't trust nobody to get it right but me." She smiled to show she meant no harm. Torian was starting to warm up to her in a big way.

She felt a tinge of excitement as she realized, *I've never met anyone like this.*

"How'd you learn to make gumbo?" she asked. "I don't know how."

Why didn't Lise teach me? What are mothers for?

"My ontee teach me. Way a long time ago—before I start school."

"Your ontee?"

Faylice nodded. "Auntie Shaunna." Torian finally got it. "My mama's baby sister. Ain't it funny she be the one?"

"Your mom doesn't cook? Mine doesn't either."

Faylice was stirring the roux now, her back to the table, so that Torian couldn't see her face. "Nooooo, my mama don't cook. My mama too busy with her rock and her men frien's. My mama sho' don' cook."

Torian was dying to know everything about this girl who was younger than she was and even more alone in the world—except perhaps for a nice aunt. "What about your dad?"

"Ain't got no dad. Ain't got no brothers, ain't got no sisters. I did have a baby brother, but he die."

Torian looked at Paulette, needing some kind of grounding. She nodded. "Tha's right. Faylice has had it real hard. And no matter what happens, she always makes straight A's. Idn't that right, Faylice?"

"Well, I try. I shore do try." Something in her voice—so un-sure of herself, so unaware of what a miracle she was—devastated Torian.

Paulette said, "What'sa matter, chile?"

Humiliated, Torian picked up her paper napkin and swiped at the tears that had run down her cheeks. "I don't know. I . . . noth-ing, I guess."

Paulette patted her wrist. "It's gonna be all right. Everything's gonna be fine."

Torian said, "Faylice. I have two baby sisters." That was funny—Joy certainly wasn't her sister. "I don't know what I'd do if something happened to them."

"I had a real hard time when Demas died. We woke up one mornin' and he was dead in his bed. Jus' like that. No reason for it."

"I've heard of that. Sudden infant death."

"That's what they call it. Sometime, I think it jus' be the Lord lookin' after him."

Is she saying what I think she's saying?

Torian waited for her to go on, but Faylice just kept stirring the roux. She said, "You mean you think he's better off dead?"

"Sometime I do. Sometime I don' know how he would have made it. My mama didn't have no milk to nurse him. She had to give him a bottle and sometimes she forget; most times she forget. And I was just a little bitty girl—eight years old then—and they make me go to school. How'm I gon' take care of him when I'm at school?"

"Your aunt—um—"

"Oh, Auntie move away just as soon as she get married. And when she move, she say, 'Faylice, honey, I wish I could take you with me, but I can't right now. I gotta go, I'm real sorry, but you promise me one thing. You promise you'll always make all A's, and then I know you gon' get a good job and I rest easy.' "

Faylice turned to face her. "See, we live in St. Thomas." One of the city's worst slums. "She want me to get out. She couldn't take me, but she want to let me know I can do it myself. So I say to myself, 'Okay, I will. Faylice ain' gon' be no crack whore.

Faylice gon' get a job and go to a office and wear nice clothes.'
Auntie Shaunna, she be a insurance adjuster. Maybe tha's what I be
one day."

"That's what my mom is."

Faylice turned around again, face animated. "Oh, yeah? She like
her job?"

Torian stared at the floor. Lise called it "a piddlin' little job a
twelve-year-old could do." "I don't think so," she said. "My mom
doesn't like much of anything."

"Mmmph. Maybe she on drugs."

"Alcohol."

Faylice nodded. "Tha's no good. Mmmm, mmm. Tha's
no good."

Torian realized Faylice talked like a much older person. She
said, "Faylice, how old are you?"

"Thirteen and a half. You?"

"Fifteen. But I don't think I know as much as you."

Paulette snorted. "Honey, you don' want to."

Faylice said. "No, you don't. 'Specially as much as I learn last
couple days."

Torian was dying to know what had happened, what had finally pushed her over the edge and made her leave home, but she
didn't feel she could ask. Maybe it was too painful, or too private.

But Faylice said, still stirring the roux, "My mama boyfrien'
rape me and beat me up day before yesterday." She turned around
and raised her T-shirt, showing a bandage on her midriff. "He try
to cut me too, only I got the knife. I jus' get a scratch. But then he
knock the knife out of my hand, and he so mad he pull off my
clothes and stick his thing in me."

Torian gasped. "Where was your mom?"

"Oh, she went out to the store. They smokin' rock together,
then she go out to get cigarettes, and he start tearin' the house
apart, lookin' for money. I come home from school 'bout that
time, and he start beatin' me and . . . the rest of it."

She had been matter-of-fact up to that point, but Torian noticed her voice getting lower on the last phrase, as if she were
deeply ashamed. "My mama come home and start beatin' on him

with her hands, her fists, some ol' ashtray she pick up, anything she can, and I run away. I jus' run away without a stitch on. Neighbor lady let me in, and I call my auntie. She say her church take care of me, and tha's how I got here."

She had added her vegetables to the roux—all but her tomatoes and okra—and there was a great sizzling and smoking.

Torian said, "Faylice? Could you teach me to make gumbo?"

"Sho', girl. You didn't have no auntie?"

Torian shook her head, feeling inadequate, unable to speak. Finally she said, "I've got a stepmother."

"See, your vegetables have to wilt. You like her better'n your mama?"

Torian stared into the pot, as if the green peppers and onions would give up the secrets of the universe along with their fragrance.

"Well?" said Faylice. "You don't like her either?"

"Sure I like her. I like Carol."

"Okay, now the tomatoes."

"What?"

Faylice nodded at the kitchen counter. "The tomatoes. And that pile of sausage."

Finally comprehending, Torian began tossing the piles into the pot. For the first time it occurred to her that she really didn't like Carol.

She's better than Lise. At least she doesn't hit me.

But I don't think she loves me, I really don't.

Nobody does.

Noel did, she was pretty sure, and her dad and Joy and Marly to the extent that they were capable, but at the moment she doubted them all.

Sheila! Sheila loves me.

Well, at least she likes me a lot. She's a true friend, she'd do anything for me.

She wasn't entirely sure of that, it hadn't been tested, but she needed to think it right now.

I'd do anything for her. She knows that, doesn't she?

"Now we gon' put in the water. And the okra and some of the shrimp; and we gon' season it."

Once again, Torian dumped in the piles Faylice had readied. She watched as the other girl ground bay leaves, measured thyme and pepper, counted little balls she said were allspice.

"Hey, y'all. What's for dinner?" A new girl had arrived, probably the owner of the suitcase and underwear Torian had seen in the other bedroom.

Paulette said, "Where've you been, young lady?"

"Went for a bike ride. Saw your bike and went for a spin. Rides pretty good."

Faylice turned around. "How you know how to ride a bike?" She sounded furious.

"Everybody know how to ride a bike. You tellin' me you don't?" The girl started to laugh.

Faylice looked as if she could fall through the floor; Torian thought she would have turned bright red if she'd been white.

The new girl was the color that black people call red, and she had a few freckles on her nose. She looked much younger even than Faylice, only eleven or twelve, and she was skinny, with legs that went on and on like stilts. Like Faylice, she was wearing white shorts, but hers were very short, and her little buttoned sleeveless top, though made of T-shirt knit, fit snugly and was clearly meant to be sexy. Since the girl hadn't yet grown breasts, it wasn't quite that, but Torian gave her points for intent.

Her hair, which had apparently been straightened, was held back with a yellow print cotton scarf tied on the side. She was young, but she had a lot of fashion sense. When she smiled, as she was doing now, you could see a gap between her front teeth, which gave her a perennially delighted look. She looked like a kid without a care in the world.

"Who you?" she said.

"I'm Torian. Who you?" Something about the girl made her laugh.

"Adonis."

"Adonis?"

"Somethin' wrong with that?" Adonis was suddenly a little package of muscle and gristle.

"No, it's a beautiful name."

"Faylice say it be a boy's name."

Torian kept quiet. She desperately wanted Faylice's respect—and friendship if she could have it—but she couldn't see lining up with her on this one. Something about Adonis, cheerful, freckled little biker that she was, was a tiny bit threatening.

Adonis opened the refrigerator and came out with a handful of carrot sticks. "Y'all want some?"

Faylice and Torian shook their heads, all but turning up their noses. Adonis sat down hard on one of the kitchen chairs. "So what chew doin' here, little white ghost? Tha's what the Chinese call y'all—you know that?"

"I needed to be away awhile."

"Why?" Adonis put a foot on the table, but removed it at a look from Paulette.

"I don't want—I don't think I can talk about it yet." She hoped that didn't sound too lame. The truth was, she was embarrassed to talk about it in front of Faylice, whose life seemed so much harsher, whose courage so much stronger. "What about you?" she asked.

Adonis stood up again, looked in the gumbo pot, grabbed a spoon, and tasted. "Bleeaghh."

"You don' have to eat it, Miss Smartie," huffed Faylice.

Adonis spun around to face Torian. "Ain' nobody home where I live."

"You can say that again. Ain' nobody home in ya haid," Faylice cut in.

Torian said, "I don't see what you mean."

"I come home from school one day; they all gone."

"I don't understand."

"My mama, her man friend, my two little brothers. They all gone." For a moment she looked like the forlorn child she was. Then she turned back to the gumbo and began shaking pepper into it. Faylice got up and wrestled the shaker from her hand, not speaking, just doing what had to be done.

"What do you mean? Was—um—was there a fire or something?" Torian's imagination was going wild. A fire was the least of the possibilities that occurred to her.

Something like a bark came out of Adonis, something that was probably supposed to pass for a laugh. "No. There wadn't no fire. Jus' wadn't nothin'. Nobody home. No furniture. Oh, yeah, there was some piles of dirt and cardboard. And a broom. Case I wanted to neaten things up."

Torian was still trying to wrap her mind around this one. "What happened. Where were they?"

Adonis shrugged. "Don' know. Lady nex' door say she saw 'em loadin' up and leavin'. I ran all the way back to school. Thought maybe they meant to pick me up there, but I was already gone." She shrugged again. "They wadn't there."

Torian looked beseechingly at Paulette. Could she be hearing right?

Paulette said, "The two boys are the boyfriend's children; Adonis isn't."

"He like me! I know he like me. Too much, my mama say."

Paulette raised an eyebrow and bit her lip, as if to keep from saying the wrong thing.

Torian had been horrified by Faylice's story, but this was the one that haunted her as she tried to go to sleep that night. She tried to imagine arriving home to find your family had left you, leaving not so much as a note or a message with a neighbor.

Just split. Gone.

If that doesn't make you feel like a piece of shit, what does?

She wondered how Adonis could keep smiling, could do anything at all except lie down and feel sorry for herself. She hadn't found out how she came to be at Paulette's and couldn't imagine what would become of her.

Maybe Paulette'll adopt her.

But she knew that wasn't going to happen. Paulette had probably seen a dozen kids like Adonis. She didn't keep her strays. She just fed them and patched them up.

I can't stay here. I'm ridiculous.

At breakfast the next morning, she stared into her coffee cup— Paulette was letting her drink regular coffee; Lise made her dilute it. "I think I better go home."

She had deliberately gotten up before her two companions.

"Why?" said Paulette. "You think anything's better today?"

"I think I've got to be better."

"You're the child. The folks around you are s'posed to be the grown-ups."

"I'm not like Faylice and Adonis."

"Oh? You too good for 'em?"

"No! They're—they've got real problems. I'm just some spoiled white kid."

Paulette was standing at the stove. She looked over her shoulder. "Is that what ya mama says? Ya daddy, too, maybe? Listen, darlin', ya lucky ya don' have problems like those girls got problems, but ya got ya own problems. Don' feel like ya haven't." She turned around. "You want some toast?"

Torian didn't, especially, but she nodded. What she wanted was Paulette's continued attention, this unexpected mother kind of thing. Paulette didn't speak while she made the toast, but when she had two perfect golden pieces, she put each of them on a plate, gave one to Torian and sat down across from her.

Lise never makes me toast. And certainly never has breakfast with me. Thank God for that part.

"Ya came here, now ya know ya aren't the only one with problems. But ya do have problems, baby. I'm not sayin' ya don'. Me, I used to be a drug addict."

"You? But you look so healthy."

Paulette nodded, as if proud of her addiction. "I did every drug I could get my hands on, till I met Daddy. Reverend Jacomine. I owe my life to that man. You ever do drugs, baby?"

Puzzled, Torian shook her head.

"That's my girl. Don't you ever start, either. It's just a way of not thinking about what ya real problem is. Trouble is, it dodn't solve it. Postpones it, tha's all. I'd give my life for Daddy, you know that? He helped me that much; he means that much to me."

Torian felt slightly tense, not sure whether this was the standard antidrug lecture or some bid to become a disciple of Errol Jacomine. She sort of hoped it was the latter.

"He's a wonderful man," she said, hoping the simple sentence wouldn't convey her deep longing for someone wonderful in her life, someone she could believe in completely, not just a little bit in a certain area at a certain time of day if she were lucky.

But Paulette seemed ready to go on to other things. "What happened to me was somethin' like what happened to Adonis, 'cept I was much older. I was about your age, and I had two loves in my life—my little brother and my little sister. I was those kids' mama. Really. My mama never stopped to think about that—she jus' up and left." She took a bite of toast and looked thoughtful while she chewed it. "I don't know. I jus' don't know who took care of them later on."

"You mean you just came home one day and everybody was gone—like Adonis did?" Surely something that cold couldn't have happened twice.

"She took me to my daddy's house and never came back for me."

"I wish my mama'd do that."

"Thought you had baby sisters. Wouldn't ya miss 'em?"

"My dad's kids." She guessed she had to stick to her story about having two of them.

Paulette nodded. "Well, I understand, then. Because it was my sister and brother I missed. My mama never was much of a mama. My dad—he drank, and he didn't have no interest in me, so I ran away. Tha's how I got to New Orleans. I hitchhiked down here, and I didn't have a penny, and I met a man who said he'd take care of me. He turned me out and got me on drugs."

"He was a pimp?"

"Sho' was, baby. He was a pimp. Finally, when I met Daddy through a friend, and I got off drugs, I knew what I wanted. Know what it was?"

Torian shook her head.

"I wanted my little brother and sister back again. So tha's what I told Daddy and he told me he could give me that. And he did. He helped me open up this place for kids like you—every day a new kid comes, I get my little brother or sister back."

"Do you get paid for this?"

"No, baby, I don't get paid. I got to work full-time, doin' somethin' else, just to keep it open. I'm a carpenter, baby. Tha's where I got these muscles. You ever seen a lady carpenter? Daddy told me I could do it. He encouraged me even though I thought I'd never get a job. But he said he'd give me one. Sho' enough, he did, and now I do a lot of work for folks in the church. But, listen, tha's not what I want to say to you.

"I know ya thinkin' of goin' back, but I want ya to stay here a few days and think about things. Ya know, Daddy's real worried about ya, and so am I. Because ya got a problem ya don't even know about. Ya main problem's not ya mama, honey, it's ya boyfriend."

"What are you talking about? I haven't even got a boyfriend."

"Sure you have. Noel Treadaway's ya boy friend. Ya know when I met that man who turned me out? I was jus' your age and he was Noel's."

"Noel's not a pimp!"

"No, sweetheart, I didn't mean that. But there's somethin' wrong with a grown man who's hanging with a kid."

"We're in love." Torian could feel herself slouching, pouting, behaving like the kid Paulette described.

"Yeah. That's what my man said, too."

"He's not trying to get me to have sex. He refuses to have sex with me."

"That's a funny kind of love, ain't it, baby? Look, all I'm sayin'—this dude's trouble for ya, one way or another. I just want ya to think about that, okay?

Torian got up. "I'm leaving." She was pulling her few things together when Paulette called up to her.

"Torian. Somebody to see you."

Noel! It had to be. No one else knew she was there.

She raced down like a kid whose dad has come home, but it wasn't Noel at the bottom of the stairs.

"Reverend Jacomine! I look terrible. I mean—"

"I just came by to make sure you're comfortable."

"You did? You came by to see me?"

"Of course. Why wouldn't I?"

"I don't know. You're busy."

"Well, you were a mighty upset young lady yesterday. I was hopin' you'd be feeling better today."

Torian gave Paulette a glance. Had she called him? No, there wasn't time.

A funny thing, though—Paulette was looking at the Rev as if he were God.

But he was looking at her, Torian. As if she were the center of the universe. "You feelin' better, Miss Gernhard?"

She loved the way he called her that. She still couldn't figure out why he was here. She couldn't believe he cared so much—about her, a perfect stranger—that he'd come out to see her.

"I feel—fine."

"Paulette said you're 'bout ready to go home. I thought maybe you didn't like it here."

"Oh, I do. I love it. I just thought—I mean, everyone else has *real* problems. I just felt kind of trivial, I guess."

"Well, not at all, Miss Gernhard. We'd love for you to stay as long as you like."

"Thank you, but—"

"One more night? Just to get a fresh perspective? For me?"

Torian smiled. "Sure. What can that hurt?" The longer she was away, the more Lise and her father would worry. Who knew? They might even miss her.

16

• •

Lise thought: *Have I got a sinus headache? I must have a sinus headache. My head couldn't hurt like this if I didn't.*

Her cranium felt as if it would explode, which was the way sinus headaches made her feel, but at the same time, veins throbbed; muscles twitched.

She held some ice to her head, and when that didn't help, she got out some more ice and poured vodka over it. She had called her ex-husband, but he didn't answer. Somehow, that was a relief. She didn't think Torian was with him—whatever else you said about him, at least he had a rudimentary sense of responsibility, meaning he'd probably have let her know if Torian were there.

She had called Sheila, of course, but the little bitch denied even talking to Torian in two days, which Lise didn't believe. They spent hours on the phone every day and if each didn't know every move the other made, Lise would be astonished.

Suddenly she thought, *I know! The babysitting people. She likes that woman.*

"Mrs. Treadaway? Oh, right, Miss Leydecker. Dr. Leydecker, I mean—you're a shrink, aren't you?"

"Not really. But I am a therapist. May I ask who's calling?"

"Sorry. It's Lise Gernhard. Torian's mother. I haven't seen Torian and I wondered—"

"Haven't seen her? Since when?"

"Well, I—" She stopped, too ashamed to tell the truth. "This morning." Lise hadn't seen Torian the morning after the fight—she'd spent the night at Charles's. Then the next night, she'd come home late and assumed her daughter was asleep—now it was the morning after that. She had no idea how long she'd been gone.

"I'm sorry. We haven't seen her today."

"I just thought—she and I had a fight last night, and she's told me about your talks."

"Talks?"

"Oh, yes. She idolizes you. I think you're the only adult she listens to."

The woman—her name was Boo, wasn't it?—laughed in a way that wasn't a laugh, that came out like a snort, as if she were just filling the air until she thought of something to say.

Lise thought, *I wonder what I did to make her nervous.*

Finally Boo said, "I'm sure that can't be true." Then, quickly, "Listen, I'll send her home right away if I see her."

Well, Lise hadn't really thought she was there. Discouraged, she had another drink and thought about it.

That proved the right thing to do, because once she thought it through, there was really only one explanation. She ran a comb through her hair and walked over to Sheila's.

The uncle answered the door, and Lise recognized him. "Oh, hi. I've seen you at Matassa's."

"Hi. Yes. What can I do for you?"

"I'm Torian's mother. Sheila's friend?"

"Oh, of course. Come in."

He's kind of cute. A little old for me and a little short, but—wait a minute, isn't he gay? Didn't Torian say that?

She really had no idea, but someone might have said it if Torian hadn't—it was that kind of neighborhood. He wasn't married, that part Lise was pretty sure of. Which probably meant he was gay—that was where she'd probably gotten the idea.

He said, "Do you mind coming in the kitchen? I'm making dinner."

She followed him into as beautifully equipped a kitchen as she'd seen in the French Quarter. He was cleaning up after breakfast. An enormous woman stood against a counter, wearing jeans and holding her purse, as if waiting for him.

"Skip Langdon," he said. "This is Torian's mother—uh—"

"Lise. Are you Sheila's aunt?"

Sheila, coming into the room, snorted.

Lise turned around. "There you are. Listen, it's you I want to talk to."

The girl smiled. "Hi, Mrs. Gernhard." She was maddening. There was no question she knew where Torian was—hiding out in Sheila's room, probably.

"*Where* is Torian?" Only when Sheila stepped back, as if frightened, did Lise realize she was shouting.

The large woman took a step toward her, and Lise remembered who she was—the cop who lived in back. In fact, now that Lise saw the cop and heard her name, she realized the cop was someone she had seen on television. She was quite a famous cop in New Orleans, and not only that, she was at least six feet tall.

Wait a minute, I haven't done anything illegal. I'm just here to find my kid.

A wave of righteousness washed over her. She saw no need to do anything different.

"I don't know where she is," said Sheila, and her voice was whiny. She was a little younger than Torian; Lise remembered what an awful age fifteen was.

"She has a boyfriend, hasn't she?"

Good. The girl looked alarmed.

"She's probably holed up in some fleabag with some dude with dreadlocks and nipple piercings. Right, Sheila?" Lise was deliberately exaggerating, making it worse than it could possibly be, to back Sheila in a corner, make her want to explain how cute and clean-cut little Jeffrey or Jason really was. But oddly, the girl seemed to be relaxing.

She said, "No. She isn't. Torian's not like that."

Lise took a step toward her. "Well, she has other friends, right?"

Sheila shrugged. "Mrs. Gernhard, I don't know where she is. I swear it."

"Yes, you do. Goddammit, Sheila, you do and you're going to tell me now!"

The uncle put a hand on her shoulder. Funny, she'd almost forgotten about him. "Lise, I'm giving Skip a ride to the airport. Sorry, but we're right down to the wire." He removed his hand and spoke very quietly, as if trying to calm her. "I'm really sorry Sheila doesn't know where Torian is, but it can't be helped. She just doesn't."

To her horror, Lise started to sob. "Oh, God, my baby's gone, and it's all my fault. Oh, God, she's really gone!" She turned to the cop. "Can't the police do anything?"

"How long has she been missing?"

"Is that all you can do? Ask stupid questions?"

She saw Sheila look beseechingly at Skip Langdon, as if begging the cop to rescue her friend from the madwoman, and that frightened her.

"I'm sorry," she said. "I didn't mean that. I'm just upset."

Skip Langdon nodded. "I understand—everybody gets upset about that one. If your kid's been missing an hour, it seems like a day and a half. Have you filed a report?"

"A report?" Lise wiped her eyes with a tissue the uncle handed her.

"With the police. Maybe they can help."

"Skip. Come on." The uncle was standing at the door, jingling keys. The cop left.

"Lise?" said Sheila. "Can you get home okay?"

Lise nodded, puzzled at the question. But in fact it was hard to get home, picking her way through a sort of Impressionist landscape, made fuzzy and strange by her tears.

And when she arrived, the apartment seemed like a cave—dank and uninhabited. She called, "Torian? Torian?" knowing it was futile. She would know if her daughter were there.

She sank down on the couch and cried some more, finally getting up and pouring a drink to give her the courage to call Wilson again.

But she had not yet found the courage when there was a great banging on the door. "Lise! Goddammit, Lise, let me in."

Wilson. How he'd gotten in the front door she didn't know—probably told a neighbor he was her husband.

"What in the fuck is this about losing Torian?"

She'd left a message on his machine. "She's not with you?"

"With me? Would I be here if she were with me? What the fuck do you mean?"

"She ran away. She hates me."

His face said he could understand perfectly. "Has her bed been slept in?"

"She made it up. She does that."

"Goddammit, Lise, I haven't got time for this crap! Don't you think I have anything else to do?"

"This is your daughter, you asshole."

"Have you called the police?"

"No, I—"

"Well, why not, goddammit?"

"Stop firing questions at me—I can't think."

"Oh, shit. You're shit, you know that? You make Medea look like a great little mom." He turned around and walked out.

What was he going to do? she wondered. The answer came to her, clear as sunlight in the garden: *Nothing. Make me do all the work as usual. Blame me if anything happens.*

She started to cry again, only this time she poured a drink right away, hoping it would make her sleep, at least. True, it was mid-morning, but Lise felt a great urge to go back to bed and stay there for about six hours. If Torian weren't home by then, she could call the police.

In fact, maybe it would be a good idea to take some aspirin. She went into the bathroom and took six or eight of them.

● ●

Hanging up the phone, Boo turned to Noel. "That's odd. That was Mrs. Gernhard."

He looked up from his Times-Picayune. "Torian's mother?"

"Seems the kid didn't come home last night."

"Why'd she call here?"

"That's the odd part. She said something about our talks—Torian's and mine. I wonder what she meant by that?"

He turned back to the paper. "I don't know. Maybe you said something wise to her once."

Boo began unloading the dishwasher, trying to call up Torian's face. She couldn't quite picture it.

It's funny, she thought, how you can have an effect on a kid and be completely unaware of it? I hardly even noticed her.

But if she's that influenced by the tiny little bit of contact we've had, she must have a pretty hellish home life. Of course she does, she's a runaway.

Boo felt a terrible pang at not having been more receptive, more nurturing. I'm supposed to be a therapist after all. But I guess, when you get down to it, I'm not a very maternal person. Too bad for Joy.

She was never more aware of how hard she had to work at mothering, how it didn't come naturally to her. Is my daughter going to need a therapist when she's Torian's age? Or is she going to make friends with some neighbor lady—maybe it'll be Torian. Maybe she'll be Mrs. Smith or Mrs. Jones by then—she'll be thirty—and maybe Joy will be babysitting for her. Maybe she'll unwittingly say wise things to Joy—and anyway, they'll have this bond because Torian babysat her . . .

Suddenly she realized they probably did have such a bond. Already. For all she knew, Torian was better with the kid than she was.

After all, Noel is. He knows how to play with kids. The simple fact is, he's a better father than I am a mother. You can even see it with Torian—the way he laughs and jokes with her. Mostly, I don't feel I have a damn thing to say to her. Well, face it, I'm not interested. What do I care about CDs and makeup? Isn't that what they're into at her age?

Oh, can it, Boo, you're projecting. Who knows what they're into?

I would if I'd take the trouble to find out. Face it, I'm still closed down. After all the fancy shrinking I've had myself. I'm smothering but not nurturing.

Goddammit, I can be nurturing. You don't have to go to nurturing school. You just do it.

A woman with a mission, she found some eggs and started

breaking them. She couldn't remember the last time she'd made Noel anything more for breakfast than toast and coffee.

She scrambled the eggs with green onions, tomatoes, and some feta she found in the back of the refrigerator. Simultaneously, she toasted an English muffin and when she had the whole meal ready, she set it in front of her husband.

"*Voilà.*"

"For me?"

"*Oui. Bon appétit.*"

"But honey—" he looked as if he had some news he didn't know how to break. "I already had cereal."

"Oh." She tried not to show her disappointment. "Well, I— that's okay, I'll eat it."

"No, what the hell, I'll eat it."

"No, you don't want it."

"I do want it."

"No, you don't."

"What the hell are you doing telling me what I don't want?" The words said he might have been kidding, but his voice had a dangerous quality.

"Look, I'm sorry. You don't want breakfast, you don't have to eat it."

He stood up, furious. "Why the hell did you make these eggs, Boo?"

"What? I just—"

"Did I say I wanted eggs? Why'd you have to make the goddamn eggs? I'll tell you why. Because you're strangling me. You're smothering me, inch by inch. You're going to kill me, you know that? With your goddamn control.

"Always have to be in control. Even control what I *eat.* It's not enough you have to pick this house, have to remodel it just so, have it paint it certain colors; not enough you kept on me to get a job until I took one I hated. Not enough you got pregnant and there was no talk of abortion. Never any doubt but that we were about to be parents.

"Did it ever occur to you I didn't want a kid? We never even talked about it, remember that? I bet you didn't even notice."

"I don't remember cutting your tongue out. You could have said something."

"Oh, Little Miss Perfect. I'm sure you would have. It would have been oh-so-rational, oh-so-perfectly reasoned. Well, I'm not like that, okay? Do you have to stick your fucking perfection in my face every time I sit down to read the paper? In my face, in my face, all the time in my fucking face. Just so fucking perfect! Perfect, perfect, perfect!

"Well, fuck perfect!"

He threw his napkin on the table and began walking toward the door.

Joy started to cry.

17

• •

"Mr. Treadaway."

"What, for Christ's sake?" He was still steaming, knew he was going to have to walk for at least an hour to calm down. He was in no mood to be accosted. He kept walking.

"Listen, I have to talk to Torian. You have to tell me where she is."

He stopped dead and looked for the first time at the person who was talking to him. It was a child.

Not actually a child, but a young teenager. Very young. But she was big, this one, as tall as an adult woman, taller than most, and outweighing a good fifty percent of them. A hefty girl, but not un-attractive. In fact, she was rather beautiful if you looked right at her face. She had extremely vivid coloring, and huge, gorgeous lips. "Who are you?"

"I'm Sheila." She waited, as if expecting him to understand. "Torian's friend."

Had Torian ever mentioned her? He didn't think so. But she must have friends. It just surprised him that they'd be so young.

Suddenly he realized this girl must know. Torian must have

told her. He felt as if his chest were caving in, a visceral sense of betrayal.

How could she? I wouldn't have. How could she possibly?

He turned his head nervously, automatically, checking to see if Boo had followed him out.

No, but she might be watching. "Meet me around the corner," he said, and crossed the street. She was waiting for him on Dauphine, near one of the gay bars that anchored nearly every block.

He said, "Tell me about Torian."

"You tell me."

He stared at her. She was proud and defiant, her pouty lips slightly pursed—in determination, he thought. A very bad kid. He couldn't believe someone her age could speak to him like that.

"How old are you?"

"Fifteen. Torian's age."

He felt his cheeks go hot, and hoped it didn't show. He said, "You wear too much makeup." At the time he thought he'd lost his mind; later he realized it was the giant lips that had prompted him to say such a bizarre thing. All that lipstick.

She gaped at him. "I really don't know—"

She didn't finish her sentence but he knew what she was thinking: *I don't know what Torian sees in you.*

She had every right to think that. He was making an ass of himself. He simply couldn't cope with this, didn't have the slightest idea how to behave.

"Look, if I don't know where Torian is, you do. You're the only other person she's close to. I know what happened with Lise the other night. She called me yesterday and said she was going to talk to you. I begged her not to, but if she didn't call me back, she did. I know that, and I'm going to tell her mother if you don't tell me where she is."

"You're crazy, you know that? You're just a crazy little kid."

"Well, your girlfriend's a kid, too, Noel."

"Girlfriend! What—Torian? Is that what you think? You could get in big trouble spreading rumors like that."

She smiled a canary-feather smile that also managed to be seductive. How could a kid her age behave like this? She said: "I think you're the one who'd get in trouble."

"You can't spread lies about me! You go around spreading lies, and I swear to God you"—he stepped back and pointed a finger at her—"are the one who's going to be in trouble. Big trouble."

"Are you threatening me?"

He couldn't believe this kid. "You watch yourself or you'll be sorry." He turned around and started walking. He had had quite enough of Miss Sheila, whoever the fuck she was. She couldn't be a friend of Torian's, he was sure of that. Torian had never mentioned her.

He'd gone about three steps when he realized how crazy he'd acted. He was terrified. *Jesus Christ, I'm nuts. I'm completely nuts. I did threaten her, for Christ's sake. And she's got all the power. If she blows the whistle on Torian and me, there goes my life.*

He called her name and spun around. "Sheila!"

She wasn't there.

Where the hell did she get to so quickly? He went to the corner and looked down the street: no Sheila.

Maybe she lives around here. Maybe she went in a house, or a store.

Dejectedly he turned back toward Canal Street.

What the hell could I have done, anyway? I don't know where Torian is, or how to call her. Why the hell didn't I get her number? I had it, right in my hand. I even had the address, and I just gave it to her, without thinking about it.

He replayed the scene in his mind. He couldn't remember anything, even the name of the woman Torian was staying with. He had a strange sense of being out of control, or being manipulated.

But the thing had happened so fast. Nobody could have planned it. Could they?

He walked toward the Central Business District and kept walking to the area of Lee Circle, where his office was. And Jacomine's.

The walk had calmed him down a little, but he was still on edge, not in the mood for making nice. He got right to the point: "I wonder if you could give me Miss Gernhard's phone number? I'd like to see how she's doing."

A smile spread slowly across Jacomine's face, a nasty smile,

Noel thought, a kind of "gotcha." He said, "She's perfectly fine, I assure you. I went out to see her today, and she's happy and comfortable."

"Her mother's pretty worried about her."

"Her mother hit her, if you recall."

"She's still her mother."

Jacomine didn't answer.

Noel said, "I'd really appreciate it if you'd give me the phone number."

"I can't do that, Noel. She'll be much safer this way."

"What do you mean by that?" He felt his cheeks warming again.

Jacomine shrugged, looking smug. "I mean, the fewer people who know where she is, the safer she'll be."

"But I know her—I'm the only person who actually knows her who even knows for sure that she's run away."

"I'm sorry. I really can't help you."

Where the hell does he get off? Noel was close to decking him. He said, "You're harboring a minor, Jacomine. You let me call and make sure she's all right, or I'll drop a dime on you."

Jacomine glared at him. Seizing the advantage, Noel said, "I mean that."

"Mr. Treadaway, things are simply not working out between us," said Jacomine. "If you persist in this, I'm afraid I'll have to let you go."

"You aren't kidding, things aren't working out. I should have gone to work for Perretti."

"He made you an offer?"

Noel nodded. "I'm sure it's still open."

Jacomine shrugged. "Perhaps you should take it, then."

"Good-bye." It was the one word he could manage.

He walked toward—what? Where the hell could he go?

He simply walked, not caring if he ever got anywhere. His life was in shambles.

I don't want the damn job anyway. But I don't want to work for Perretti either.

Fuck!

What do I want?

I don't want Boo. I've outgrown her. Whatever we had, we just don't anymore. I don't even remember why I married her.

And it was true I didn't want a baby, but the irony is, I do want Joy. I can't live without Joy.

But do I want to live?

The thought shocked him. Suicide had never occurred to him. Not even suicide—death. He had simply never thought of not living.

If I weren't alive, I couldn't see Joy grow up.

I'd never make love to Torian.

Torian! Now there's something I want.

But face it, Noel, how can you have her? She's fifteen. It'll be three years before you can even be seen in public with her without running the risk of getting locked up, and then she's still not out of high school.

Am I crazy or what? What kind of future could we have?

Oh, who the fuck needs a future.

● ●

Potter was thinking this was about the worst job he'd ever had, tailing a man who wasn't going anywhere. A man on foot when Potter was in a car.

Damn. How did I know he was going to do this?

Disgusted, he turned on the radio. A newscaster was saying, "Hurricane Hannah is expected to strike New Orleans early Friday morning."

Oh, sure, Potter thought. It was the third time that summer. Because the area flooded so badly, evacuation warnings generally came three days early, so people really could leave if they wanted to. But so far no hurricanes.

"The hurricane is traveling at a rate of thirteen miles per hour, with winds up to ninety miles per hour."

That's a pretty good hurricane. Where's that sucker going now?

Treadaway had entered a convenience store.

Potter parked and waited. *The things I do for Daddy!* But the truth

195

was, he'd have held his own gun to his head and pulled the trigger if Errol Jacomine had asked him to. He trusted Daddy that much. He didn't for a second doubt that if Daddy asked him for that, for his life, he'd have a damn good reason.

Daddy's the only hope, that's the thing. Be different if there was some alternative.

Potter had grown up in the Fisher Project across the river. He'd never even seen a backyard till he was six. But he'd seen plenty of shootings. He'd seen his own apartment, the one he shared with his mother and three sisters and brothers, he'd seen it filthy and stinking, piled waist-high with dirty clothes, dirty plates full of half-eaten food and the roaches it drew. If he needed a T-shirt, he had to pull it out of the pile on the floor, and it was as likely as not to have two or three roaches on it.

Somehow, he didn't know how—maybe from television— Potter knew this was not how it was supposed to be. He knew his mama wasn't supposed to be sick all the time, and the kids weren't supposed to have to do everything themselves. He even knew he was supposed to have a daddy. Kids on TV did.

He didn't think there were supposed to be so many shootings, either. He didn't think people you knew were supposed to die.

My whole life might have been different if it hadn't been for Ms. Myers.

She was his first-grade teacher. She had read stories to the class, the first he'd heard, and he was desperate to be able to do that himself. And so she had taught him. All the kids were supposed to learn, but he threw a fit one day because he couldn't do it, because it wasn't coming fast enough, and she had asked him if he wanted to stay after school until he learned how.

He had simply nodded, not thinking words were necessary, and after that, he had stayed twice a week. Ms. Myers brought him home herself.

She taught him how to read and other things. She even took him home one day, to show him where she lived, and that was how he found out what a backyard was like. He saw where her kids lived, too, each in his or her own spotless room, and then he knew for sure it didn't have to be the way it was at home.

For some people there were other ways.

"Why not me," he had asked her. "Why is my life ugly and bleak?"

He hadn't actually put it that way. He had pitched another fit, screaming incoherently, but she understood. She saw what he was trying to ask.

"It will get better," she said. "You can get out of this. But you have to promise me two things. First, do well in school."

He had simply nodded, impatient. All you had to do to do well in school was show up.

"And second, never, never, never under any circumstances, do drugs."

"Drugs?" he had said. "What that be?"

He had found out. When his mother died, his grandmother had come, and she had said his mother died of drugs. He still didn't know what they were, but he saw why Ms. Myers objected.

His grandmother couldn't keep the kids, and they were split up. Potter was sent to a foster home, and then another and another.

Pretty soon every kid he knew was doing something, pot at least, but all Potter could think about was that Ms. Myers said he could get out.

He had gotten out of the project, out of the filth and squalor, but they beat him in some of the homes, in the one where he was living when he decided to run away.

I can get out, he thought. *She told me I can. I do well in school and I don't do drugs.*

He was twelve years old at the time. He lived on the streets for three weeks before it occurred to him to find his grandmother. He knew she lived somewhere in New Orleans, in the lower Ninth Ward she had told him once, so he asked where that was, and he went there. He never did find her, but he did find someone who reminded him of her, an older woman who found him sleeping in a doorway and took him home. He didn't know why except that Miss Rose was a Christian.

She told him that right away and immediately began taking him to church. She said he should thank God for his food and shelter and clothing and the truth was, he was so grateful, he didn't care who he thanked.

That was how he found out about God. He liked the idea that someone was looking out for him. Maybe that was how he'd gotten out of the Fisher, maybe God had sent Ms. Myers.

He did well in school, just like she said, and even got into Xavier, where he went for a year. Miss Rose helped him out a little, but she couldn't really afford it, and Potter had to work his butt off doing various jobs that paid pennies just to stay in school.

That summer he got a real job working for a lawyer. And from there his life went fast—he met the guy who did the lawyer's investigations, and they got to talking. Potter got fascinated, so the guy hired him, and that was it. Potter never went back to school.

It paid seven-fifty an hour, but he figured he could learn fast and open his own agency, which indeed had happened. And that had led to other things, things he'd never have imagined—lucrative government contracts, some of them in foreign countries. Potter had done things he couldn't tell Yolanda about, but Daddy—now that was different. He could talk to Daddy about anything and not feel judged, not feel he'd be any less loved—either by Daddy or the Lord—if Daddy knew everything he'd ever done for money.

"You did what you had to do, son," Daddy had said, and it was true. Potter had gotten out of the Fisher, and had gotten his wife and kids a nice house in Eastover. And he'd made enough money to take a few months off and help Daddy get elected.

What Potter had liked first about being a detective was playing with the surveillance equipment. He still loved the stuff (which had improved markedly since he'd been in the business), but now what he liked was the sheer joy of being good at it. He had never played football in any formal sense, but he watched athletes, even at the high school level—the way they used their bodies, their grace and confidence, their surefootedness, and he felt their exhilaration; it was his life.

Treadaway came out of the store, apparently having gotten change. He made a call at the booth outside and then began taking notes from the Yellow Pages, making more calls. Most of the numbers he called evidently didn't answer, but one or two seemed to.

In a few minutes a cab pulled up, and Treadaway got in.

Potter followed the cab to a pawn shop in Harahan. He got out and watched through the window as Treadaway bought a handgun, and then he followed the cab back to Treadaway's house in the French Quarter.

He reported instantly to Daddy, whose mouth turned grim at the news. "He's coming after me."

Potter nodded. "It's possible, yes."

"What do you think we should do about it?"

Potter shrugged. "Terminate him."

"Very good. But how, Mr. Menard?"

"I have to think about that."

"You do that. And come up with a plan."

18

• •

Skip had gotten an early start—semi-early anyway—because Steve Steinman was coming that night. It was going to be a tight squeeze—New Orleans to Atlanta, Atlanta to Savannah, interview a woman who wasn't expecting her, and back again in time for dinner at Jimmy Dee's.

If Aunt Alice would see her—and Hurricane Hannah didn't disrupt plane schedules—she'd make it. According to the weatherman, Hannah was still headed for the Gulf Coast rather than the Atlantic, which meant that, as long as the storm didn't take a sudden turn, Savannah was out of danger.

But if anything went wrong, she'd have to spend the night. It wasn't a hospitable way to greet a guest. She had phoned in advance—found an Alice Sherman in Information, and gotten an answer, but as Theo Jackson had warned, she was deaf as a store dummy.

When stating her business didn't seem to work, Skip had simply said she was coming Wednesday morning, but she wasn't sure that got through either. She had called Theo back, asked him to run it down for Aunt Alice, then spent fifteen minutes explaining why she wouldn't be needing to be picked up at the airport, and in fact really wouldn't be able to see Theo at all this time. He seemed a little miffed, and Skip wasn't sure he'd speak to his aunt.

Aunt Alice was there when she showed up, though, resplendent in light blue, apparently dressed for receiving a guest. She was a large woman, either built so top-heavy she was a freak of nature or the victim of bizarre and sadistic corsetry.

"I'm Skip Langdon."

"Alice Sherman. Not at all sure why you're here, but come on in."

Aunt Alice had a lot of extra fat, extra skin, and extra makeup. Her skin had been powdered a sweet shell-pink, and it hung off her chin in wattles. She had white hair curled much too tight and an absolutely beatific expression. Skip wondered if perfect happiness came from being able to tune out what you didn't want to hear.

Her living room was so full of tiny things that had to be dusted, Skip didn't see how she could have time for anything else. She sat in a rocker and motioned Skip to a stiff, hard-sitting sofa.

"What can I do for you, Ms. Langdon? My, you have pretty skin."

"Thank you. Thank you. I've come about—"

Sherman began waving her arms for quiet. "Sorry. I almost forgot your paper." She handed over a small lined pad. "In the pleasure of having a visitor, I nearly forgot my infirmity. I can still talk, praise the good Lord, but I'm as deaf as that girl in the picture."

She pointed to the wall behind Skip, where an ancient print of Lawrence's Pinkie hung.

"Just write down your half of the conversation. And while you're doing that, I'll fix us some lemonade." She heaved her bulk out of the chair and waddled to the kitchen, legs unsteady though she wore the heaviest of orthopedic shoes.

Skip wrote, "I'm here about your nephew, Earl Jackson. I understand he was quite a hellion in his time."

She wanted to test the waters before plunging in.

When Aunt Alice had returned with the lemonade, and had read the note, she wrinkled her nose. "Theo told me what you said about him being a small-town preacher who just got elected president of something. Is that true? Earl Jackson's actually a solid citizen somewhere?"

Skip wrote, "I'm afraid I lied to Theo. Earl Jackson's a preacher, but I think he's a con man and worse."

Aunt Alice said. "Now that sounds more like him. Meanest kid I ever saw. Only mean kid I ever saw. You ever meet anybody you thought was really a bad person? I mean, actually evil?"

Skip said, "I think so. Earl Jackson."

"Write it! Write it!"

When she had, Aunt Alice nodded. "The family thought it was a big joke about the kittens and fish and everything—Theo said he told you about that. They always play it for laughs. But I say, "Taint funny, McGee.'"

At Skip's puzzled expression, she said, "That's something left over from radio. You're not supposed to understand it. I wonder why families do those things? He was a very, very dangerous little boy—always in trouble, too."

Skip wrote. "What sort?"

"At first, it was just stuff like getting sent to the principal's office—you know, for disrupting the class, things like that. Then he started actually getting arrested."

"For what?" Skip was so excited she spoke, but Sherman nodded, evidently having understood.

"Oh, things like breaking into the school." She shrugged. "Personally, I think that was just a prank. What really bothered me was that he hit other kids. And then there was the time he set fire to his parents' mattress. 'Course, no one knew about that but the family. Then later on, when he was in high school, there was the usual stuff—marijuana, illegal possession of alcohol, car-stealing once. Nothing much." She stopped and frowned. "I notice you're not taking notes. You're not a reporter, are you?"

Skip laughed and shook her head. She wrote, "I'm a police officer on leave. This is a private job. To tell you the truth I'm working for myself. I think he's incredibly dangerous and he's running for mayor of New Orleans."

Sherman let out a loud breath. "God help that city if he gets elected."

"That's what I think."

"He did threaten a kid with a gun once, but that's not gon' help you. I know something that might, though." She put a hand over her mouth for a moment. "I know he's dangerous, always knew he was dangerous, but I don't know about this one."

"What was it?"

"He was accused of murder once."

"What!"

Sherman held her ears, and then laughed. It was her little joke. "Well, I wasn't gon' tell you over some silly small-town club election, but I just never did think that was what you were here about. Nobody'd fly a reporter clear to Savannah for that. Anyway, you're older than Theo thinks you are. Didn't quite make sense."

Skip smiled. She had underestimated Alice Sherman, and she was kicking herself for it: Deaf didn't mean stupid, and neither did old. She wrote: "Why'd you decide to talk to me?"

"Liked you," Sherman said simply. "I knew you were a good person, even if you were lying."

Skip smiled again and wrote, "You must be psychic."

"Nope. Just smart." She rocked a bit, intertwining her fingers. "Don't know about that murder charge. In the first place, I don't know much about it—even where it was, I mean. Only reason I know about it at all is, Earl's mother had to hire a lawyer for him, and the lawyer got him off. She always said it was an accident." She rocked some more. "Maybe it was. Might have been, I just don't know."

"Do you have any other details?" Skip wrote.

"Nope. Not a one. Wish I did, but that's all I know. Right after that he became a preacher, and Blanche—that's his mother— begged me to forget about it. You know what, about Blanche? When he was a little bitty boy, she dreamed he was the Messiah. Can you beat that? Now there's a dream shoulda never been told."

Skip was wondering if Blanche were alive when Sherman said, "'Course, poor Blanche is long gone. I'm the oldest one left—in fact, the only one left who'd know about that. And I sure don't know much about it."

Skip thanked her and drove to the airport in her rental car, thinking she'd have to write Alice Sherman a big fat thank-you note, even if she didn't find out another thing. Sherman was a sharply intelligent woman who didn't try to brush things under the carpet—*evil* under the carpet. She liked the way Sherman had put it, what she saw in Jacomine.

Skip had seen it only a couple of times, and she knew what courage it took to face it—to say, *this is it, that thing you've read about.*

This is pure evil.

She called Jane Storey from the airport. "I've got something good, but I can't prove it. A murder charge, no conviction."

"Dynamite! Who needs a conviction? It's not libelous to say he stood trial—and the testimony's public record. If there's anything good, I can use it."

"Here's the problem. I don't know where it was."

"Wait a minute. We know his real name. Wouldn't it be in a data bank somewhere?"

"Uh-huh. In any one of fifty."

"You mean there's no central Hall of Records?"

"There's a federal wanted system, but I've already checked it under both names we know. The problem is, some small towns don't report—this could have slipped by. Or, he might have had a third name at the time. I'll check southern states—Louisiana and Georgia, for sure. Maybe a few others."

"I'd appreciate it. I'd love to get that bastard."

"Careful. In his case, the walls really do have ears."

"Listen, I've got a tidbit for you. Do you have time? Is your flight being called or anything?"

"Shoot. I've got half an hour."

"I just got a call from a source in Perretti's campaign. Get this—Jacomine's new press secretary quit. He wants to go to work for Perretti."

"Noel Treadaway?" Skip whistled. "Thereby hangs a tale, I bet."

"Don't you imagine. I've got a call in to him right now."

• •

She'd been gone two days. Maybe that was long enough. Torian called her mother.

"Torian? Torian, is it really you?"

Did her mother sound slightly concerned? Maybe just a little bit as if she'd been worried?

"It's really me."

"Are you all right?" Lise's voice was slurred—that was what was off.

"Fine."

"Where are you?"

"I just thought I'd call and—"

"Where are you, Torian?"

"I'm in a nice place. Someone nice is taking care of me."

"Some kid with a pierced nose? You little whore, you probably—"

"What?"

"You'd probably shack up with the first thing in trousers—"

"What did you call me?"

"Torian, you brat. Do you have any idea what you've put me through? Tell me where the hell you are, and I'll come get your sorry ass."

Even Lise wasn't usually this nasty—or this loaded, from the sound of things.

Torian said, "You couldn't even walk, much less drive."

She hung up.

Faylice said, "Ain' nothin' change, huh?"

Torian turned away, blinking tears.

Faylice came and sat on the bed next to her. "Hey. It be okay to cry. That what my auntie say."

Shyly, she put an arm around Torian's shoulders, and without thinking, Torian put her arms around her. She buried her face in Faylice's soft, fleshy shoulder. It was oddly, almost unbearably comforting. There was a pleasure in it that took Torian by surprise, not like what she felt when she held Noel, but not so different either. It was something more basic, something primeval.

205

It came to her suddenly: *This is what a mother feels like.*

In the realization were the ironies of it, and all the pain of them: That she shouldn't find out till she was nearly an adult; that the maternal object should be a child younger than she; that she should discover it only because Lise had hurt her so much and so often.

Faylice had given her permission to cry, and she took it, with utter abandon and without self-consciousness. The other girl held her and stroked her hair as if Torian were a younger sister.

When she had exhausted her tears, Torian pulled away, a little embarrassed. "Thank you," she whispered.

"You sure got silky hair, you know that?"

Torian laughed. "I feel better." In fact, she felt as if a dense black thing in her heart had dissolved.

Can a person have heartstones? she wondered. *Like gallstones?*

Faylice said, "You ain' goin' home yet, I guess."

For some reason, that didn't depress Torian. She felt she could cope with whatever happened. "You got that right."

I'm happy here, she thought. *I wonder how long I can stay?*

The notion of simply staying, of not thinking for a while of Lise, or her father, or school, or even Noel was wonderfully appealing.

I wonder if I could just stay forever.

I'd miss Sheila, though. And then, as if it were a sudden revelation: *That's who I'll call.*

"Sheila?"

"Torian! Thank God. Listen, your boyfriend's a jerk."

"What?"

"All hell's broken loose here. Lise came over and made a scene—"

"What kind of scene?"

"She yelled at everybody. I thought Skip was going to arrest her."

Torian giggled.

"But listen, she is your mother. It's not right for her not to know—"

"I just called her."

"You did?"

"Yeah. She called me a whore."

"Omigod. She found out about Noel."

"I don't think so. She seems to think I'm shacked up with some pierced-noser."

"Oh yeah. She mentioned that to us."

"She did?"

"Except I think it was pierced nipples in that version." They both giggled.

Sheila said, "Wonder what she'd think if she did know?"

"She'd probably be jealous. Why is he a jerk, by the way?"

"Well, I figured he knows where you are—"

"He sent me here."

"—so I went to find out. He told me I wear too much makeup."

"No!"

"And I'm just a crazy little kid—"

"Little. You're my age."

"And he threatened me. He said to watch myself or I'll be sorry."

Torian was suddenly depressed again. "Oh, shit. Just when I was beginning to feel better."

"I think you should dump that dude."

Torian was quiet.

Sheila said, "Are you there?"

"I was just thinking. He might be a little nuts."

"He's not exactly Mr. Normal. I mean, first of all—"

"I know, I know. What's he doing with a kid half his age?"

"I wasn't going to say it."

"I know it's crazy—maybe we're both crazy. But we're in love. You can't control who you fall in love with. Can you?"

"I don't know."

"Well, anyway, he sent me to a great place."

"What kind of place?"

"Oh, yeah, I want to give you the address. I want somebody to know where I am."

"Wait a minute. You just said Noel sent you. Doesn't he know?"

"I don't know." Torian realized she was confused about it. "I thought it was his friend's house, but now I'm not so sure. Maybe it's the Rev's friend. Anyway, she's somebody really nice. From the church."

"The church?"

"You know. The Rev's church. There's these two black girls here. If you think *we've* got problems . . . I'll tell you about them later. Anyway, here's my address." She read it off. "*Promise* you won't tell Lise—I don't care if she rips your fingernails out."

"Don't be silly. I'm your friend."

"Well, how are you, anyway? Have you been out with Joe Eddie yet?"

"Not yet. He cancelled on me."

"Shit."

"But we've rescheduled for tonight."

"Cool. I'll call back. You have to tell me everything."

"I hope it doesn't rain—that hurricane's supposed to be coming."

"Not till tomorrow, I thought."

"Yes, but you know how storms are—rain and wind forever. Anyway, give me your number. I'll call you when I get back."

When she hung up, she called Noel at the office.

"I'm sorry," said an icy voice. "Mr. Treadaway is no longer with us."

She was so freaked she called him at home, thinking to hang up if Boo answered. His voice came urgently over the line: "Torian. Torian, I love you."

"Oh, Noel. Oh, God, Noel, I miss you." She hadn't realized how much; how familiar and comforting he had become to her. Before this, when she thought of him, it was with passion. He seemed suddenly like a relative, someone who'd always been there, who'd protect her when she needed it.

For the first time, she was homesick, rather than plagued by the nagging feeling that she ought to get home. A sudden desperate urge came over her—to get back to normal, just to be home again, going to school, seeing Sheila, home in her own room, where her cigarettes were hidden.

But I *can't. Lise is there.*

"Torian, let me come get you. Everyone's really worried."

"Oh, Noel, I don't know. I just don't know. A part of me really wants to come home. I desperately want to see you; and I want to see Sheila, but I don't see how I can go back to Lise. I just can't see it."

"She'll talk to you now. I think you finally got her attention."

"You'd think so, wouldn't you? You'd really think so. But she's meaner than ever, Noel, I swear it. I called her. I talked to her. Do you know what she called me? Whore! She called me a whore."

"Does she know about us?"

"Of course not. That's just her little way of showing affection."

"Torian, please. I think you should come home. I miss you so much."

"Oh, Noel. Oh God, I love you." Something clicked on the line. "What was that?"

"I don't know. Don't worry about it. Boo's at Whole Foods—it couldn't have been her."

●　●

Boo had had to hang up and run to the bathroom to vomit.

Washing her face, she fought for balance. She was dizzy, barely able to stand; a pulse pounded in her scalp.

I'm going to fall on the floor. I have to get control.

For the first time, she understood what it meant when someone said her head was spinning. She couldn't focus, felt her head literally moving back and forth as her eyes sought . . . what? A sign, maybe? A billboard that said: *You didn't hear your husband declaring his love to the fifteen-year-old babysitter. It's all a big mistake.*

Get a grip, Boo. Come on. Chill. Her hands were shaking.

She heard Noel coming down the stairs. Moving very slowly, she dried her face, patting it with a pink towel. Then she closed the toilet seat and sat, staring at a space on the wall, saying over and over, *I can handle this. I am calm and adult; I can handle anything.*

When she had sat there ten minutes or more, maybe twenty, when she had said the mantra so many times it bored her, she saw that her hands had stopped shaking and realized she no longer felt the pulse in her scalp.

She stood up. That was tricky, but she managed it. When she felt steady, she looked in the mirror. She said again, *I am an adult. I am going out there, and I'm going to handle this with dignity.*

She went out to the courtyard, where Noel was reading last Sunday's papers, catching up, the sort of thing a person did who'd just been fired. He was sitting at a round wrought iron table, sections on the table, on the ground, lying all around him like so much shed skin. He said, "Honey. I didn't hear you come home."

He looked a little uncertain, but probably not because he suspected anything. He had apologized after his tantrum, but they were still uneasy with each other.

"Obviously not." She watched his smile fade, though probably, she thought, because of the ominous tone of her voice. He hadn't yet caught on. "The phone was ringing when I came in. I guess we picked up at the same time."

She watched fear fill his eyes. And regret? Or was that her imagination? His mouth started to work, but no words came out. Probably he couldn't think what to say.

"Excuse me. I didn't have time to unpack the groceries." She went into the kitchen and started taking things out of bags. But she left them on the table, unable to put them in the proper cabinets or the refrigerator. She couldn't really think where anything belonged.

Noel followed her in. He said, "Look, I didn't mean for this to happen. Certain things you just . . . can't control."

"Oh, really? Then I suppose no babysitter in America's safe." Ice cream. That had to go in the freezer. She opened the door and shoved it in.

Frozen pizza. That, too.

Noel said, "What's that supposed to mean?"

"What it means, Noel, is that ninety-nine percent of grown men manage to keep their hands off the babysitter. In other words, do control 'certain things.' These are the ones who've grown up."

"Boo, this isn't some frivolous little flirtation."

"I heard you declaring your 'love.' Christ! You stupid fuck! Who do you think you are? The captain of the football team? Think you can fuck her and nobody'll find out? Then when you break her heart, she quits babysitting and you just grope the next little cutie who comes over to take care of your darling baby daughter?"

Cereal. The cabinet to the left of the sink.

"Boo, you're not getting the hang of this. You're treating it way too lightly." She had been staring down at a packet of sundried tomatoes, trying to remember why she'd bought them and what she planned to do with them.

His tone made her look at him. It was measured—not angry, not whiny, simply straightforward; the last thing she'd have expected. His face was immeasurably sad, and she had the oddest feeling that it was on her account, that he felt badly for her.

"Lightly? You're quite mistaken. I haven't even begun to figure out how to treat it. But lightly isn't one of the options I'm considering."

He walked over to her and took both her hands. "Boo, I love her. Please try to understand that."

She jerked away and spun around, bracing her arms on the sink. She stared down at the drain. "She's fifteen! She's a baby!"

"She's the most extraordinary human being I've ever met. I love her more deeply than I would have thought possible." There was a calm in the way he spoke, an unexpected dignity.

"You don't love her! You can't. You're just projecting." She heard the whininess in her voice. Her eyes flicked to the counter, where dishes had been left—her cup and saucer, the plate she'd put her toast on, the knife she'd cut the bread with. She looked at the serrated edge of the knife and thought about it tearing human flesh. It wouldn't be a swift, clean cut; it would be slow and jagged.

"I'm sorry you had to find out."

"Sorry I had to find out! What were you planning to do, live this little lie until she graduates?"

Some expression that she couldn't name crossed his face. She had a sudden intuitive flash: *That is what he meant to do. Omigod, what have I married?*

Despair gripped her for a second, and then it let go, forced out by raging, pounding fury. "Let me ask you something. What's so extraordinary about this child? Just what could a grown man possibly see in a skinny kid—except a real docile lay, I mean."

She thought, *I'm a pretty docile lay myself,* and she hated herself for getting hooked. She knew perfectly well what he saw in the girl. If he'd been her client he'd have been as transparent as a fishpond—with someone that young, he'd be a hero, he'd always be in control, he'd always be right, he'd be worshiped, he could do no wrong, he could dominate her utterly.

How strange, she thought. *He's passive as hell with me.*

He said, "I don't think I can explain it. We're soul mates, that's all." He grinned. "Isn't it ironic? What a weird twist of fate I had to get one who's fifteen. I mean, it's not like I asked for this."

"You *idiot!*" She picked up the knife and raised it, blind with rage, not at his infidelity, but at his inconceivable stupidity. Furious with herself as well—for failing to see what a perennial adolescent he was, for getting involved with someone so passive, so unformed.

"Watch it, Boo! Watch it, watch it!" He grabbed her wrist and the knife fell. He stepped back, staring at her as if she were a murderer.

For Christ's sake. He looks like he's got a two-figure IQ, and for all I know he has.

She hated him. Without realizing what she was doing she balled up her hands and threw herself at him, pounding on his chest as hard as she could.

He didn't do anything. Didn't raise a hand to stop her, didn't open his mouth, just stood there and let her pound. She found it curiously unsatisfying.

"Goddammit, fight back."

He sighed. "I guess I deserve it."

"Damn right you deserve it." She was just getting down to the second level of what this thing meant—it not only meant her marriage was over, her husband was an adolescent, it meant . . .

"Oh, shit. You bastard." She pounded harder, beginning to enjoy it, especially as he was finally wincing.

. . . when you got right down to it, it meant he'd seduced a child.

"I can never trust you with Joy! I can't even leave your own daughter alone with you."

He caught her wrist. "Joy? What does she have to do with this?"

"She's a child. Obviously you're attracted to children, and you have no impulse control."

"She's a baby, for Christ's sake!"

She pulled away from him. "Where do you draw the line, Noel?"

"What?"

"You heard me. I said, where do you draw the line?"

"You vindictive bitch!" He stepped toward her, looking around, she thought, for a weapon. Frightened, she stepped back.

But he didn't so much as raise his arm. He let his shoulders sag, turned around, and left by the front door.

19

• •

Steve was in the courtyard when Skip arrived home from Savannah. He had changed to khaki shorts, found himself a Turbo Dog, and was drinking it with Angel at his feet.

He got up as she came in, ready to engulf her. "You look better."

"Better than what?"

"Better than a rag, a bone, and a hank of hair."

"I was that bad?"

"Worse. I'm just too polite to mention it."

"Then I guess I am better." She stepped into his arms. Angel's tail thumped against her legs as she and Steve kissed. "I really think I am."

"Shall we go inside?"

"Does that mean what I think?"

"Happy women turn me on." He held up the beer. "Besides I've had two of these. I have no inhibitions."

"Better seize the day, then." She was surprised at how much the idea of making love appealed to her.

Steve walked behind her to the second floor and when they

were in her bedroom, it was she who moved toward him, pro-
pelled by a sudden electric surge.

"You smell like beer," she said, the instant before their lips met.

Steve broke away. "I'll brush my teeth."

"No. I like it. I want you now."

He took on a mischievous look. "Maybe we should wait till tomorrow. Think how great it'll be in a hurricane."

"We'll try it both ways." She had a hand under his T-shirt,
feeling the depression of his spine, pushing his body closer to hers.
She hadn't felt like this in months, not since . . . *since I fell into the*
depression.

But what the hell, I used to smoke pot when I got depressed. Sex is healthier.

She let him bend her backward so that they were lying on the
bed, his body on top of hers. "Take your shirt off."

He stood up and obeyed. He was a large man, several inches
taller than her own six feet, and he was well filled-out—a bear,
Jimmy Dee called him. He had a good coat of fur on his chest, and
apparently knew it. He posed for a moment, letting Skip absorb the
effect.

She said, "Come here, bear."

He straddled her, a hand closing over each breast, obeying
but doing it his way. She stared at him as he caressed her, their
eyes locked, and when he said, "Show me," she took off her T-
shirt and bra.

His mouth closed over her nipple, and she felt herself slide into
a different consciousness. She had always hallucinated when they
made love, and this time she saw a river of honey flowing in a
ruby canyon, felt herself flowing with it, falling over the edge as
the honey reached the end and cascaded downward, riding on it,
tossed gently, as if by soft breezes and waves, face glowing in the
warm sun.

Steve took off his khaki shorts. She couldn't believe he still had
them on. She had been in another world.

She went away again. She could have sworn she could taste
honey, but it was probably Turbo Dog, she thought, holding
Steve's shoulders with her right arm, not letting him get off her.

"You missed me," he said.

"What makes you think that?"

"We were due at Jimmy Dee's five minutes ago."

She bit his ear. "You're lying."

"No, I mean it."

"Damn." She let him go, wriggled out from under, and reached for the phone. "Dee-Dee, listen . . ."

"Are you going to be the teeniest bit late? You young people have fun now." He hung up.

Steve looked at her quizzically.

"He was pretty understanding. Want to flip for the shower?"

"You go first. You probably want to wash your hair."

Later, as she was drying it, and Steve was unpacking, he asked her about Jacomine. She told him what Alice Sherman had said. "It kills me. Every day I become more and more convinced he's dangerous as a scorpion. But I can't seem to get anything Jane can print."

"Why don't you just give the stuff to Perretti?"

"For one thing, I don't like him."

Steve nodded.

"For another, I'm still a police officer. Which means I can't work for a political candidate. Even if I wasn't working for him when I did the investigation, I don't see how I could suddenly turn over my results to him."

"On the other hand if you don't do something, a maniac is going to be elected mayor."

"Well, that's my dilemma. You think I was depressed before . . ."

He was serious a moment. "Hey. Did you find a new therapist?"

"I didn't look. Hey, wait a minute. I bet I could go back to Boo."

"This is moving too fast for me."

"Her husband was Jacomine's press secretary. But Jane Storey just told me he quit."

"Listen, maybe you should get together with the husband. He must have quit for a reason."

She considered. "Not a bad idea—Jane's probably all over him, but I'm sort of a friend of the family; that might help." She looked at her watch. "Let's go, though. Dee-Dee's probably getting restless."

"Half-drunk," Jimmy Dee said when they arrived. "I find a glass of wine distracts from restlessness. On the other hand, it has a price."

Skip's head swivelled. "Where's Layne?"

Dee-Dee turned his palms up, casual, but there was a catch in his voice: "The Angel problem. He can handle about an hour, so he's coming for dessert."

"I really must get those witches on this."

" 'Eye of newt and toe of frog. Wool of bat and tongue of dog.' "

Steve said, "Is that what we're having for dinner?

"We are having my justly famous couscous."

"Funny you've never mentioned it before."

"I've never made it before. But it will be famous, I'm quite sure. Kenny will tell all his little friends how awful it is."

Skip thought she saw a desperate look in Steve's eyes. She said "The kids are—?"

"Kenny's desperate to see Steve. I hope you don't mind. And I'm trying to teach Sheila manners."

Steve said, "Kenny wants to see me?"

"Frankly, I think he wants an update on Napoleon."

When they were all seated and Kenny had been filled in on Steve's German shepherd, Jimmy Dee said, "How's L.A.?" in a way that made Skip suspicious.

He and Steve had never really hit it off—out of jealousy, she was pretty sure—but things had gotten better after Layne came on the scene. Still, Skip wouldn't have expected the line of questioning she thought he was about to pursue.

"Same old rat race," said Steve.

"Still thinking about moving to New Orleans?"

I was right. I must really be pathetic if Dee-Dee thinks he can't take care of me himself.

"I just have to salt away a few more pennies, and then I think it's really going to happen." Steve was a documentary filmmaker who'd one day stumbled into a lucrative career as a film editor—a career he wanted to milk thoroughly before making the move he'd long talked about.

"Phooey," said Kenny. "Napoleon's probably dying to come back—it's his home town."

"Yeah, he mentions it pretty often. Actually, I might be able to come for a few weeks now and then if I get my new project going."

Sheila said, "May I be excused?"

"Sheila, we just sat down." Dee-Dee couldn't keep the impatience out of his voice.

"Look, my plate's clean." She held it up. "It was delicious, Uncle Jimmy."

"You must want something."

"No, I liked it. Honest. But—you know—dinner was way late and I have homework."

Kenny said, "Me, too?"

"Okay, then. Since you ask so nicely."

When they had gone, he shrugged. "What are you gonna do—chain 'em to a chair?"

Skip said, "Well, anyway, they made a clean getaway. Manners lessons workin' out."

"Am I a great father or what?" He looked the slightest bit smug. "It was easy. I promised to send them to manners camp if they didn't shape up." He looked at his watch. "May I be excused, too? I need to call Layne."

An hour and a half later, full of couscous and Jimmy Dee's chess pie, feeling mellow and talkative, Skip and Steve returned to the garçonnière. They sat on Skip's bed, cross-legged, facing each other. Steve took her hand. "You seem almost . . . okay."

She pulled back, slightly embarrassed. "Nothing like building up a good head of anger to make you forget your troubles."

"I guess the shrink knew what she was doing."

"It's weird, isn't it? I could have done volunteer work—or come out to L.A. to visit you . . ."

"A great idea."

She shrugged. "I don't know, there's a million things I could have done, but I didn't have the energy or the inclination."

"Thanks a lot."

"I can't help it. If I could have, I would have. I just couldn't move. Have you ever been that way?"

"When I've had the flu."

"It was like that. It seems so strange that getting good and mad is the only thing that could get me out of it."

"Oh, come on, it isn't only that. You're trying to prevent something terrible."

"Mighty Mouse, that's me."

"Tell me something. Do you ever think about . . ."

"Shavonne crawling across the floor?" She felt her eyes close for a moment. "Yes. I still do. What's that?"

"It sounds like someone knocking."

"Dee-Dee!" She stepped onto the balcony. "What is it?"

"Can we come in a minute?" Layne was with him.

As she opened the door, he said, "Guess who's missing?"

"Well, not Kenny. Must be Little Miss Manners, who really liked the couscous—'honest'."

He put a hand to his head. "How could I have been so dumb?"

"I would've fallen for it. I mean, I did."

"What do you think I ought to do?"

"I don't think she's run away, Dee-Dee. Remember how she said, 'dinner was way late'? She must have had a date."

"A date! She's supposed to get picked up at the house."

"Maybe she thinks the guy's socially unacceptable."

"You mean like, my age, say? A pervert? It's that damned teenage computer conference—she probably met some pedophile."

Layne said, "James, will you calm down? She's only been missing an hour or two. She'll probably be home by midnight."

Skip nodded. "We'll go stay with Kenny while you take Layne home. That's what you came for, isn't it?"

Dee-Dee nodded.

"And if she's not home by the time you get back, I honestly think the best thing is just to go to bed—and give her what-for in the morning."

"What-for indeed. She's grounded till the next century."

• •

"Torian! Come down, quick! Somebody to see you." Paulette sounded unlike herself, almost frightened.

Torian thought: *The Rev again?* She was reading in bed, wearing a T-shirt and panties, Faylice asleep in the next bed. She didn't answer, not wanting to wake her roommate, just pulled on yesterday's shorts and hit the stairs.

"Sheila!" Torian's bare feet moved so fast the worn carpet burned them. She'd never seen Sheila like this, hair unkempt, cheeks wet from crying. "Sheila, what is it?"

Sheila glanced at Paulette and didn't answer, just threw her arms around her friend. "Oh, Torian, I'm so stupid."

Torian also looked at Paulette, but not distrustfully—beseechingly. She couldn't imagine anything happening to Sheila. What on Earth should she do? For the moment, she just held her.

When Sheila pulled away, Torian said, "This is Paulette. She's so cool." And then she noticed her friend's jaw was swollen. "What's this?" Impulsively, she touched it.

Sheila winced.

Paulette didn't offer to shake, didn't even acknowledge the introduction, simply said, "Honey, you need a place to stay?"

"Yes! Can I really stay here?"

Torian was going crazy. "Sheila, what's wrong?"

Paulette said, "Better get some ice on that. Come on. Let's go on in the kitchen. I'll make y'all some hot chocolate."

It wasn't really hot chocolate weather, New Orleans being a September furnace. But the AC was on, and nothing she could have mentioned would have been so perfect, so comforting.

This must be what a real mom is like, Torian thought.

She couldn't wait to question Sheila till they were sitting civilized around the table. "What's wrong?" she said again.

Paulette said, "Come on, y'all."

They followed her to the kitchen, and by the time they were there, Sheila seemed to be recovering her composure. She looked very pale.

Torian remembered something. "You were supposed to meet Joe Eddie . . . oh, no! You got mugged on the way."

Sheila shook her head, wiping tears with the back of her hand. "He tried to rape me."

"Joe Eddie?" Torian couldn't take it in.

Paulette, fooling with ice trays, spun around, alert, "Sheila. You really okay? He just tried, or he did?"

"Oh, he didn't. Uh-uh." She shook her head vigorously. "Listen, I don't weigh a hundred and forty-five pounds for nothing."

Paulette gave her a dish towel full of ice cubes. "Sit down, baby. Hold that on ya jaw." She busied herself at the stove.

Torian sat down with Sheila. "What happened?"

"Well, I went to meet him when he was getting off work, and he said, 'Let's take a walk.' So we walked to an apartment building, and he started to unlock the door. I said, 'Where are we going?' and he said, 'My friend lives here. He's letting us use the apartment.' "

Paulette said, "Uh-oh."

Sheila nodded. "That's what I thought. So I said, 'I don't think we know each other well enough,' and he turned around and he hit me. Just like that." Her face wore a look of utter bewilderment. "He didn't say a word. Just hit me." She rubbed her jaw.

Paulette said, "Mmmm. Mmmm. Mmmm," as if she had heard it all before.

"Omigod. Then what?" said Torian.

"Well, I was so surprised, I grabbed my chin and said something dumb like, 'What'd you do that for?' And he backed me up in the entryway and groped my boobs. I was trying to fight him off, and he was laughing. Then he put an arm around my back to hold me and with the other, he tried to unzip my jeans. And suddenly I thought, 'Holy shit, he's trying to rape me.' It just never occurred to me, you know?"

"Did he say anything?"

"Yeah, he said, 'Come on, baby, you know you love it.' Anyway, when it occurred to me what he was trying to do, I kneed him."

221

Torian giggled. "Just like they tell you."

"Guess what? It works. He fell back, and then I hit him in the stomach."

Paulette said, "Good for you, girl," and set a cup of cocoa in front of her.

"There was a taxi going by, so I just grabbed it. I told him to go to my house, and we were almost there when I thought of what was going to happen when I got there."

"What?" said Paulette.

"Well, see, I sneaked out for my date, so they were going to kill me for that. And then I went out with someone I didn't run by Uncle Jimmy first."

"Why'd you do that, baby?"

"Well . . . I sort of knew they weren't going to like him."

"Why?"

"You know—he doesn't go to high school, his family doesn't know my family, all those stupid things."

Torian said, "He's quite a bit older, too."

"But I never thought he was *dangerous.*"

"Honey," Paulette said gently, "there might be a reason they got those rules."

Sheila looked into her cup. "I know," she said in a small voice.

Paulette got up again, as if repenting of bringing up an unpleasant subject. "Let me get ya some whipped cream for that."

She squirted some into Sheila's, then Torian's cup. She looked at Torian when she spoke again. "Whenever an older dude goes out with a young girl, ya know what? He controls her."

Sheila stuck out her jaw. "He didn't control *me.*"

"Well, he tried, baby. He thought he could. He was cruder about it than most, but, believe me, they're all like that, whether they mean to be or not—"

"Mean to rape you?"

"No. Mean to be the one in charge. It's real dangerous and real bad." She glanced at Sheila quickly. "Now, honey, don't think I'm judging ya. I know why ya don't want to go home. Ya think they will judge ya there. And punish ya, too—right?"

Sheila looked miserable. "I don't know. I just feel like it's my fault." Her eyes filled and a sob came out of her throat.

Paulette put an arm around her. "Well, it's not, baby. Don't you forget that. It's just plain not."

"I feel like somehow they'd make it my fault."

"Ya might be wrong about that, but we're not gon' argue about it. I'm gon' give you a nice warm place to stay, but ya gotta do two things—first, don't say where ya stayed, okay? 'Cause this is illegal. I do it because I think there's a need." She smiled. "And I love kids.

"Second, do ya want to call the cops? They can't come here, but ya might want to think about whether ya want to let that bastard get away with this."

"Well, I don't want him to get killed."

"The cops won't kill him, baby, why do ya think that?"

Sheila laughed. "'Cause my Aunt Skip's the cops—and she'd murder him."

"Ya never going to tell her?"

Sheila shook her head. "Oh, I don't know. I feel so mixed up. I just don't want to *deal* with it."

"I know how ya feel, honey. But they might worry about ya. Want to give 'em a call or anything?"

"I just can't . . . talk about it yet. To them, I mean."

"Well, what if I call 'em? I'll just say you're all right and y'll call back tomorrow or somethin'."

Sheila looked uncertain, but a sudden calm had come over Torian, now that she knew her friend wasn't badly hurt and hadn't been raped. Somehow, she knew exactly what to do. She said, "No, I'll call," and Sheila shot her a grateful look.

"I'm going to call Skip instead of Uncle Jimmy."

She got no answer, but left a message saying Sheila was with her, and they'd be in touch soon. "Is she working tonight?" she said when she was done.

Sheila shook her head. "Probably out looking for me." And then she smiled for the first time. "Or screwing. Steve just got here."

Paulette winced. "Girl, girl. Y'all talk like sailors." When they had finished their cocoa, Paulette said, "Torian's already got a roommate, so I'm puttin' ya in with Adonis."

"That's a girl?"

"That's what Torian said. Why's that a boy's name?"

"Guess it isn't."

Torian slept as soundly as if she'd run a marathon.

20

• •

Boo thought: Is it raining? She listened, but heard nothing.

Why did I think that?

I must have heard something.

She saw that she was alone. *Something didn't feel right—that must have been it.*

She remembered why Noel had left and she thought then that perhaps a dream had awakened her, that surely she had dreamed after so shattering a revelation, that her psyche must be struggling like a child thrown in the ocean to understand the thing that had happened to her.

What did I marry? Was I molested as a child and I've set up a replay?

Her gut told her it wasn't that. It was something even harder and less acceptable, something about power, about control, something it made her angry even to consider. Angry at herself, mostly.

Shit. I'm supposed to know what I'm doing. I'm supposed to have some sense. What in the hell am I going to do now?

Get a divorce, I guess.

The answer—so simple, so straightforward—filled her with unutterable despair—not pain, but a feeling of clammy emptiness.

She had a vision suddenly, a sort of hallucination, of a terra-cotta pipe that sweated freezing, filthy, foul-smelling liquid.

Stumbling, not really knowing what she was doing, she found her way to Joy's room and nearly picked up the sleeping baby, wanting desperately to hold the child to her heart and hug her like a teddy bear.

She caught herself. That's right, Boo, pass on the pain to your daughter. Real mature idea.

Oh, shit, I need the cat.

She padded to the living room, turned on a light, and checked Melpomene's favorite chair, an ancient rocker with a red cushion. It was empty.

I know where she is. She probably slipped out when I went to turn off the light in the slave quarters.

The red pillow on the rocking chair was an old one, having once been retired because of a cat-sized indentation in its middle. Boo had bought a new pillow, exactly like the old one, but during the renovation had put it on a shelf in the garage, giving Melpomene the old one out of pity. More than once, though, she'd found the cat on the shelf when Melpomene got caught between the house and its outbuilding.

She opened the door to the garage and there was Melpomene, curled up on the pillow, at eye level. But at the same instant she registered something else—the car was running.

The garage was filled with exhaust.

She held her nose and slipped into the garage, intending to circle the car from the back and turn it off. She didn't look at the floor, so she actually tripped over her husband's body before she saw it.

She knew that he was probably dead, but she didn't stop—turned off the car as planned, and opened the garage door into the courtyard. Air rushed in as she knelt beside Noel. His body was cold.

Her scalp prickled and she began to sweat. Not knowing why, moving like a robot, she picked up the red pillow with the cat on it and brought it out onto the flagstones. The disheveled corpse of the cat made a tiny, agonized sound, and she was suddenly galvanized, no longer moving like a robot, but leaning over Noel, meaning to breathe into his mouth. She nearly vomited, realizing that he was dead before her lips met his. She was aware, as she bent over him, that his crotch was wet, that he had emptied his bladder in death. Yet her hand, having already begun the action, opened his mouth to clear it of obstructions. The night—early morning now—was warm, yet his skin was deadly cold.

Revolted, she fell back on her heels, then stood and staggered out to the courtyard. She touched the cat. Again, it made a feline moan.

She went in and sat by the phone, not wanting to phone 911, wanting more personal attention.

Why don't I know any cops?

Her brain made a leap and she reached for her Rolodex. Langdon!

"Skip? I know it's the middle of the night, but please pick up if you're home. This is Boo Leydecker and my husband's dead. Please pick up . . ."

"Boo, what's going on?"

"Noel's lying on the floor of the garage. The car was on."

"Did you call nine-one-one?"

"He's dead," Boo said simply. "I'm calling you."

"Call nine-one-one now. I'll be right there. Stay out of the garage. Don't touch anything."

As she hung up, Boo felt taken care of, as if things were in someone else's hands at last.

For once.

But what about when she leaves?

She felt the beginnings of panic and fought it off. *Okay, she'll come; she'll leave. I'm going to need someone. My mother lives in Alabama.*

Noel's mother?

Of course not.

Who then?

She couldn't think of a soul. She realized with amazement: *I have no friends.*

In a moment she heard sirens and went to get a robe. Looking out the window, she saw the pathetic furry lump on the red pillow.

• •

Not knowing what Boo would do, Skip called 911 as she pulled on a pair of shorts and a T-shirt. The dispatcher would call Homicide, but Skip called as well, as a courtesy.

Steve heard the whole thing, of course. "Can I do anything? Drive you over?"

She considered. "I don't think so. By the time we got the car, I could be there."

She appreciated the fact that he hadn't asked her why she was going. He would have gone for the excitement alone, she was pretty sure.

There was an element of that in her decision, as well—or at least, of curiosity; Noel was a major player in the Jacomine drama.

But mostly, she wanted to help Boo out, partly because she'd helped with Skip's own problem, but it was more than that. Boo was a neighbor.

She ran the few blocks to Boo's, hearing the sirens of emergency vehicles on their way as well.

A police car was already parked in front of the house. It was muggy out, with a slight drizzle, perhaps the beginning of the hurricane. The air felt edgy.

Boo was on the sidewalk, in a terry cloth robe that was much too hot for the morning. She was holding her baby—no, it was the cat, but she held it like a baby.

Skip said, "You okay?" *Inane question,* she thought. *How could she be?*

Yet Boo said she was, as if they were standing in line at a bank.

She shook her head, her face tragic, but her eyes dry. "I never thought he'd do this. I don't know why, it just didn't occur to me."

"You think he committed suicide?"

Boo nodded. "Oh, God, we had a horrible fight. Will I have to tell them?"

"What was it about?" Skip felt let down, and she was ashamed—she simply saw no way this could connect with Jacomine.

"I said I couldn't trust him with the baby—not to molest her."

"Did you have evidence that he *had* molested her?"

"No, but . . . he was having an affair with the babysitter."

"*Torian?*" It was out of Skip's mouth before she could stop herself.

"You know Torian?"

Skip shrugged. "You know what the French Quarter's like."

"Omigod. Does everyone know she and Noel . . ."

"No. Someone would have said something."

"Did you know Torian's run away? She called here—for Noel. Can you believe that? I picked up to make a call just as she was declaring her love."

"Do you think it was one-sided? Girls do get crushes."

"Oh, no, I listened to the whole conversation. They were having a thing."

"So you told him you heard it."

Boo nodded.

"And what did he say?"

"He said he loved her and wanted to be with her. Something like that."

"That doesn't sound like a man about to commit suicide."

"Well, there's Joy. And my unbelievably stupid remark."

"Don't be so hard on yourself." Skip saw the other woman's sniff of impatience and realized how lame she sounded. "Where is Joy, anyway? She can't be sleeping through all this."

"She is. I was dying to pick her up. I'm making do with Melpomene."

"Pretty docile cat."

"Well, actually she's not usually like this. She's still recovering—she was in the garage, too."

"She was?"

"Uh-huh. At least I got there in time for one of them." She was quiet a moment, staring into space. "The car woke me up, I guess."

A couple of policemen walked toward them, and Skip knew what they were going to say—that Noel was officially dead, that the coroner had said so.

Far from losing her cool, Boo simply thanked them, behaving as if she'd already accepted the fact. Skip wondered if she was too cool, or was simply in shock. Probably the latter, she thought—she'd seen it a lot.

While they waited for the Homicide detectives, she managed to steer the conversation back to Torian. "Did she say where she was?"

Boo shook her head, looking momentarily more miserable.

It's going to hit her soon, Skip thought.

"Look," she said, "let me call someone to come sit with you. I've got a feeling you're going to need help with Joy."

"I'll be okay." She spoke like a robot.

"I'll go talk to the detectives then. Unless there's something I can do."

Boo shook her head.

"By the way, does Torian's mother know about any of this?"

"Not yet. I was going to call her in the morning." She hesitated. "Did you really mean it—about anything you could do?"

"Of course."

"You could let her mother know. Would you mind?"

"Of course not. I'll be glad to."

The night was turning from black to gray as Skip slipped back into bed beside Steve. He turned on his side and wrapped his arms around her. "You okay?"

"Jacomine killed him."

"Yeah? They arrest him yet?"

"Don't be so sarcastic. There's hope—I'm not kidding. Listen to this." She broke away and faced him. "Two animals were locked in a garage full of carbon monoxide, one a full-sized man, the other a seven-pound cat. The cat survived, the man didn't. What does that mean to you?"

"The car wasn't running long enough to kill the cat."

"Right. Therefore—"

"It couldn't have killed the man."

"It must have just been turned on. I'll bet that's what woke Boo up in the first place. Also, the body was on the floor at the street side of the garage."

"Instead of sitting up in the car?"

"Uh-huh. Just as if it was dumped there."

21

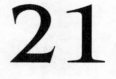

Lise was awakened by a terrifying banging.

The door. Maybe it's Charles.

But she knew it wasn't. It was too insistent and loud—too angry. It must be Wilson.

I'm damned if I'm opening the door in my underwear. She already had on a
T-shirt. She found a pair of shorts and ran a comb through her hair.

"Who is it?"

"Skip Langdon."

Who the fuck is Skip Langdon?

The cop! Sheila's aunt or whoever she is.

"What is it?" she said.

"Could you open the door, please? I need to talk to you."

"It's not a good time right now."

"I wanted to tell you some things. Torian called me last night."

Lise flung open the door. "Torian called *you?*"

The cop seemed startled. She took a step back, but recovered
her composure and even ventured a smile. "There's a lot to talk
about. May I come in?"

Lise stepped aside, hoping she didn't seem too sulky. She didn't want to let the cop in at all. The place was a wreck and even if it hadn't been, it wasn't exactly a showplace. And then, whenever you had someone in your house you had to offer them coffee or something, and that meant work. It also meant they tended to settle in and stay.

The cop came in and closed the door behind her. She had on shorts and a dark green T-shirt.

"Sheila's missing, too. Torian called to say they're together."

"Well, where are they?"

"Torian didn't say. She left a message on my machine." The cop held up a hand. "Don't ask why she didn't call Uncle Jimmy. I wouldn't know."

It had never occurred to Lise to ask that. She barely knew Uncle Jimmy's name.

Langdon said, "Where do you think they are?"

"Where do I think they are? If I knew, I'd be there right now, tanning their little butts. Listen, Officer, this has been my problem for a while—don't you think I've pretty well been back and forth on it by now?"

Once again the big woman, presumably a pistol-packin' mama and a veteran of the mean streets, took a step backward. *What's with her?* Lise thought.

"I just thought you were in the best position to know what her interests are."

"Her interests." The notion made Lise oddly uncomfortable.

Who on God's green Earth knows what Torian's interests are? Other than smoking and giggling with Sheila.

Ah. There's one thing.

She shrugged. "Only the mayor's campaign. But I hardly think this is some kind of political protest."

"Whose campaign?"

Lise thought. "That . . . uh . . . the priest or whoever he is."

"Errol Jacomine?"

"Exactly."

"What kind of interest did she take in the campaign?"

"She was volunteering. I don't know—stuffing envelopes, I guess. Whatever they do."

"Did you know anyone she was working with?"

"No. It was something she did after school. I was at work."

"Did you ever hear her mention anyone's name—either from the campaign or the church?"

"Church?"

"Jacomine's church."

"Oh. No, I never did."

"Not even Noel Treadaway?"

"He's the man she babysits for."

"He was also Jacomine's campaign manager."

"I didn't know that."

"Mrs. Gernhard, can we sit down for a minute?"

Lise shrugged. "Okay." It meant she had to clear newspapers off the sofa. She was damned if she was going to offer coffee or lemonade.

She motioned Langdon to the sofa and took a straight chair for herself.

The cop said, "Did you know your daughter was involved with Noel Treadaway?"

"Involved? What do you mean, 'involved'?"

"Romantically involved."

"Oh, come on, she's just a kid."

The cop didn't speak, just stared back at her until she burst out, "What the fuck are you talking about? How could you know a thing like that? I'll tell you—you couldn't. You've been listening to some lying little . . . Sheila! She's probably jealous just because Torian . . ."

The cop was standing up. "I guess you were right. This isn't the best time to talk about it."

"Wait. Wait a minute. I'm sorry if I was rude."

The cop didn't sit again, simply stood there, towering. "I'm telling you this because I promised Boo Leydecker I would—Noel Treadaway's wife. She felt it was her responsibility, only she isn't quite up to it. Her husband died last night."

"Noel Treadaway's dead?" She waved her hands in front of her, crossing them in the air, like some demented referee to whom no one was paying the least attention. "What are you saying to me? First my daughter's having an affair with a married man twice her age—my God, he could go to jail for this!—and then you tell me he's dead."

"I'm sorry."

Lise sucked air, trying to take this in, not having any idea how to do it.

Could this be true?

Little Torian? She's just a baby.

"Tell me, Mrs. Gernhard—did Sheila work on the Jacomine campaign as well?"

"How would I know? What the fuck do I care about Sheila?"

"Mrs. Gernhard, listen to me. Two girls are missing and a man is dead. This is serious, do you understand that?"

"Of course I understand it." Lise turned her voice to ice. "Torian is my daughter."

"Did Sheila work on the campaign?"

"I really don't know a thing about Sheila."

"Can you think of any reason why she'd run away from home?"

"Perhaps . . ." Lise raised her head and looked down her nose ". . . perhaps she's desperately unhappy."

"I'm sorry you don't feel like cooperating. I'm doing my best to find Sheila, and I've just told you Torian's with her. Don't you want to find your daughter?"

"Of course I want to find my daughter." Lise heard the defiance in her own voice. She sounded like some yappy little dog—all defense, no offense. "You're really being quite offensive."

The big woman shrugged and left a card on the table. "If you change your mind, give me a call."

In a pig's eye, you condescending bitch.

●   ●

Skip left running, heart pounding, feeling desperate to do something. Almost anything.

If this were someone else's kid you'd be cool, right? So be cool.

Deliberately, she slowed her pace, but her heart still pounded.

It had simply never occurred to her to connect the girls' disappearance with Jacomine. The suspicion that this had something to do with Torian's volunteer job, with Noel's death, filled her with panic.

God, he's dangerous! I think he's one of the most dangerous people I ever saw.

Sheila, Sheila, what were you thinking of?

And Torian. She could have killed Torian. What the hell was she doing involved with a married man twice her age, a man with many times her experience and no ability whatsoever to make her happy or even take her on a date? The years between thirty and forty-five were one thing, but the gap between a kid of fifteen and an adult was almost like the gulf between being five and being twenty.

Jacomine's church had a million group homes, and probably safehouses and just plain hidey-holes. Sheila could be anywhere.

If she's with them. The Treadaway connection could be a coincidence.

She sighed. *Face it, it's the best lead you have.*

Why the hell would she run away, dammit? Things were going fine. Weren't they?

Sheila had run away once before, but that was when she was thirteen and had just come to live with Jimmy Dee, still struggling with the death of her mother. They had found her sleeping near St. Louis Cathedral.

In Skip's heart of hearts, she thought the reason must be very different from the other time—that had been to demonstrate how unhappy she was. This time it must have to do with Torian.

She must have known all along where Torian was. And then something set her off. Maybe a call for help. Maybe Torian needed her.

Something, anyhow. Some incident.

She knocked on Jimmy Dee's back door and entered without waiting for an answer. "Is she back?"

Kenny came running down the hall. His sweet freckled face was pinched and a little pale. "No. She hasn't even called."

He's scared to death.

Well, no wonder, poor baby. His daddy left and his mother died, and then he had to leave everyone else he knew to come here. The thought of losing someone is probably a lot more real to him than it is to most kids.

She smiled, keeping up a good front. "Torian did, though. Uncle Jimmy didn't tell you?" Torian had called while Skip and Steve were babysitting Kenny, and they had phoned Jimmy Dee as soon as they picked up the message.

"Yeah, he told me." His face said he wasn't reassured.

"Don't worry about it, sweetheart, she's just a teenager. You know how they are."

"Hey. I'm one, too."

"That's what I mean."

He opened the referigerator, which she took for a good sign.

"Where's Uncle Jimmy?"

"He went out to get milk. He thinks I can't go to school without it."

"How's he doing?"

"He's trying to act cool, but he keeps dropping things and he put on one blue and one black sock—he's so weirded out, I didn't even say anything."

Skip's heart went out to both of them—each pretending for the other. "Tell him to chill out, will you? And you chill yourself— she'll probably be back by noon."

Steve was in the shower, but he'd made coffee. She poured herself some and found some bread for toast. Steve came out drying his hair. "News?"

"The worst." She filled him in.

"So," he said, "you think Jacomine killed Noel and probably kidnapped Torian. Then he got her to call Sheila and ask for help, whereupon he snatched her, too."

She stared at him, surprised he'd spoken so bluntly. "Yes. In my darker moments. Talk me out of it—go ahead."

"Let's kick it around a little. What would be the motive for such a dastardly deed?"

"Don't joke about it."

"Sorry. I'm trying to cheer you up."

Skip barely heard. Her mind was on his question. "Maybe it's something to do with Noel's leaving the campaign. Did we talk about that?"

"You said Jane Storey told you."

"Okay. That was yesterday. He died yesterday. Cause and effect?"

"Listen, I know you think Jacomine's the Prince of Darkness, but that's a pretty extreme reaction to a person quitting a job."

She chewed a bite of toast and considered. "Honestly, I don't know that he's not capable of it. The man is not normal—extreme is his middle name. But that's not what I was really suggesting. I was thinking maybe Noel quit because of a disagreement over policy. Maybe he simply refused to play Jacomine's games—which were no doubt illegal. Do you see what I'm getting at?"

Steve nodded, looking serious. "Yeah. He knew too much. I'm sorry to say that sounds all too much like Jacomine's form of craziness."

"Did I ever tell you about Nikki?"

"Who?"

"Nikki's the woman from the church who told me all the stories about Jacomine—how he sexually abused his followers and tortured them. Remember?"

He nodded.

"Well, she's dead. When I first started working on this, I tried to find her—she was my only witness. And I did, all right. In the morgue." She sat back and looked at him. "So now we have two bodies."

"Oh, God. You must be terrified for Sheila."

"Who, me? Feel my heart." He reached a hand out. "On second thought, don't. We can't lose any time here."

"Hey, I just thought of something. If Sheila knew where Torian was, someone else might too."

"Right. I was going to talk to her other friends today. That is, if I could figure out who they were. I guess I'll start with the kids who came to her birthday party." She picked up the phone and called Jimmy Dee. "Kenny. You still there? Listen, does Sheila talk about her friends at all? Did she mention anyone in particular in the last few days?"

"I don't know, I never listen to that crap. I mean . . . uh . . . excuse my French. Hey, some dude called last night. Hold it, I got a name." He left and came back. "Joe Eddie. Does that help?"

"He didn't say his last name?"

"You mean it isn't Eddie?"

"Go to school, kid."

She did the same herself, after she had cornered Jimmy Dee for the party guest list. The second kid she interviewed—an elegant blonde named Mallory—placed Joe Eddie instantly. Mallory tossed her white locks over her shoulder. "Well, yeah. He's her boyfriend, I think. She talks about him all the time. Listen, she's not getting in trouble, is she?"

Skip thought, *Now there's an irrelevant question.* She said, "Does he go to Newman?"

"Uh . . . no."

"Well, where does he go."

"He . . . um . . . well, I don't know."

"Mallory. How does she know him?"

Mallory looked at her lap, aware she was tattling. "I think he just . . . um . . . from the deli."

"What deli?" Hardly any Newman kids lived in the Quarter. They couldn't know what a way of life delis were.

"I don't know . . . wait! A new place. Does that help?"

"On Dumaine?"

"I don't know."

The sky was clear as she drove to the French Quarter. If the hurricane were really coming—and the forecasters were still saying it was—it would be squally all day. It would rain awhile and then quit, and then do it again. Each squall would get more intense, the rain more persistent, the wind faster and nastier, until it finally reached hurricane force—seventy-four miles per hour, or more if Hannah kept up her strength.

The deli was the one on Dumaine. Joe Eddie was due at work that afternoon at three. Skip, pulling out her badge for the occasion, had no trouble getting his address.

She was delighted to hear he worked late. With any luck at all, it meant he slept till noon. So he'd be easy to find and if her luck held, a little groggy.

She was right on almost all counts. Though she got there considerably before noon, Joe Eddie was most assuredly up—and smoking pot, if the dense atmosphere was any indication.

Not one to pass up an opportunity, Skip said by way of greeting, "You been smokin' pot?"

"'Course not."

But now she had the advantage. "Tell me about Sheila Ritter."

"Huh?" He looked stunned, but there was also fear in his face—as if he knew exactly what she meant, he just couldn't believe she could know.

She rapped her knuckles on the pine kitchen table—a table several steps up from one a struggling kid with his job would be likely to have. The other furnishings also exhibited stolid blue-collar taste. He probably lived with his parents, which gave her even more leverage.

"Talk fast, or you're going to Headquarters. Look, you're due at work at three o'clock. You're going to miss work, and you're going to get fired. And your mom's gonna find out what you smoke when she's not home."

He looked absolutely incredulous, as if he'd somehow stepped into the presence of an amazing and astounding psychic.

She said, "When's the last time you saw her?"

"Yesterday, okay?" He was as sullen as a five-year-old. "You know that, anyhow. We went for a walk, I said something she didn't like, and she got mad." He shrugged. "That was that. She tells you any different, she's lying."

From years of experience and hundreds of war stories, Skip had come there with a pretty good idea of what had happened; she now considered it confirmed. She grabbed his hair and shoved him up against a kitchen counter, making sure it struck him squarely in the back; his head banged into the cabinet above. "Hey!" he yelled.

"Is that what you did to her? Huh? Something like that? And then you unzipped her jeans—right?"

"No!"

"She yelled, but you hit her to make her shut up." Once more, Skip banged his head against the cabinet. "Like that."

240

"She asked for it, goddammit. Little bitch been hustlin' me for months now . . ."

"So you just thought you'd rape her."

"Rape! Goddammit! I got a little affectionate, and she ran away. Shit! Lying little bitch!"

Get a grip, Skip. Walk out, now. If he did rape her, he's going to jail—and I don't mean juvie. If he didn't, whatever he did do's at least going to cost him his job. You don't need to beat him up. Okay?

But she banged him one more time for good measure.

"Where'd she go when she left?"

"I don't know. To Torian's probably. They're two of a kind. Little flirtboxes."

"Let me tell you something, Don Juan. You ever lay a hand on either of those girls, or any girl in the state of Louisiana you meet on that job of yours, and I personally will cut your nuts off. Understand?"

He nodded sullenly.

"Say it!"

"Understood."

"Understood, Detective Langdon, ma'am."

He repeated it, but she left still fuming, not even remorseful for banging him around. She was toying with the idea of returning with a baseball bat.

22

• •

Daddy had had a breakfast talk followed by a meeting with some pol or other, and by the time he arrived, Potter had a wild woman for him. He was sitting in his own office, trying to cool her down, when he saw Daddy walk behind her, waving on the way to his office. Potter kept a poker face. Good thing the cop couldn't see behind her or she'd have turned around and attacked. Potter excused himself.

"I got some good news and some bad news."

"Gimme the good." He didn't like the look on Daddy's face. Irritated. The meeting must not have gone well.

"It's done."

Daddy did not change expression, just blinked and nodded slightly, but Potter thought he saw a slight lowering of the shoulders, the tiniest sign of tension leaving the candidate's body, and he rejoiced in it. "The bad?"

"The cop's here."

"Langdon? Here, in this office?"

"Hello, Mr. Jacomine." She was standing in the doorway behind Potter, had probably heard Daddy's voice.

"Detective Langdon, what on Earth can we do for you?"

"Mr. Menard didn't tell you?"

"He hasn't had a chance."

"I want Torian Gernhard and Sheila Ritter."

"I beg your pardon?"

"Come on, Jacomine, I know you're hiding them. They've got problems, and you're taking care of them. Harboring a minor is a criminal offense, as you will undoubtedly claim you didn't know. Personally, I don't give a shit about that, I just want the girls. Now."

"Officer Langdon, I believe you're on leave from the police department."

Potter could have sworn that surprised her. Daddy pressed his advantage. "Which makes me wonder what makes you think you have a right to be here."

"Call me a concerned citizen. Where are the kids?"

"What kids?"

"Don't play games with me, Jacomine. Sheila and Torian."

"Oh. Those are the names of kids. I'm afraid I never heard of either of them."

Potter said, "May I show you out, Detective Langdon?"

"Look, guys, it's like this. You give me the kids and I never bother you again. Do you understand what I'm saying? I leave you completely alone. You don't give me the kids and I report you for kidnapping."

Daddy actually laughed. Potter had to give him credit. "On what evidence, Officer?"

"Don't fuck with me, Jacomine. You're running for office; there's lots of ways I could get to you—starting with the Times-Picayune."

"Have at it, Langdon. I have a thousand bigger fish to fry." Potter held himself very stiff, to keep his muscles from twitching.

The cop didn't answer, simply turned around and left, but in a cloud of something Potter could almost feel. Anger, he thought. The cop would as soon bust up the office as not. He made sure she was gone, and then he rejoined Daddy.

Lightning blazed from Daddy's eyes. "Shut the door, Potter."

And when he had: "Who the fuck is Sheila Ritter?"

"Uh . . . well . . . yes, Paulette called this morning. She's . . . uh . . . she's the kid Langdon's landlord adopted."

"Langdon's kid then."

"No, she's . . ."

"Don't 'no' me. She's Langdon's fucking kid, the little bitch!" He lowered his voice and repeated the phrase, as if thinking. "Langdon's fucking kid."

He raised it again: "Tell me she's full of shit. Tell me Paulette doesn't have her."

Potter raised his shoulders, trying to show the thing was out of his control. "The kid showed up at Paulette's. Totally unexpectedly. Torian must have . . ."

"Torian! Goddammit! What kind of fucking security do you have over there? None, right? None! What kind of operation you running, Mr. Menard? Is this a campaign or a motherfucking kindergarten?" His voice was so loud on the last word that Potter feared everyone in the office would hear. He was desperate to shush Daddy, but nobody shushed Daddy.

"Do I have to draw you a picture? She's a fucking spy, you idiot."

"With all due respect, Daddy, I don't think so. She had some trouble with a boy . . ."

Daddy was shaking his head, as if unable to fathom how Potter could be so slow.

"I can't believe you ever worked for the government. Sometimes I just can't believe it. Langdon's a cop who's trying to bring me down; so she plants a mole in our organization. Her own kid, for convenience' sake. But even she thinks that's a little too obvious. So she comes by and kicks up some big stink, says she'll leave us alone if we'll just give up the kid—oh, shit, Potter, I don't know why the fuck I keep you around."

Potter stared at him, astounded. Could Daddy be right?

Surely not. Paulette had said the kid was pretty upset, and Paulette knew kids. But suppose this one had been coached.

He was starting to feel foolish. The thing was starting to look as obvious as a pigeon drop.

"Daddy, I . . . I don't know what to say."

"You big fat idiot, Potter Menard. I swear to God I don't know why I hired you. Biggest mistake of my life, I say this before Jesus. If you'd had one grain of sense, you'd have had that girl out of there and that detective out of our office. You'd have fucking taken care of it all by the time I came in. What the fuck is wrong with you?"

Potter was wondering that himself. He hated it when Daddy got like this, it made him feel bad about himself; made him doubt his training. Daddy had instincts, intuition that Potter simply didn't. Potter ran on rote learning. What he did, he was good at; he had no qualms about what he was trained for, but it just wasn't enough. Things escaped him.

The only thing to do was redouble his efforts.

"Goddammit, let's go to Paulette's."

"What?"

"Get the car, Potter. Just get the car." Daddy was shaking his head, as if at a half-wit.

Potter wasn't quite sure why they were going to Paulette's, but it wasn't his job to question Daddy's decisions. His job right now was to drive.

Daddy didn't say a word on the way over, and when they parked in front of Paulette's, he simply got out of the car, slammed the door, and stalked up the walk, Potter at his heels like a puppy.

"Paulette! Paulette, what the fuck is going on here?"

"Daddy? What's wrong?" Paulette came out of the kitchen wearing an apron. She'd probably been fixing lunch for the kids.

"What in the name of God are you doin' shelterin' the spawn of the enemy?"

Paulette's face was gray. "What are you talking about?"

"Miss Sheila Ritter, that's what the fuck I'm fucking talking about."

Two white girls came out of the kitchen. A black one started down the stairs, then thought better of it and stopped halfway.

One of the white ones was Torian, the other was much bigger—overweight and awkward. She looked like any kid—no smarter, no more evil—just a kid.

Daddy raised a finger and pointed it—Jesus accusing the money changers. "Miss Sheila Ritter, I presume."

The girl, who had looked only confused till a moment ago, now turned to Jell-O. She looked around frantically for an escape.

Potter saw instantly that Daddy was right. The minute he called her name, she knew the game was up. She panicked.

"Sheila Ritter. Come here to destroy everything we've built." The finger moved to Torian. "And you, Torian Gernhard—this is how you repay us. We give you shelter, and you strive only to bring forth our destruction."

Paulette said, "Daddy, wait a minute. Hold on."

"Traitor!" His face was an electrical storm. He pushed Paulette aside and strolled toward the white girls, now huddling together in terror.

"Sheila Ritter, I demand to know who sent you and what your orders are."

"Orders? What kind of orders?" The girl looked at Potter, as if he could answer her question.

"You tell me, you little spy."

Daddy moved closer to her, brushing aside Paulette, who deferred to him, though in truth she was taller than he was, probably outweighed him, and could certainly take him in a fight—at least Potter thought so.

The girl took a step back, and so did her friend. They still clung together, as if one could protect the other.

"Torian Gernhard, move out of my way."

White people were so transparent, the way their blood betrayed them. They either blushed or turned pale. Torian was the color of a calla lily—a pure, stark white. And so thin, her little collarbone sticking out at the top of her T-shirt. Potter felt for her.

She did not move. "No! Sheila's my friend."

"No? Excuse me, did you tell me no?" This was the one thing Daddy found intolerable. Did not forgive. "Did you say no to Errol Jacomine, soon-to-be mayor of New Orleans?"

Sheila Ritter stepped forward. She had recovered from her initial panic—probably thought Paulette wouldn't let anything happen to her.

She squeezed her hands tight around something she was holding—what, Potter couldn't see. Great red apples grew wild on her cheeks: she was furious.

Look out, girl, he thought, and the thought surprised him.

"Why shouldn't she?" said Sheila. "You're not the mayor yet, and what if you were? That doesn't give you the right . . ."

Daddy said, "Do you know who you're talking to? Do you really have any idea?"

The girl stepped back, the apples fading, a new wariness settling in. He moved toward her, and Potter saw the wariness deepen to fear. Daddy grabbed her elbow, but she twisted away, stumbling backwards. "I am your *Daddy!*"

The divine fire was in Daddy's eyes.

The girl made an inquisitive sound that ended up a whimper.

"I am your father on this Earth!" He was using his preaching voice now, singsonging his words. It sounded sonorous and powerful from the pulpit, but this was a front hallway. Sheila was nearly as pale as Torian.

Paulette stepped forward. "Daddy, I don't think . . ."

He turned on her: "Leave me be, whore! 'Yours is a harlot's brow and you are resolved to know no shame.' " When he got started on Bible verses, there was no stopping him. " 'Your adulteries, your lustful whoring, your wanton lewdness are an offense to me.' "

He was trying to get past her, but Paulette had maneuvered herself between him and Sheila.

The girl bolted.

Ran right past them both as they struggled. Potter reached out for her, but she threw something at him—the something she had been holding. Not knowing what it was, wincing, he lost his opportunity.

It was an open jar of mustard, which splattered him with rich, golden gunk. Further disconcerted, as if it were some kind of toxin, he hesitated another split second, enough for her to get out the door. Its bang woke him up.

He yelled, "Stay here, y'all!" knowing Paulette, at least, would give chase and possibly Daddy would as well. The last thing they needed to do was present a roaring spectacle in Paulette's mostly white neighborhood.

Sheila was down the steps, heading across the street by the time Potter got out the door. It was pouring rain. As Potter got to the curb, she made the other side, and simultaneously, a white Cadillac bore down on him.

He thought: *Fuck! Chasing a kid in a residential neighborhood. What in hell am I doing?*

But it wasn't like she ever had a chance. She was a somewhat overweight teenage girl and he was a trained agent. He simply loped the few paces it took him to catch up with her, but rather than do anything crude, he ran along behind her so he could reason with her. It was bad enough, a large black man covered with mustard chasing an underage white girl—he didn't want to have to struggle with her, especially didn't want to have to put his arm in her mouth to keep her quiet.

She had yelled only once, as the Cadillac came into sight, but he hadn't heard what she said. That was good. Maybe nobody else had either. Why she was quiet now he didn't know, but he suspected it had to do with breathing. He could hear her gasping.

He said, "Sheila, you got to give us a chance. We helped Torian when no one else would, you know that. We don't mean you any harm, girl. Just come back and talk with us."

She glanced around briefly, and he saw the terror in her eyes. Okay, that wasn't working. He stepped up his pace and jogged alongside her.

"You can't outrun me, girl. You see that? Let's say for a minute you're right. You're in big trouble, just like you think. Say I'm as mean as I look. I'm big, you can see that, can't you? Say in a minute I'm gon' reach over and grab you, take you back to Paulette's and have a nice little talk with you and your girlfriend. Just for a minute say all that's true. Then, what's gon' happen is this: I'm gon' reach out and grab you and that's gon' be that.

"But I'm real, *real* mean. For every second you struggle with me, every sound you utter, and I do mean *every* sound . . ."

She screamed.

Apparently he'd given her the idea.

He reached out and hugged her close. "Okay, that's *one* for your buddy Torian. Do it again and that's two."

He could see the fight ebb out of her. She collapsed against him, tears streaming, sounds coming out of her, but soft ones. Mostly, she was just trying to catch her breath. She'd probably never run that hard in her life. She was exhausted, apparently unable even to stand, and that was excellent.

It meant he could hold her like a little girl, helping her walk, a benevolent uncle rather than the neighborhood terror.

Still, someone might have seen and called the police. Unwilling to go to Paulette's house, he put Sheila in his car, which was wedged between two others, so that reading the plate would be pretty hard. He peeled out of there and circled the block, coming in the back way.

When he got her inside she recovered her voice. "Where's Torian?"

Daddy was sitting at the kitchen table, Paulette hovering, fixing him something to drink.

Daddy gave her a narrow-eyed, appraising look that found a world of fault. The "evil eye," Potter might have said, if he'd associated the phrase with the man he worked for.

"Lock her up," he said.

The girl was pathetic—hair wet and dripping, eyes darting. She looked frantically at Paulette, who gave her the same harsh look Daddy had. Then she nodded and reached out a hand.

"Here's the key."

● ●

"Okay," said Steve Steinman, "so now you know why she ran away—some sort of trauma with a boy."

"Steve, she might have been raped."

"I didn't mean to make light of it. I just don't want to assume the worst."

Skip smiled. A good quality, optimism. Steve could keep it up when she couldn't.

"Yeah, that's got to be it. It happened yesterday, she disappeared yesterday. She knew where Torian was—which wasn't home—which meant she had some place to go. So she went there."

"So if we knew where Torian was—"

"Listen, I want you to help me on this."

He tried not to look too pleased—she could actually see the parade of emotions on his face—surprise, then pleasure, then his need to cover it up. There had been arguments in the past over his eagerness to help her. "Me?" he said. "Sure. I'll do anything."

"What I have in mind is right up your alley. First a little breaking and entering—"

"Hey, I'm not all that experienced."

"Followed by some computer expertise."

"Really?" His smile was like something on Christmas morning. Computers were his love.

"Really. We might need to copy some stuff. Do you need any disks or anything?"

"Depends. I only have the little ones."

"How many kinds are there?"

"Two."

"Better get both kinds."

"Right." He stood, saluted, kissed her hand, and left.

She dialed Jimmy Dee. "Who installed your alarm system?"

"Why?"

"Let's put it this way—was it someone who might do a little illegal job in the interests of finding a lost kid?"

"Oh my God," he said as he got her drift. "What's going on, Skip? I'm going crazy over here."

"Listen, I know why she left, and it has to do with a boy. I've got a plan to find her. Just bear with me, okay? I'll explain later."

He sighed. "I know someone who's actually served time for little illegal jobs. Rodney Parrott."

"Can I trust him?"

"Are you kidding? I've known him for years. I've got enough on him to send him to Angola for the rest of his life. Also, he owes me *beaucoup* favors. Let me give him a call and explain how he not only doesn't mess with my best friend Skip for any reason, ever, he gives her a tape accepting all responsibility for certain jobs I happen to know about, and on which the statute of limitations has not expired. And then he does everything she says."

Skip had rarely heard Dee-Dee so grimly serious. She said finally, "Since when do you consort with criminals?"

"His mom's a family friend—I've done her some favors."

He might have given her a bantering answer, but he hadn't. "Dee-Dee?" she said. "It'll be okay. Believe me."

"You're gonna love this guy. Cutest drag queen you ever want to meet." That was more like him—if he'd been on the Titanic, he would have danced all night.

In five minutes her phone rang. "Rodney Parrott. Jimmy Dee said you had an emergency."

"Yeah. Here's the deal." She explained what she wanted.

"When do you want to do it?"

"Tonight. Two places—or only one if we get what we want the first time out. An office and a church."

"Woo. Are we in luck. No way in hell we could do it without a hurricane. But you know what? I see something beautiful coming together here; a crime of rare beauty and distinction; a crime for the annals of crime."

"Hey, I just need a simple B and E."

"Listen, we gotta get started right away. Where can we meet?"

"Here. Come on over."

"Be there in an hour. Give me addresses on the targets."

When she had, she said to Steve: "He doesn't exactly talk like a common criminal. Or even your ordinary drag queen."

"What does he talk like?"

"Professor's kid, maybe."

He was about an hour late, but well worth the wait. He looked like neither that nor a drag queen—certainly not bookish, decidedly not effeminate. First of all, he could have been a movie star. Second, he was black. He was stocky—buffed, in fact—and drop-dead gorgeous. He had dark, dark skin and close-cropped hair. Skip just couldn't see him in feathers and sequins—and certainly not lurking in libraries.

Then she had another little surprise. She had simply thought of herself as chief of this operation. It hadn't occurred to her that outside the department, democracy prevailed. Rodney roared in like a lion—a lion on speed, chain-smoking, talking nonstop, carrying pencils, pens, papers, and the tape Dee-Dee had promised, which he turned over immediately.

"Okay, we got to hit the church. The office building might be a much harder hit—might take some planning." This would have been her call, but she resented Rodney's making it—she and Steve had talked it out in advance and decided Jacomine would probably keep church records at the church.

Still she said, "Wait a minute. What if what we want's not there?"

"Don't worry, don't worry. I got a backup plan. But we might have to wait till the power goes off."

"What if it doesn't?"

He looked at her with pity. "Sugar, are we gonna have a hurricane or not? You need this ASAP, right?"

"Right."

"Well, we can probably get in the church by about nine-thirty—the other one's problematical."

"Keep talking."

"See, the key to busting a security system is electricity, pure and simple. And phones, of course. You know why most burglars get caught? The halfway smart ones, I mean—not the crackhead amateurs. Because they forget the phone lines. Now what happens when your alarm goes off?"

Skip started to answer, but it became evident that wasn't necessary.

"What happens is, your monitoring service is notified, and they in turn call the cops. Now, how is your service notified? Over the phone wire." He checked out his audience, possibly expecting applause.

Skip and Steve contented themselves with appreciative nods, which seemed to be enough.

"So the first thing is to cut the phone lines. Fortunatement—"

he gave the word a faux French pronunciation—"about eighty percent of those are outside. All you have to do is take your clipboard
and you can get to 'em—probably for both jobs—certainly for the
church. Follow me so far?"

"We're riveted. But what makes you so sure about the church?"

"'Cause it's done."

"What's done?"

"The lines are cut, everybody's gone home, and the power's off."

"What?"

"Hey—this is Rodney. And this is the greatest job I ever
pulled—bar none, I tell you. Bar none."

"You want to explain?"

"Oh, man, a hurricane! I'm only working in storms from now
on. I've got a whole new lease on life."

"Are you forgetting I'm a police officer?"

"Hey, sugar, you're not about to turn me in—you're commit-
ting the same felony I am."

"Don't get too cocky. Your word against mine, remember. Then
there's the tape."

"Hey, I'm saving your kid. You're going to be grateful the rest
of your life."

She stayed silent on that one.

"Hello? Okay, to explain. See, all alarm systems have a backup
battery—even the cheapies. And churches usually put out good
money for their systems—they go in for quality. The quick and
dirty companies sometimes use four-amp-hour batteries. The good
ones are seven-amp-hours—so you gotta figure on that. Meant I had
to move fast, right? You want to save your kid, and everything."

Skip nodded, trying to keep her face neutral.

"So I said to myself, how many people are going to be working in a church when a hurricane's on the way? One or two,
maybe—skeleton staff at best. I figured whoever was there was just
looking for an excuse to go home, and there was no chance in hell
of getting a phone repair on Hurricane Hannah day. Sure enough,
two people came strolling out two minutes after I hit the phone

line. So then I reconnected it, and gave the church a call. Nothing. After that, I marched up and knocked. *Nada.*

"So I cut it again, got out my trusty bolt cutters, and cut the padlock on the utility room—just about all buildings have them, and inside's the power switch. You just throw it, and *voilà!* Power's history. Seven hours till blastoff." He looked at his watch. "You roll at nine-thirty."

"Well, now, I don't want to seem picky, but what if we have to do the damned office building as well?"

"*Naturellement,* I checked it out. Trouble is, they got lots of rent-a-cops, and they're probably monitoring closed circuit TV. Get my drift? Can't really prowl the perimeter."

"That's a problem."

"Ah, but not on Hannah night. A beautiful thing, isn't it? All we have to do is wait till Mother Nature herself takes the power away." He frowned. "'Course the downside is, we have to wait seven hours after that."

"Maybe not."

"What you got in mind?"

"Well, if the phones are out, who cares if the alarm goes off? Sure, we have to work with a lot of noise, but who's going to call the cops? All the phone lines'll be out."

"I am majorly impressed. You got a great criminal mind on you."

Steve said, "You know what they say about cops and crooks. So all we have to do is wait, huh? And hit the church at nine-thirty?"

"How you going to get in?"

Skip said, "I've got picks."

Rodney shook his head. "I don't know. What if something goes wrong?"

"Nothing will."

"I better go with you."

$\bullet \quad \bullet$

The hardest part was waiting. But at nine-fifteen, they were assembled at Skip's, all in dark clothes, Skip with her burglar tools and Steve with a backpack full of disks.

It was barely drizzling when they left the French Quarter, but raining hard by the time they got to Metairie. There was hardly anyone on the streets.

Rodney was exultant. "Man, would you look at this? I'm gonna pray for a hurricane every day."

"How do we make sure the alarm's disabled?"

"See? I knew you were gon' need me." He produced a flashlight, which he shined through a glass pane in the side door. "See that? It's a dead key panel."

"Meaning?"

"If the alarm were on, the red light would be blinking. Ergo, Rodney rules."

"Hope you're right."

"Ah, ah, ah. Dis Rodney, and I don't help you when you can't work those picks."

In fact, she couldn't work the picks, though she was convinced it was because she was nervous, having a genuine burglar there. Expertly, Rodney took over and then said he'd stand guard.

Once inside, Skip again felt like a fifth wheel. She and Steve found what appeared to be an office, and Steve immediately set to work at the computer, cool as a master criminal. Skip busied herself with files, but she didn't have much hope for them.

"Skip. Look at this." Steve had turned up a list of church properties.

"Can you copy it?"

"Already have."

Desultorily, wishing she had a skill for the occasion, she began to go through desk drawers—the property, she suspected, of some innocent secretary.

But there, right in the middle drawer, waiting to be mailed—was an envelope addressed to Potter Menard, with a Post-it attached. It was unsealed; the Post-it read: "cut check for hit." Inside was a note: "Daddy asked me to send you a little bonus for a job well done. He wants to thank you for keeping the unpleasantness in the family."

She was beside herself. Who would leave a record of a hit?

Someone so confident she'd gotten sloppy. Someone a little out of touch with reality, which of course was what happened to cult members.

And someone in Jacomine's confidence. She'd have to find out who this secretary was.

The thing just might be real, and it might refer to Noel Treadaway—in fact probably did, given the timing. But she could think of absolutely no way—considering her own criminal status—of getting it into evidence. Yet it certainly told her where to look. Somehow it might be proved later on that Menard had gotten a bonus right after Treadaway was killed—there might be a record in the church checkbook, for instance. With other evidence, it might add up to something.

And the secretary might be squeezeable.

Steve said, "Oh, wow."

"What?"

"Pay dirt. Check this out."

It was a list headed INACTIVE MEMBERS. "As in 'ex,' " Steve said. "Or anyway, let's hope so. Anything else we need?"

"Sure. Let's scour the whole damn system."

"I more or less have."

"You're kidding."

"It's this way—Rodney just said we had sixty seconds at the outside."

"Sixty seconds till what? Till he calls the cops?"

"Let's go, dammit."

I hate democracy. But she went.

And Rodney was having a small conniption. "Do you know how long you were in there? Five and a half minutes. I can't believe it—five and a half!"

It had seemed like half an hour, at least.

Rodney said, "'Course nobody came by—who'd be out in this?"

"Then what are you so upset about?"

"Rules is rules. We do it again, and you toe the line or I spank you."

23

• •

They dropped Rodney off and started calling names on the "inactive" list. After two hang-ups, one "fuck-you," and three "don't-know-what-you're-talking-abouts," Skip decided to go visiting.

"How can you do that?" Steve protested. "It's after ten o'clock."

"I'm a mother whose child is missing. Is that an emergency or not?"

He shrugged.

"You want to be the father?"

Again, he tried to conceal his pleased look.

First they tried Betty Landry, who lived in Mid-City. It was pouring rain as they walked to her front steps.

A man opened the door, a black man about fifty-eight, Skip would have said, starting to go gray at the temples. He was a huge man, and the fact that he wore only jockey shorts made him look like a sumo wrestler. His belly was like a great black cauldron, so smooth and round it was all Skip could do not to reach out and touch it.

"We're looking for Betty Landry. I know it's late, but our daughter's missing and . . ."

"She don' know nothin' 'bout that."

They heard a voice behind him: "Lemme talk to the people, James Allen."

"You don't want nothin' to do with this."

"Well, how do I know till I find out?"

He stepped aside for a woman in a pink flowered robe. "Oh." She looked very surprised. "I thought you were a lady I used to work for."

Skip saw she was losing interest fast. "Our daughter's only fifteen, and she's been missing a week. We're terrified, Ms. Landry. Somehow she got involved with this church that we understood—"

Landry's eyes turned to hard, nasty black beans. "Who give you my name?"

"I tol' you . . ."

"Shut up, James Allen." To Skip, she said, "You tell me who give you my name 'fore I call the po-lice."

The po-lice were the last people Skip wanted to see. She made her voice as soft as she could. "Nobody. I got it off a list."

"What list?"

"Look. My daughter's been missing a week."

The eyes turned harder still, to glittery glass.

"I don't know nothin' about your daughter." She slammed the door.

Steve said, "I get a feeling people who've been involved with Jacomine would just as soon you didn't bring it up."

"I liked it better when I was a cop. Warmer welcome. On the other hand, the next address is in Metairie. Tonight I don't have to worry about jurisdiction. It's a couple—maybe they have children."

"Hot dog—the lights are on," said Steve when they found the house.

A white woman came to the door, looked out through a peephole.

"Mrs. Todd?" Skip repeated the little speech she'd given Landry.

"I'm sorry, my husband's not in right now—he's gone out for candles. For when the power goes."

Skip had a brainstorm. She said, "Sheila's never been in a hurricane. She'll be so scared. You see, she got mixed up with this crazy church—"

"Did you say church?"

"Yes, ma'am. Something about a lamb."

"Get out of here. Get off my property now!"

A car turned into the driveway. A man got out carrying a paper bag. The woman flung open the door. "Paul! They're from Daddy."

Without hesitation, he shouted, "Call the police! Now!"

The woman slammed the door shut. Steve whispered, "Let's get out of here," but Skip shouted, "We're not from Jacomine. He's got our daughter and we're desperate. We'll do anything we can to find her."

"You get away from here." There was no mistaking the expression on his face: it was terror.

• •

The good-looking black dude locked Sheila in with Torian. Torian had been alone till then, ushered upstairs when Sheila ran away. She wasn't even in her own room, she was in Sheila and Adonis's. She was so scared she'd have called Lise if she'd had a telephone.

Torian ran to her. Though they'd been separated only a few minutes, the two girls hugged. "Sheila, what's going on? The Rev acted like a maniac. What did I do wrong?"

"I think trusting these people was the only thing we did wrong. Auntie Skip's always thought he was crazy. But Paulette! She seemed so nice."

"Oh, so did he! He called me 'Miss Gernhard.' He treated me like a real person. I thought he was the greatest man I'd ever known."

Sheila walked to the window.

"What are you doing?"

"Trying to see if there's a way out. Look, I'll bet I could get down that drainpipe."

Torian went over to look. "You've got to be kidding. I couldn't do that in a million years." She was overcome with the sadness of feeling unequal to the situation.

"Too bad. I could do it, but it might not hold my weight."

She snapped her fingers. "You know what? I've got a better idea—why not just open the window and yell? If I'd yelled a few minutes ago, the cops would probably be here now."

She tugged at the sash. Torian bent to help, but the window didn't budge.

Sheila said, "Damn. Painted shut." She turned around and sat on the bed.

"Why didn't you yell out there?"

"At first I didn't think of it, and by the time I did, I needed everything to keep breathing. I thought if I did, it would slow me down, and all I wanted was to get away."

"I wonder if Jacomine and the mustard dude are still downstairs?"

They could hear very little from where they were.

After awhile Paulette brought them some sandwiches and milk. She opened the door and stood there blocking it. "Torian, take this."

"I'm not hungry."

"Take it, you little shit, or suffer the consequences."

Not wanting to find out what she meant, Torian took the tray.

Paulette said, "When I come back that stuff better be gone."

When she had left, Sheila took a sandwich and held it up—not quite ready to eat, but working up to it. "Look at it this way," she said. "If they're feeding us, maybe they're not planning to kill us."

"Maybe that stuff's poisoned."

Sheila shrugged and ate. When she didn't keel over, Torian did, too.

Paulette came back and took Torian's arm. "Come with me."

She locked the door behind her, holding tightly. "Okay, I want you to go to the bathroom."

Torian didn't believe what she was hearing. "What?"

The woman shoved her in the right direction. "Get in there and pee. Leave the door open."

She did the same thing with Sheila, and then she left again.

When she came back, she had some lengths of clothesline with her. "Sheila. Tie Torian's arms behind her back."

Sheila had that sullen look she got. "Why should I?"

"Because I'm going to beat the living hell out of you if ya don't."

Sheila got up and walked over to Paulette. But instead of taking the clothesline, she kicked Paulette in the shin.

Torian saw instantly that it wasn't the wisest tactical move—it warned Paulette that Sheila wasn't going to cooperate, yet it left her undamaged. Paulette lunged forward. It was the first time in her life Torian had seen her friend look frightened.

But Sheila fought. Torian could see her suck in her breath. She doubled up her fist and landed it on Paulette's arm.

I should do something. What should I do? The lamp! I'll bash her with the lamp. Torian picked it up and prepared to smash it on Paulette's head, but the cord was too short. She tugged hard, but the plug wouldn't come out.

Panicked, she bent down and tried to unplug it. Behind her, she heard a crash, and looked back to see Sheila down on the floor, Paulette straddling her, holding Sheila's head in her hands. She started to bang it against the floor, and then stopped. Very deliberately, she doubled up her fist and socked Sheila in the jaw.

Sheila's eyes closed. Her head hit the floor, hard. Torian thought she was almost certainly unconscious.

"Sheila!" she yelled, but her friend didn't respond.

Paulette did instead. "Torian, get up off that floor."

Torian noticed that she was still down there, where she'd been trying to get the lamp plug out of the socket so she could unplug it.

Paulette went over to the door and locked it. "Listen, baby, I'm gonna have to tie ya up. I know that scared ya, what I did with Sheila, but I wouldn't hurt ya for the world. You gon' be okay, ya know that?"

Torian was frozen with terror. She was still while Paulette tied her hands behind her back and she sat quietly, watching Paulette turn Sheila over and truss her as well. "I had to do that, ya know, girl? You be okay; I swear."

She was different from the way she'd been a few minutes ago, before she knocked Sheila out. As if she'd calmed down—or simply changed tactics.

She left and came back with some water, which she sponged on Sheila's face till the girl came around. "Ya gon' have a sore chin, baby, but ya be all right."

Sheila said, "Oh, sure. I'm sure I'll be just fine."

"You shut up, girl, and do what ya told. Turn around." She tied a bandanna around Sheila's mouth, so she couldn't make much noise, and then she did the same thing to Torian.

"Okay, girls, y'all come on now, one at a time." She herded them into her van, which had been drawn up close to the house. Torian was first. She saw that Faylice was already there, feet tied as well. Paulette tied Torian's feet. Then she left, came back with Sheila, and tied her feet, nearly suffering a nasty kick for her trouble.

"Y'all lie down now, the best way ya can." When they were jackknifed to her satisfaction, she covered them with blankets. It was raining hard, but still fairly warm—the blankets were smothering. Torian was so unhappy she almost forgot to be scared.

They drove a long time, start-and-stop at first, then fast. Paulette turned the air-conditioning up high, possibly to offset the heat from the blankets. Now it was so cold Torian's teeth chattered, but it was better than the stifling heat.

Paulette played the radio loud, listening to the country music Torian and Noel thought so trashy. Sometimes she sang along.

Torian tried to hear when the news came on, wondering if her disappearance, or Sheila's, would be reported.

But why should it? she remembered. I disappeared days ago. And I called Sheila's house to let them know where she was. Nobody knows we've been kidnapped.

She wondered where Adonis was.

"Hurricane Hannah is expected to hit New Orleans at approximately three-thirty A.M." said the announcer. "The storm is traveling at twelve miles per hour with winds up to eighty miles an hour."

Torian felt another of the fear leaps that were beginning to seem familiar, but then she thought, What the hell do I care? We're not even in New Orleans. We couldn't be.

She didn't have the least idea where she'd be at three-thirty A.M. Or if she'd be alive.

• •

Next on Skip's list was a Gloria Holmes, who lived in the French Quarter. *Funny I don't know her,* she thought.

Holmes was on Burgundy Street, near Orleans. She lived in a neat Creole cottage with three units—three units, three doorbells, all unmarked. Skip pressed them all.

A door opened near the gate. A tousled man in shorts and a white undershirt stood there, not speaking, jut squinting into the night.

"We're looking for Gloria Holmes."

"Shit, it's raining," he said, and closed the door.

Skip shrugged and kept pressing the other two bells, knowing that, because passing drunks love to punch buttons, French Quarter residents often don't answer unless they're expecting someone.

Finally a female voice called, *"What?"*

"We're looking for Gloria Holmes. It's an emergency."

"St. Ann." Loud and irritated. A door slammed.

Skip was about to lean on the buzzer again, but Steve said, "The deli?"

"Oh, hey. Maybe so." He gave her one of his pleased-but-hiding-it looks.

She slipped her hand in his as they walked the two blocks to the deli, scurrying in the rain. "You're semi-useful, you know that?"

"Don't get all carried away."

The St. Ann Deli was known for its bountiful, frequently quite decent food, and in Skip's experience, snail-like service. Whether Gloria was a slow server, slow cook, or patient customer remained to be seen. It even occurred to Skip that maybe her roommate said "St. Ann" whenever Gloria was missing, on the theory that she was probably sitting there waiting for her order.

The woman behind the counter had some kind of tooth around her neck and about eight ornaments in each ear, nicely displayed with the help of a buzz haircut. She wore a faded lavender T-shirt that announced she was gay and proud, and that barely covered a pair of free-swinging breasts too large to be wrestled into a bra. Skip knew her by sight—they always exchanged greetings when they ran into each other.

"Are you Gloria Holmes?"

"Uh-huh. You live up the block, don't you?"

"On St. Philip. I'm Skip Langdon."

"What can I do you for?" Her voice was hearty, said she was ready for anything.

Skip liked the setup. They were in a public place so Gloria couldn't slam any doors on her.

"We've got a little problem we hope you can help us with. Our daughter has disappeared and . . ."

"Oh. You're from P-FLAG. Sure. Be with you in a minute." She disappeared into the kitchen.

Steve turned to Skip: "We're from pea flag?"

"Beats me. All I know is, she hasn't threatened to call the po-lice."

Gloria came back with someone's corn chowder. When she had served it, she said, "You can't be Susan's parents—you don't look any older than she is."

"Listen, please talk to us for a minute. We're desperate."

Gloria nodded, all sympathy. "I know. It's really hard when you first find out—"

"We think she's mixed up with a man named Jacomine."

"Oh shit. You're not from P-FLAG."

Steve said, "What's pea flag?" making Skip impatient again; she hated getting off-track.

"Parents and Friends of Lesbians and Gays. Too bad. If your kid was a dyke, I'd know what to do. But the Blood of the Lamb? That's something else again. Kidnap her, deprogram her, and move to another country. That's my advice." She strode back into the kitchen, clearly enjoying the way her body moved.

Besides the T-shirt, she wore a pair of baggy khaki shorts and lace-up boots with heavy socks. Her hips probably wouldn't fit into a smallish chair, and her butt jiggled. Her leg hair would have flapped in the breeze if there'd been one.

"Pinch me," Skip said. "She didn't haul out the garlic and crucifixes."

"Probably sneaking out the back right now."

But she came back with a burger and a plate of red beans and rice, served them, and rejoined the ersatz parents with a grin.

Steve said, "We really have to thank you. You're the only person we've talked to who hasn't threatened to call the police."

"Oh, honestly. They've got this ex-members' support group that's more like a cult than the Jacomeanies. They think every stranger's a spy for the church. Does paranoia breed paranoia, or what? Of course, what do I know? I was never really in it myself— I just went with my mom sometimes. See, my dad was a butt about me coming out, but Mom was great. Went to P-FLAG, and got right with the program. So when she joined this liberal, progressive new church, I tried to support her.

"She said the reason it attracted her was they had lots of gays— the Rev talked to her about me being gay and—you know—was cool about it. I mean, kind of aggressively cool. Well, Mom was probably vulnerable to anything that might help her deal with it— but anyway, she didn't last long either. I mean, it was pretty obvious it was a cult."

"What tipped your mom?"

"Oh, the usual, I guess. They wanted too much time and too much money. And I guess it got kind of old having to call Jacomine 'Daddy.' Oh, yeah, and she never did buy the healings. Simple laying on of hands, yes, no problem, she said. But when he pulled tumors out of people, it kind of compromised credibility." She shrugged. "The truth was, neither of us ever got deep into it. It was no more than an episode."

"We think they've got our daughter someplace. Do you know of any—I don't know—runaway programs they have? Anything like that?"

"My mom might. Want me to give you her number?"

"Please."

Gloria scribbled something. "Her name's different from mine. Sauter. Sylvia Sauter. You can call her now if you like. She stays up all night—her clock's backwards or something."

"Thanks," Skip said, though at this point she hadn't the least concern about Mrs. Sauter's sleep habits.

She and Steve went to her house to make the call. As advertised, Mrs. Sauter seemed ready and happy to talk. She said they hadn't disturbed her, she was just ironing. "Errol Jacomine. A bad man. A very bad man."

"Why do you say so, Mrs. Sauter?"

"He got people's money. Old people's. Mine—he got some of mine, in fact. With his phony healing and his seductions . . ."

"You know about that?"

"Oh, yes. Yes. It happened to friends of mine."

"Listen, do you have any idea where my daughter might be? Is there some kind of quasi-legal shelter they run?"

"You know it's strange you brought it up. My friend Paulette . . . and the other thing, too."

"Could you say all that slowly?"

"Well, they used to list their projects every Sunday at church, and you were supposed to pick the ones you wanted to contribute to. So I picked several, including this sort of little shelter they had—I mean, basically it was just one woman—Paulette Thibodeaux—and I took her some food one day, for the kids."

"Why is it strange that I'd mention her?"

"Oh. Because there were rumors."

"Rumors?"

"Listen, I really don't want to be that kind of person. Would you let me off the hook, by any chance?"

Since you ask so nicely—and since I don't care anyway. "Sure. Can you remember where she lives?"

Mrs. Sauter gave her the address.

"Okay, Steve. Commando raid. Let's look sharp."

"What's our plan?"

"Good question. Sheila's been gone twenty-four hours. We could get the police in on this. I could call in a favor or two." She thought a minute. "You know what? I don't see any way around it. Forget the commando raid."

She called a friend in Juvenile to meet her there.

The place was on the other side of town, near Aububon Park,

266

but they were there in about twelve minutes. The block was dark, including the Thibodeaux house. It was raining harder.

The officer rang the doorbell—getting no answer. The three of them looked around the house, then in the garage. No car. No one home.

They all left.

In the officer's absence, Steve said, "What now?"

"Now the commando raid."

"Another B and E? Two in one night?"

"You up to it?"

They simply broke a window in the back and went in. In one bedroom, they found a pair of earrings lying on the bureau—Sheila's turquoise studs.

Or rather, earrings like hers—inexpensive, mass-produced turquoise studs of a type that could be purchased at any store in America that catered to teenagers.

Sheila said the posts were so cheap they hurt her ears. She was always taking them out and leaving them on the bureau.

24

• •

Let's talk to the neighbors. You take the left side and I'll take the right."

"Are you crazy? It's the middle of the night."

"Forget it—I'll do it. Wait for me in the car."

He did it, of course. Skip was rather enjoying working with him. He did things efficiently and well—he simply wasn't used to the privilege a cop enjoys.

And face it, he doesn't have confidence yet.

She could remember all too well when she didn't have it either. Now it was like a muscle she'd built up—something that came in handy and felt great when you had to swim or leap a fence.

Most people on the block either hadn't been home or hadn't seen anything—one or two knew Paulette Thibodeaux and said she ran a "halfway house for delinquents."

One had seen Sheila arrive the other night—either Sheila or a girl a lot like her. The neighbor had taken special notice, because most of "Paulette's kids" were black.

"These people are a lot nicer than the religious fanatics," Steve said when they had finished and met back at her car.

"People love to help. It can be a pain in the ass sometimes."

"I hope you didn't mean anything personal."

She had to smile. Steve's helping instincts had often been a pain.

He said, "Listen, I got something. The lady across the street saw Sheila cross to her side this afternoon. I mean a girl who looked like her."

Skip perked up, "Really?"

"Apparently, she was being pursued by a black man in a suit. She ran a long way, but he caught up and ran with her awhile, evidently just talking to her. Then she stopped and let him help her back to Paulette's."

"Shit."

"Yeah. The neighbor said she didn't call the police because she knows Paulette works with delinquent kids—"

"Really great cover story—it explains any erratic behavior on the kids' parts, and lets the adults do anything they want."

"—and Sheila wasn't screaming. I wonder why she wasn't."

"One of life's little ironies. When I think of all the times she's screamed for no particular reason . . ." Skip stopped, realizing she was getting angry, and seeing no point in it. "What about the black man—any more description?"

"Tall, thin, glasses, that's about it. He looked real respectable, she said—another reason she didn't call the cops."

"Potter Menard. It's gotta be."

"Who?"

"Jacomine's hired thug. The good reverend calls him a 'campaign aide.' "

"So what does all this mean?"

"She must have been here. And sometime between this afternoon and now, they moved her. Presumably Torian, too."

"Moved her where?"

"Maybe to some other 'home for delinquent kids.' Shit."

"What about Potter Menard?"

"I already ran a check on him. He's Mr. Clean. Wife and two little kids—I don't think they could hide two white teenagers. And no point waking him up in the middle of the night. He's not going to invite us in to take a look around. Someone from Juvenile might take a gander, but not tonight—we need something more definite connecting Sheila with Jacomine's group."

"We've got Paulette. What more do we need?"

Skip really didn't want to talk about it. Her instincts told her that the more policemen who came around knocking on doors, the more paranoid—and thus the more dangerous—Jacomine was going to get. He was already several steps ahead—had probably moved the girls before the church break-in. She had to catch up somehow.

"Let's stop at a pay phone."

Steve didn't ask questions, just drove to the nearest K&B. Skip got out and called Mrs. Sauter again. "Do you know of anyone else in the church who was doing the same kind of work Paulette was?"

"Why, no. I don't think anyone was."

"Look, Mrs. Sauter. Paulette apparently left in a hurry—with my daughter. Does the church have—what would you say?—safehouses? Something like that? Where would Paulette take her?"

Mrs. Sauter mused. "I don't know about safehouses. Maybe they have them. There were lots of things I didn't know. But I know a little about Paulette, and I can tell you exactly what she'd do."

Skip's stomach hopped. "What?"

"Wherever Jacomine told her to."

"Thanks, Mrs. Sauter."

But she had a thought: *Suppose he just said, "Get those kids somewhere safe; I don't care where, the farther from the church the better."*

When you get down to it, Paulette's my only lead—unless you count Potter, and he can't be tackled till tomorrow.

Without much hope, she dialed Homicide, thinking that the way things were going, her nemesis, Frank O'Rourke, would pick up the phone. Instead a man named Myers did, someone just transferred in. She asked for her buddy, Adam Abasolo.

His lazy voice came over the line, and her heart pounded. Something was working right. "Hey, baby, What's all that noise in the background?"

"Just rain and stuff. I'm at a pay phone."

"Don't you have enough sense to get in out of a hurricane?"

"Listen, Adam, I need you to run a sheet on somebody."

"I'm not even going to ask why."

"Well, I'm going to tell you. It looks like Sheila's been kidnapped."

"My God. You've reported it?"

"Yes on missing—no on kidnapped. The way I found out wasn't exactly legal."

He sighed. "I sure hope you're wrong. Listen, I see a free computer. Whose record are we checking?"

"A Paulette Thibodeaux."

"Back in five."

It was more like ten. "Couple of arrests for prostitution. That's about it. Want her address?"

"Sure."

"Looks like she's on Martin Luther King near South Rampart." He gave her a number.

"Isn't that the corner they call the Kill Zone?"

"Uh-huh. But big deal. You're gonna have a lot more trouble with Mother Nature than the neighborhood gangsters. Know what my advice to you is? Go home and batten your hatches."

Back in the car, Steve put an arm around her. "Any luck?"

"Not to speak of."

"Let's go get a few hours' sleep."

She started the car. "Great idea—for you. I personally intend to run around like a chicken with my head cut off."

"Oh, well, I guess I will, too."

"Uh-uh. I'm sending you home in a taxi,"

He protested, but their deal was she gave the orders, and she could see that he was flagging. He wasn't used to the grind of police work—and also Sheila wasn't his kid.

Those arrests for prostitution worried her. She could just see Paulette recruiting and training a corps of baby hookers under the guise of helping runaways.

As she transferred Steve to a cab, she noticed the wind was getting stronger. She wanted desperately to go home with him.

On Martin Luther King, a male voice answered her knock.

"Whatchew want?"

271

The man was clearly asleep and clearly not thrilled to be disturbed. He probably wasn't going to let her in unless . . . she hesitated only a moment. "Police."

There followed a great banging, as if the man wanted to make the point that he really couldn't get out of bed without falling and that the police were a great inconvenience.

"Yeah?" He was short and scrawny, and he wore only shorts.

"I'm looking for Paulette."

"Paulette? That white bitch been gone two-three year. Ain' nothin' here for you."

Skip couldn't believe she'd actually made contact with someone who knew Paulette—she'd half expected an abandoned building. "Oh, yes, there is," she said, and wedged her foot firmly in the door. "Where is she?"

"I'm tellin' you she ain' here. Foxy here, though. Say hello, Foxy."

A very young-sounding girl said hello, probably from a bare mattress.

"I ain' seen'r in so long, I wouldn' know her ugly face no more. Whatchew want with her?"

"What's your name?"

"Mitchell Taylor. What yours? Paulette about your size."

"I'm Skip Langdon." She paused to take a breath, about to tell him how desperately she needed his help, but he seemed to be on a tear.

"Can you believe me and Paulette . . . I mean, she so tall and . . . big and everything . . ."

"You were her pimp."

"What you know about it, Miss Smarty-Pants? Yeah, I was her pimp. So what? Think I didn' care about Paulette? Think she didn' care about me? She be my main woman, that one. But we look pretty funny together. Paulette, she had a real unhappy life."

"What do you mean 'had'?"

"Back where she come from. Her daddy screwed all the kids or somep'n. I never did know quite what. But somep'n make her real unhappy. Well, she got Jesus now. Hallelujah . . . that be her life now. Maybe she happy, I don' know. She be back, though. Paulette be back. She care too much about ol' Mitch not to come back. We got somethin' special together."

"I thought you said she was ugly and a white bitch."

"Oh. Well. That just be the way I talk."

Since he had on nothing but shorts, Skip couldn't grab him by the shirtfront. She settled for taking a step forward, getting right in his face. (Though in this case that more or less meant putting her breasts in his face.) "Is she here, Mitchell?"

"You just axt that, you cain't remember? No, she ain' here. You crazy or somethin', Miss White Po-lice? I swear you don' get outta my face I turn yo' ass in to Public Fuckin' Integrity." With some editing, that was the new name for Internal Affairs.

"You're a spunky little devil, I'll give you that."

"Been arrested much as I have, get to know ya rights."

"Where's Paulette from?"

"Whatcha mean where she from? How I know somep'n like that?"

"The place where her daddy screwed the kids."

"We didn' talk about nothin' like that."

"Does she have any good friends? Somebody she'd go to if she needed a place to stay?"

"Yeah. Me. She need a place, she come right here."

"We've been over that one. How old's Foxy, anyhow? Fifteen or sixteen? Maybe I better find out."

"Okay, okay. Lemme think now. 'Nother girl used to work for me—thousand years ago. Turned up at that same church Paulette did. They be real close, over there, in the fuckin' God-box. I try to get Paulette back, she send Miss Nikki over, threaten to break my kneecaps; maybe toes, I forget which."

"Nikki?"

"Yeah. Nikki. Hope she die a horrible death."

Skip shivered. "Last name?"

He didn't even hesitate. "Pigeon—like the bird. I remember specially 'cause she call it 'P'jhone,' like she think she the Queen of Fuckin' France."

Nikki Pigeon was the first of Jacomine's followers Skip had met—the one she'd seen the video of in the coroner's office.

● ●

"She's fucking *disappeared*? A fucking six-foot woman and four fucking kids? Potter Menard, I swear to God I'm gonna kick your sorry ass to kingdom come. When the fuck you gon' start to earn your salary? You are the sorriest excuse for an employee I've ever had in all my life—I pay you premium wages, and this is what I get. I might as well hire teenage girls. Why, little Abby's a better detective than you are."

Daddy had fits.

Potter was used to that. He didn't let it bother him, knew Daddy was under more pressure than any human could take. He'd just let it dissipate, and then he'd do something to remind Daddy how good he was, and he'd get a pat on the back. Daddy seldom apologized—Potter could remember only once or twice—but he'd do something to show he was sorry, and let Potter know he appreciated him. Sometimes it took the form of a little bonus in Potter's pay envelope, which was especially nice because Daddy most certainly didn't pay premium wages. Potter did this for love, and Daddy knew it. He just said things like that when he was upset.

Nonetheless, Potter found himself feeling defensive. Usually he prided himself on riding out the storms—that was part of his professionalism—something he could do that very few others could. Yet this morning, this particular morning, Daddy's tirade felt like too much.

He'd worked for hours, concocting a plan for those kids—he knew exactly what to do. Leave it to Potter, and they'd never be heard from again, never be traced—and neither would Paulette Thibodeaux. It was simple, it was neat, above all it was clean. Better, it was ingenious. Potter had truly outdone himself this time. And then when he'd called, no one was there. He'd gone over—with tropical storm-force winds already blowing—and discovered it was worse than he thought. Not only was no one there, somebody'd been there who wasn't supposed to be.

Potter didn't know what to make of the break-in. There were no signs of violence, which might mean it occurred after Paulette left. And if she left on her own, that meant she was one step ahead of him. Maybe Daddy was right, maybe Potter was an idiot. Maybe he should have locked them all up when he left yesterday.

Yeah, he should have. Daddy was goddamn right. This shouldn't have happened. Potter had moved too slow. The kids and Paulette should be history by now.

He'd been so full of himself and his little plan, and God had sent him this to teach him humility. Well, it worked. He was humble now.

"You listening to me? Potter, goddamn it. I don't think you're even listenin'. I don't know why I don't just fire your ass right now."

"Daddy, you're right. You're right. I don't know why you don't."

"Well, I'll tell you why I don't. It's because I don't have anybody else to do your sorry job. I'm gon' tell you one damn thing and I'm gon' tell you right now. You gon' get us out of this mess. You got us in it and you gon' damn well get us out of it. And you gon' do it now! Before this night is over. Is that clear, Potter Menard?"

"Yeah, Daddy." His voice sounded grim even to him. "I'm going to get us out of this or die tryin'. Tonight. Hannah or no Hannah."

"Who the fuck is Hannah?"

"The hurricane, Daddy." Potter was sorry to have mentioned it, knowing Daddy had more important matters to think about.

"Potter, I want to spell somethin' out for you. I'm within a hairsbreadth of bein' mayor of this city, do you understand that?"

Potter nodded.

"You realize what that could do for race relations? For social justice? For all the things we've worked for? This is the moment we been workin' years to get to. If you don't solve this, that moment's lost. Do you take my meaning, Potter?"

"Yes sir, I do."

"I want those three people dead, you hear me? I want 'em never heard from again. Paulette Thibodeaux and the two witnesses. You find Paulette and you're gon' find Sheila Ritter and Torian Gernhard. I repeat—those girls are witnesses. I told you I was gon' spell it out, and I am. Those three people, and the other two girls if they're there. I want 'em dead. That's as plain as I can make it."

"I understand, Daddy." Sometime during the evening, after much praying and soul-searching, Potter had come to the conclusion that this was the only way out. He hated it, but it was the way it was. "I need your help."

Daddy opened his arms, as if offering a kingdom. "Anything, son."

"We need to plot some strategy." He knew Daddy loved that word. "I think what happened is, Paulette realized what was in the cards. In other words, I think she left of her own accord, taking the children with her. The question is, where would she go?"

"We got a dossier on her."

"Yes sir, I have it right here. It just doesn't have very much personal information in it."

"She had some kind of sweetheart, didn't she?"

"I don't know much about that." What he did know was that she'd been Daddy's favorite for a while, but it wasn't his place to bring that up.

"Maybe she went to see him."

"I wonder how I'd find out who he is." Other than the Daddy story, he knew absolutely nothing about Paulette Thibodeaux's personal life—in fact, hadn't really thought she had one outside the church.

"Ask her friends."

"It's funny. I never think of her as having any." He hated the position he was in. It made him look like a bad detective.

The hell with it, he decided. *If she was anybody else, I'd just come out with it. That's the professional way to handle it.*

"Daddy, I'm wondering if she confided anything in you— anything that might help me."

"Paulette Thibodeaux? Are you crazy, boy?"

"Any kind of thing like—you know—who her friends are. Just little things I could use to jump off from."

"Now why would Paulette Thibodeaux talk to me about personal matters?"

He'd done it, and Daddy was mad. "I guess she wouldn't."

"You must have had some reason for thinking that."

"Well, you're a minister and all, I thought what we're talking about might cancel out confidentiality. I mean if she came to you for pastoral counseling."

But Daddy wasn't letting him off the hook. "Now that wasn't what you thought, was it, Potter? You heard some rumor or other and you believed it, wasn't that it?"

Actually, among other things, Potter had stood guard outside Daddy's parked car while Paulette gave him a blow job. Had Daddy forgotten that?

He said, very formally, treading on eggs, "No, sir, you brought me into your confidence on that matter."

"*What matter?* What *matter*, Potter Menard?" Daddy was shouting. "I am a minister and must be above reproach. Did you forget that for one tiny minute?"

"I guess I did, Daddy. I apologize, sir."

"Don't 'sir' me. You only call me sir when you know damn well you've done something wrong. Potter, I just don't know what I'm gon' do with you. I can't take your insubordination too much longer. Some things you just don't do. And *you* do 'em anyway. I swear to God, I'd fire your ass if I could."

The thing about Daddy was, he was always right. Potter had known better than to pry into his private life.

25

• •

They drove for a long time. Torian had to go to the bathroom so bad she whimpered inside her gag.

Finally, Paulette stopped the car, went somewhere, came back and said, "Y'all must be 'bout to die back here, po' little things."

She was the old Paulette, the one who was like a nice mom.

"I'm gon' untie ya, and we gon' go in and pee."

It was still dark, and the rain was relentless now. The wind was so fierce the girls staggered on the short walk to a small asbestos-shingled house. It was as poor a little shack as Torian had ever seen, and there didn't seem to be much else around. It was too dark to tell, but there weren't streetlights. Torian didn't think they were in a city.

Her muscles were so cramped from the ropes and from lying down in the van, her bladder so stretched, that at first she was aware only of herself. Her body. She realized gradually that there were other people here, a man and a woman, who'd obviously been waked from a sound—and possibly drunken—sleep.

The man wore an ancient plaid flannel robe, too hot for early

September, now worn so thin it was probably fine. He was dark and tall, but lean, his longish hair graying, his mustache still dark. Torian classified him as semi-old—fifty-five, perhaps.

The woman was also dark and thin, the kind of thin that derives partly from genes and partly from smoking too many cigarettes. She looked stringy to Torian—her face was long, her hair lank, her body bony. She wore a garment Torian had seen in plenty of stores and catalogues, but rarely on a human being: a nightgown. This was a thin cotton one, white with tiny green polka dots, sleeveless, with some sort of inset under the boobs—a satin ribbon, perhaps, so that it was vaguely A-shaped. On her feet she wore fuzzy pink slippers in the shape of pig heads. A haze of cigarette smoke engulfed her.

The man seemed to be keeping up a relentless, angry harangue, the woman interjecting shrill comments whenever she saw fit. Both spoke with a heavy Cajun accent.

"Paulette, Paulette, Paulette." The man shook his head in thorough disapproval. "Years we don't see ya, and then ya come running from the law. What ya got, two girls? Three? What we gon' do with ya, huh?"

"Black as the ace of spades," said the woman. Her voice had the clipped, hard cadence, the perennial anger and heavy judgment developed over a lifetime of unhappiness and disappointment.

Faylice put a hand on her hip. "I s'pose *your* shit don't stink." Her shorts looked as if they'd been worn for a week. In spite of her weariness, Torian half smiled: *Go, Faylice.*

"Denis, ya hear that? Ya hear? Comes right in my house, talks ta me like that. Little fat nigra girl." Her already irritating voice now carried a note of outrage—the world had treated her as badly as she feared it would.

Torian tuned the others out, trying to take in the inside of the shack.

The furniture was worse than hers and Lise's—older and cheaper, if that were possible, and in much worse taste. Covered with that rough, ugly fabric that seemed to come always in plaid. Herculon? She wasn't sure. There were doilies, too. This was something she'd only read about. The place smelled musty, and dirty somehow, as if there were a huge accumulation of dust under beds and on baseboards, caught in curtains and on doodads, permanently embedded in sofas and chairs. An old stained blanket was spread on the sofa, making her think that whatever was under it was even worse. She didn't want to sit down.

"So, Paulette, why ya kidnap these girls?"

"Daddy, look. Ya my blood kin. I got no one else. We got to have a place to stay for a while."

"We gon' be in jail by mornin', every one of us," said the woman. "If we're not dead from that hurricane." She took a long drag on her cigarette and blew it out fast.

Denis said, "Ya gon' bring bad things on all of us. Ya got to get these chirren out of here."

"Daddy, ya gon' throw ya only kin out in a hurricane?"

"Hurricane! Pah. They always say there's gon' be a hurricane, it never comes. Look—we still got power. There ain't gon' be no hurricane, Paulette. Ya b'lieve everything ya hear on TV?"

"It's supposed to hit New Orleans at three-thirty. Look at that rain. You don't b'lieve—?" Paulette shook her head. "It's comin', Daddy."

"Goddammit, Denis, I tol' you! Ya wouldn't b'lieve me and we gon' be killed. Now it's too late to get anywhere."

"Tootie, shut up! I gotta think."

It occurred to Torian that these two had probably done quite a bit of drinking before going to bed.

The smoking woman looked panic-stricken. "My daddy was killed in a hurricane, ya know that, Denis. I don't take no chances with 'em. Denis, we got to get out of here. We can't stay here in no hurricane."

Denis was fumbling with a radio. "Shut up, Tootie. Tootie, will ya just shut up?"

"Daddy, listen. I been working with the Reverend Errol Jacomine. Ya know? Who's runnin' for mayor?"

"Oh, yeah? He used to stay in St. Martinville—ya cousin Eddie knew him, got us over there to see him once."

Tootie said, "Ya just had to go to that revival. Wrecked ya car on the way back."

"You the one got rid ya arthritis."

"I did not—my left shoulder's been killin' me."

"Daddy, I been doin' this work for him, with runaway kids. He axed me to bring these girls up for a few days. They're in some kind of trouble—"

Tootie said, "You rite they in some kind of trouble."

"You tellin' me the truth? That Reverend Jacomine sent these kids up here?"

"That's what I been trying to tell you."

"He remember me, then? He remember that night we came up to hear him?"

"Sure. Course he did, Daddy." Torian thought Paulette looked at him for the first time with affection.

"Listen." He turned on the radio. "Y'all be quiet. Here comes the weather report."

Hurricane Hannah was still headed toward New Orleans, coming in up Barataria Bay. Winds were still about ninety miles per hour, but she might be slowing a bit.

Denis said, "That puts her just west of New Orleans and east of Houma. Guess she'll get us about the same time she gets New Orleans."

Paulette said, "Daddy, ya gotta let us stay. Ya wouldn't throw ya only kin out in a storm, would ya?"

Tootie was having a small conniption. "Girl, nobody can stay here in a hurricane. Ya must take after ya mama. Don't have the sense God gave . . ."

Denis hit her. Not hard, Torian thought, and not on the face, but she heard flesh connect with flesh. She turned away.

"Ya know better than to talk about Marie. I don't know why I ever married ya. Ya not fit to wipe her shoes."

"Daddy! After the way you treated Mama!" Denis looked as if he might come after Paulette next. She took a step back and composed herself. "Now listen, y'all. I got three chirren here and a hurricane's comin'. Could y'all pick another time to fight?"

Denis said, "Tootie, get ready. We gotta get outta here. Paulette, ya comin' with us. We can't none of us stay here in that storm."

● ●

Skip thought: *I can call Jane Storey. Like people in AA; whenever the thing's got you . . .*

Wait a minute! Gloria mentioned a support group for former church members. If she knows about it, Mrs. Sauter probably does.

Quickly, Skip found a pay phone, but it was dead. She found another—also dead. And suddenly, it began to dawn on her that she was soaked to the skin; Spanish moss was blowing off the trees, some of which were straining, as if limbs were soon to follow.

Is this really it? she thought.

Already?

She looked at her watch.

Yes. The beginning of it anyway. The storm was going to get worse, and already the phone lines were out.

I wonder if they're down at Headquarters?

Or home. I should go to the Quarter. If I can't get Mrs. Sauter, I can try Gloria.

Electricity was out in most of the city. It was eerie driving the deserted streets, a tempest blowing—the "felon winds" of some forgotten poem—the city dark as the sea. Skip had a sudden surge of loneliness—and of fear, not for Sheila, but for herself. It wasn't fear of Jacomine or Menard, or even fear of the storm. It was more an existential kind of fear, a sense of being a grain of sand and knowing it would soon be high tide.

"Paranoia," she muttered to herself, and rocked in her seat, trying literally to shake it.

I wonder if I should just go get some sleep for a couple of hours? Or turn it over to the real cops.

Uh-uh. The only advantage I've got—if I have any—is that the bad guys are asleep and I'm on the road.

There were no lights in the French Quarter, which meant Gloria's doorbell wouldn't be working. Shouting was a possibility, but she didn't think she could be heard above the wind.

Well, first things first.

Skip went home and tried her phone—dead. She picked up her gun, flashlight, and radio and left again, not even waking Steve.

She dragged her gun back and forth on Gloria's metal gate until finally the tousle-headed man opened his door. This time, he came awake instantly: "Oh, shit. Don't shoot."

She was on the verge of saying she was a cop, but stopped herself at the last second. With Mitchell, she might get away with it. But for all she knew, this guy was a cop himself.

She tried to hold the gun in such a way as to suggest she hardly knew what it was. "Sorry, I just needed to make a lot of noise. I know it's late, I'd never have done it except . . . it's about Gloria's mother."

"Oh, shit," he said again, and started to close the door.

"I can shoot through it, you know." His eyes jerked from his task back to her and registered that she was now holding the gun very professionally indeed.

"Uh . . . I guess you want to get in."

"You got it."

He opened the gate and went back to his warm bed—or more likely, fled into the night, convinced she'd shoot him as soon as she'd finished off Gloria.

The setup was like Skip's and Jimmy Dee's, Big House in front, slave quarters in back; Gloria and her roommate apparently lived in the latter.

The ground floor was lit up, and loud music poured out of it. Pam Tillis singing "Mi Vida Loca."

Skip banged out the police knock.

Gloria pulled the curtain aside, then flung open the door. "Get your butt in here. There's a storm, girl. Haven't you heard?"

"Hurricane party?"

"Old New Orleans thang. You met my roommate? Suzanne Shasta."

"Skip Langdon. Listen, Gloria, I have to throw myself on your mercy."

"What you drinkin'?"

"I'd love to, but I can't, thanks. I'm still looking for my kid."

"Hey, Suzanne, she's the one I thought was from P-FLAG."

"Gloria, this is serious."

Gloria's tone changed instantly. "Hey, I don't think we invited you."

Skip made her voice extremely low, trying not to sound melodramatic. "My daughter's life may be at stake."

The roommate intervened. "Hey. Hey, sit down, okay?"

Skip looked at Suzanne for the first time. In some ways, she was almost indistinguishable from Gloria—hugely overweight, large of tit, buzz cut, a lot of earrings. But her face was rounder and softer. Her hair—what there was of it—was dark like Sheila's, and her cheeks were as red, her skin as white. She was probably in her late twenties, but to Skip she looked like her kid. Skip sat down, feeling a sudden wave of something like defeat.

Suzanne turned down the CD player. "Would you like some tea? Gloria! Put some water on."

Her friend obeyed, slightly sullen.

"I know it's awful to turn up at midnight, but all the phones are dead. I can't get your mother."

"I thought you were going to call her right away."

"I did, and she gave me a lead that—frankly—might save Sheila . . ."

"Sheila! That's right, you said you lived in the Quarter. Chubby girl, looks like Suzanne? Hangs with that skinny little Torian. The two of 'em call me St. Ann."

"That's her. Torian's missing too."

"God, they practically live at the deli."

"Yeah, that's probably what folks at Croissant D'Or say."

"Torian came in once with a blond guy about twice her age."

"That man was Errol Jacomine's campaign manager. He was murdered yesterday. He introduced Torian and Sheila to a woman in the church, and now they're all missing."

Suzanne said, "My God," and Gloria turned around to stare at her."

Apparently, that put things in perspective. Gloria seemed to sober up instantly. "What woman?"

"Paulette Thibodeaux."

"You've got to be kidding!"

Skip's pulse speeded up. "You knew her?"

"Yeah. Yeah. I'm just trying to get the hang of this."

"Listen, time's running short. Tell me everything you know about her."

"We sang in the choir together. And we were both in this church support group. All the Jacomeanies had to be in one. Kind of a cross between a twelve-step program and an old-time therapy group. Personally I think it was just their way of spying on people; finding out their weak spots."

"You talked about personal stuff in the group?"

"Mostly, yeah. Relationship stuff." She cut her eyes at Suzanne.

Skip could barely speak in a normal tone. "So you know something about Paulette's personal life?"

"It was awhile ago." She put a hand to her head and closed her eyes. "Boyfriend. Yeah. You know there were always rumors about her and Daddy—that's what they call Jacomine, did you know that?"

Skip only nodded, not wanting to stop the flow.

"She said she'd had a terrible disappointment—I guess Daddy must have dumped her. And she met this dude, Mike, when she had a broken heart. He was real nice to her, but there were problems. See, he was a former dope dealer. . ."

Skip couldn't stand the suspense. "Mike who?"

"Oh, Aaron; Mike Aaron. I know because he sang in the choir too—I used to see them together. I guess that's how they met."

"You wouldn't know where he lives, by any chance?"

"Sure. He had a little picnic at his house once, for the choir. Let's see—was Paulette there? No, I don't think so. She probably didn't want Daddy to know about him—probably didn't realize somebody in the group was reporting every word."

"How do you know that?"

She shrugged. "It just stands to reason."

"Listen, can I have his address?"

She could hardly sit still while Gloria got her Rolodex and looked it up.

As soon as Skip opened the door, she realized that the full force of the hurricane had hit. She was nearly blown over the second she stepped onto the flagstones. Her umbrella was stupid, worthless against the downpour, a joke in the wind.

Her hair flew in her face and wind blew up her nose, forcing her to open her mouth. She could feel her cheeks puff out, and she realized her eyelids wouldn't work, her eyes were pasted open. *This, she thought, is why bikers wear goggles.*

She let the wind take her to the far wall of the courtyard, which fortunately was on the side with the gate. There she held onto the wall, to the patio furniture, to anything she could until she reached the shelter of the narrow passage between the wall and the main house. Unwilling to go out themselves, Suzanne and Gloria had lent her a key. Struggling to unlock the gate, she could feel minutes ticking away.

She had to get to her car by the same method she'd used in the courtyard—leaning against walls, holding onto whatever was there. Almost everyone had closed their shutters against the storm, but one home owner, evidently away, had left his to flap in the gale. Skip watched as the wind ripped it off its hinges, and hoped the power lines wouldn't be next. Random debris already clogged the street, mostly small branches. Driving was going to be hell.

Because no one was out, even in the French Quarter, she'd been able to park close by. Bits of trees and plant debris formed a light carpet on her car.

Mike Aaron lived in Bucktown, out by Lake Pontchartrain. *There might not be flooding there,* she thought. *Part of Bucktown's within the levee system.*

It didn't matter. She was going to try anyway.

Surprisingly, the streets were fairly clear. There were no floods and only smallish branches. She had to stop only once to clear a path.

Not wanting to walk in on a band of armed fanatics, she cased the house like a burglar. She wished she'd thought to ask what kind of car Paulette drove. But there was one car in the driveway, and one parked in front; she drew hope from that.

Sunrise was still hours away, the sky still dark with the storm, the lights still out. With her flashlight, she could see that Mike

Aaron took pride in his house. It was neat and newly painted. The front curtains were drawn.

She moved to the side, using her now-familiar method of hanging onto anything that wasn't flying through the air. The curtains were drawn here as well.

Damn. I'm out here without backup. I wish I'd brought Steve. But I can't go back in this storm.

The backyard—probably where the choir had had its picnic—was enclosed by a Cyclone fence. She opened the gate and nearly slipped on a carpet of wet grass—more evidence of Aaron's house pride.

She wonderd what kind of man he was—former dope dealer was all she knew. On the surface, he was somebody who had simply "found Jesus" and used religion to leave behind an old way of life. He could be an innocent drawn to Jacomine's good works— and possibly their beneficiary. Or he could know all too well about the violence; be a willing participant in it.

The same went for Paulette.

How far, she thought, *are these people willing to go? Are they planning to kill these children?*

She knew enough about cults to dread the answer.

The kitchen door was solid at the bottom, with nine small window panes on top. There was no curtain.

She cupped her eyes with her hands and looked in, daring to shine her light. The kitchen, unlike the neat exterior of the house, was a wreck. The contents of the cabinets had been more or less dumped on the floor. Broken dishes were everywhere.

Though it looked as if the kitchen opened into the living room, it was difficult to see in there. Skip strained her eyes, but couldn't make out much at first. Gradually, as she adjusted, she saw that this room was also a wreck—something white was everywhere, maybe feathers from pillows. Furniture was overturned. It was definitely a scene more appropriate to an earthquake than a hurricane.

Who could go to sleep with a mess like that? So they must not be home, right?

She knew that was a load of manure, but she also knew she was going in that house, one way or another. First, she tried the door, which was locked.

But the front door might not be. If it isn't, nobody's home, because that would mean the last person to leave wasn't Mike Aaron.

It opened.

A man was lying on the floor, arms outstretched.

Head blown off.

In each palm was a knife, nailing it to the floor. Tiny x's had been cut on the chest, like the x's on the tomb of Marie Laveau—but Skip didn't think these were there for religious reasons.

She had entered the house with her gun drawn. Automatically, she moved through the rooms, making sure they were empty. There were only two others—bedrooms, separated by a bathroom. One was decorated with posters; littered with toys—footballs; baseballs and bats.

A boy's room. The bed hadn't been slept in.

The other was obviously Aaron's. It had an odd feature for a small house—a walk-in closet. At the back of the closet was a wall hanging, a beach towel with a scene from *Aladdin* on it, held up by pushpins. That struck her as so odd she took it down.

Behind it, there was a small door cut in the closet—a square, something like a pet door, but bigger. She opened it, stuck her gun in, and shined her light.

Huddled up, trying to make himself as small as the mouse whose hole this resembled, was a boy. Every muscle was tensed. His face was in profile, and he didn't turn towards her, didn't want to face his killer. A single tear progressed down his cheek.

"Oh my God, you poor baby." She lowered the gun and tried to get him to look at her, but he refused.

If I were this kid, I wouldn't look at me, either.

"Look, whoever was here before, I wasn't with them."

A sound came out of him, an intake of breath, tears being swallowed. It was a hopeless sound.

"Something real bad happened here, but you're gon' be all right. You hear that, baby? Nobody's gon' hurt you, now; you're okay now." Her voice sounded like something she'd heard before, from someone else's mouth. Its cadences were those of a black person.

Betty Ann.

The near-forgotten name slipped into her brain like a soothing unguent. Betty Ann was a woman who'd worked for the Langdons when Skip and her brother were preschoolers. While their mother was out doing volunteer work to raise her social status, Betty Ann had taken care of skinned knees and cut fingers. She must have talked like Skip was talking now.

"I need you to stay here one more minute, sweetheart, then I'll be back to get you. Can you do that for me?" Eyes still straight ahead, the kid nodded.

Skip went and got a sheet to cover what was almost certainly the body of the boy's father. It was hard to do, harder than looking at the shell that had been a person, harder even than finding the boy who'd lost his father. She was trained for these situations. But covering the body was tampering with a crime scene.

Still, she simply wasn't prepared to take a chance on that quivering kid seeing the mess that had been his father.

If the scene hadn't been so grim, she'd have had to laugh at herself. This was the third building she'd broken into in the last eight hours. She'd left her training pretty far behind.

The boy was letting go a little now; still trying to hold back sobs, but no longer trying to be heroic about it. He looked at her. He was a pale little kid, ten or eleven maybe, his brown hair fashionably clipped so his scalp showed through, a mole near his mouth that somehow underscored his vulnerability. He was dressed like a skateboarder, in long, loose shorts and oversized T-shirt. "I heard the shot. Is he dead?"

"Yes. I'm sorry." Kneeling, Skip held out her arms. "Come here, honey."

He didn't hug her, but for the briefest of moments he let his head fall against her body.

She said, "We've got to get you out of here."

"I don't have anyplace to go."

"Honey, come on." She tugged at his arm, and he unfolded. She saw that he was taller than she'd thought, and skinny, a little awkward, shoulders slightly hunched. He was barefoot.

"Where are your shoes?"

"In my room."

"You're Mike Aaron's son?"

"Yeah. Billy." He sniffed, the mention of his dad setting off more tears. "Who are you?"

"Come on, let's go get your shoes."

She sat on his bed and fiddled with her radio while he searched for his shoes and put them on. "My name's Skip Langdon. I'm a cop some of the time." To her dismay, the radio was dead, too—the tower must be out.

She thought about it: no power, no phones, no radio. She couldn't imagine what Headquarters would be like right now.

I'm not taking him there. Not after what he's been through. The realization was like a weight lifting, but it brought up a question: *What the hell am I doing with him?*

I can't take him to Steve. I need him myself.

Jimmy Dee? Uh-uh. Kenny's got enough trouble right now. She sighed. *Cindy Lou, I guess. But kids aren't her thing—and she lives so damn far.*

She said, "What happened tonight? Why were you in that little hidey-hole?"

"Daddy and I were doing a storm-watch—you know? And then this car came along in the rain, and he told me to go get in the hole and don't come out, no matter what. See, it's a place he had put in. He was a drug dealer. When Mom died, he wanted me to come here, but he was afraid of some people he used to do business with. So we worked out this system." He shrugged. "Daddy said it wasn't perfect, but it was better than a foster home." There was something about the kid that was a lot older than his years—he'd learned to accept what life sent him.

"He told you he was a drug dealer?"

"Well, it wasn't like I didn't know. My mom died of an overdose." He tied his shoe and stood up. "Where are we going? I've got to call somebody."

"Right now, we have to get to the car. But we're going to be soaked. Put some dry clothes in a backpack." Though it meant a much longer trek to the car, she took him out through the kitchen. She couldn't stand to think of him bearing for the rest of his life the memory of the bloody sheet in the shape of a cross.

The wind seemed heavier, and probably was—the worst winds

usually came at this end of the storm. The kid held one of Skip's belt loops, and slipped once, nearly taking her down with him.

Once in the car, she drove a few blocks and parked, wanting to think a little more about what to do with him. "Okay, let's talk a minute. Who do you need to call?"

He bowed his head and stared at his lap.

He doesn't trust me, she thought.

She said, "Look, the phones are out. My police radio's out. We can't call anybody, but I could take you somewhere."

Cindy Lou's.

"Okay, the police station."

That was the last thing she expected to hear. She realized with surprise how resistant she was to it—aside from what he'd go through, Skip would be there for hours. She couldn't afford the time. "Why are you so eager to go to the cops?"

"A friend of mine's in trouble."

"Look. Billy. A friend of mine's in trouble, too. In fact, two friends, and they're both kids. I have a feeling whoever got your dad is after my kids."

"Your kids?"

"Yeah. One of 'em's mine—or sort of mine. She's like you— her mom's dead."

"What about her dad?"

"He's somewhere else."

"Oh. Deserter, huh?"

"Billy, we have to talk. What happened in there?"

He started to cry again. "They searched the house—to find Paulette. Dad's girlfriend."

Skip's heart pounded. "Was she there?"

"No, but they thought she was. They didn't find me, anyway. Dad said I was at a friend's. They kept asking where was she, and had she been there, and I heard them hit him. I think . . ." he lowered his head and eyes again ". . . I think they did other stuff to him, too."

"Did he tell them anything?"

"He didn't *know* anything. That's what they kept saying—tell them *anything*. Anything he knew about her."

"She was his girlfriend. He must have known something."

The kid didn't speak, just looked away. She'd lost him.

"Look. I think Paulette's got my kid—these guys are after her, do you understand? I've got to get there first."

"Oh, come on. Think this is a movie or something?"

"Billy, listen. There are no phones or radios. There's no *way* to call the police. At this point, I'm her only hope.

"If your dad told them anything, tell me."

She watched the complex play of emotions on his face, from hopelessness to wariness to a little bit of hope.

She said, "You like Paulette, don't you?"

"Yeah. She took care of me."

"Took care of you?"

"You know. Cooking dinner and stuff. Dad tried, but he didn't really know how."

"Have you any idea where she is?"

He bit his lip. "My dad finally said . . . he said . . . her dad lives in Lockport. You know where that is?"

To her dismay, she did. It was in that part of Cajun country known as LaFourche Parish, for Bayou LaFourche—maybe forty, fifty miles away, an hour or so in good weather. The problem was, you had to take Highway 90 to get there, and 90 flooded—might already be impassable.

That settled it. She didn't have time to slog either to the police station, or to Cindy Lou's. She had to get Steve and get on the road.

She racked her brain and finally came up with a possible baby-sitter. She had a neighbor who was both a mother and a therapist.

26
• •

They had long since lost power. They were sitting on the floor, the four of them, around a single candle, though there were others burning in the room. Paulette had made it as nice as she could, transparently trying to cheer the girls up.

First, there had been a screaming fight with her parents, ending in her father getting so mad he pushed her. But he'd forgotten what a powerful woman his daughter was. She had picked up a kitchen knife and threatened him with it, cool as a moose. There was no doubt in Torian's mind she'd have jammed it right in his stomach if he hadn't backed down.

Denis apparently thought so, too. He said, "That's it, Paulette. Ya not my daughter anymore. Ya stay in this house and drown, you and ya little kidnap victims."

Tootie, with a look of hate, had stabbed out her cigarette on her own floor and ground it with her heel, apparently to mark the transfer of ownership to Paulette.

They must really think the place is going to float away, Torian thought.

When Tootie and Denis had gone off to their hurricane shelter,

Paulette took the girls outside and made them look at the house. "See that? Two feet off the ground. Water's gon' come up past that? Naaaaah."

Faylice said, "Paulette, it does. I've seen it on television. And the windows aren't boarded. We ain't ready for this."

It was Sheila who asked what Torian was wondering: "Why couldn't we just go with them to the shelter?"

"Le's go back inside, and we'll talk about it."

When she had them gathered around her, she said, "Because I did kidnap y'all. We don't know what police we gon' run into, or who mighta seen ya pictures on television."

"But Paulette—why'd you do it?" Sheila's voice got that desperate, whiny tone it took on when she was frightened.

"Ya know that man ya got the mustard on? That was real good work, by the way. That's some dangerous man."

Torian said, "How about the Rev?" Her illusions had pretty well been shattered, but she had to check.

"Oh, yeah. Daddy. That's what we call him in the church. Y'all know that?"

"Well, what about him?"

"I guess y'all need to know. Daddy can do anything. I mean sure, he can heal the sick and all that kind of stuff, but the other thing he can do is anything he wants. If he wants something done, it gets done. He doesn't want something, that thing's gon' disappear."

Torian felt a prickling at the top of her head, as if some loathsome bug had gotten into her hair. She had a bad feeling Paulette had used "something" as a euphemism for "someone."

She said, "But . . . the police . . ." She didn't want to confront it either.

"He's got church members everywhere ya look—probably in that police department, I wouldn't be surprised. Worse yet—he's got judges, people like that. Y'all hear what I'm sayin'? He gets away with things."

Sheila said, "Wait a minute. Hold it. We're just kids. Why would he want to kill us?"

"I'm not sayin' he does, precious. I'm just sayin' if he did, can't no cops protect ya."

"And he might."

"Well, now, I don't know." But she did, Torian was sure. What had seemed to her fury that afternoon was really fear, she thought. At that moment, she knew she'd do anything for Paulette—because she was surer than sure that her own mother would never have done such a thing, would have been too drunk to summon the energy.

Sheila wasn't going to let it drop. "Paulette, come on. Why would he want to kill us?"

She sighed. " 'Cause he's gone crazy, sugarplum. Y'all know stuff that could wreck his damn ol' campaign."

"We don't know anything! And anyway, you don't kill people over stuff like that."

"Well, okay, precious lamb, then Paulette's gone crazy."

"I don't see why we can't just go to the regular police and say we need protection. My aunt's a cop, you know."

"Honey, half the time he's got somebody watchin' ya aunt."

Torian said, "But there's Noel. Noel wouldn't let him get away with anything."

Paulette shook her head; her eyes were so sad Torian thought she must be thinking of all the bad things that had happened to her; she knew thinking of Noel set off that reaction in her.

"Y'all just don' understand what you're up against here." She seemed to curl into herself. "Killin'. I could see killin'. Some things got to be done. But killin' children? Uh-uh. No, ma'am on that one."

"Adonis," said Torian. "What happened to Adonis?"

"She got away, honey. Daddy didn't know she was there, and she saw what was happenin' and hid till they left; and then she snuck out. She didn't think I saw her. It's better that way." Her smile was so big that Torian didn't doubt her.

Faylice, who had been rocking herself, her eyes as sad as Paulette's, spoke for the first time in a while. "Suppose he doesn't catch us? What are you going to do with us?"

"Well, idn't that the truth? What am I gon' do with y'all?" She was trying to be hearty, but, finding she couldn't make it fly, she switched gears. "Le's just get through the storm, okay? Then we'll worry about that."

Shortly after that, the lights went out. Paulette made a big thing about how they had to eat everything in the refrigerator or it would spoil, and sure enough, they'd found some potato salad and ham in there that really did need to be eaten. And then Paulette had tried to get them to sleep, but they were too keyed up.

So they drank some leftover coffee they found, and Torian and Sheila taught the other two to play hearts. Paulette didn't really cotton to it, but Faylice shot the moon about an hour into the game, and that got everyone's competitive spirit up. They played through the night, listening to the wind rip branches from trees, the rain like a drum, sitting on the floor in case something flew through a window. Every now and then one of them would go to the window to check on flooding.

Halfway through the night, Torian became alarmed—the water was getting high, and the worst part of the storm was yet to come. Paulette pooh-poohed it, saying you could drive a car through that, no problem. "You know what y'all's trouble is, Toreen?" This was the nickname she had given her charge. "Y'all are just ol' city gals. Growin' up here in bayou country, the way I did, ya get on speakin' terms with nature. This is nothin' but a l'il ol' storm. Storms come and storms go, and Lockport stays. It's here now and it'll be here tomorrow. So y'all just settle in and enjoy it. Ya hear that creakin' and groanin'? When we were kids, we used to think that was just good entertainment. Le's tell ghost stories, why don' we? Y'all know about the *loup-garou*?"

A tree fell against the house. One of its limbs came through the kitchen window, shattering their nerves along with the glass. Torian saw Paulette start, and watched her mouth tighten, trying to keep up a front for the kids, who screamed unabashedly.

Rain poured in; the candles blew out. The howling and groaning was in the room with them.

But they all broke up when Faylice said, "Yeah, Paulette. This be a great time for ghost stories."

They got the candle lit again, the one on the floor, and kept it shielded with their bodies. Paulette brought quilts from the beds, not so much because they were cold, as for comfort. Then she did tell about the *loup-garou*.

"Really, really bad people who want to do really, really bad stuff, go rub themselves with voodoo grease, and then their eyes get red and their nose gets pointy and they grow fur, just like a wolf."

Sheila doubled over. "Gimme a break, a Cajun werewolf? He doesn't say 'I'm going to eat you all up,' he's like, 'Ya gumbo or ya life.' "

"You laugh. He's a werewolf, but he's like a vampire, too. Giant bats drop them down ya chimney, and they suck ya blood and turn ya into a *loup-garou*."

"Yeek, I'm terrified."

"After he sucks your blood," said Faylice, "he goes, '*Merci bien. Laissez les bon temps rouler.*' "

Torian said, "I hear something," and went to the window. "Headlights."

"What?" Paulette stood up slowly, an impressive form in the candlelight. She muttered, "I got to get something," and she went to a round table with a drawer in it, a shiny-finished table, maybe the best piece in the room. The thing she got was a gun.

She said to Torian, "Get away from that window."

Torian moved to her left, in front of an old-fashioned, dark-stained china cabinet. Another tree crashed onto the house, which shook so hard the cabinet fell over, taking Torian with it. The cabinet, filled with dishes, had a glass front. The noise it made as it hit the floor was about twice as loud as the tree crash, and full of the ominous jingle of breaking glass and crockery.

Not sure where she was cut, or how badly, Torian was afraid to move. Her left leg was numb, her right one hurt so bad she wanted to howl like a *loup-garou*, but she stuck her fist in her mouth instead. Lying face up, she could see through the window as the approaching car stopped and someone got out.

Paulette fired.

• •

When she knocked at Boo Leydecker's door, for a minute Skip questioned her own good sense. Here was a woman she hardly knew who'd just lost her husband. What made Skip think she could show up with a strange kid?

297

She'd left Billy in the car, and talked fast. "Boo, listen, I need an emergency therapist. I found this kid hiding in the closet of a house where he heard his father getting killed. Apparently, he doesn't have any family, and I can't get to the police station."

All her instincts had been right. She saw Boo's horror give way to compassion, and then that replaced by something else, something like hunger. She needed someone she could help—maybe that was how she got through crises.

"Of course. Bring him in."

"The phones are out, and so's the radio tower. I need you to call my sergeant and fill her in as soon as you can."

"Certainly. But why are you out in this?"

"Emergency. I have to get to LaFourche Parish."

"You can't go in that."

Skip stared down at her drenched clothes. "I'm going home to change."

"I meant your car. There might be flooding—you need four-wheel drive."

Skip realized she was probably right.

"Take mine. I have an Explorer."

Skip accepted quickly. *What a mom*, she thought. *Cindy Lou's a therapist who's always attracted to the wrong man—here's one who's got to take care of you.*

"There's a gun in the glove compartment—normally I'd remove it, but I guess with you it'll be okay."

Skip only nodded, barely registering the information. Lots of middle-class women carried guns in their cars. She'd gotten used to it.

She parked the Explorer on the sidewalk, which was strictly illegal.

She heard Steve stirring as she came in the house and started up the stairs. As she came in the bedroom, he said, "I'm awake. You can turn on the light."

"There aren't any lights. Listen, I need you."

"You sure do. You look like you've been out in a hurricane."

"I've got to go back out. I think Sheila's in Lockport."

"Where the hell's that?"

"LaFourche Parish—near Houma. About forty or fifty miles on Highway 90."

"You've got to be crazy. You can't drive that far in a hurricane. There'll be flooding."

"So we'll wade." She was peeling clothes as they talked. She now pulled on a dry pair of jeans, T-shirt, sweatshirt, and a pair of rain boots. She got out her rain parka. In its pockets, she slipped her gun, a couple of pairs of handcuffs, and, just for good measure, her radio. "You in or out?"

He swung his legs onto the floor. "I'm your man."

She stopped long enough to give him a lazy smile. "You sure are, baby."

"Hey, we've got a gas stove. Let's have some coffee. Dee-Dee called, by the way. Ten or eleven times."

"Oh, God. What'd you tell him?"

"The first time or the last? I started out with 'Don't worry, everything's under control,' and progressed to . . ."

"Spare me, okay?"

While he made coffee and dressed, Skip tried her radio and phone once again, to no avail. It bothered her to leave Mike Aaron's murder unreported, but it bothered her a lot more to imagine the animals who'd tortured Aaron getting hold of Sheila and Torian. No way was she going to pop by Headquarters and fill them in—they probably couldn't do anything till the storm was over, anyway.

● ●

Highway 90 was a sometimes desolate stretch of road, lined near New Orleans with junk-food joints and minimalls, finally giving way to swampland. This part was pretty in the daytime, but so low that water could be seen a few feet from the road at the best of times. A boat might have been a better idea than a car.

Skip and Steve took turns driving, Steve first. Skip filled him in, then napped for a while, but it was a very little while. She was bone weary, but she was also wired.

When she woke up, she looked through Boo's collection of CDs and chose Bonnie Raitt for boogying down the road. Steve said, "Here's the part I don't get. When we get to Lockport, how do we find Paulette's old man's house?"

"Well, I've thought about that. We could ask somebody."

"Just any old body who happens to be out walking in a hurricane?"

"Yikes! You'd better stop and let me get that." A huge limb was blocking the road. It took both of them to move it.

The wind was so strong they had to lean on each other to get back to the car.

Skip said grimly, "It's getting worse."

"Maybe we can outrun it."

But there was no outrunning it. What with flooding and debris in the road, they were crawling. The only good news was that they might just avoid the heaviest and deadliest part, what meteorologists call "the eyewall of the storm," the part that surrounds the eye, at least till they got to Lockport.

After an hour, they changed places, and Skip realized instantly that Boo was right—she'd never have made it in her own car. The Explorer was much higher off the ground, so that they could go through deeper water than most cars could handle. Road conditions being what they were, a couple of pontoons wouldn't have hurt either.

The flooding could have been a lot worse—they were plain lucky—but there was certainly debris. Occasionally there was the shock of something hitting the car—and not always branches. Pieces of houses and boats were in the air as well. And tires, for some reason. With the rain pounding down, visibility was nearly nonexistent. About the best she could do was follow the white line whenever she could find it.

But for the first time that night, Skip felt like a police officer again—like the well-oiled machine that knew how to get the job done, no matter how dangerous, no matter how sticky. Like she could get enough distance not to blow it.

She had been operating in a panic for hours, adrenaline pumping through her veins, and along with it the heightened awareness and almost superhuman performance it can bring. It was a drug, though, and it could make you edgy.

After Steve had made the coffee, he had pressed his large, comforting frame to hers long enough for her body to absorb some of his calm and strength. It was funny—she usually thought of herself as the one who had to handle crises, but she was beginning to develop a new respect for Steve—to see him in a different light entirely. Just because he wasn't a cop didn't mean he couldn't handle emergencies—he'd already proven himself a cool and competent burglar.

At the moment she was almost pathetically grateful for his presence—and for the coffee he'd made and packed in a thermos. The music was helping, too.

They had made it nearly to Des Allemands when they saw light ahead.

Steve said, "Roadblock."

Hope flickered briefly in Skip's vitals. *Backup?* she thought, and then realized it was a pipe dream. Every available state and local policeman would be dealing with the storm. She could plead on her knees, and it wouldn't do any good.

The officer standing in the rain looked about twenty. He had a chubby, pink-cheeked face and a haircut that looked as if it had been done by a girl friend with a razor. He also had a don't-fuck-with-me look about the eyes that plainly announced he wasn't enjoying his day.

She said, "Hi. Kind of wet out, huh?"

He didn't answer, instead let his nasty eyes bore through her, silently asking how this uppity piece of road furniture dared address him.

Skip recognized the expression: it was one way of dealing with intrusive civilians. It was no fun on this side of it. Quickly, she produced her badge. "New Orleans police. I've got an emergency in Lockport."

"Let me see your commission card."

She showed him that as well, but instead of glancing at it, he studied it for a long, maddening time, looking back and forth from her picture to her face.

Does the word "emergency" have too many syllables for you? she thought, and gritted her teeth to keep from saying it.

Finally, he said, "What kind of emergency you got?"

"Kidnapping. Three teenage girls."

"Kidnapper's not goin' nowhere. This road's impassable. We been here for four hours, issuing warnings—just closed it half an hour ago."

"You've been here four hours?"

"Sure have."

"Have you seen a white female adult, late twenties, with two white female juveniles and one black one?"

"Plate number?"

He had to be kidding. She answered in bureaucratese, a language she thought he might be able to grasp. "That information is not available."

"Make and model of car?"

"Look, if you've stopped every car, you've looked inside. Just tell me—have you seen anybody like that?"

"Nope." He spread his hands. "No mixed groups at all. Doesn't matter, nohow. The problem is, you're not listening. What I'm trying to tell you, this road's impassable."

She was tired of playing games with him. "I'm a police officer. Let me through, please."

"Now you know I can't do that. How you gonna drive on a road that's impassable?"

"That's my problem."

His tone changed from a kind of neutral stubbornness to a sort of nasty triumphant purring. "Listen, be a good little girl, why don't you. You're a New Orleans police officer. So why don't you just go on home to New Orleans? When the storm's over, we'll handle your little kidnapping for you, right up here."

"Let me get this straight. You're preventing another officer from doing her job? Is that what I just heard?"

He turned red. "You bitch." He responded more to her tone than anything else, she thought. She sounded like a schoolteacher dressing down a class.

"Call your commander and ask him what to do, please." She knew he had to do it, and so did he. He turned redder still, and when he was in the car, he fumbled in his pockets for a long time, finally extracted a cigarette, lit it, and sat there smoking, not making a move for his radio. It was probably out anyway.

She mouthed, "Fuck you, asshole!" not even bothering to shout, and drove through the roadblock.

The young cop leaned on the horn, but that was all he could do.

Steve leaned out the window and hollered, "Fuck yooooooooooou!"

"I already said that."

"It needed saying again. Besides, you ever seen a grown man explode in an Explorer? Not a pretty sight."

She put a hand on his knee. "Hey. Thanks for keeping your mouth shut."

"I'll probably recover in fifteen years or so."

As they crossed the Company Canal, Steve asked for the second time, "How're you going to find Paulette's dad's house?"

"I'm going to ask somebody."

"Like maybe a cop?"

"Well, I thought of that. Don't think I didn't think long and hard about it. The trouble is, you can't know how these small-town guys are going to respond. They might say, 'let's go, not a minute to waste'; or they might keep me around for hours asking questions and waiting for the rain to stop or their shift to be over." She glanced at him. "We've got to move now, Steve. You game?"

"Hey, I didn't get up in the middle of the night so I could wimp out at the last minute. Hey, stop!"

Skip slammed on the brakes. "What's going on?"

He pointed. "There's a light in that window."

The windows of the house had been taped rather than boarded, and from one came a glow, probably produced by a hurricane lamp.

"And there's a boat in the yard. Obviously these people didn't want to evacuate—they must think they can get away in the boat if things get tough."

Skip went in alone. She was met at the door by a man in T-shirt and shorts. Though it wasn't cold, further back in the room a woman huddled under a blanket. "I saw your lights, and I'm desperate. Do you have a phone book? Or better yet, do you know Denis Thibodeaux?"

The man shook his head, puzzled. "Come in, come in. Renee—she needs a phone book."

The woman moved fast. She brought the book, looking worried. "Ya all right, out in that? Ya want to stay here with us?"

Skip didn't have to fake looking regretful. "I have an emergency. Here's the address—where's Terrebonne Street?"

The man nodded vigorously, indicating he was now in control. "Ya keep goin' on Highway 1. Ya gon' pass a lot of streets with women's names and some named fa trees. Ya keep gon' and gon', and finally ya gon' come to a house already decorated fa Hallowe'en. And here it is, first week o' September!"

"Decorated how?"

"Bats and pumpkins and things in da windows. Ya see dat, and da next street's gon' be Terrebonne. If ya pass da Valentine Bridge, ya've gone too far."

Terrebonne was a mean little road, pebbles dumped on dirt. The car shook. If they'd crawled before, they were snails now.

The night was black as dirt, but they could make out a little by their headlights. Homes were mingy little dwellings, many of them trailers, windows boarded against disaster.

As they drew near, they heard gunshots, close together.

27

• •

The man's voice was so loud Torian thought he must have brought a megaphone. She hadn't heard his car over the noise of the storm, but his voice was deep and commanding; terrifying. "Paulette. Don't shoot, baby. We're here to help you."

Sheila and Faylice had lifted the cabinet off her, just a little, and Sheila was looking under it. "I think you're cut. I think I see blood. I'm pretty sure."

"Ya'll stay down," Paulette snapped.

"We're got to get this thing off her."

"Be careful, that's all." Her gaze never left the window.

Between them, the girls righted the thing and Torian looked at her legs. The right one was cut, the one that hurt so bad, but the cut didn't seem to be in the same place that hurt. She tried moving the left one and found the feeling gradually returning to it.

"Oh, shit, look at that," said Faylice, and went into the kitchen. Kneeling, Sheila held Torian's hand, her body between Torian's face and her leg, shielding her from her own wound. But Torian could feel the sticky wetness.

Paulette said, "Y'all stay down!" Then to Torian's surprise, she answered the man outside. "Who's that—Potter Menard? Is Daddy with you? I need to talk to Daddy. Bad. Lemme talk to Daddy."

Faylice socked a folded dish towel on to Torian's leg. Torian winced.

"I gotta apply pressure."

The man shouted: "Give up the girls, Paulette. Kidnapping is nothing to mess with."

"Y'all really think you can get 'em away?"

Sheila whispered, "Why is she talking to him?"

"She must be tryin' to find out somethin'—like where he standin'," said Faylice. "So she can shoot him."

Torian's leg hardly hurt at all now, except where Faylice had her hand, was pressing as hard as she could.

A tinkling sound made her neck prickle. "What's that?"

Faylice's eyes were huge. "It come from the back."

Paulette apparently hadn't heard it.

Sheila pinched the flame of the candle they were using, wax poured into heavy glass, the kind carried both by botanicas and by convenience stores in hurricane country—good for magic spells and storms. She flattened herself against the wall next to the doorway from the hall. A man stepped into the doorframe, and Sheila swung the candle like a baseball bat.

The man doubled over, just as the first shot came through the window. Paulette shot back and almost immediately started cursing.

Seizing the advantage, Sheila whacked the man on the head, now at her chest level. He staggered a little, and she hit him again. A third time.

"Shit," said Paulette. "Shit! How the fuck I'm s'posed to know how many of 'em out there?"

The man staggered a moment more before his knees buckled. He thudded to the floor, his head rolling to the side. Torian couldn't see his face.

She tried again with her left leg, gradually trying to get some feeling back, to get it moving. She heard a slight something behind her, she never knew what—perhaps it was a man brushing the wall as he tried to keep quiet.

She saw him come through the door, and she saw Sheila swing, but this time he saw it, too. A hand darted out and caught the heavy candle. The other arm caught Sheila. The hand in it held a gun.

Torian saw that he was a white man, more broad than tall, but definitely the sort you'd want to avoid on a poorly lit street. He reminded her of Stanley Kowalski—not the Brando Kowalski, but Stanley as she pictured him—ugly and brutal.

Paulette spun around, mouth open with shock, no words coming out. The man said, "Put the gun down, or I'll kill her."

Paulette didn't speak, just let her eyes pierce his body with a thousand astral arrows, none of which drew a drop of blood. Torian couldn't believe she had the guts to try.

A great weight fell across the front door, which flew open with a rush of wind and rain. The tall black man from Paulette's, the one who had chased and caught Sheila, stepped in and closed the door behind him. He trained his gun on Paulette.

He spoke very fast, but somehow the words came out lazy. "You could get me with that thing, but Rob's gonna waste that kid simultaneously." He nodded at Sheila, now tight in the white man's grip. "You Cajuns know that word? Means 'at exactly the same time.' "

Sheila's cheeks flamed watermelon. Her eyes were dark pools, big as sand dollars. Her body was tense with fear, but she wasn't shaking, she wasn't crying. For a second, Torian wondered if she could be that brave, and give it up; she knew she couldn't. She *was* shaking.

But *I've lost blood*, she thought, and saw that Faylice was still holding the cloth tight to her leg, her face down, looking at it. *Her way of escaping. Wish I could do it.*

She couldn't. She wanted to know if she was going to die.

Paulette dropped the gun. "I know the word, Potter. We're colorful, we're not dumb."

The black man said, "Let her go."

The white man, Rob, gave Sheila a nasty little push, so that she stumbled toward Torian and Faylice, had to fall to the right to avoid hitting them. Torian gasped at the cruelty of it.

Sheila sat rubbing her leg, slightly hurt from the fall, as the white man picked up the gun. He tucked it into his waistband and turned towards Sheila. "I kind of liked the way that one felt when I was holding her."

Paulette said. "Ya take one step toward her and I swear I'll . . ."

Rob interrupted her. "You'll what? Get killed. That's all you'll do. And I wouldn't like that at all, because I want to fuck you before I kill you.

"Fact, I'd like to fuck every one of you girls, 'cept maybe the dark meat over there." He glanced at Potter. "Hey, no offense, man. It ain't her color, it's her fat bottom."

Potter said, "Look after Gerard."

"Oh, man, you ain't no fun at all. Which one do you want? I'll let you have first pick—go on ahead. You want that little one with the hurt leg? She's skinny, but she's mighty pretty."

"Have you lost your mind, man? I want no talk of rape, do you understand me?" The black man was furious. "I want you to remember who you represent and what. If you're not a Christian, get out of here. Gerard and I'll handle this."

"Since when aren't Christians entitled to a little poon?"

The man on the floor stirred, turned his head toward Torian. He was black, but that was about all she could tell about him.

Potter said, "Gerard. You all right?"

Slowly, the man folded himself to a sitting position. "Head hurts."

Rob jerked his shin towards Sheila. "You can thank that little bitch over there."

Potter said, "See if you can get up. We've got to take these people out and get out of here."

Take us out? thought Torian, her pulse pounding in her ear. *These are church people. He couldn't mean—*

Sheila said, "Excuse me . . ." in a voice like a toddler's. She cleared her throat and spoke up. "Excuse me. Where are you taking us?"

Rob laughed in that cruel way that gives rednecks a bad name. "You ain't even gonna care, sweet baby. You ain't even gonna care."

• •

The water was higher here, so high that even with the Explorer, Skip was afraid it would reach her tailpipe and kill her engine.

But it's that or walk, she thought, panicked after what they'd heard. Her thoughts whirled.

Steve said, "Maybe we should wade. At least we'd have a car to come back to."

"Just what I was thinking." *Along with fifty other things.*

There were no more gunshots, and in moments they saw the house, candlelight streaming serenely from one or two of the windows. They were in a cul-de-sac.

Who the hell is in there? Skip dreaded finding out, noticed there were two cars in the front yard, looking driveable. Where she had parked must be a low spot, she thought, and realized that leaving the Explorer there meant no one else could leave. Maybe that was good.

She remembered Boo's gun in the glove box and thought hard about giving it to Steve.

These people are armed—I sure can't let him go in there without it. The question is, can I let him go in at all?

"Do you know how to shoot?" she finally asked.

"Why? Is there another gun?"

"Do you?"

"Not really."

"Forget it then. You stand guard."

"Uh-uh. If you've got a gun, give it to me. I'm not watching you commit suicide."

He's got a point. I can't go in there without backup, but I am going in there.

She taught him the rudiments and crossed her fingers. "You cover the back."

The storm was getting worse. Walking was a nightmare, involving quite a bit of falling—as well as dodging foreign objects. The good news was, the wind and rain were so loud the perps probably hadn't heard the car.

As they approached, she and Steve could make do with the

light from the house, so they almost certainly couldn't be seen from inside. Thus, they might make it without getting shot.

But then what?

She thought, *What are we going to do? Giving the police knock just doesn't seem like a way to live very long.*

But what else? Break a window? Climb up on the roof and slide down the chimney?

Tear gas would be good, but I'm fresh out.

Firebomb? Not with Sheila in there.

Suddenly, the situation seemed futile.

Fuck. Am I going to have to wait them out after all? With the worst part of the storm yet to come?

No! What do I have that they haven't got?

Steve. That's about it—and he doesn't even know how to shoot.

Wait a minute!

It's not Steve himself. It's the fact that he's here.

She saw there was only one way to play it—as a solo. Which meant back to Plan A—the police knock.

Steve said, "Are you out of your mind? What's to keep them from killing you?"

It was a real possibility. When she didn't answer, he said, "Hey, why don't I do it? They don't know me. I could be a guy lost in the storm. Or better yet—I'm a neighbor with an emergency."

"They probably do know you. They've been having me tailed."

"Well, it'll take them a while to figure out it's me. I can do a Cajun accent."

"Do me a favor and forget that part."

"Aha. Like the plan, do you?"

She did. But she couldn't believe she'd more or less just acquiesced to it. Everything in her said not to put a civilian in that kind of danger.

But what choice have I got? He's right—they'd be downright delighted to shoot me on sight. Steve could buy us a couple of minutes.

Deep down, she knew the truth, and it had nothing whatsoever to do with putting a civilian in danger. It was too late to worry about that one: Both their lives were on the line.

She said, "Okay, forget the back. It's mine. But make sure you know I'm there before showtime."

"How am I going to know? I can't see doing bird calls above this."

"Why don't we just set a time limit? Give me ten minutes to reach the back. That should work even if I twist an ankle."

"Ha. I knew there was a use for my Timex Indiglo feature."

Good old Steve. Making jokes in the heat of battle.

She couldn't help wondering if he had any idea how much danger they were in. But he was a grown-up—he must.

After they split, on higher ground so that at least she was no longer knee-deep, she pulled off her boots, emptied them, and put them back on. After that, she kept up a steady crawl, holding onto the house the way she'd learned in New Orleans, trying not to splash. Yet the storm was so loud it probably didn't matter about the noise. By the same token, no matter how she strained, she couldn't hear a sound from inside.

On the side of the house, where there was no light from candles, it was pitch-dark, and she could see nothing.

She'd progressed past what she thought was less than a third of the house when she hit her forehead on something big. What? She could get her arms around it.

Exploring a little more with her hands, feeling bark and then branches, she realized it was a tree that had fallen against the house. It took her awhile to get around it, but she made it to the back with no further obstacles. She should be well within her ten-minute limit.

There were steps leading to a back door. As soon as she put her foot up, she crunched glass. She knew instantly what it meant—an earlier forced entry.

Good—that'll just make it easier.

Steve started to holler. "Denis!" The house shook as he pounded the door. "Denis, it's Etienne. Open up, goddammit! Let me in."

Etienne! It was as if he were trying to make her laugh—at least to amuse her, to remind her it was Steve out there, that he was with her. Skip recognized that and drew strength from it. Perhaps unintentionally, the small joke, the spark of humor in the face of adversity, reminded her how good life could be.

Adversity, hell, she thought. *That sounds pretty trivial—like ants at a picnic.*

She tried not to let the rest of the thought materialize into words, but in the back of her mind she knew: He could be dead in five minutes.

However, the perps had done her a favor. Effortlessly, she found the hole in the door where the glass had broken. She stuck her hand in, opened the door, and slipped in. Simple as that.

"Denis, I've lost my house. Tree crashed in and hit my wife. I think her hip's broken. Denis, goddammit, I fixed ya boat that time. Ya owe me, man!"

It was dark as a cave in the kitchen. The door to the living space had been closed, probably against the storm.

Slowly, silently, she cracked it.

A storm blast came from the front—the door opening to Steve. Skip breathed deeply, grateful they hadn't shot him.

A thick-bodied white man was speaking to him. "Denis ain't here. Look, we got our own emergency . . ."

Skip surveyed the scene quickly, knowing she had to move before they shut the door on him. There were two other men there.

Potter was one, holding a gun on a tall woman, her arm twisted behind her back. He was facing the door, intent on the intruder.

Another black man held Sheila's arm, much the same way. He had his gun trained on Torian, who sat on the floor hugging a cloth to her leg, having evidently hurt it. A black girl Skip didn't know was gaping at the door. The gunman was, too.

Steve butted the white man back into the room. At almost the same moment, Torian, so motionless and white-faced, seemingly so frightened, leaped for the black man's gun, got his hand in her mouth, and bit him hard, judging from his howl. Sheila seized the moment to jerk away; he still held on, but by this time the black girl had also joined the fray.

Skip hesitated a moment, thinking to help the children first, but really there was no choice—she stepped up behind Potter, stuck her gun in his neck, and said, "Let her go or you're dead."

He said, "If you were going to shoot me, you would have already."

That was the signal to pull the trigger.

Oh, God, I can't do this again. I can't.

Sheila hit him like a cannonball, having wrenched away from the other one. He was knocked off balance, which gave Paulette a chance to knee him.

Steve yelled, "Skip!" Only one word, but the urgency in it was riveting.

She could almost feel the adrenaline course through her blood-stream, take over her mind and body. As fast as her eyes could flick to Steve, could take in the sight of the white man holding a gun on him, she fired and watched him fall.

Oh, shit, it's like before.

She thought later that it was amazingly like the time she had killed before. It was not like shooting Potter in the back would have been. That time she had been immediately threatened, this time Steve was, and neither time had she hesitated.

There's no way out. I just go through life killing and killing . . .

Another shot, this one behind her, cut through her thoughts. She whirled to see Paulette holding Potter's gun, Potter bleeding on the floor. Sheila was sitting beside him, trying to catch her breath.

That left the second black man. The black girl was squeezing him around the waist, as if she could make him stop breathing. Torian still had his hand in her mouth, the hand with the gun.

Skip realized only a few seconds had passed. *Two seconds; two men killed,* she thought.

Steve said, "Drop it," and she saw that he had the white man's gun, had it pointed at the black man. For the first time she looked at the black man's face and saw how wide his eyes were, how frightened.

This is not a professional thug. This is just some kid from the church.

"Police," she said. "Do what the man said."

His eyes flicked to her, took in her gun, and the fight went out of them—fear turned to relief. The game was up, and he didn't have to keep trying to play it.

The gun slipped from his grip. Torian kicked it toward Steve, but she must have bitten down once more for good measure: the man yelped like a struck dog.

Another noise covered his voice—a ripping sound overhead. They all stared up as a chunk of the roof opened up and blew away. Papers and garments flew about the room, as well as some of the crockery from the broken china cabinet—anything small enough to fly flew. The candles went out.

Skip grabbed the standing man's arm, so he'd know how close she was. "Steve, I need you." When he had stepped closer, she pulled a pair of handcuffs from her pocket. "Get these on him," she said, and turned quickly, wildly uncomfortable, knowing there was still one loose gun in the room. "Paulette, drop the gun and kick it over."

She breathed easy when she heard a thunk and a dragging noise. Paulette wasn't going to fight—at least not right now. "Sheila, pick it up and give it to me."

When she had the gun, she said, "Okay, everybody into the kitchen." Where there was a roof. "Steve, handcuff that dude to something in there. Girls, get the candles and matches. Can you do that?"

"Sure can," said the black girl. "But Torian better sit still. Her leg bleedin' again."

Skip kept Paulette covered, Paulette and the two fallen men, while Sheila and Faylice lit up the kitchen. Then she, Steve, and Paulette examined Potter and Rob. Both were alive and bleeding. Thank God, Skip thought. Thank God! I couldn't handle that again. They dragged them into the kitchen and did what they could to stop the bleeding.

As soon as she could take a break, Skip said, "Sheila, you all right, sweetheart?" To her surprise, the girl leaped into her arms.

"Auntie Skip. Thank you for coming."

"It's okay now, baby."

"Torian's hurt."

Faylice said, "Jus' about stopped bleedin' again. She gon' be okay."

Sheila looked at Skip with as bewildered a look as Skip had ever seen on the girl's face. "I don't understand what's happening."

Skip hugged her harder and looked at Paulette. She said, "Maybe you could fill us in."

Paulette's face was tragic in the candlelight, cheeks drawn, dark eyes sunk into their sockets. "I had to get the kids. These people, they don't mess around. You know how they are. They killed Noel Treadaway—they just as soon kill anybody got in their way. Kids? Ha. That ain't nothin' to them. They kill *anybody*—"

"They did not! They did not kill Noel Treadaway! Noel Treadaway is fine! Noel Treadaway is not dead—do you hear me? I talked to him two days ago." Torian was standing up, Faylice at her feet. Hands over her ears, she was screaming as loud as the wind.

28

• •

When Torian had been calmed, and Paulette, distraught at upsetting her, had been taken care of as well, day was breaking, and the storm was still blowing.

Skip desperately wanted to get Potter and Rob to a hospital. She looked at Steve: "Think we could get out of here?"

His face was grim. "I don't know. I just don't think—" but seeing her face, seeing her glance at the man she had shot, he stopped in mid-sentence and nodded. "I'm going to go take a look."

It took him nearly a minute to get the door closed behind him. He came back shaking his head. "Water's up. We can't get the Explorer any closer—and there's no way to carry them out to it."

Skip nodded. She had expected it, but the idea of waiting out the storm made her want to scream.

He said, "Let's get everyone as comfortable as we can, and one of us can go for help."

Skip hadn't handcuffed Paulette, taking her at her word for the moment, but she didn't feel comfortable leaving the woman alone. She left Steve with her and the three prisoners while she braved the storm within the house to find pillows and blankets for the wounded men and the girls, dry clothes for herself and Steve. Paulette settled the girls and herself while Skip and Steve did what they could for the men. Half-conscious, Potter moaned as Skip tucked a blanket around him, brushing at an area under his hip. Readjusting his clothes, she felt something hard in his pocket—the thing digging into his hip. It was a tiny tape recorder.

It was evidence, she knew she shouldn't touch it, and if anyone had asked why she pushed the "play" button, she could have supplied only one answer—she couldn't help it. It was like a junkie going for junk, a woman for a man, a cat for a bird—no thought behind it, only compulsion. If she hadn't been so tired, and coming off an adrenaline high, she might have palmed it and turned it meekly over to the proper authorities at the proper time.

She didn't think so, though. This thing was way too personal.

To her surprise, Paulette's voice came through on the tape, loud and clear: "I carried out Daddy's order."

"Shit!" Paulette threw the covers off, leaped up off the floor in her shirt and socks, having shed jeans and shoes, and pounced on the thing.

But she wasn't quick enough to stop the next voice: Potter's saying: "Treadaway's dead?"

Torian leaped up as well, grasping instantly what Skip was still grappling with: "You killed him!"

Paulette wrenched the machine away and opened the door. She splashed out into the storm, pursued by Torian.

For one mad moment Skip thought: Let them go. Who cares? And then she was out the door herself, the rain hitting her like a blast from a fire hose, the wind puffing her cheeks.

By the time she got her bearings, Paulette had already fallen, probably stumbled on a rock or root under the water. Torian had caught up with her and was beating her, hitting her in the face with doubled fists.

The sky was gray now, the light was soft and lazy. Even the air seemed gray, the rain steel instead of silver. Torian wore a T-shirt and shorts, soaked and clinging to her skinny little bones. Paulette sat in about a foot of water, facing into the wind, thick short hair blowing back in such a solid, constant mass, her head and upper body looked like a bust of some wind goddess. Her legs, folded in a kind of semi-lotus, thighs and knees sticking up out of the water, were perfectly muscled, strong as a dancer's.

And little Torian, skinny, fragile little Torian, hair hanging wet and stringy, looking much more the pathetic drowned rodent than any goddess-kin, was battering the statue's chiseled visage as methodically as if she were working out. Paulette did not move, didn't turn her face to avoid the blows, didn't raise a hand to stop them. She simply sat there, staring into the wind, features immobile.

Torian's face was transformed as well. By a trick of the light, perhaps, it seemed as black as Paulette's hair.

Skip heard sloshing behind her—Steve, she hoped. She grabbed Torian's hands and turned the girl around. Her eyebrows, still knit together, relaxed and the rage left her face, replaced instantly by pain.

Her body went slack, and Skip had to pull up on her arms, to put her arms round her shoulders, literally to hug her to keep her from falling. She smoothed the girl's hair like a mom. "It's all right. It's okay, sweetheart."

Torian's voice was strangely matter-of-fact as she said, "It'll never be all right. He's dead."

Without being asked, Steve was gathering Paulette out of the mud. Skip said, "Take her inside. I've got another pair of handcuffs."

"What about the tape recorder?"

Paulette said, "I threw it away."

Maybe she had, maybe she hadn't, but the tape wasn't on her.

"Torian. Did you see her?"

"Yes, she threw it that way." She pointed towards a stand of trees about fifty feet from the house.

"Did you see it land?"

The girl shook her head.

When the floodwaters dried up, it would be easy to find.

As Steve, gripping her elbow hard, passed Skip and Torian, Paulette reached out a hand to the girl and spoke in such a soft voice she could barely be heard. "I'm so sorry, baby. I'm so sorry ya have to feel like this. But it had to be done, sugar. You just didn't know he was fuckin' you up."

"You don't know anything about it! He was all I had in the whole fucking world."

"Just know this, baby—when you think about it later, just know this—I did it for you. I do things for Daddy, sure I do, but that's not why I did this. I did it for you."

Great. That's all she needs on her conscience.

Skip hugged the girl like she was five years old. Torian held on like a baby for a long time in the wind and rain, as if they could wear away her pain. When Skip loosened her grip, Torian would tighten hers, and Skip would let her hold on awhile longer. Finally she said, "Come on. Let's go inside."

Faylice and Sheila found Torian some dry clothes and got her into them.

Skip saw that Steve had handcuffed Paulette on the side of the kitchen opposite from Gerard. Both were attached to cabinet handles, neither of which looked too stable. They wanted watching.

She was itching to get back to New Orleans, to get backup and go get Jacomine, but there was no way right now. She'd have to send Steve for help while she watched the prisoners.

She had him take the girls as well, thinking it was far too dangerous to keep them with her—both wounded men were stirring and moaning, the other two might try to break loose at any moment.

As they got on such coats as they had, she thought about the tape. No way Potter was going to testify against Jacomine, even if he survived. What Paulette would do was anybody's guess. The tape might be all they had against him and soaking in a foot of water couldn't be doing it any good.

Restlessly, she went outside. Why, she wasn't sure—she was never going to find it in the storm. She saw that there were utility shelves by the porch, to the right, the direction Paulette had taken. And Paulette had had time, she had a head start on Torian—she could have faked the throw once she had an audience.

Not daring to hope, Skip let her gaze wander over the shelves. Nothing was there but a few old paint cans, gardening tools, a couple of stacked flower pots. Just to be sure, Skip moved everything, looked behind each item. Almost as an afterthought, she stuck her hand in the topmost flower pot, on a shelf over her head. Her fingers closed around hard plastic.

Once again, she pressed the "play" button. Paulette's voice alternated with Potter's.

"I carried out Daddy's order."

"Treadaway's dead?"

"Yes."

"Report."

"Broad outline or details?"

"Details."

Paulette's voice settled into a kind of professional singsong, like a salesman making a pitch, an anchorman reading news; simply the rhythm of the job. Skip didn't like the sound of it at all—it was obvious she and Potter had worked together before.

"Well, I got this kid to help me."

"Are you crazy? You weren't supposed to involve anyone else."

"This was one of my kids—a kid I took off the streets a few years ago who got molested by an uncle, didn't want to tell anybody. He curled up in a kind of mental shell. He's doin' good now, but he'll always be a little mad. Angry mad, not crazy. Ya know? Doesn't seem like that ever goes away. I told him Noel was a molester."

"Get on with it, Paulette."

"I got him to help me tie him up."

"On what pretext?"

"What do ya mean what pretext? I said it was Daddy's orders, and not to ask questions."

"He's one of ours?"

"Oh, yes."

"Go back to the beginning."

"I got my gun and waited for Noel to come home, just in my car. I leaned out and I said, 'I need to talk to ya about Torian. I'm the woman who's taking care of her.' He got in the car and I took him to my garage.

"I held the gun on him while the kid tied him up. Then I verbally abused him awhile, so the kid would think that's what it was about. Like those sessions we had last year—with the people who tried to leave the church. Remember that?"

"Paulette, I ran those sessions."

"Then I said he could go, I'd take him home, and that would be that. When the kid was gone, I shut up the garage and ran the car till Treadaway died. Didn't take long."

"Doesn't."

"Then I took off the ropes so he wouldn't have marks, searched him, and got the key to his garage. I took him home and unlocked it. Then all I had to do was drag him out and put him in it. If anybody saw me, I was helping a drunk to bed—how often do ya see that in the French Quarter?"

"Uh—tell me you didn't forget anything."

"What?"

"You can't commit suicide without turning on your car."

"For heaven's sake, Potter, you think I'm simple or somethin'? Of course I turned on his car. Pretty slick, huh?"

"Satisfactory. I'll tell Daddy it's done."

Skip could almost see him nodding. It was pretty slick. Provided the kid didn't talk, it was beautiful. And the kid had no reason to connect the death of Treadaway, clear across town, with Jacomine's berserk idea of discipline.

She clicked the machine off, wiped it clean of prints, and put it back in the pot—might as well let the local guys find it with plenty of witnesses. She didn't want some lawyer accusing her of planting it.

Knowing Paulette had heard, she didn't bother to conceal her anger. She banged the back door behind her. "Paulette, where do you draw the line? You killed Treadaway for Jacomine, why not Sheila and Torian?"

"You crazy, girl? Ya think I'd hurt a kid? Anyway, I didn't kill him for Daddy—I already told Torian. I killed him for her—so he'd keep his mitts off her."

"I talked to Mitchell last night—your former pimp. He thinks you had a great relationship. Thinks you'll be back."

She didn't quite manage a laugh, but an amused grunt came out of her. "I'd rather go where they're gonna send me."

● ●

It was two hours before Steve made it back with two ambulances and three sheriff's cars. The storm was slacking off by then, the winds no longer hurricane strength, the rain no more than a steady drizzle.

But the water was still high, and the ambulances couldn't get close. The paramedics had to lift the men out by stretcher.

Skip turned over her other two prisoners and asked to speak to the highest-ranking officer at the scene. Feeling more desperate by the moment, she wasted no words:

"I'm a New Orleans homicide detective on leave. This thing involves a murder-for-hire, and—with luck—the guy doing the hiring is still in New Orleans. I need to call my sergeant—bad."

He had looked impatient all through her speech. Now he shook his head in pity. "We're probably not gonna have phones for three days. We got radio, but you can't get New Orleans with it."

"E-mail. Something."

"No power. No nothin'."

"Then let's drive."

"You crazy? There's flooding all the way to the city."

"We drove here in it."

He shook his head again, giving her the kind of contemptuous smile adults reserve for stubborn children.

"Look. Let me try alone. You know who I am. You can question me any time."

"I don't know who you are. I only know who you say you are."

He let them go by noon, but he was right—the roads were impassable.

Skip, Steve, and all three girls ended up collapsing at a motel, Skip waking up every hour to try the phone again, Torian zonked out on painkillers from the emergency room.

Skip got through at five A.M., and Cappello called back at seven. She had sent raiding parties simultaneously to Jacomine's church, his house, and his office. Jacomine was gone, his wife was gone, and most of their belongings were gone. The church database, the one she and Steve had raided, was wiped out.

29

• •

Lise stood in line at Matassa's, having made a special trip for the instant oatmeal Torian liked, the kind that came in little envelopes and had dried bits of things in it, like apples and raisins. She was also nearly out of gin and was picking up a bottle of that as well.

She was thinking of Charles, largely because she'd spent so much time with him in there. Whenever he came over, they nearly always came down for a six-pack of beer, something she never could seem to remember to pick up.

Well, I could remember, she thought, *if there weren't so damn many other things to do.*

I wonder if life will be simpler in L.A. And then: *I wonder if Charles and I could have worked it out.*

Probably not, with Torian underfoot.

Lise had a sister in L.A., someone to stay with while she got on her feet—an advertising executive, maybe a role model for Torian.

God knows she needs something—she doesn't appreciate anything she's had so far.

The time was right—because of a personality conflict (meaning her boss was a bitch), Lise had been fired again. The decision to move was for and about Torian—New Orleans had simply turned too nasty lately. The girl's values were fucked up.

Try as she might, Lise couldn't see how it had happened—that is, until she started to look at the world around her.

First, there was the larger society. The economy was based on the pleasures of the senses—what the hell was a young girl supposed to think?

Then there was Torian's own father—a married man who'd ended up with a younger woman. That's how she thought men were, and how she thought women were. She probably aspired to be another Carol, grab the prize right out from under the wife, never mind that Lise had dumped Wilson.

How could Torian have overlooked that tiny detail?

Who knew? She was fucked up, that was all Lise knew. Not only that, she'd pretty much disgraced both of them in the neighborhood. For Christ's sake, you just didn't waltz away with the husband of the woman you babysat for.

I'd think she was raised in a barn if I hadn't raised her myself. I don't see why I should have to leave.

I could always get another job. I've got roots here. I've got Charles.

That is, I did have Charles until he dumped me because I got so depressed over that child of mine. It's hard being a mother. Why doesn't anybody get that?

Especially being the mother of a really difficult child, a kid who basically doesn't know her ass from her elbow.

Well, all you can do is do the best for them.

Lise truly believed that, even though it was obvious to everyone what an ungrateful little bitch she'd been cursed with. There was no question Torian had deliberately provoked Lise into hitting her that time. It was a ploy to get sympathy from her married lover—to get him to leave his wife and child. Nothing could be more transparent, and yet Lise's efforts to get Torian to see it, to accept herself as she was, had failed.

Let's face it—along with most things I've ever done as a mother.

I wish to hell I'd never met Wilson Gernhard and never had his damn devil-child.

She nearly tripped, going down Dauphine Street. *I don't mean* that. *I love her. Every mother loves her child. I just wish I could get something back from her. Why does it have to be all one way?*

• •

Feeling numb, trying to hold back tears because Sheila was there, Torian pulled clothes out of her closet, armfuls at a time, and folded them into cardboard boxes. Lise had said she could take only one suitcase with her—the rest would have to come with the movers.

There was something about the work that was soothing, that kept her from falling apart altogether, so in a way she was glad.

She wasn't sure this great lump in her throat, this ugly thing the size of a grapefruit, was ever going to go away. She needed to say good-bye to Sheila—that's what Sheila was here for—but she couldn't bring herself to do it.

Sheila was nattering on, and she wasn't listening. It was something about all the stupid stuff Torian wouldn't have to do anymore—like put up with asshole tourists who peed on your house at Mardi Gras. It was meant to cheer Torian up.

If she only knew—if I listened, I'd melt in a puddle.

She wasn't sure why she felt so lonely right now, so absolutely alone and desperate—she was going off to have a new life, as Lise had said.

In California.

Great.

She'd thought she hated this life, but at least her dad was here, and Carol and Marly.

And Sheila. Most of all, Sheila.

When you go through something like that with someone, they're like your sister. Nobody can ever understand how close it makes you.

I don't know anyone in California. Why would I fucking want to go there?

Sheila said, "Hey. You okay?"

Torian realized she was leaking from the eyes again. "Oh, God. Maybe I better not think about it."

"I better go."

"No!"

"Oh, rats. I have to babysit." She paused. "I mean . . . I'm taking care of Kenny," she said quickly, as if suddenly remembering that 'babysit' was a word bound to be fraught for Torian.

Torian could see the sympathy in her eyes, the pain. She knew it reflected her own eyes, that she had bags under them big enough to haul groceries, that her arms were thin as noodles, that her hair had all the luster of something from a broom closet. In short, that she was an object of pity.

That made her feel sorry for herself all over again. And angry. But not angry the way Sheila got, with balled-up fists and red cheeks. Just hot beneath the eyelids, where the tears nearly reached boiling point. She had to keep her eyes closed to keep them from overflowing, and even that didn't work.

Damn! Shitfire.

Being mad felt better than what it really was. Torian knew, deep down, but she wasn't about to name it: It was the shame of it all. She hated being pitied, hated having Sheila see her like this, knowing this would be her friend's last memory of her.

"Will you come back this summer?" Sheila was saying. "Uncle Jimmy said to ask you. He said you can stay as long as you like. Oh, please, Torian, we'd love to have you."

Torian tried to smile. Lise would never be able to afford it. And wouldn't let her anyway. "Sure," she said.

She thought: *Things are so easy for Sheila.*

Then: *But she has no mother.*

Wish I didn't.

She knew that in reality things were not easy for Sheila, and even that she loved Lise in some twisted way that kids do love their mothers no matter how badly they're treated, but she couldn't help it, she just couldn't be brave right now.

She wanted Sheila to go. It was a horrible feeling, because she also wanted her to stay—she wanted that a whole lot more. But since she couldn't stay, Torian wanted her out of there, wanted it over and done with, and that made her sadder almost than Sheila's going.

When she was finally alone, floods broke forth past the grapefruit in her throat, tissues full of slobber and snot and tears.

Sobs on the Richter scale.

Revolting.

And when she was done, the grapefruit had not dissolved.

Maybe, she thought, *I have throat cancer.*

She slept.

In her dream, someone chased her, someone dressed in black, someone so terrifying Torian couldn't even have guessed at the magnitude of her fear. Finally, she saw who it was, and it was only Paulette. At first she relaxed, smiling, and then she jerked awake, outraged. Really mad this time. Sheila's kind of mad.

Goddammit, she was the only adult I ever thought I could trust.

She killed my lover!

Somehow, this made her feel better. The melodrama of it. It felt . . . removed, somehow.

She thought of Noel's face, their time together, the things they'd done.

Did I really love him? She wasn't sure anymore.

But I must have. How can something that feels like that not be love?

Sex, Sheila would say, but how does she know? She's never been in love.

Their love, the most vivid thing in her young life, was starting to fade in her memory.

A random thought crossed her mind: *I wonder if it's because of Boo?*

She had gone to see Boo, at Skip's request. It was about a week after they'd been rescued—after Skip had broken the news about Noel and Paulette.

Torian had been at Sheila's, and Skip had come in and said she had a message for her. She said Boo wanted to see her, and that she, Skip, thought Torian should call on her.

Torian had said sarcastically, "I'm *sure* she really means it."

"She does. Listen, she's cool. You'd be surprised."

And because Skip currently got Torian's vote as Most Evolved Homo Sapien over the Age of Twenty, she went.

The older woman, her lover's wife, greeted her with a hug. "Torian, I'm so sorry this happened to you."

Torian was speechless.

"Come in, will you? I made some coffee."

Torian liked that. Coffee. If it had been lemonade, she would have understood the subtle put-down. Coffee meant Boo wanted to treat her as an adult.

Torian followed her into the kitchen, but Boo said, "I'm just going to put things on a tray—we can sit upstairs if you like. In the meantime, would you like to see Joy? Go on up if you want to. Her nap's about over—you can wake her up."

"Okay." It felt weird in Boo's kitchen. And the truth was, she was dying to see Joy—she hadn't realized how strong the need was till she actually saw the baby, sleeping as if nothing had happened.

"Joy? Hey, Joy girl, wake up." Torian used to sing "Summertime" to her, with its references to enviable parents; the words flitted through her neurons, and she found that she could bear them. She changed Joy's diaper, just as she used to do, and brought her in to Boo, now in the library beyond the bedroom.

Boo said, "I wanted to apologize to you," and Torian felt her cheeks turn red.

She stammered. "I . . . uh . . ." Surely she was the one who should apologize. That is, if they were going to have the bad taste to talk about Noel.

Boo put up a hand, stopping traffic: "I didn't see what was happening. Adults are supposed to protect children. I didn't do a very good job of protecting you."

"But . . . uh . . ."

"Yes. Noel was my husband. But what he did was pretty bad to both of us, don't you agree?"

"I'm not sure I . . . no. I don't see how."

"You agree he was bad to me?"

Torian nodded.

"Okay, that leaves you. Look. He had some need for you, so he took you. What do you think would have happened eventually?"

He would have dumped you and married me. She couldn't say that, of course.

"Suppose he dumped me and married you—he still couldn't do that for years. You're fifteen, Torian. You're a sophomore in high school. Do you really want to be married?"

In fact, before she met Noel she had no desire at all to be

married. She wanted to sail the seven seas, go to college, get a job—
be somebody who'd made it on her own. Somebody far away
from Lise.

Marriage was the last thing on her mind.

"I just thought . . . I thought . . . it was the only way to be
with him."

"Look, you don't really get along with your mom, do you?"

That made her a little mad. "How'd you know that?"

"Ohhhh . . ." She drew it out. "I know Lise."

That was interesting. Did other people see what Torian saw?

"Also, I've been a kid. I know what it's like to want to get
away from something. Maybe that's more what you really wanted.
And Noel wanted to help you. I feel sure he did."

"Yes! He did."

"Listen, it's none of my business . . ." She paused, holding her
breath, evidently calculating something. "Well, no, I think it is.
You're a child who should have been protected in my house, and
we've gone through a tragedy together. So I'm going out on a limb
here. Do you know what Ala-Teen is?"

Torian shook her head, too dazed to have any idea where this
was going.

"It's a group for kids whose parents are alcoholics."

All Torian could think was, *How on Earth does she know Lise drinks?*
She felt oddly defensive about it.

Boo went on a bit, telling her about the organization, in which
Torian hadn't the least interest, and then she said, "Okay, that's
enough of me being mom."

Surprised to hear the word, Torian looked at her face and
thought how gentle she looked, how much like a nice person. And
for the first time came out of her daze long enough really to see
her, to understand what it had probably cost her to ask Torian to
visit, to talk to her husband's lover.

I'm really not, though, Torian thought, and for the first time, she
knew it was true. She and Noel hadn't made love, and probably
never would have. They were having a flirtation, that was all.

For him.

But deep down, somewhere on the wrong side of her belly, she knew that maybe it was true for her, too—that this wasn't true love, that even she would have tired of it soon.

Yet she wouldn't tire of his memory. For now, she loved him desperately.

I have to hold onto something, she thought.

As she was walking home, she had an odd idea about Boo: *I wish she were my mother.*

●　●

Boo looked in the mirror and was almost disappointed to see her same old face. She had taken to doing this several times a day—examining her visage as if she were a doctor looking for disease.

But it was not disease she expected to find. She felt like a snake leaving its skin in a scaly curl on the floor of the forest. She could not look the same. Surely no one who had been through what she had, was still going through it, could look the same.

And yet she did.

My hair didn't even turn gray overnight.

She was changing from minute to minute and not always, she thought, for the better. Things were battling within her, almost as if there were a good Boo and a bad Boo.

The good one—*oh, hell, don't be so Christian! At least say the healthy one and the . . . what? . . . the sicko?*—The healthy one could see it all so plain: white sand stretching for miles in every direction.

The sicko was lost in the thicket, a pathetic, gnarled crone, all-over warts, unable to straighten her warped body.

The healthy one had invited Torian over, had spoken to her in so civilized a fashion, indeed felt for her, loved her, wanted to give back what Noel had robbed her of. Oh so generous.

Oh yes! This was the one who took care of Joy, ever so bravely, who went about her day picking up the pieces. She was the kind lady to whom the neighborhood cop had brought a little boy who needed shelter the night of the hurricane, the lady you could depend on, who could take care of a second kid with one hand and make her husband's funeral arrangements with the other.

(As it happened, she'd had to take care of burying the kid's dad as well.)

This one could cope like crazy, might even give therapists a good name if anyone were watching. God, she was adult!

She missed Noel. She lay awake at night, missing him, crying over him, yet so furious she didn't know why the sheets didn't catch fire.

How could a grown man be such an idiot? Not to get himself killed, anyone could have done that, Skip had explained that—this guy Jacomine was like those traffic demons who'd shoot you if you got in their face while they were trying to get your parking spot.

Getting killed wasn't Noel's fault—even Sicko Boo didn't think that. But Torian! Where did a grown man, the father of a baby who could barely walk, get off seducing a fifteen-year-old girl?

Noel, why in the hell don't you grow up? she wanted to holler, and it saddened her all the more that now he wasn't going to get the chance.

Okay, okay, the healthy one knew that he was never going to anyway, and that she had a part in that—she didn't want to let him grow up, she knew that; she could see that.

Oh, yes, yes, yes. She could see it all so plain, she was so very rational.

And if anyone ever found out how attached she was to little Billy Aaron, they'd take him away from her.

As it turned out, he had no relatives. None. Not one. Or at least no one close enough to give a rat's ass. He'd been born to a couple of junkies, one of whom had waited just a little too long to straighten out, and one of whom never had. Each of them had one living parent, neither of whom had the money or inclination to take on a child, and there were no kindly uncles or aunts in either family.

Boo wanted to adopt him, and that would be a good thing, a very good thing, if she could manage to get the sicko under control.

When she saw him in the rain that night, his little white face so tragic, his tiny shoulders trying so hard to straighten up, despite what he'd been through, she'd felt everything fall away except a need to take care of him.

Everything. Even her love for Joy.

She wanted to hold him until they melted together.

That was the sicko in action—she had to help out, she had to fix, she had to solve and straighten, she had to be Big Mama.

It was the thing that had drawn Noel to her, and the thing that had driven him away. If he had gone because he'd outgrown her, that would have been a different matter. Instead, he was still the child she'd made him—or helped to make him—even she knew she didn't do it all herself. And he'd found himself a playmate. She could not forgive herself, or Noel. It pissed her off that he was dead, so she couldn't at least have at him with a baseball bat.

But the thing was, the whole thing, was not to do it to Billy— fix him when he didn't need it; rip him up and put him together again. This kid was so lovable. He wanted love so bad he had put his arms around her that night—that very first night, when his dad had just been killed and she was a stranger.

Talk about responsive. He needed a mom so bad he practically trailed her like a puppy.

And she needed him just as badly.

Joy was healthy. Boo was doing a good job with her, raising her right. She was in great shape, and couldn't answer any of the sicko's needs right now. This kid Billy needed fixing.

The part of her that could see things so plainly, laid out bald on that great desert of white sand, was trying hard to hold the other one down, to protect Billy from strangling in a barrel of honey, but the fight exhausted her.

She wanted to look in the mirror and see naked baby skin, shining soft, the new Boo out from under the dry curl on the forest floor.

Every day she was disappointed.

She wanted to rip out the mirror and throw it on the flagstones of the courtyard. But that would be seven years' bad luck, and she couldn't afford it.

30

Cappello called. "So how're you feeling?"

"Fine." Skip answered automatically before she realized it wasn't a rhetorical question. "Wait a minute, let me revise that. Not bad. For me, not bad."

"Recovering?"

"It's a damn good thing that man didn't die, or I'd probably be in the bathtub with a razor."

"The man you shot? No, you wouldn't, you'd just be on Prozac like everyone else."

Skip sighed. "I wonder if I could get Sheila on it."

"She's not doing too well?"

"Actually, she's doing fine in most ways—she almost got raped, did get kidnapped, then almost got murdered. She seems perfectly able to cope with that, but her best friend's moving away. You'd think it was the last act of *Hamlet*—high tragedy time."

"Ah, she's a kid. Say, how's Faylice?" Cappello had gotten to know the girl in the aftermath of Lockport.

"She's fine. She came to dinner last night, along with Torian. Lots of tears—everyone saying good-bye to the California Kid."

"Where's she living?"

"Well, now, that one had a happy ending. She has this nice aunt who finally realized the kid can't make it with her drugged-out mom. Faylice is with her now, and the aunt's trying to get custody."

"I like that kid." Cappello had kids of her own, but she didn't believe in getting too sentimental about them. She switched to professional mode. "Back to your mental health."

"Well, I now get out of bed on weekends and hardly ever dream about Shavonne—or even think about her. Although, ouch; I wish I hadn't said her name. Yeah, I'm better. Some therapy, huh? Head-to-head with a lunatic. Cops are not normal people."

"Listen, Joe asked me to call you. He said to get you back in here before you blow up the state or something."

"He did? He wants me to come back?"

"Christ, even the chief wants you to come back. You're kind of a folk hero right now." Skip could almost see her grinning.

"Now I get it. He wants me back in the office so he can take me down a peg or two."

"You got it."

"I'll think about it."

She could hear the sergeant's sharp inhalation.

"Oh, Sylvia, you know I'm coming back. I just don't know if I'm ready yet."

"Hey, don't be ridiculous. You're out there doing police work without a badge. You're just going to keep on embarrassing us."

"I'll have my people call your people."

She hung up and padded barefoot into the kitchen for a Diet Coke. The nice tiles Jimmy Dee had installed back when he occupied the apartment were cool to her feet. The white of the cabinets against the green of her hanging plants was pleasing to her eye. The Diet Coke could have been champagne.

Her mood had nothing to do with the phone call—she was simply pervaded by a sense of well-being, an appreciation of this moment in this day.

But because of the call, she noticed the moment. *I'm alive*, she thought. *I'm snapping back.*

The thought saddened her a little, and that told her she'd grown used to her melancholy—even, possibly, come to enjoy it in some way.

She had a new thing these days to brood over—Jacomine's disappearance. After what happened in Lockport, she wanted him all the more. She wanted him in a cell, and she wanted to cuff him herself, to feel those metal circles closing around her wrists. Failing that, she could at least go look at him in jail.

She had tracked down the murder charge against him, but big deal—the point of that was to ruin his campaign. It was laughable now: *I have a thousand bigger fish to fry.*

Her scalp prickled as she remembered where she'd heard the phrase. *Shit! He said it himself. He's in my brain.*

Cindy Lou had suggested, in her shrinky way, that maybe being vindictive wasn't the healthiest thing in the world, but her obsession wasn't that.

It was fear. Skip simply didn't believe she could ever feel safe again until Jacomine was behind bars. What she had seen, the machinery he could put in motion, the vast energy he was willing to exert on anything in his way, or anything that might conceivably get in his way, was bewildering at first. Bewildering before you even noticed it was frightening—because no sane person would do it, because it really was what it seemed.

Pure evil.

The devil in human form.

The bogeyman come to life.

You didn't see something like that every day.

After she came back from Lockport, the only people she had wanted to see were Steve and Sheila, because they'd been through it with her, and Jane Storey, because she knew. She understood. Skip could maunder on and on about Jacomine, and Jane would listen attentively, would swear she needed it as much as Skip did, to confirm her own experience.

When she was able to look past the bewilderment, fear grabbed her with a thousand tiny suction cups, like the things on the wrong side of an octopus. Cindy Lou was damned right vindictiveness wasn't healthy, and who did Skip know who wasn't the poster boy for mental stability? Jacomine was perfectly capable of marshaling his resources against her and hers under any rationale his twisted mind could invent.

He might decide she was still dangerous to him—and if she could in any way arrange it, she most assuredly was.

Or he might simply decide he wanted revenge.

And he knew exactly how to get her: Get Sheila, get Kenny. Get Steve or Jimmy Dee.

How in hell could she protect them?

"You can't," said Boo, who agreed to take her on again, at least for a few sessions, after the night of the hurricane. "You have to live life, Skip. You can take precautions—burglar alarms, things like that, but unless he's actively threatening their lives, you have to let it go. Especially with the kids—you want them to grow up as paranoid as he is?"

"I just want them to grow up."

Her hair stood up when she thought of what Sheila had told her. How, when Jacomine had come for her, he had ranted, "Do you know who you're talking to? I am your Daddy! I am your father on this Earth!"

The man thought he was God, and that made him as scary as the devil.

But she saw the sense of what Boo said. With the resilience of youth, and certainly its callousness, its surpassing capacity for denial, Sheila, rather than brood on her various fortuitous escapes, was reveling in her current notoriety.

Kenny was pissed because he'd missed all the fun.

Jimmy Dee was threatening playfully to go back to pot-smoking (something he'd given up when he got the kids) on grounds his nerves needed calming.

Steve wanted to know when he could partner up with her again.

Nobody wanted Skip on their back about security.

And there wasn't really very much she could do anyway. Except one thing, and she did it: She took a private vow that she'd never let down her guard, never forget Jacomine and what he was capable of—that somehow or other she'd get him before he got her and hers.

• •

She took her Coke out to the courtyard, where Steve was making notes, having just interviewed some kids for his project.

"Want anything?"

"No thanks. I've got iced tea." He had looked at her only a moment. Now he turned back, fast, doing almost a classic double take. "What?"

"I don't know. I was just thinking—I better get hold of those witches. For Layne's allergy."

"Uh-uh."

"You don't believe in magic?"

"That's not what's on your mind."

"Well, what is, big boy?"

"You know how some machines have a 'ready' light? You're blinking one, baby—want to spend the afternoon in bed?"

"I thought you'd never ask." She sat down next to him and took a pull on her Coke.

"Uh-uh again. That's not it. You didn't sit in my lap. You're not following up."

She shrugged, but she couldn't hide her excitement. "I guess I'm a little distracted."

He drew away a little bit, so as to get a better look at her face. "You think you know how to get him!"

Jacomine, he meant. She didn't have to ask.

"I wish. Cappello called, that's all. I think I'll go to work Monday."

ABOUT THE AUTHOR

Julie Smith's other Skip Langdon novels, all set in New Orleans, include *House of Blues*, *New Orleans Beat*, *Jazz Funeral*, *The Axeman's Jazz*, and *New Orleans Mourning*, for which she was given the Edgar Award for Best Novel. A former reporter for the *New Orleans Times-Picayune* and the *San Francisco Chronicle*, Julie Smith is also the creator of the Rebecca Schwartz series of mysteries set in San Francisco. Ms. Smith lives in New Orleans.